RA

Frank Lean, the per...   n
in Bolton and educ...   d
Keele University. F...   y
schools in Manchest...   ...e
1990s. His third novel, *The Reluctant Investigator*, was a
runner-up for the Golden Dagger award of the Crime
Writers' Association. Frank divides his time between crime
writing, teaching and family life.

Praise for Frank Lean

'One of the most engaging of fictional detectives'
— *The Times*

'Frank Lean's novels, featuring stroppy Manchester private
eye Dave Cunane, have evolved into beguiling entertainments, skilfully interweaving the righting of wrongs with
knockabout violence and comic dialogue' — *Sunday Times*

'This is the kind of stuff the English thriller has been
begging for' — *GQ*

'Witty, fast and thoroughly gripping' — *Arcade*

'Lean can still run rings around most of the opposition,
showing the way that the modern whodunit must go'
— *Yorkshire Evening Post*

'Sharp, hip-shooting prose with a refreshingly nasty twist'
— *Arena*

RAISED IN SILENCE

Frank Lean

arrow books

Published by Arrow Books in 2004

1 3 5 7 9 10 8 6 4 2

First published in the United Kingdom in 2004 by William Heinemann

Arrow Books
The Random House Group Limited
20 Vauxhall Bridge Road, London, SW1V 2SA

Random House Australia (Pty) Limited
20 Alfred Street, Milsons Point, Sydney,
New South Wales 2061, Australia

Random House New Zealand Limited
18 Poland Road, Glenfield
Auckland 10, New Zealand

Random House South Africa (Pty) Limited
Endulini, 5a Jubilee Road, Parktown 2193, South Africa

Random House UK Group Limited Reg. No. 954009

www.randomhouse.co.uk

A CIP catalogue record for this book
is available from the British Library

Papers used by Random House UK Limited
are natural, recyclable products made from wood grown in
sustainable forests. The manufacturing processes conform to
the environmental regulations of the country of origin

ISBN 0 0994 2728 1

Typeset by Palimpsest Book Production Limited,
Polmont, Stirlingshire
Printed and bound in Great Britain by
Bookmarque Ltd, Croydon, Surrey

This book is dedicated to the memory of
James P. F. Leneghan
and Stephen R. McClean

1

'The Manchester Mangler

'A fourth woman has disappeared. Is this linked with three other brutal murders? We demand answers. The public is impatient with the stonewalling tactics of the Manchester police. Is a single killer responsible, as the *Sun* believes? Tell us now! The public image of a city must not stand in the way of the truth.'
Headline story in the *Sun*

'Come on, Dave, do the right thing for once,' my secretary, Celeste Williams-Coe, insisted. Celeste, a member of Manchester's black community, has a way of twisting me round her little finger that suggests future success in a career requiring persuasive skills.

'What do you mean, for once?' I grumbled. 'I always do the right thing.'

'She's been given the brush-off by the Five-Oh and now you won't see her. A poor widow . . .'

'Not poor from what I hear, and if the police won't help her . . .'

'Whatever, but she needs your help. What are you? A socialist or something? Are you turning her down because she's rich?'

'You do understand that I'm running a business here . . .'

'Come off it, Boss! You know you're going to see her. Stop stalling.'

I looked at Celeste and I knew she was right, but pride demanded a show of continued resistance.

I racked my brain to think of something convincing to say. It was true that we were busy. The firm was inundated

1

with insurance fraud cases, but it was also correct that I now employed people to sort those out and that I was bored to the back teeth by the sheer pettiness of it all.

No words came.

A slow grin spread across Celeste's face. Then she was smiling broadly, giving me the full benefit of her perfect pearlies.

'OK, OK,' I growled. 'Where and when?'

Celeste picked up her phone. 'She's waiting just across the street.' Her face creased into a scornful grin.

'You sly monkey,' I muttered.

'Well, somebody's got to organise you,' she said as she dialled. 'The file's on your desk.'

'Tell her to give me a minute or two,' I yelped as I dashed out. Back in my own office I grabbed the file that Ruth Hands had sent with her request for an interview and began riffling through the pages. It was a hopeless task. The thing was a mass of scientific jargon. Gone were the days when coppers like my dad operated by guess and by God. Still, they got a hell of a lot more things right than wrong in those days. Criminals were frightened of the Law rather than the other way round. Anyway, that was irrelevant.

From what I could gather, Ruth Hands was complaining that a crime was being ignored.

I stopped scanning when I reached an extract from the pathologist's report.

Its author was the attractive Dr Ashley Gribbin, a lady who'd put some personal business my way a few months previously. Ashley's like Celeste. She's black, ambitious and bursting with the ability that has already carried her to a high position in the pathology service. I'd helped her deal with a little problem that could have put a brake on her upward progress and she'd made it clear that she was prepared to show gratitude in other ways than the purely financial.

2

I'd had to tell her that I wasn't free – not that that put her off. To be fair, she may have sensed that my protests were a little half-hearted. Things hadn't been going too well between myself and Janine White, my partner of several years.

So now, knowing that Ashley was dealing with the Hands case, I read on with redoubled interest. I put it to myself this way: a strictly professional reunion with the delicious Dr Gribbin didn't seem to contradict the hopes I had about the way things would develop with Janine. My problem with Janine was that our vows were still unspoken despite my wish to have them made official.

I read:

. . . There are no obvious indications that the subject, Miss M. Hands, was strangled, deliberately drowned, was unconscious before she hit the water, or went into the canal as a result of a sexual assault, etc. She died by asphyxiation as a result of 'wet' drowning, in which water fills the lungs, rather than 'dry' drowning, when the cause of death is cardiac arrest due to the shock of immersion in freezing water.

Following immersion in the cold water of the canal in mid-November Miss Hands struggled for a brief time. Then her lungs filled up with water and she drowned. During her death throes she gripped weeds and stones in her hands. Injuries revealed at the autopsy were post mortem, caused by her body bumping against the side of the canal.

Freshwater diatoms (microscopic algae of the class *Bacillariophyceae*) were present in her blood. During the 'wet' drowning process, diatoms pass into the bloodstream, lungs, heart and even the bone marrow. They are detectable after death because they are jacketed with virtually indestructible siliceous cell walls. A dead person dumped into water as opposed to a person accidentally drowned will only show a few diatoms present entirely in the throat.

The presence of diatoms suggests that Miss Hands was alive when she went into the water although it is noted that these were recorded in lower concentrations than might have been expected from the Bridgewater Canal, which is unusually rich in diatoms since the water came 'back to life' a few years ago.

The final sentence had been underlined and there were question marks in the margin. The implications had barely penetrated my not-very-acute intellect when the woman in question, the mother, not the daughter, that is, was ushered in by Celeste.

I flinched.

Why? Was my fate walking into my room? The pale rider?

I still don't know exactly what the chemistry between myself and Ruth Hands was, but I'm sure that even at that first sighting I knew she was trouble. She radiated certainty, courage, and conviction, all positive qualities; so why didn't I respond with approval? If I'd known the answer to that I might have saved myself an ocean of trouble, but then if we all had perfect foresight none of us would ever need to get up in the morning to do anything.

Ruth Hands was a tall woman in her late thirties. Her hair was raven black, without the attentions of a hairdresser, I guessed. Her cheekbones were prominent, as was her nose. North American Indian genes, possibly. She held herself well, almost with an arrogant swagger. Her dark green clothes were utilitarian in style, an expensive designers' version of safari kit. They were loose fitting,

4

almost as if intended to disguise the fact that she had a very voluptuous figure. I can't help noticing such minor details.

There was something about her shoulders-back, chest-out posture that set my teeth slightly on edge. She seemed to stand in a way that said 'look at me,' as if inviting admiration, like a small child being paraded by its parents. The woman was presenting herself as a picture. She wore her long jacket with the collar turned up, framing her face, and complementing her good bone structure. Her long black hair was tightly gathered at the back of her neck in a red bobble. The splash of colour brought a touch of the exotic to a typically dull Manchester morning, as did her well-maintained tan. If her eyes had been brown I might have thought she had Spanish, as well as native American blood, but they were startlingly transparent, very light blue.

There was nothing in her hands, no bag or purse, though I fancied she ought to be carrying a riding crop. She looked as if she'd be happy on horseback.

As I scrutinised her, she studied me in return.

'At least you can read,' she said dismissively. 'That's the censored version but I'm supposed to be too dumb to know that.' She spoke in a non-regional American accent. 'I suppose you must represent an up-grade.'

'On what?' I asked.

'On the so-called law enforcement that exists in this wretched, rain-soaked patch of England that you call Manchester.'

'Ouch,' I murmured, miming a slap on the wrist.

This brought no response from Mrs Hands. Obviously she wasn't here for jokes, however feeble.

'We do our best,' I continued, trying not to sound like a spokesman for the local tourist department.

'Do you?' she demanded, her eyes fixing on me as if she really expected a reply. 'All I can tell you is that I wish to God that my family had never set foot in this damnable place and that if I don't get –'

'Mrs Hands, I understand that you're upset, but you must realise that I can only do whatever is humanly possible to sort out your problem.'

'My problem!' she said, drawling the syllables to exaggerated length. Then she laughed bitterly. 'Dear God Almighty, that's cute coming from one of you natives. My problem is your problem, Mr Cunane, and your problem is that there's an undetected murderer prowling the streets of this hellhole with a licence to do as he pleases.'

'If you mean the so-called Mangler, the police are denying that he exists.'

'Yes, denying. They're in denial, all right.'

I nodded my head as if in full agreement and this seemed to cool her anger to the degree that she was prepared to sit in the chair opposite my desk.

'Can I get you a coffee or something?' I asked soothingly.

'Coffee!' she said, her voice again rising almost to a shriek. 'If you think I came here to drink the dishwater you people call coffee –'

'Sorry, sorry!' I murmured.

'And that's another thing. I can't stand you people saying sorry all the time. Do you need my permission to carry on breathing?'

'Sorry,' I said firmly and then sprang to my feet. 'If we're going to carry on like this maybe we'd better adjourn to a gym and do three rounds in the ring.'

She looked startled by this suggestion.

'No, you're quite right,' she agreed after a moment, but without a trace of sincerity. 'It's just that there are times when I wish that this whole island would slip beneath the sea.'

'What, all of it?' I queried sceptically.

My reply produced the faintest shadow of a smile. Her

6

face was gaunt with grief. Swollen eyelids and dark shadows under her eyes told me that she'd been weeping very recently.

'You're all right, Mr Cunane. I need someone who'll stand up to me. I don't really hate England. I was married to an Englishman, after all.'

'I see,' I muttered, although I didn't. 'Can I offer you a drink then? Something stronger than coffee that's made in Scotland . . .'

'You're offering me alcohol, now?' she asked with a laugh. 'I love this. Have none of your buddies on the incompetence squad given you a heads-up about me being teetotal?'

'I don't have "buddies" in the way you mean and I only know what I've read about you in the papers. They didn't go into detail about your drinking habits.'

'Sorry,' she countered; again, there was the briefest possible flicker of a smile. 'Look, you can tell that I'm almost Anglicised. You've got me saying the s-word now. Have you read the report?'

'Some of it,' I admitted cautiously.

'Have you got to the part where they say my totally abstinent daughter was pickled in alcohol when she went into that canal?' she demanded angrily, plucking the report out of my fingers.

'I've reached that part but I haven't studied the case in detail yet, Mrs Hands.'

'I think we can make do with just Ruth, don't you?' she stated crisply, extending her right hand across the desk. 'Hands is such a silly name. Meg wanted me to change it.'

'To what?'

'My maiden name was Muenzendorfer . . . it's Swiss.'

Keeping my face straight, I looked at her.

Sticking her lower lip out, she blew the hair from her face.

'Yeah, well. It doesn't arise now.'

'I can manage to say Ruth, and we're all used to Hands, Hands Jam. Who hasn't heard of that?'

'That's been in back of all my troubles, I guess,' she said.

Despite her refusal of alcoholic refreshment it seemed as if the suggestion had relaxed her. She was no longer sitting to attention.

There was still a strong undercurrent of bitterness but no self-pity that I could detect. I felt myself warming slightly. The late Mr Hands was a lucky man but – hell's teeth! – he must have been a patient one.

'Every meeting I've had with your Keystone Kops has been bedevilled by good old English inverted snobbery. If I was the widow of some ordinary Joe those lobotomised creeps would have moved heaven and earth for me. But no, when you're credited with great wealth and have a name that's a household word, and you're a foreigner as well, then you're just another rich nut demanding more police manpower than you're entitled to. They're sneaky too. I keep finding things about myself in the papers that could only have come from them.'

'I'm not the police,' I said quietly. I didn't care to mention the long line of coppers that I spring from, an heredity at least as crucial as any soft fruit bottler's.

'Right,' she said with approval. 'I suppose you're an expert in these things,' she continued, indicating the forensic texts on my shelves. Their main purpose was for detecting inconsistencies in the endless flow of bogus compensation claims that provide me with an income but she didn't need to know that either.

'Not really,' I said modestly. 'Most of my work involves insurance fraud.'

It was as if I'd turned a light on. Her face became animated. The hostility faded.

'Fraud, the *mot juste*, Mr Cunane,' she commented, tossing her ponytail back with a certain satisfaction. 'You said it, Mr Cunane. Yes, fraud, that is the heart, centre and beginning and end of this investigation.'

'Yes?'

'I know you think I'm bitter and twisted and just a Brit-hating Yankee but if I am it's because of that. All I've had from the police and everyone else I've turned to is fraud and evasion and weasel words.'

'Surely –'

'Oh yes, I may be foreign but I'm not dumb. I want you to investigate this completely fraudulent claim that my daughter's death was an accident. Meg was murdered – I know she was – and I want the case investigated by someone who's not so lazy that he gives up before he's even started.'

'They're not all lazy or incompetent,' I retorted.

'Possibly not,' she conceded, 'but they're totally wrong about Meg.'

'Can you be specific?'

'Alcohol,' she muttered, waving her hand towards the whisky bottle I'd forgotten to put away from a previous client's visit.

My brow must have furrowed. 'In what way –' I started.

'No,' she said imperiously, raising the little fingers of each hand. There was no nail varnish but the fingernails were exquisitely manicured.

She stood up. 'What do you make of me?'

I shifted uncomfortably on my chair. 'You're a very attractive person.'

'Yeah, yeah, whatever, but that's not what I mean. What do you think I am?'

'Well, er . . .'

'I'll tell you. I'm a life-long campaigner against alcohol and so was my husband, and I can give you my Bible

9

oath that my daughter would not have consumed alcohol willingly.'

'But the report –'

'Yes, it says she had alcohol in her bloodstream, so why aren't the police trying to track down who made her drink? I mean, do I look like an untruthful person? Why do they get all antsy and start shuffling papers when the issue comes up? Is it totally unheard of in England for someone to force drink down an unwilling girl's throat?'

I felt as if someone had unzipped the bottom of my stomach. I continued to stare at her with the fixity of a rabbit studying a boa constrictor, aware of what was coming next.

'Have you seen anything that might give you some indication?' she asked falteringly. The overbearing tone had disappeared, suggesting that despite her earlier claim she did have doubts of her own. 'I mean, you've had experience reading these things. There must be something that will give you a clue because I know that Meg's death was no accident.'

She gazed at me expectantly as if she was trying to drown me in the limpid pools of those opalescent blue eyes. Her expression was filled with intelligence and hope.

I was supposed to come up with some brilliant insight.

I had to say something. I wanted to say goodbye, but . . .

'It is true that the pathologist noted that the number of diatoms found in your daughter's tissues was on the low side although the canal was unusually rich in them,' I said, measuring my words.

'So?' she responded eagerly.

'Well, that opens up a remote possibility that someone . . .'

'Go on,' she commanded when I hesitated.

10

'It's difficult to explain,' I said. I didn't want to be too explicit.

'Please carry on,' she said in a voice as hard as granite. 'Whatever you have to say can't be worse than what I've imagined.'

Experience has taught me that some things can be very much worse than any normal person's imaginings, but she wanted my opinion.

'OK, straight on the chin then, Ruth . . . There have been cases, a very few cases, where a killer drowned or half drowned his victim in fresh water, such as a swimming pool, or even a bath, and then dumped them in a river or canal to make it look like an accident. I'm not saying this happened to your Meg, mind you.'

'It's what I guessed,' she said in a half-whisper. 'You can't imagine what it means to me to have that confirmed by an expert.' She was now sitting on the edge of her seat, twisting her hands and looking like a child whose parents had just abandoned her in a crowded street. I should have denied that I had expert status but vanity makes fools of us all.

I was hooked.

'Now hold on,' I cautioned. 'We can't be certain that's what happened to Meg. It's only one possibility. The level of diatoms didn't quite match what Dr Gribbin expected but they were present. If there was foul play, then Meg was still alive when she entered the canal.'

'I knew it! Meg was a fighter. She wouldn't have given in without a struggle.'

'Ruth, don't get your hopes up. Don't forget there was drink as well. She might have been – '

'No, intoxicated is the one thing she wasn't! Why do you think I'm saying your wonderful British justice system has fumbled the field pass on this one? I know as surely as I know that my name's Ruth Hands that drink never passed Meg's lips. Not voluntarily, that is.'

11

'May I be frank?'

'Sure, it'll be a relief if you'll stop being so British and polite. I'm not made of cotton wool.'

'Meg was here in Manchester; you were away . . .'

'In South Africa.'

'Exactly.'

'And your point, Mr Cunane?' she said stubbornly.

'Dave, please.'

'Listen, *Dave*, don't keep on giving me this *oh so polite* run-around. Why do you think I've come to you? It's what I've been getting from that complacent pig Rix. You guys must take lessons in handing out bullshit. Just say what you've got to say and I'll be on my way.'

'Excuse me,' I flared up, 'all I was going to say was that if you take a stroll round central Manchester any Friday or Saturday night in term time you'll think the streets have been resurfaced in technicoloured slime. There are so many students puking up their guts it's like a scene from a horror film about the Black Death. Alcoholic excess is the name of the game where those kiddies are concerned, whatever parents may believe.'

'But I'm not just your average ultra-permissive British parent!' Ruth snapped. 'I knew my daughter. There wasn't a day went by without us being in touch. Meg would have told me if she wanted to go out drinking. I didn't expect her to be a saint, but we had no secrets. In her last phone call she told me over and over again that she was scared that someone or something was following her. Then she turns up in some God-awful canal.'

'Some*thing*?' I repeated. I was startled. Was Ruth about to claim that her daughter was a victim of alien abduction? Was I going to be asked to investigate the Manchester UFO scene?

She looked at me resentfully.

'You said some*thing* might be following her. Such as what?' I repeated.

12

'Don't look at me like that,' she snapped back. 'Meg also sent me several emails saying that she was aware of being followed. She felt she was being watched for some purpose. If anyone but Meg had said it I'd have wondered if she needed medication, but Meg was normally so cool and in charge. I blame myself for not coming straight back to England to get to the bottom of this stalking or whatever it was. Something caused the death of a healthy, strong-minded girl.'

'But a *thing*? What are you thinking of?'

'OK, OK, I expect you're another conventional little British atheist, brainwashed by the media here. Shakespeare would have understood. There are more things in heaven and earth –'

'I get the picture,' I said impatiently. 'And for your information, I'm not a conventional little British atheist, or any kind of an atheist.'

'No, you're right. I'm sure you're not. I shouldn't have said "thing" like that. I meant something in her mind, something intangible.'

I didn't believe her for a moment. In one corner of my mind I was taken by the novelty of the situation. It was the first time in my career that someone had asked me to track down a ghost.

'The police . . .' I muttered, to hide my confusion.

'The police think I'm making it all up about Meg's fears. They've studied the CCTV recordings of her walking home and there was no one following her, therefore I'm just a hysterical bereaved parent and a rich Yankee foreigner to make things worse.'

I picked up the file from my desk and put it in a drawer. 'To be honest, I haven't studied this all that closely . . .'

'What does that mean, "To be honest"? Do you make a habit of lying?'

'There's no need to be so hostile, Ruth. I'm on your side. What I was going to say is that I'll investigate the case without reference to the previous findings.'

'Progress at last,' she said with a sigh. For a moment her grim expression relaxed. 'I know you limeys think we colonials are pushy and crass but does it take half an hour to tell me something you could have said in the first minute?'

I shrugged. It was going to be one step forward, two steps back with Ruth Hands.

'At the risk of sounding "Olde Worlde", we do say "More haste, less speed" on this side of the Pond and, being honest again, I hadn't decided to take the case until I heard your version of events –'

'Which you haven't really done yet.'

'No, my idea was to let you take me through what you think happened and then see if there are any leads I can usefully follow. After all, despite what you seem to think, I'm not a policeman. It does appear that there are one or two things I can look into in your daughter's case so I'll be charging you by the hour for my services and I don't come cheap. I wouldn't like you to think I'd left any stone unturned . . .'

'Money's not a problem.'

'That's nice.'

'Listen, *Dave*,' she said with a glare. 'Whatever you may believe, I'm not one of the idle rich. Thomas, that's my late husband, left me very well fixed but I haven't got money to burn. He inherited a significant shareholding in his family business but there are so many cousins and aunts, et cetera, that the jam's spread quite thin these days.'

'OK, you'll get a fully specified invoice of all charges. I'm not a crook.'

This produced another sceptical lifting of the eyebrow by my client. I felt irritated. I took out one of our standard contracts and indicated where she should sign, but she wasn't ready for business yet.

'And another thing,' she continued, with her eyes focused on the ceiling, 'if you're thinking of taking this case as a way of getting into the little widow's pants, think again!'

'Now that is uncalled for,' I spluttered. 'I already have a partner.'

'Since when did that slow your type down? I saw the glint in your eye when I came in.'

'If you don't want men to look at you, you should be wearing a burka. And while we're at it, what is my type?'

'You look like the sort who's up for anything and is ready to swallow an unwary female for breakfast.'

'Thanks! I suppose that about clears the air.'

To be honest again, but only with myself this time, although I wasn't inclined to leap over the desk and pin her to the floor, her challenge had stimulated a certain amount of interest in the libido department. I firmly repressed the feeling.

'You're welcome,' she said. 'Now where do I sign?'

2

'Moral Panic in Manchester? Manchester police are baffled by the outbreak of "Mangler Madness" in the northern football fastness, which likes to claim the title of England's second city. Although the tabloids have done their torrid best to fan the flames of popular indignation, the police claim that four recent deaths of young women are either unrelated sex murders, or, in one case, an accident. Statistics show that . . .'
Editorial in the *Guardian*

A challenging woman in every sense of the word, I thought when she'd gone. Getting into her pants, indeed! Would that be worth the confusion, general mayhem and wreckage that it would cause to my life style? Rich and nicely packaged though Ruth Hands was, she came along with a bundle of opinions that would make her an awkward companion at best. Sleeping with her would be like sharing a bed with that Hindu goddess with all the arms: sharp elbows at every turn. Not that I was thinking of any kind of rupture with my girlfriend, the delightful Janine. Far from it. Permanence was what I was looking for there.

There was no obstacle on my part.

I was earning enough for both of us if she wanted to give up journalism but every time I put the proposition something else came up. Like the grain of sand that irritates an oyster to make a pearl, there was a tiny fragment of grit in my relationship with Janine. Only I wasn't sure that a gem was going to be the end result.

According to the folk wisdom that my parents dispense at the drop of a hat, I'm in need of an anchor to fix me in my moorings. I was more than half convinced that they were right. Janine's steady refusal to steer into harbour with me was having an effect.

For some time I'd been catching myself eyeing other suitable females in a certain way. That's what Ruth Hands had detected. It was embarrassing and I felt like a daft teenager. I just wished Janine would stop havering and let us get on with the 'happily ever after' part of our lives.

Anyway, it was as a detective that Ruth Hands required my services and so I picked up the phone and asked Celeste to get her husband to come into the office. Celeste married Michael Coe two years ago. A Londoner who knows his way round the low spots of our beloved capital, a skill that we've used more than once, Michael represents the technical branch of my little firm. He served as a surveillance operative with the army in Northern Ireland and what he doesn't know about all forms of electronic snooping isn't worth knowing. There's a high turnover of staff in all detective firms because anyone who's any good is soon tempted to set up on his own. I don't mind this. It means they're keen. Michael is amongst the keenest, but his marriage and the arrival of a baby seem to have made him less anxious to give up whatever security working for me provides. Also, he likes working with his wife. Celeste recently returned to work part time while they save for a house.

So, while I've got him, I might as well use him.

I read as much as I could of the rest of the report while I was waiting for him to arrive from his current job in Angel Meadow.

'Boss?' Michael said quietly when he eventually poked his head round the door. Michael's like that. He always uses part of his body for reconnaissance before fully committing the rest of himself.

'Yes, downtrodden worker?' I rapped back. I've never been entirely comfortable with my managerial status.

'Er, Celeste, er, she said you wanted to see me.'

'Did she? You'd better come in then,' I said in a mock hostile way. 'I'm not going to sack the pair of you just yet.'

As soon as I spoke I realised it was the wrong thing to say.

Michael looked stricken. His John Lennon-style glasses steamed up.

'Joke, Michael! Joke!' I said apologetically.

'Yes,' he agreed doubtfully.

'CCTV. Is it possible to follow someone through streets buzzing with cameras and avoid appearing on screen yourself?' I demanded.

'I suppose so. It depends which streets you're talking about.'

'That's what I thought, but why would the police totally rubbish the idea? I want your expert opinion.'

I passed him the report open at the page where Ruth's claim that her daughter could have been followed was dismissed because there was no sighting of her alleged stalker.

'I don't know,' he commented inconclusively when he'd finished reading. 'The police must have reason for saying she wasn't followed, but if this was down to me I wouldn't dare be as definite as this.'

'Explain,' I ordered.

'Anywhere else but Manchester I'd say there are so many gaps in CCTV coverage that you couldn't make a definite statement one way or the other. All you could say is that absence of an image proves that no one was caught on camera. But in Manchester the police are claiming that CCTV coverage is virtually total. So, they can be definite that there wasn't a stalker.'

'But is that credible?'

'Dave, asking them to deny it's like asking the Pope if he's agnostic. The investment's been made and now the

18

city council's spent millions on a control room covering the whole city centre. It's comprehensive.'

'Not for every street.'

'There are four hundred cameras.'

'Yes, but a lot of them are in car parks.'

'True, but all the main streets are well covered, especially at pub closing time, which is when this girl took her last stroll.'

I scratched my head. It looked as if Ruth Hands' case had fallen at the first hurdle. The trouble with experts like Michael Coe is that they'll never give a definite answer. I tried to frame the problem another way.

'Is it possible that somehow all the cameras were pointing the wrong way just at the instant after Meg Hands had passed and so they didn't pick up this geezer?'

'You mean like driving through a dozen sets of traffic lights one after another at green? Lucky coincidence, like?'

'You're the expert. You tell me.'

'No, that's not possible, Dave. The cameras are carefully sited to cover a large area. The fields of view overlap. If there was a stalker following this girl closely enough for her to notice they'd have spotted him. Obviously they tracked the Hands girl, and before your suspicious mind goes into overdrive, these cameras aren't worked by individual operators, so there's no one to bribe. At the time she was on the streets the monitors would have been following a pre-set operation which scanned all the main pubs and clubs simultaneously.'

I tried to find a flaw in his logic. I felt in my bones that there must be one. Michael and his fellow technicians believe that when they pit technology against humanity it's always technology that wins. I can't accept that. I must have frowned because Michael continued.

'Dave, I know you feel sorry for Mrs Hands – Celeste filled me in on the phone on my way over – but this line of enquiry is a no-no. Imagining that you're being followed is one of the classic signs of mental illness. Face it, the girl was probably – '

'No,' I said sharply. 'If I start believing that I might as well phone Ruth Hands now and tell her to forget the job. Your reasoning's wrong, anyway. It isn't just the night of Meg's death that we're considering. She claimed that she was aware of being followed, or at least observed, for some time before her death.'

'Presumably CCTV hasn't picked up a stalker on those occasions either. So, now we're talking about going through a hundred sets of traffic lights all on green, not just twelve?' This comment was accompanied by a tolerant smile at my old-fashioned attitude.

I felt my collar tightening as my neck swelled.

'Listen, Michael, for the sake of argument assume there was a stalker. How could he do it without leaving a record on the tapes?'

'They don't use tape any more, Dave. That was in the Stone Age. It's all digital now, stored in a huge computer memory for ninety-two days.'

'Computers – ' I probed – 'surely, they're vulnerable? What about all these hackers and viruses and suchlike?'

'You don't understand. The CCTV system's meant to be a deterrent. Suppose someone mugs you on Deansgate. The operator might miss it happening in real time and so you hit the deck and get a sore head. Then you report the assault. The police are on the case. They punch in the co-ordinates and time of the incident, and lo and behold, they get the action replay. The image quality's so good you can tell whether the victim's watch is a Rolex or a Tag Heuer. No one knows all this better than the crooks, so they keep their hands in their pockets until they're out of range. That's why crime's down in the city centre.'

'You're not much use to me, are you?' I complained, only half in jest.

'All right,' he said wearily, as if to appease someone who wasn't quite up to speed on modern life, 'I promise I'll try and come up with a technically feasible way that someone could make themselves invisible to a whole battery of CCTV systems but don't hold your breath. It'll take me some time in the technical library. Do you want me to come off the job in Angel Meadow?'

Technically illiterate I may be, but I knew that Michael didn't think there was a chance in a million of finding a solution.

He was currently investigating stock leakage in a warehouse company. The suspects were all employees of the firm concerned. The job was nearly complete. I'd once performed similar tasks by disguising myself as an employee or by staking the place out for up to twenty-four hours at a stretch, Michael now did the same job with electronic aids and using about a quarter of the effort.

'Decisions, decisions,' I moaned. 'No, you'd better stay with it, but keep thinking about my little problem. Meanwhile, I want you to take me for a drink, if you can spare half an hour.'

He looked at me with raised eyebrows.

'I need to visit the CCTV centre.'

'Dave, it's in a secret location. I don't know where it is.'

'Humour me again, Michael. Take me to the pub where all these computer nerds from the CCTV centre hang out, and don't tell me you don't know where that is. Even computer experts must need occasional liquid refreshment.'

'Dave, you're barking up the wrong tree.'

'Humour me,' I insisted quietly. I could see that my talk of nerds wasn't going down too well.

Ten minutes later we entered a small pub not far from the Town Hall. Following current fashion it had a modish name, the 'Mouse and Pixel'.

It was almost empty apart from two young men each nursing a half of lager and earnestly discussing some problem. They looked like the genuine article to me. Both of them were wearing specs. One of them was writing something on the back of a beermat. I felt like a hunter in range of his prey.

'This is ridiculous, Boss,' Michael protested in a forced whisper. 'What am I supposed to do? Start questioning them about shortcomings in the CCTV system?'

'No, you can leave any questioning to me,' I said evenly. 'Do you think they're from the CCTV centre?'

'How do I know?' he said with a shrug.

I favoured him with one of my honest and open smiles.

'They might be,' he agreed through clenched teeth, 'but the guy I know who used to work at the centre's on holiday.'

The phrasing of this answer was just a shade too careful to be convincing. He obviously knew that the pair sitting across from us were nerds on the loose.

'My mate Gareth was what you'd call a nerd, I suppose. Degree in computer science from Cambridge. He helped to install the terabyte memory and design the system architecture. I met up with him in here a few times and he had his workmates with him but that wasn't in the middle of the afternoon like this.'

I sipped the pint of Guinness I'd ordered and studied Michael's face. I wasn't trying to give him the third degree, it was just that I wasn't used to being treated as a source of embarrassment by one of my employees. Perhaps he'd been too long in the army because he certainly wasn't thinking in the subversive way I do.

'It's high security, you know,' he said defensively. 'They'll have been briefed not to talk about their work.'

I nodded. 'Tell me about these terror-bites, then,' I suggested.

'Er, you are joking, Boss?' he asked uncertainly.

22

'No, terror sounds as if it's right up my street.'

'It's *b y t e s* not bites! D'oh! . . . You are joking, aren't you?'

'Just give me the facts.'

'The memory on a household computer might be five hundred and twelve megabytes, that is five hundred and twelve million bytes where each byte is –'

'Skip to the terror-bites – they sound like hot stuff.'

'OK,' he said, his face a study as he grappled with my ignorance. 'The hard disc on a household computer might be eighty gigabytes where each gigabyte is a thousand million bytes. Now the CCTV operates with a storage system that uses terabytes, where each terabyte is one million million bytes. Get it? It's big. It can store all those images and retrieve them almost instantly.'

'Wonderful,' I said curtly. 'I get the picture. You'd better get back to Angel Meadow now.'

'You'll be careful about approaching those two,' he cautioned.

'I'll be fine,' I assured him.

He cast a final furtive glance in the direction of my intended prey before departing with a shake of his head. Michael was all right. He'd be fine if there was any rough stuff. He'd been in the army, after all. He'd never trawled around the mean streets to break a case as I had in the days before everything went electronic.

I sipped my drink.

I didn't have a clue what I was going to do. By coming down here I was following rule ten in the *Private Detectives' Handbook*: 'When totally confused, put yourself where you think the action is and hope that something falls into your lap.'

Half an hour passed with excruciating slowness.

I tried not to stare at the pair in the corner, but my eyes were constantly being drawn towards them.

I don't know what I hoped was going to happen,

23

perhaps something that would give me an excuse to engage them in conversation. Perhaps they would start taking drugs and give me the opening I needed to put pressure on. But no, they were as blameless a pair of nerds as ever donned anoraks. They had their heads together the whole time discussing whatever was so urgent. Then suddenly one of them looked at his watch.

They both hurriedly got up and left.

I followed, stooping to pick up the beermat as I passed their table. It was covered in technical notation that might as well have been hieroglyphics, as far as I was concerned. I put it in my inside pocket.

They strode across Albert Square and up Tib Street into the financial district. My heart sank. They were probably just a couple of trainee merchant bankers.

I followed at a distance but one of them kept casting furtive glances over his shoulder. It could only be a matter of time before he clocked me. Right on cue a *Big Issue* seller came forward, looking for trade. The *Big Issue* sellers we always have with us, at least on the streets of Manchester. I took advantage of the momentary diversion to stand behind the poor guy while my quarry scanned the street. Then I whipped off the fawn raincoat I was wearing and thrust it into the arms of the startled seller.

'Here, wrap yourself up in this,' I grunted, thrusting the coat into the astonished man's hands.

I closed in on the prey, worried lest I lose them in the tangle of intersecting streets.

Suddenly they halted at an unobtrusive-looking doorway. The careful way they scrutinised the area before punching a number into the keypad told me that I might be about to score. It flashed through my mind that otherwise I might have to follow dozens of nerdish types from the Mouse and Pixel before I found the right place.

However good these two were at surveillance in front

of a screen, they were novices here on the street. I kneeled to fasten a nonexistent untied shoelace as soon as they turned to give the street the once-over. They both ignored me. I doubt if they even saw me.

I rushed up behind them just as they pushed the heavy door open.

'Excuse me,' I shouted.

They jumped like a brace of frightened rabbits.

'You left this behind in the pub,' I said, brandishing the beermat. 'We can't be too careful about security, can we?'

By this time they were almost inside the building. Whatever wonderland it led to, they were about to disappear down the rabbit hole. The taller of the duo reluctantly held the entrance open to see what the fuss was all about. Beyond them I could see a small lobby from which the only exit was the stainless-steel door of a lift.

Bingo! Hole in one! I was sure I was right. This must be the CCTV control centre.

I could feel the blood pounding in my ears. I hadn't felt so chuffed for months. This was infinitely better than poring over a balance sheet.

The taller of the two, a thin heron-like creature, impatiently extended his hand to take the offending article.

I snatched it away.

'Oh, no you don't, sunshine,' I said confidently. 'I'm going to show this to your operations manager. Then he'll know how careful about security his employees are.'

'It's only – ' the lanky nerd started to say, but his shorter companion pulled him down and whispered something in his ear. They looked me up and down as they conferred. I was wearing an elegant navy-blue suit. My black leather Oxford shoes were shiny and polished. I didn't fit into the category of street people.

I caught the words 'police' , 'some sort of security drill', 'Heritage'.

'That's right, sonny,' I said in a spirit of reckless adventure. 'This goes straight to the boss-man.' I pushed my way into the lobby behind them. The beanpole released his grip on the door and it slammed shut.

Red-faced and breathless, the tall youth turned indecisively to his partner. This was not the sort of problem he could solve with a pencil and paper. I nodded in the direction of the lift.

'I'm sure it's just a mix-up,' the shorter man said. 'We can clear it up in a moment.' He then punched a number into the keypad. The lift opened and all three of us entered in a stony silence. I avoided showing any surprise when the lift descended rather than ascended as I'd expected.

It really was a rabbit hole.

We emerged into a glass-sided box. It was the CCTV control centre. Either that or the North American Air Defence system had relocated to central Manchester, because a massive wall of separate screens filled the shorter side of a huge rectangular room as big as a five-a-side football pitch. Low beams supported the weight of the building above. The rest of the area was filled with desks, monitors, cabinets, and men and women lounging about.

Meanwhile, I wasn't home free.

The shorter, more capable-looking man was speaking into a phone.

'We've picked up a visitor on the way in,' he announced to an unseen supervisor. 'He claims he wants to report a security breach to Mr Heritage.'

He listened to the reply for a moment.

'Who are you?' he asked.

'That's for me to know and you to find out,' I said jokily. 'Security's the name of the game.'

He looked at me uncertainly, fidgeting with the security ID dangling from a chain round his neck.

'You're not press, or one of these right-to-privacy activists, are you?' he queried.

I shook my head, pleased that the range of possibilities was apparently so limited.

'I think you'd better see him yourself, Mr Heritage,' he said into the phone.

There was a buzz and the door opened. My two new friends scurried into their haven and I followed.

An officious-looking type approached; obviously management, he was clad in a charcoal-grey suit unlike the casual jeans and sweatshirts others were wearing. Slightly older than the two I'd conned, he nevertheless had the same nerdish, absorbed look that they did. He also wore specs. I thought there was something ferret-like and thin-lipped about his face. They say dog owners begin to resemble their pets and certainly Heritage, if this was him, fitted the super-snooper role perfectly. In case anyone forgot his rank he was festooned with several large security passes. I peered at the largest. His name was Heritage, right enough.

'Who are you?' he barked in a rather high-pitched voice.

'Spot check,' I announced.

'Police or Home Office? It's most inconsiderate of you to arrive unannounced.'

He put his hand out for my ID but I'd been in this position before.

'If you want to stay in charge of this unit for much longer you'd better have a good explanation of why your employees are littering the pubs of Manchester with classified information,' I countered boldly. Then I allowed him a two nanosecond squint at my Pimpernel Investigations pass.

'What!' he spluttered, instantly on the defensive.

I waved the beermat at him.

'What is it?' he muttered, biting his lip nervously.

'Ask those two,' I suggested, pointing at my two former companions. Like a pair of naughty schoolboys escaping wrath to come, they were rapidly dodging towards the corner of the room.

'Roberts and Conlon!' Heritage bellowed.

They froze and Heritage abandoned me and trotted towards them. He held a hurried conference with the duo, leaving me unattended. I studied the room. The inhabitants, male and female, were mostly in their twenties and thirties, not a grey head in sight. One or two could have been plainclothes police officers. My bold front took a dent but I gritted my teeth and stayed where I was. What could they do me for, after all?

Some, but not all, of the workers were studying the displays that each contained sixteen images of the outer world.

A group were gathered around an object resembling a large double-doored refrigerator. It stood about six feet tall with blinking lights on top. As I watched, an individual opened one of the smoked-glass doors and pulled out a rack, one of many inside the unit.

I guessed what it was.

Heritage returned. This time those sharp teeth were hidden behind an ingratiating smile.

'I'm sure it's a misunderstanding,' he gushed. 'Not that we take off-site security lightly. Did you say you were with the police or the Home Office?'

'City council,' I said bravely. This produced a furrowing of the brow. 'You know anyone could get in here and damage that thing. We're concerned about our investment.'

'The terabyte storage array's monitored continuously. No unauthorised person can get near it.'

'I have.'

He had no immediate answer for this.

While he was framing his reply I went on the offensive

28

again. 'I want to see the material relating to the Hands case. The City's concerned about adverse effects of publicity in America.'

'The police –'

'I know what they say but the chief executive wants my personal assurance that there'll be no comeback on this accident story. The publicity's ruining business.'

Heritage pursed his lips so severely that they almost vanished, then made his mind up. He parked me in front of a monitor and rapidly typed a password.

'I know this location off by heart,' he commented, as his fingers flew over the keyboard. Almost instantly a picture appeared. It showed a young woman walking slowly along Whitworth Street West – I recognised the bars reached by walkways over the Rochdale Canal. She looked over her shoulder along the street she'd just walked down. The view changed and showed the whole street. The girl looked back again and then broke into a run. There was nothing behind her.

The images ran on. She waited at a pedestrian crossing. There was still no one else in sight. Then the screen went blank.

'What about where she was found?' I asked.

'Our coverage ends on the other side of Deansgate. There are CCTV cameras in Castlefields but they're not yet linked into our system. That's the next development,' Heritage said proudly.

'I want to see the earlier stuff as well,' I demanded.

'One moment,' my guide replied. 'I need to look up those co-ordinates in my office.'

He departed, leaving me in front of the monitor. Using the on-screen toolbar I ran the pictures again. I may know nothing about terabytes but that girl's body language spoke of terror, yet there was no other person in view. The time logged on the screen was ten forty-five on the Friday night of her presumed accident just before the pubs shut. The streets were deserted. There wasn't even a dog on the move. Meg Hands was the only living soul stirring. That struck me as somehow odd.

Then on my third run through I noticed something. As she walked along Whitworth Street West past the bridges leading to the canal-side club scene, Meg seemed steady enough on her feet. She was walking briskly, flashing quick desperate glances over her shoulder at the real, or imagined, but certainly invisible stalker. I wanted to reach out and say, 'Go into one of the bars,' but she didn't.

Then the point of view changed from one camera to another. She was now standing unsteadily at a pedestrian crossing on Deansgate that would take her down to the Castlefields Canal Basin area where her body was found. She was swaying, actually clinging to the traffic light. It was possible that the effect of alcohol consumed earlier had just kicked in. There was a definite contrast with the first frames in which she looked much more sober.

I was considering all this when my luck ran out.

Heritage returned flanked by two beefy security men, ex-Royal Marines, judging by their closely cropped heads and military posture.

'I want to see your ID again, Mr . . . you didn't give me your name.'

'Cunane,' I announced, handing him my ID.

'You said you were from the council!' he gasped indignantly as his eyes took in the information.

Undaunted, I rapped, 'I pay plenty of council tax and I live in Manchester.'

'You're a private detective. You've no right to be in here.'

'I'm investigating that girl's murder.'

'You're working for the gutter press, aren't you? You're one of the scum who're making up all these lies about a Mangler.'

'No, but I want to know the reason why you claim there was no one following Miss Hands when clearly someone hounded her to her death.'

His jaw dropped at this idea. His glasses began to get steamed up.

'How dare you imply that we're incompetent?' he gobbled, his face puce with fury. 'No one followed her. The woman was demented. Get out of that seat!'

The heavies laid their horny hands on my shoulders and yanked me out of the swivel chair. I tried to hang on to the desk and the whole thing tipped over. Heritage leaped forward to prevent the monitor, an expensive-looking flat screen job, from crashing onto the floor. A curious three-sided wrestling match then followed. Heritage battled to save the monitor and his henchmen fought to restrain me. All the workers gathered round. No blows were struck but I was soon overwhelmed.

'Take your hands off me. This is assault,' I warned. 'I'm not going until I get some answers about how you've faked those images.'

'Yes, you are,' Heritage screeched. 'This is a restricted area as defined by European legislation. You're going to be sued for breach of security and trespass.'

'Your security's rubbish!' I replied. 'The press'll have a field day with you.'

My empty threat made everything worse. The grip on my arms tightened and the security men ground their teeth. Heritage threw a tantrum. He danced from toe to toe, hugging the monitor he'd rescued like a shipwreck survivor clinging to a life raft. He was beside himself.

'Remove this man at once,' he wailed to the guards. 'I shall hold you two fools personally responsible if he isn't on the street within the next thirty seconds.'

The guards now had a firm grip on my jacket. They marched me to the entrance, into the lift, and out into the street. Before they released me they gave me a powerful shove. One hooked my legs from under me as he pushed. I lurched forward and landed on my knees.

I felt the fine worsted material of my trousers tear as I skidded across the pavement. When I staggered to my feet and turned I was confronted by a blank door. It was as if the whole event had never happened.

I was more annoyed about the trousers than about the assault. The raw and bleeding flesh of my knees was visible to the world. A Greek tailor in Chorlton had spent a long time getting those trousers to hang perfectly but they were well beyond invisible mending now. As the thought of having another pair made to match the surviving jacket arrived I noticed that my right sleeve had parted company with the shoulder.

I retraced my steps towards my office. I stumbled once or twice. My knees hurt like hell. Passers-by avoided eye contact with me. A mother shepherded her children off the pavement as I passed.

The *Big Issue* seller spoke.

'Here you,' he said, slinging my fawn raincoat back at me. 'I don't need charity from falling-down drunks.'

3

'Repeated and strident claims by Manchester Police that the reported deaths of young women in the city are accidental are undermining the credibility of the police and forensic science service. Yesterday police again tried to hide behind statistics, claiming that with eighty thousand students in the city accidental deaths should be expected. We say, murder will out, and there should be an immediate inquiry into the behaviour of our smug so-called guardians of the law ...'

Editorial in the *Sun*

The raincoat disguised my dishevelled state when I reached the office.

Celeste was just getting ready to leave. I helped her on with her coat, noticing the Prada label.

'Very nice,' I commented.

'Now, Dave, you pay me a good clothing allowance to look nice for clients but not enough for Prada coats. I got this in Selfridges sale.'

'All I said was that it was nice, and it is,' I said, holding up my hands. 'No reflection was intended.'

This produced the well-practised smile. There was something almost frightening about the perfection of Celeste's teeth. Orthodontist, look and weep, I thought. Intelligent, attractive and well-dressed as she was, Mrs Celeste Williams-Coe had her sights on higher things than managing a small office. I knew if she found a job that did run to Prada coats there'd be no holding her back.

My remark had put her in a talkative mood and she leaned against the door of my office. I didn't reveal anything of my recent adventure. Obviously she wasn't in too much of a hurry to get to her childminder.

'What do you make of Mrs Hands, then?' she asked coyly.

This was unusual. Celeste normally discussed practical details. We weren't Holmes and Watson. I wasn't in need of a sounding board. I was curious about her interest.

'Just what was the idea in pressuring me to take her case?' I asked quizzically.

She pulled a face. 'I thought Mrs Hands deserved a fair crack of the whip.'

'Whip! She certainly looks as if she knows how to crack the whip. She's a very uninhibited type. Why, she practically accused me of wanting to sleep with her.'

'Well, don't you end up sleeping with some of the clients?' she asked with a sly grin.

'So that's where she got the idea. That's libel! You'd better consult that solicitor cousin of yours.'

'Marvin would tell you straight away that if it was untrue, which we both know it isn't, it would be slander, not libel.'

'OK,' I said, putting up my hands in surrender, 'but tell me, why were you so anxious for me to take the case? Apart from being barking mad with grief, the woman's asking me to prove a scientific impossibility and take on the GMP, who've staked the force's reputation on her daughter's death being an accident. You must know – '

'Excuse me!' she broke in. 'I know that Ruth Hands has done wonderful work for Aids sufferers in Africa,' she said. Her eyes had suddenly developed that guarded look that's usually a sign of danger with her. 'She's been to my church to talk about that.'

'Oh,' I murmured, and blundered blindly on. 'She belongs to the same church?'

'What does that mean?' Celeste erupted. 'Do you think

you can dismiss her because I know her through my church? Would you say the same if she was black? – "Oh! Another crazy Sambo!"'

'Er . . .'

'No, Dave, I'm serious. There's too much of this pigeon-holing of people.'

'I wasn't – '

'Yes, you were. Everyone does it, the police most of all.'

'Celeste, it was just an innocent remark.'

'Dave, get real!' she shouted. Her eyes were blazing. 'My five-year-old niece makes innocent remarks, but not someone of your age. What you meant was that if I know Ruth Hands through my church then she must be just another dyed-in-the-wool fundamentalist like me. As it happens she isn't a member of my church. We just support the work she's doing for Aids sufferers.'

'Celeste, dear girl,' I spluttered, trying to recapture the friendly mood, 'you're making too much of this.'

'Not at all! You said she's barking mad – '

'With grief.'

'Not just that. You meant in general. Well, if it's barking mad to want to help people suffering from a deadly disease and barking mad to believe that there may be more to your own daughter's death than the Five-Oh care to credit, then I hope I'm barking mad too.'

I know Celeste well enough to realise that I wouldn't beat her in argument. If things got too confrontational she'd just storm out and come back at her leisure, leaving the office to run itself. If anyone's barking mad, it must be me. I've surrounded myself with a whole posse of headstrong females.

Fortunately, hard experience has taught me when to pull my horns in. 'Celeste, I'm terribly sorry if I upset you,' I said sweetly. 'You can tell that I'm not just stereotyping Mrs Hands as a religious nut because, after all, I agreed to take her case.'

35

'Oh, yes,' she mocked. 'They do say love of money is the root of all evil.'

'Celeste, I haven't taken the case just for money. I need a change . . . these fraud cases, each one's the same as the one before.'

'Very noble, Dave. So Mrs Hands' problems are going to provide you with occupational therapy?'

'I know when I can't win. Tell me what it is you want to get off your chest.'

'Ruth Hands isn't mad, whatever you may think about so-called scientific impossibilities. She believes someone or something was stalking Meg.'

'I've already been through all this with Ruth. She's prepared to concede that Meg was being stalked by something in her mind, something intangible . . .'

Celeste pursed her lips and released a sceptical gasp. 'Intangible rubbish!' she snarled.

'There's certainly no sign of anything on the video recording.'

'And you accept the word of our great white police force for that?' she demanded caustically.

'Seeing that I've just gatecrashed the CCTV control centre and seen the recordings for myself I can tell you, Ruth Hands, and your whole assembled congregation, gospel choir included, that there was no one following Meg Hands. For your further information there's nothing "white" about this case. Last time I saw her Ruth Hands was looking pretty white herself.'

'She may be white to you but she's devoted her whole life to helping black people and there's some would like to see her fail.'

I stood up and the mac fell open, revealing my torn suit.

Celeste's eyes widened. She came forward and gazed at my ripped trousers. 'And you're saying that Ruth's mad,' she said with a wild laugh. 'Are the Five-Oh on their way?'

'I don't know,' I said with a shrug.

She looked at me appraisingly. 'Well, Dave Cunane, I suppose your heart's in the right place even if you are as crazy as a screech owl. Just so long as you don't forget that the Devil might not care to show himself on a VCR recording.'

With that she turned on her heel and headed to the door.

Since she got married, the religious side of Celeste's life seems to have flared up like a raging fire, but I wasn't about to let her have the last word. If there's one thing I do believe, it's the evidence of my own eyes.

'Fine,' I shouted at her retreating figure, gritting my teeth to avoid yelping at the pain from my battered knees, 'Christian Ruth Hands may be, but charity case she ain't! She gets charged top whack.'

Signalling acceptance of this command with a pout, Celeste departed. She refrained from slamming the door, so I guessed she'd be back at work on Monday.

I slumped into my chair and after an inner struggle resisted the urge to reach for the nearest whisky bottle. Instead, I rummaged through my desk for the case notes, or rather the photocopied case notes. I needed to see the statement in black and white that there was no evidence, either from VCR or any other source, that Meg Hands was followed.

As I grabbed the file it struck me how unusual it was for a civilian to be in possession of such a document. All I could put it down to was Ruth having some political influence with the authorities that was denied to the native population. Possibly the American Embassy had exerted pressure.

I was impressed.

I riffled through the pages before deciding what I was going to do next.

A change of trousers seemed like a good idea.

I keep spare clothes in the office. Living in Manchester, you never know when you might be suddenly soaked to the skin in a downpour of semitropical intensity. So I stripped off the ruined suit and threw it in the bin. I wondered whether that was a good omen or a bad omen. I reckon to have a suit ripped off my back in every major case, usually at a later stage in the proceedings. So, did the early shredding of expensive threads mean that I was now through the woods, or was it a sign that worse was to come, much worse?

As well as being severely grazed, my knees had now turned a deep shade of purple and were unpleasantly swollen. The thought of a visit to the A&E department at Manchester Royal Infirmary was unwelcome. I told myself that I'd taken worse knocks in a rugby match. I got out the first aid kit and made what repairs I could. I could still move and the more I thought about it the more I realised that I might have to move rapidly to avoid a visit from the constabulary because of my afternoon's amusements.

It was surprising that they weren't on scene already.

I put on a pair of cord trousers.

These had some history behind them. My father, Paddy Cunane, as well as being a retired cop, is a keen amateur builder. He's added so many extensions to his weaver's cottage on the moors above Bolton that he's had enquiries from the tourist authorities about taking in coach parties. In pursuit of authenticity in this role, or as I prefer to believe because he's as loopy as a crazed ferret, he wanted to look the part of a builder's labourer, circa 1900. He ordered a pair of heavy-duty cords from a specialist trouser-making firm in Hebden Bridge, Yorkshire.

When he unpacked the awaited parcel he discovered that they were of a bold yellow tint and made of such heavy material as to be arrow proof, if not bullet proof.

38

My mother and I teased him about his 'super-kecks', with the result that next birthday I was presented with a similar, but mercifully less luridly shaded pair myself.

These were what I now selected. I was hopeful that they might offer some protection for my wounded knees.

I chose a blue shirt, black leather jacket and a pair of industrial boots to complete the ensemble. The boots were an afterthought. Not being a criminal or a policeman, I don't carry lethal weapons, but if any eager security guard decided to mess with my knee caps he'd end up hobbling.

Pondering the wrath of Celeste, I left a message on Janine's answerphone to say that I'd be home late.

Dressed for action, I quit the office and headed for Castlefields. That's about a mile away but I didn't even consider going for my car. The trigonometry of the problem is that a trip to the car park would take almost as long as a walk to Castlefields and then I couldn't be sure of finding anywhere to park nearer than the car park my Mondeo already resided in. When I finally poked my head round the corner of the street there was no sign of police interest in my premises but then there are CCTV cameras everywhere. Possibly my every move was being translated into bits and bytes.

Lurching towards Deansgate because I was trying not to bend my knees, I quickly discovered that my choice of foot and leg wear was a mistake. The heavy boots and thick material impeded mobility but I decided to press on. I tried to walk normally. If Heritage was observing me I wanted to deny him the satisfaction of seeing me staggering along like a drunken sailor on a pair of peg legs.

After a few minutes the pain began to ease. I stamped along the crowded pavements stoically. Now that we've adopted the Euro-American way of life and graze in countless coffee shops and snack bars, there's always movement in this part of town.

Deansgate's like a long narrow canyon with tall Victorian and modern buildings on either side but it widens towards the viaduct, which passes over the canals and rivers of Castlefields. It's much lighter and you get an open prospect of the sky that is lacking in central Manchester. In the last rays of evening sun the sky took on a surrealistic glow. It was filled with a mass of individual fleecy clouds sailing in from the west. Each looked as if it had been carefully painted by René Magritte. Usually in Manchester, if it's not actually raining the clouds are all joined up into a dull grey blanket. For once it was bright and my heart lightened a little.

How did Meg Hands end up in that canal? Suicide was the possibility that I feared. Hard to believe, but had she thrown herself into the canal, having sinned against Mom's high expectations by getting plastered for the first time? Perhaps she hadn't intended a fatal result.

But what did I know? I knew little about the motivation of highly religious people.

I looked up at the clouded sky with a sigh. I'd warned Ruth but she was so fixated that it hadn't occurred to her that the results of an investigation might not be to her liking. I fancied I heard the whine of an aircraft heading for sunnier climes. Why wasn't I on it?

I trudged along Deansgate, passing Victorian buildings transformed from grandiose temples of trade into greasy spoon restaurants. The Canal Basin I was heading towards is another resurrected slice of local history. Where dockers once sweated, yuppies now play.

When I arrived things were just beginning to warm up for the evening. Offices were closing early for the weekend and the moneyed young were gathering round the waterholes. The main action is provided by bar restaurants – La Venezia, Coleman's Wharf and the Bargee's Rest. Audi Quattros, Porsches, and Golf GTIs jammed the cobbled streets. I decided to give La Venezia a visit first because it was slightly less crowded than the rival establishments. A modern stainless-steel and glass establishment, it blends well into Castlefield's mixture of old and new. Despite its name, there are more locomotives trundling over the viaducts than there are gondolas or barges in the canal. The basin pool is dominated by a cantilevered steel foot bridge that hangs over the murky waters like an abstract sculpture.

These were the waters that I was interested in. Any similarity to the lagoons of Venice began and ended with their colour.

'I'm enquiring about a woman who was found drowned out there last month,' I said to the crop-headed youth who served me in the ultra-modern bar. I showed him a photo of Meg. His bat-like ears twitched. He took a very quick squint at the picture and then looked away through the plate glass at the waters beyond. His features screwed up into a frown.

'Nothing to do with us,' he said sourly.

'I was only asking,' I replied, 'I'm not making accusations.'

'Sorry, but we've had a lot of press in here, what with that missionary woman kicking off. The manager doesn't want to encourage gawpers.'

'Really,' I murmured encouragingly.

'Yeah. You're not press, are you?'

'I don't think so. I'm not wearing a dirty raincoat, am I?'

He shot me a suspicious look. I realised that he'd interpreted my remark as meaning that I wasn't an active paedophile.

'Yeah,' he said, looking me over with narrowed eyes. He didn't know what to make of me. 'Well, it's just that we get a lot of celebs in here and they'll stop coming if there's too much of the wrong sort of news and wrong sort of people.'

Teetotal Ruth Hands was certainly the wrong sort as far as a boozing-den was concerned but the lad was coming on a little strong. I wondered why.

I gave an expressive shrug and moved away. I headed towards the stairs leading to the upper bar and restaurant. The youthful barman hopped from behind his counter and blocked my path.

'You can't go up there. It's a private meeting,' he said.

'What? Some of the old celebs?' I joked.

'You can't go up there,' he barked roughly.

There was something about his expression and the way his hands had formed into fists that cautioned me against further argument. It wasn't cold so I went outside to the beer garden. It was one of those days when a westerly wind brings mild pure air to Manchester. It was pleasant sitting in the gathering dusk. I tried to get the feel of the place where Meg Hands had met her death.

Situated on wharfs formerly pulsing with industry, this is now one of the most popular meeting points in Manchester. A gigantic wedding cake of railway viaducts layered one on top of the other provides an interesting backdrop.

Apart from La Venezia, a renovated building, nothing much has changed since the railway navvies hacked their way through here.

The Canal Basin is a weird spot to choose for a swim, or even a suicide attempt. To get to the water's edge involved a walk down a flight of uneven stone steps. Even for the able-bodied it's an obstacle race. It was too much for my aching knees, but apparently the police believed that a girl so drunk that she'd had to cling to a lamppost had been able to take a header into the canal.

Something didn't quite compute, as Michael Coe might say. Judging by the state of Meg Hands in those last shots of her on Deansgate she couldn't have crawled here. Not unless she had some help, that is.

42

There was another puzzle.

It was getting quite gloomy now in the spaces between the buildings, yet the canal surface was well lit from all sides, and even from above by the lights on the cantilever bridge. The waters were the main attraction of the spot.

How was it possible Meg wasn't seen as she struggled?

I felt a tingling sensation in all my nerves as the answer came to me. It wasn't possible. I could hear car doors slamming and the excited voices of young people greeting each other as the place revved up for the evening's fun. It just wasn't possible that a person drowning in the canal wouldn't be noticed. If that's what had happened the police had to come up with an explanation of why not one of the hundreds of potential spectators had seen anything. Was there some other event, some massive diversion, that captured everyone's attention at the time of Meg's death? If so, there was no mention of it in the report given to Ruth Hands.

First the invisible stalker and now the invisible victim.

That was just one too many invisible for me to accept.

Even now, early on a winter evening, there were gleaming reflections on the impenetrably dark surfaces. There were streetlights, lights all over the beer garden, lights from the nearby flats. Anyone splashing about in that water was bound to be seen.

'A proper puzzle, in't it?' a sallow-complexioned young man in a dark suit said. He'd suddenly turned up at my side, apparently endowed with the powers of a mind reader. Looking past him, towards the doorway of La Venezia, I could make out the shapes of two burly door stewards. I read the words 'Ted Cosgrove, Manager' on a black plastic badge on his lapel. One of his Myrmidons came closer, an individual only about two inches taller than me but with massively overdeveloped arms, resembling a child's drawing of a comic-book hero. The bouncer's bald head gleamed like a shiny golden helmet in the sodium lights. He was not the type you'd quickly forget.

'Like that, is it?' I asked.

'Oh, them,' he said, turning to glance at the hulking shadows, 'they're only here as a precaution. We get a lot of famous people down here.'

'So I was told.'

'Sports people, people from the *Street* . . . *Corrie*, you know, and media types, important, like.'

'Are they the ones having the private meeting? What is it? Celebs Anonymous? They all gather to decide how to cope with fame?'

'It's none of your damn business,' he said evenly.

'Right,' I agreed. 'While we're on the subject of famous people, Mr Cosgrove, how did a famous person's daughter manage to get herself drowned in that pool with this pub going full blast?'

'I don't know, mate. That's what I mean. It's a right puzzle.'

He stared at me coldly. I was intended to get the feeling that I wasn't welcome but that sort of thing doesn't get through to me. I stared right back at him. His face was long and narrow with a lantern jaw and a big nose. Fronds of black gelled hair covered his narrow forehead and poked out onto his prominent cheekbones. Dark, close-set eyes gleamed at me. I amused myself by considering which member of the animal kingdom he most resembled. The best I could come up with was a particularly ill-favoured horse. One thing was clear to me: this guy wouldn't give a damn if a missionary's daughter had been deliberately drowned here. No, not if one girl had been drowned or a hundred more like her.

Uncaring, that was the word. He gave off that hard nasty emanation that I was so familiar with in my meetings with the underworld.

Seeing his boss apparently at a loose end, the more

44

ferocious-looking of the two bouncers, the bald-headed one, came forward. I tensed for action.

'Leave it, Neville,' Cosgrove grated.

The brute retreated but I fancied he left an odour behind him. Testosterone or just plain old halitosis, I wondered.

'Has he got a problem his best friends won't tell him about then?' I joked.

'You want to watch what you say to Neville. He can be impulsive.' Cosgrove made a gesture with his hands to signify something being broken.

'I was only offering advice on personal hygiene.'

'You the police, then?' Cosgrove asked out of the side of his mouth.

When I'm asked this question I know what's coming next: a flow of information or the bum's rush.

'Private, actually,' I said, offering him one of my cards.

He carefully scrutinised this before putting it in his wallet, then cleared his throat. I looked up at him with mixed feelings. Having suffered at the hands of security guards once today, I knew I could be in for either revelation or elevation.

'Cunane, are you working for the mother,' he asked cautiously, 'or is it someone else?'

'The victim's mother.'

'Victim, eh?' he said scornfully. 'Well, I don't know anything about how the daft tart managed to get herself drowned but the police have investigated thoroughly and no one at La Venezia, staff or customers, knows anything either.'

'Really?' I said.

'Yes, *really*, and I'll tell you something else for free. We're sick to the back teeth of people coming asking stupid questions about what we did or didn't see. I'm running a pub, not the bloody lifeguard service.'

'Pretty inconsiderate of her, wasn't it?'

'All right then, sarky-gob, ask your questions, but I'm not guaranteeing any answers.'

'Someone must have seen Meg Hands, either here, or in the street, or when she was in the water. This area's well lit. Even if it was chucking it down and everyone was inside, somebody must have seen a drunk wandering down onto the canal bank.'

'They didn't. Nobody saw nothing. Before you ask the next question, the answer is this: no, I am not, repeat not, covering up for some telly star who came on to this girl and then threw her in the water when she blew him out. I know nothing, full stop.'

I thought this just a little too well rehearsed. He knew something.

'Oh, come on,' I urged. 'It was a Friday night. Rain or fine, the place must've been buzzing. What about your security people? They must be on the lookout for people wandering near the water's edge.'

'They saw nothing,' he insisted doggedly.

'So, how's your hearing, then? I'm not saying she took the plunge outside La Venezia. It could have been somewhere else, but you must have heard a whisper from someone.'

'We saw nothing. We heard nothing.'

'I'm only asking, not accusing. I'm not the police. Anything you tell me's in confidence and there might even be a reward. Think of the girl's mother. Do you have children yourself? Don't you think the mother's entitled to find out everything she can?'

'Maybe she is, but there are some people who think the Hands woman has more money than sense, the way she keeps raking over things. I suppose you're down here trying to get your fingers into her jam?' He laughed at his own wit, an unpleasant sniggering sound.

'I have my job, you have yours,' I said levelly.

'Listen, I'll give you some friendly advice,' he offered.

46

It crossed my mind to get him by the scruff of the neck and throw him and his advice into the canal and see if his bouncers noticed him struggling, but I didn't. Instead I nodded and offered him my shell-like.

'There's people round here, nothing to do with La Venezia, or the other joints for that matter, people with money invested in property who're concerned about this area getting a bad reputation. That girl's death was an accident, a freak accident if you like, but it was nothing more. How do people get themselves drowned in public swimming pools with attendants standing around? It's a puzzle, like I said before, and if you've any sense you'll leave it at that and tell Mrs Hands to stop harping on.'

'Thanks,' I said, 'but what if I don't?'

'Don't what?' he asked.

'Leave it alone.'

He gave that same sniggering laugh he'd used earlier. 'Nothing to do with me, mate. I live in Didsbury and I don't own any waterside developments. I'm just offering a word to the wise.'

'Thanks for your concern.'

'OK!' he said with a dismissive wave as he turned. 'I'll send you another drink. All this talking must have made you thirsty.'

He strode away as swiftly as he'd arrived, a brisk young man on his way to higher things, no doubt. I wondered who was giving him his orders. The people meeting in the upper room? I decided that I'd like to see who they were. The lurking bouncers disappeared back into the shadows from which they'd emerged and a moment later a fresh new pint was sitting on the table in front of me.

It didn't take me many minutes to work out why I was being treated to a pint. It wasn't generosity. Cosgrove had that calculating look about him that suggested that he never did anything without an ulterior motive.

All I had to do was wait and see if he'd summoned

47

his heavy mob or the police. I just had to wait and see, that, or leg it as fast as my battered knees would let me.

I stayed where I was.

I didn't have long to wait.

A police car drew up on the narrow stone bridge at the end of the Rochdale Canal. Detective Chief Superintendent Jack Rix emerged. He made a tall and imposing figure in his double-breasted Hugo Boss suit. A red-faced, prematurely bald Irishman, something about his bearing signalled 'bluebottle' like a flashing neon light. He scanned the area, spotted me and signalled me to join him. I pretended I hadn't seen him and turned away to study the ripples stirring on the surface of the Bridgewater Canal.

It wasn't that I had anything special against Rix. I'd have to admit that he's one of the more congenial of the boys in blue. The big danger with 'Smiling' Jack is that he has all the charm and verbal fluency of the Irish combined with a ruthless determination to win at all costs that would make even a Prussian general blanch. Just the qualities a copper needs to succeed in Manchester, you might think.

I've never actually detected him in a lie but he's made a fine art of bending and shading the truth and has relied on his quick mind and even quicker tongue to get him out of trouble with the legal fraternity more than once.

A moment later I heard the heavy, intimidatory footsteps of a lone man approaching. They told me that I wasn't going to have my collar felt over my excursion to the 'secret' CCTV centre. Like turtle doves and Mormon missionaries, detectives always travel in pairs when coming to arrest you and Rix was alone.

'Cunane!' he snarled peevishly. 'What are you using for ears?'

I took a swallow of my drink. I tried to stay calm but I wasn't.

There was a sound similar to teeth grinding. It may just have been Rix clearing his throat. I continued to enjoy the view.

'Cunane!' he growled.

'You speaking to me?' I muttered.

'Oh, don't piss me off, Dave. I haven't time for this crap,' he scolded, sitting heavily on the seat next to me.

'You must have all the time in the world,' I quipped.

'How do you work that one out, genius?' he snarled.

'Someone phones to say I'm enquiring into the Hands case and, hey, you're here in under five minutes.'

'Rubbish!' he snorted. 'I was on my way home.'

'I see,' I said, 'and what other economies with the truth would you like me to take into consideration?'

A divorced man, he's never been known to go home before eight.

I enjoy listening to Rix spin a yarn. He speaks with a Northern Irish accent but to say that gives a false impression. There's none of that gritty old Presbyterian granite in Jack's vowels. His voice has a lilting, musical quality and he emphasises his words so clearly and with such conviction that it's easier to believe him than to doubt him. A brilliant storyteller, he could have been a great salesman.

I turned to look at him. His brows knitted unpleasantly as he trawled his extensive collection of insults for a crushing comeback, but nothing came. Instead his features melted into the famous Rix smile. I knew then that he wasn't here just to give me a rap on the knuckles.

I responded with a blank stare.

'Look, Dave, *old boy*, you may have all the time in the world to sit freezing your bum off but I don't. We can do this at Bootle Street Police Station or in my car, suit yourself.'

'I don't know what you're on about, but I'm perfectly comfortable where I am,' I said nonchalantly.

'You're an irritating sod!' he snapped. He turned and waved to his driver, who slowly pulled away from the bridge and began looking for somewhere to park. 'Christ, it's brass monkey weather out here,' he grumbled. 'At least come inside while we talk.'

I shrugged to indicate that the temperature was fine by me.

'You're working for the Hands woman, aren't you?' he declared. 'And a wee bird tells me that you've already been making trouble where you shouldn't. If there's one individual in Manchester who can always be trusted to shit in his own bed, it's you.'

'That's unkind,' I murmured.

'I'm feeling unkind. Have you seen the papers? According to them we're lying about the existence of a serial killer. You'd think all we do all day is hide evidence.'

He didn't look well. His face was pale and his nose was red as if he'd been blowing it a lot. I took pity on him, picked up my glass and strolled over to the interior of the bar. The lurking bouncers had made themselves scarce, more because of Rix's presence than mine, I guessed. I caught a glimpse of Cosgrove peering down in surprise from the top of the stairs. He bobbed back inside when he saw I was with Rix.

Rix followed me in, still whinging. 'You know, I can do without aggravation from jumped-up private detectives . . .'

'Aggravation, you say,' I commented. 'So far I've had piss, crap, rubbish and shit from you and that's just in two sentences. You're heading for a nervous breakdown.'

'Get away!' he laughed, slapping me on the shoulder like a long-lost brother as he unthawed.

'What'll you have?' I asked with an excess of that misplaced kindness that has never done me the slightest good with top plods such as Rix.

He turned eagerly to the barman, the same shaven-headed youth who'd snubbed me earlier. 'Have you got a drop of Bushmills?' Rix enquired.

The lad nodded.

'Bushmills Gold?'

The youth nodded again.

'Make that a large one, a very large one, in a shot glass. That's a triple in case you don't know, sonny. Now have you also got warm water, brown sugar and the thick end of a lemon?'

'Why don't you just grab the bottle and we can make a night of it?' I observed.

'Don't interrupt, Dave,' he ordered. 'This is serious business.'

Turning to the bar he continued to relay his instructions. The youth, who'd been so sour with me, was following Rix's commands with open-mouthed admiration. I guessed this was how he expected celebs to behave.

'Now, sonny, have you got that, a triple? No, scrap that, slip another one in there to keep the other three company, and then add the same amount of water, hot but not boiling, then the sugar, two teaspoonsful, and then squeeze the lemon juice into it and stir.'

By now the barman had an audience as he carefully followed the detective's instructions. Finally he handed a steaming glass to Rix.

'Have something yourself, my son,' Rix invited the barman, indicating that I was going to pay, 'and you too, Dave.'

I ordered another pint for myself and paid up.

We sat in the 'pointed end' of the irregular-shaped room, at a table for two overlooking the canal. I could see people crossing the white bridge. It was brilliantly illuminated.

'You're a great comedian, Dave,' Rix commented. 'I hear you had them in stitches down at the CCTV centre, so look on this wee drinkie as part of your fine.'

'OK,' I agreed.

'Well, here goes,' he said, and then drained his glass at one swallow. 'Kill or cure, that's the way to treat colds.'

I grunted something in reply.

'Am I boring you here, Dave?' he asked.

'Always ready to 'elp the Ol' Bill, guvna,' I said in my best cockney.

'I really ought to keep in with you private boys,' he opined.

'And why would that be, Jack?'

'You're the in-crowd these days, I kid you not. The way things are going, if the police service can't get the crime rate down the politicians will be putting you lot in charge.'

'Heaven forbid,' I muttered.

'No, I'm dead serious,' he insisted. 'You ought to make yourself into a big consortium and be ready for when they privatise us.'

For a moment I almost felt sorry for him.

Then it struck me that his smile was as false as the face on a photocopied twenty-pound note. With Jack, every move was calculated. His alcohol intake probably made him more, not less cunning. As I tried to think what his sly purpose might be, he looked round to make sure that no one was earwigging, and settled down for a confidential chat.

'Dave, you're right about me. You're very perceptive. I'm on a raw edge,' he whined self-pityingly. 'What with that fucking woman organising campaigns and the tabloids screaming that every accident's a bloody murder . . . I just came along to check that you were on the right lines.'

'Thanks,' I offered.

He detected no irony. No one would ever accuse Jack Rix of not taking himself seriously.

'Look, the silly heifer lived just over there.' He indicated the road bridge that bisects the Canal Basin and carries traffic into Deansgate. 'See, those flats on the other side of the viaduct,' he continued, pointing out the block, 'luxury apartments. You can tell the kid was rich – not that I hold that against her despite what the mother claims. I like Hands marmalade. No, you or I could never afford a flat there in a million years. Well, I couldn't anyway, not on police wages.'

'You poor thing,' I sympathised.

'Listen, shut your nasty mouth for a minute and I'll tell you what happened to this kid. She was pissed to the eyeballs coming home from a party. For some reason she walked, but in her alcoholic state missed the turning for her apartment, crossed the end of Deansgate and came down here, right down to the canal bank. It was a dark night. She probably didn't even realise that she was step- ping into the canal. She could have thought she was crossing a road. Easy enough if you're blotto.'

We both looked out at the still waters. It didn't sound all that likely but it was possible.

I said nothing.

'It was a filthy night,' Rix added, searching my face for some sign of agreement.

'According to her mother, Meg was as teetotal as a pub in Saudi.'

'Sez she! But I know different. The girl was at a rave-up in one of those halls of residence and it wasn't sarsa- parilla that was flowing there, I can tell you. She was with her brother but he didn't walk her home, or put her in a taxi. If you ask me that's why the woman's decided this is foul play. She wants to clear her son of any responsi- bility, but if he'd been any kind of a decent fella he'd have seen his sister home and all this would have been avoided. It was a tragic accident and nothing more.'

'Mrs Hands is very definite about the girl's drinking habits.'

'Oh, aren't they all like that? Parents are the last to know what their offspring are up to.'

'Not always,' I said, calling to mind the eagle-eyed scrutiny of my own pair.

He looked round again to check he wasn't being overheard. 'Dave,' he whispered, 'the girl'd lost her virginity some time before she drowned. I deleted that from the version of the report we let the mother have but, as I see it, the lassie was reacting against the severity of a strict home background . . .'

'So you're a social worker now, Jack?' I interjected while I took in the surprising news.

'. . . Sadly she wasn't used to drink and she took more than she should have,' he concluded complacently. Then he folded his hands round his empty glass and favoured me with a bland smile.

In this particular chess match it looked like a final score of Police 1, Private Investigator 0, and Rix knew it.

Still, Rix's move opened up new lines of thought. *Cherchez l'homme*, as we say in the private detective trade. Why hadn't the mysterious penetrator come forward? Was the deflowering of a virgin such a routine transaction that you didn't even notice when she turned up dead in a canal afterwards?

'Suppose she was raped?' I asked.

'Do you think we're a bunch of complete amateurs? Nonconsensual sex was ruled out at the post-mortem. There was no sperm in the vagina, not a sign of forcible entry.'

'Do you know the man's name?'

'Not yet,' he said complacently. 'It could be one of several and as there's no question of rape it's not a matter that we're pursuing.'

'The girl had sex for the first time not long before her death and you don't think the man's name's important?'

'Now you're jumping to conclusions. It's not like when

54

you were a kid, Dave . . . full string orchestra and a suite at the Midland. It's all casual these days.'

'Spare me the comedy, Jack. It's not that free and easy, surely?'

'You're out of touch, Dave.'

I felt the heat rising to my face. Rix had a talent to annoy.

'Have you checked out some of the bouncers round this place? There's a slap-head built like a fork-lift truck who looks as if he'd rape his own granny for tuppence.'

'I repeat, this isn't a rape case but an accidental death inquiry.'

'The bouncers –'

'No! The security staff at La Venezia are employed by a reputable agency. This young woman was drunk, possibly for the first time in her life, I'll grant you. But these things happen. She fell in. She drowned. The reason no one saw it is the same as the reason she wasn't rescued – there was no one about at the time. We've established that, so why go further?'

'What about this so-called serial-killer angle?'

'There is no serial killer. That's all got up to sell papers.'

I made no reply.

'Dave,' he said cogently, gripping my forearm, 'what if the girl celebrated cutting Mummy's apron strings by having sex with half a dozen men? Have you thought of that? Do you think that's the sort of thing Mrs Hands wishes to learn about?'

'She just wants the truth,' I snapped, shaking myself free.

'Oh, aye!'

'She claims that Meg was frightened by something or someone just before she met her death.'

Rix paused for dramatic effect and then looked round the room as if concerned that someone might overhear him. Then he caught the barman's eye and clicked his fingers.

'Same again, sonny,' he ordered.

'What's with all this checking that no one's listening?' I asked.

'It's more than my job's worth to get these fundamentalists on my back,' he insisted, tapping his nose. 'You never know who's listening.'

'You mean people like Ruth Hands, who believe in right and wrong, while you just want to list this death as a contemporary social statistic?'

'Dave, I'm telling you,' he asserted, 'the woman's out of her skull.'

'She didn't strike me that way.'

'Well,' he leaned forward and imparted his next words in a whisper, 'how else would you describe a woman who's prepared to suggest that her daughter was hounded to her death by a mysterious force? Only, it's not little green men, or even this imaginary serial killer the press boys are flogging. She's hinting at Satanism, isn't she? *The Devil Rides Out*, eh?'

I looked at him in surprise.

'Oh, so she hasn't run that one past you yet? I can tell you that even that angle has been checked out. Believe me, there's nothing in it. All that stuff was discredited years ago.'

'Still . . .' I murmured.

'Look, I'm being straight with you,' Rix said, fixing me with his beady eyes and flashing the phoney smile that's earned him the nickname of 'Smiling' Jack. I distrusted him but knew truth might pass his lips when it suited his convenience.

The barman brought our drinks on a tray.

Rix pushed the receipt at me. I paid.

'It was treated as a suspicious death from the start as there was no suicide note or anything. It was investigated in the normal way by my team. There was nothing untoward, nothing to indicate violence or foul play. We

56

kept it going longer than we normally would have because of the mother's status but it isn't as if we had to go that little bit further for a potentially racist murder . . .' He stopped, realising that his words could be misconstrued. 'Sorry, my political correctness is slipping, but you know what I mean. Some cases are more sensitive than others and this one comes into that category to an extent, but budgets are budgets. The inquiry's still officially open but that's only until we get through the formality of the coroner's verdict of accidental death, which of course your client's shenanigans have delayed.'

He paused and then squeezed my forearm again to add emphasis to his next comment. 'I don't want your name added to the list of delayers, Dave, you must see that. I mean, what did you find out by gatecrashing the CCTV centre? Nothing!'

Once again I was given the full smile. I noticed that his teeth were uneven.

I nodded my head in reluctant agreement.

'You haven't got anything that indicates foul play, have you?'

I nodded my head again, unsure of what to say. My instincts were telling me that there was more to be uncovered in this case.

Rix noted my uncertainty.

'Yes, now don't take this wrong, but you make your living by catering to these people –'

'What!'

'Rich people with problems . . . naturally you're more sympathetic than I can afford to be. Listen, Dave, we've checked and we've double-checked. Believe me, there's no mystery here, only a wealthy widow who won't accept the facts we've put before her.'

Rix was speaking in the half-conspiratorial way one 'practical' man addresses another. I had to pull myself up sharply when I almost found myself nodding in agreement again. Just in time I remembered that I was taking Ruth Hands' money to prove that there were 'facts' that hadn't been uncovered.

I battered my wits to come up with an objection to Jack's plausible spiel.

'What about the diatoms, the levels –'

'Now you're clutching at straws. The unfortunate lass probably went into shock as soon as she hit the water and died after a brief struggle. That's why the levels were lower than Doc Gribbin expected. Speaking of the good doc, didn't I hear that you were interested in our worthy pathologist? Great to see the ethnic minorities getting ahead. Very nice with it, she is too.'

He shaped his hands to indicate a voluptuous figure and licked his lips. I asked myself why a few minutes in Jack Rix's company made me feel that I needed a shower.

To my shame I rewarded his banter with a smile. If he took it into his head, he could be a nuisance in any number of ways.

'Is that all you lads at the cop shop have time for?' I asked with a grin. 'Idle gossip?'

'God! I wish it was. I could really get my teeth into a piece of idle,' he whined with genuine feeling. 'Thanks to these ten-a-penny scribblers in the tabloids, every mishap in Greater Manchester is down to this nonexistent "Mangler". There's also been a spate of mystery accidents . . . But, what the hell, you don't want to hear about my troubles. I suppose you're doing us a favour by taking this nutcase on. Keep her off our backs and you'll see that we're duly grateful.'

'Just as long as I don't find it was anything but an accident, is that it?'

'How could you? That's what it was. I mean, let's face it, Dave, you're not dishonest, are you?'

If Rix had tried to jolly her along like this, Ruth Hands' fury was understandable.

I hid my reaction but the senior detective was too astute to be deceived by a blank look.

My part in his scheme was clear. I would reassure Ruth, the coroner would do his stuff and this potentially awkward little problem would be off Rix's desk.

I might have gone along if he'd resisted the temptation to go just a little bit too far, but he didn't. He couldn't help himself putting the boot in.

'String her along for a few weeks,' he advised, struggling to keep his smile from slipping into a sneer. 'Hit her with a nice big bill if you must, but don't try any of your Lone Ranger tricks. We got this one dead right on day one and that's all you'll find, however many times you bash your head against solid objects.'

'That sounds like an order,' I commented.

I caught the dangerous gleam in his small, washed-out blue eyes as he realised that boy talk might not be enough to swing things.

'No, just the simple truth,' he said, 'and by the way, the Chief's considering whether to refer today's breach of security to the Crown Prosecution Service.'

'The implication being that if I toe the line with Ruth Hands, he won't?'

'Take it how the hell you like.'

'Fine,' I said coolly. 'Tell him to prosecute me. The publicity should really put the CCTV control centre on the map. My solicitor's already suggested that we work in tandem with the civil liberties people. They're looking for a test case. They claim the Data Protection Act gives everyone the right to check out their pictures in your little private spy box. The case might go as far as the European Court of Justice.'

'Dave, don't take this wrong because I don't mean it in the doctrinal sense, but you're one of nature's left-footers, aren't you? You're bluffing and you and I both know it.'

'As for left-footers, maybe we need one or two people breaking step with you, Mr Rix. Otherwise, call my bluff,' I invited, 'see what happens.'

'You jammy bastard,' he muttered, conceding defeat with a shake of his head. 'I've never known anyone with the ability to go face down in the horse manure as often as you, yet still come up smiling.'

'Oh, I don't know. You manage it often enough yourself.'

That wiped the phoney grin off his face.

'Fuck off, Cunane,' he said, downing his drink and heading for the exit.

As I watched his back disappear through the door I knew from the determined set of his shoulders that there'd be consequences. Jack Rix isn't the kind of man who gives that kind of advice just to hear the sound of his own voice.

I hung around La Venezia for a while, hoping to eyeball the mystery guests in the upstairs rooms. Nothing happened for ten minutes until there was a flurry of movement and Cosgrove and his crew appeared at the top of the stairs. They were barring any access from below. I emboldened myself to wait for the faces to appear. Nothing happened.

Cosgrove finally came down and gave me a genial smile.

'Still here, Cunane?' he asked, winking at his sidekick Neville, who was struggling to impersonate a human being.

The thought penetrated that there was a back exit from the restaurant. By the time I managed to scuttle out of my seat all I saw was a large limousine, possibly a Bentley, disappearing up the lane.

Walking slowly back to where I'd left my car I had plenty of time to ponder the enigma that was Jack Rix. By taking the line that sensible, 'liberal', informed opinion was preferred on the so-called Mangler killings, Jack had made himself into a progressive icon. If events proved him to be correct nothing would stop him going to the very top of the British police service. On the other hand, anyone bringing up awkward evidence might find out what happened to people who got in between Jack Rix and his ambition. Such a person would be ground 'between upper and nether millstones', as Ruth Hands might put it.

I took a deep breath and started to hurry on.

4

'The newshounds of the popular press continue to bay for red meat. Attempts by some of the print media's less than luminous elements to fight circulation wars by whipping up fears of serial killers on the loose in a northern city were yesterday condemned in Parliament by Northern MPs. Statistical evidence proves that the death rate among Greater Manchester females in the 18–25 age group is actually much lower than predicted. Deaths due to acts of violence unrelated to each other were only 4 out of 386,000, well below statistical predictions.'

Op-ed article on 'Our Mad Media' in the *Guardian*

'There's got to be some logical explanation,' I grumbled to Janine when I got home that evening. 'The accidental death story's as full of holes as a Swiss sausage.'

'It's cheese, not sausage,' Jenny, Janine's daughter, piped up from the other side of the table where she was doing her homework.

'Just checking that your ears are working!' I said, with a touch of sharpness.

Jenny gave me a very grown-up look and returned to her books with a disdainful sniff.

'Dave, calm down,' my partner advised. 'You've turned a very unpleasant shade of puce.'

'Is that all you've got to say?' I muttered indignantly. 'This woman's paying good money for results and all I've discovered so far is that the policeman in charge of the case has decided that I'm a left-footer.'

'Watch what you're saying, Dave,' Janine warned, with a nod in her daughter's direction.

'Heard it before,' Jenny said with an even louder sniff. 'It means that you can't play football properly.'

'No, dear, it means that he thinks Dave's a Roman Catholic . . .'

'Like Granny Eileen and Grand-da Paddy?' she asked, casting a speculative glance in my direction. 'But Dave doesn't go to church,' she added accusingly.

Jenny misses nothing.

'Dave's always too busy with you and Lloyd on Sundays,' Janine intervened.

'It doesn't just mean that, about church,' I explained. 'It means that you're awkward. You dig with the left foot. You won't do things in the way Jack Rix likes them done.'

'Dave, why are you worried about him? You're independent of the police.'

'Am I? Is anyone? When Big Brother's watching every move and recording it on his spy cameras?'

'Even if you pick your nose in the street?' Jenny asked wonderingly.

'Especially that.'

'Don't be horrid, Jenny,' Janine ordered. 'Of course you mustn't pick your nose in the street. Now go and see if Naomi's finished with Lloyd in the bathroom and then brush your teeth.'

Jenny departed.

'You're worried,' Janine stated firmly when the child had gone.

'A little, not enough to lose any sleep. Rix's very self-righteous. It never pays to underestimate the spite of his sort when you upset them.'

'Surely all that left-footer stuff's died out now?' Janine asked uncertainly.

'Oh, yeah,' I said gloomily. 'We're all post-modern *Guardian* readers now, but with some people in this country, bigotry's always there like wet rot in an old building. I mean, he brought it up, didn't he?'

'He's just jealous because you're doing so well.'

'Yeah, I expect that's part of it, but only part.'

'You think he's worried that you might find something and show him up?'

'Not really. He's certain he's right. He just wants to let me know who runs things on his patch.'

'And you think he's wrong about Meg Hands?'

'He could be.'

'Well, that's something, isn't it?' she observed calmly. 'All you have to do is go over everything again from the beginning and you'll see where he made his mistakes. Then if he calls you a left-footer again you can tell him he hasn't even got a leg to stand on.'

'It's all that simple, is it?' I responded gloomily.

'It is. Now be a good little man and take Naomi home, she'll have finished bathing Lloyd in a minute. You know perfectly well you're going to do everything you can for Ruth Hands and if it does turn out that Meg's death was an accident having it confirmed by you will help her to accept the truth.'

I glanced at the doorway. Naomi Carter, nanny of Janine's children, and essential creator of space and time for Janine to pursue her journalistic career, was standing in the doorway. She was holding her coat. As usual, she was frowning. For some reason my charm has never worked on Naomi. When I first met her she was crying her eyes out and I think she still subconsciously associates me with grief.

A tall, plain-looking, broad-shouldered girl of nineteen with well-developed upper arm muscles and bust to match, Naomi's definitely fallen on her feet in the White household. Sometimes I feel she gets more consideration than I do. She's probably more essential to the family's wellbeing than I am.

'Go on, Dave,' Janine coaxed. 'I've got to help Jenny finish her homework.'

Naomi had started out as a live-in nanny but that didn't work when she developed an interest in the opposite sex. So Janine had long since found Naomi somewhere of her own. The down side of this arrangement is that one of us has to ferry her back and forth all the time.

My dear partner knew well enough that I hate driving Naomi home to Stretford. Making conversation with the burly teenager's like trying to melt ice by lighting a candle on a glacier.

During the brief journey to Stretford Naomi said no more than three words until we actually arrived at her flat when she suddenly opened up like a Venus flytrap.

'Dave, I don't like to ask, but would you mind going on to my friend in Urmston's place?' was the interesting opening gambit.

'You mean to see Clint?'

Clint is the love interest in Naomi's life. The brother of a friend of mine, and physically a giant, Clint has learning difficulties.

'No, not him. It's a girl, Annie Aycliffe. She works at the animal shelter in Sale and Clint and me have got to know her through that. You know Clint works there two afternoons a week.'

'Urmston?' I asked, trying to keep a long-suffering tone from creeping into my voice.

'She's got my vacuum cleaner.'

'Oh?' I muttered.

'It's one of those Dysons. It used to belong to you but Janine said I could have it and now I've borrowed it to Annie and I need it back. My flat's a right tip. I've been at Janine's so much this week, what with babysitting while you two go out and all.'

'Right,' I mumbled, accepting my obligation. I'd vaguely noticed that my cleaner had gone from its usual cupboard. I was reduced to using Janine's even more up-to-date model.

I drove the extra miles to Urmston, following Naomi's directions until we arrived at a run-down, three-storey Edwardian house.

'She's on the top floor,' Naomi announced.

'Right,' I said, switching on the car radio for the evening news. I made no other move, expecting her to leave.

Naomi opened her mouth to speak and then paused before uttering. She closed her mouth and treated me to a rare smile.

I waited patiently.

'Er, Dave, would you mind coming up with me?' she asked in a quavering voice. 'There's this man on the first floor and he sometimes comes out and says things to me and I don't like it. I'd have asked Clint but you know what he's like. I don't want him to hurt this man.'

The curse of the Cunanes is that we always respond to a lady in distress so I switched off the radio and carted myself out of the car handily enough. My knees gave a horrible twinge and Naomi may have mistaken my grimace as an expression of displeasure.

'Sore knees,' I explained.

'Oh,' she said, without further enquiry.

'I take it you don't want me to hurt this man?' I asked as she took a key out of her purse.

'Oh no! He's just a dirty old man. He keeps saying he wants me to model for him. You know, like, with no clothes on.'

'Cheeky bugger,' I commented, eyebrows raised in mock horror. I censored any naughty thoughts such as came bouncing unbidden from my imagination.

A smell of stale cabbage and boiled potatoes assaulted our nostrils when we entered, but there was no sign of the eager old snapper himself.

Annie Aycliffe's flat was the only one on the top floor. Naomi knocked and then went in.

'Annie's at the animal shelter night and day,' she explained. 'There's a cat due to have babies.'

'How extraordinary!' I exclaimed.

Naomi's glum face lit up with a smile, as if she was being complimented on her acquaintance with such a remarkable person.

'She's not worried about her downstairs neighbour?' I queried. 'I mean leaving her door open like this?'

'Annie's a big girl,' Naomi explained, matter-of-factly. 'She'll rip the old pervert's liver and lights out if he messes with her.'

Before I could explore the concept of what Naomi might consider a big girl to be, she gave a gasp of irritation. The vacuum cleaner lay in bits in the centre of the living-room carpet.

'Oh, I thought she'd mended it,' she exclaimed. 'She's always blocking it up.'

I gave a bored smile and turned to leave.

'I don't suppose you'd like to do me a favour?' she asked. 'I expect you know how to put all it back together. I'd ask Clint, but his hands are so big I think he'd break it if he took a screwdriver to it.'

It was on the tip of my tongue to remind her that Clint is very good with his hands when the curse of the Cunanes intervened once more.

So, a moment later, I found myself on the carpeted floor of Annie Aycliffe's drab and smelly little flat about to wrestle with the guts of James Dyson's invention. Only I didn't. As I kneeled something gave way in my right knee and I let out a genuine groan of pain. I sat on my bottom and pulled the stiff cord trouser leg up as far as it would go. There was fresh blood seeping from under the plasters I'd applied earlier.

'Ooh, let me see to that,' Naomi pleaded. She dashed behind a curtain, revealing a tiny kitchen, and returned with tissues with which she mopped up the blood. When she enthusiastically started to rip off my plasters I told her to stop.

'That'll do,' I said. 'I'll fix it up at home.'

'What about the vacuum cleaner?'

'Bring it along. I'll fix that up as well.'

I dropped her off ten minutes later and took the Dyson back to my own flat for repair.

'Thanks a bunch, Janine,' I said when reinstalled in the White family's living room. Jenny had gone to bed. 'You didn't tell me you'd started giving away my household utensils. What's going next? The dishwasher?'

'Dave, you sound really Northern and purse proud. This isn't the freewheeling Dave I know and love,' she responded slyly.

'Well, you'd no right to give my stuff away without asking.'

'You're turning into a grumpy old man, and I'm not sure I like you like this.'

'Sorry, it's just this case.'

'Dave, get a grip. The case may be unpromising but you can only do your best.'

'The mother's into Satanism,' I said gloomily.

'What!'

'She believes that satanic forces had a hand in her daughter's death.' I explained Ruth's fears as relayed by Rix.

To my surprise Janine didn't reject them out of hand. She contorted her face into an expression of horror. The look was more real than pretended.

'Some things go on that are hard to explain,' she said when I pressed her.

'Such as?'

'I can't give you any actual instance, and, of course, in the past a lot of social services people went over the top with stories of ritual child abuse and such . . . I was

68

at one briefing where this wild-eyed social worker told us quite seriously that there were thousands of Satanists prowling the streets of Manchester, but with everything else that goes on these days –'

'Such as?' I interrupted.

'There've been some awful murders where a ritual element seems to be present but it's always put down to an individual act of madness,' she said vaguely. 'I mean, what about that lad who cut an old lady's heart out and drank her blood and claimed he was a vampire? Where do things like that come from? It sounds a bit like Satanism to me. So it's hard to completely discount the idea that there might be people up to no good in that particular way.'

'But it's all nonsense.'

'You and I may think that, but do they?' she retorted.

Perversely, I felt my spirit lighten as I studied the serious expression on Janine's face. I pulled her towards me.

'Shall I break out the garlic?' I asked.

'That's only for vampires,' she said at once as my hands began exploring. 'You need something more powerful for Old Nick.'

'What about Old Dave?' I asked as my fingers reached the zip of her black dress.

'I don't think a church full of archbishops could protect me from him,' she whispered. 'Not that I need protection.' She took my hand and steered me towards her bedroom. She looked in at Jenny and Lloyd on her way.

'Fast asleep,' she mouthed silently.

I'd forgotten about the children but I remembered well enough how easy it is to get a full-grown woman out of her clothes, particularly when she's helping you to get out of your own.

'Why are you wearing these things?' she asked as her fingers touched my belt buckle. 'They stand to attention without you in them.'

Stepping out of the super-kecks revealed my wounds. I think I was as upset by the sight as Janine was. The bruises had spread.

'I'm phoning for an ambulance,' she said.

'No, I'm over the worst,' I insisted. 'There's no permanent damage, just flesh wounds.'

It was almost half an hour later, after much bathing, prodding and probing, and bandaging before she was prepared to accept my word and pull back the duvet. Then things began happening very rapidly.

Afterwards we lay together in pleasurable silence for a long while.

'Dave, why do you play these idiotic games?' my partner said eventually. 'If you'd told me you were hurt when you came in tonight I'd never have sent you off with Naomi. Anyone with half a normal brain would have told me, but not you. You have to be a brave soldier and keep your mouth shut.'

'Janine,' I said reasonably, 'if I knocked off and yelled for help every time I collected a minor graze, I'd never get anything done.'

'Dave, what you did to your knees wasn't just "minor grazing". Most people would have been on crutches. Instead you get me practically naked and then reveal that you're dripping blood. What am I going to do with you?'

'You had a very good idea a few minutes ago,' I reminded her.

I kissed her but she drew back.

'There's champagne in the fridge.'

I padded out of the bedroom. I noted with interest that the champagne had been purchased that same day. I returned with flutes and the bottle.

'Two bottles?' I queried.

'There was an offer at the supermarket,' she explained with a giggle. 'You never know when they might come in handy.'

'OK, OK, I'm not complaining,' I said with a laugh as the champagne cork thudded into the ceiling. 'This is really living in the fast lane.'

We made love a second time. One bottle of champagne and then the other was consumed before we fell into a pleasantly exhausted and alcoholic sleep.

When I woke I felt refreshed and ready for anything. Janine brought me tea in bed.

'There's no need to get up in a hurry,' she said with a smile. 'Jenny and Lloyd are zonked out and Naomi's taking them to her friend's animal shelter at ten.'

'You're exploiting that girl,' I informed her.

Janine smiled enigmatically and put her finger to her lips. She gave no answer because there was none.

'I'd like to get this Hands business sorted,' I told her. 'I don't want it taking too much of my time during the week.'

'You were very inventive last night,' she commented as she slipped back into bed.

'I aim to please.'

'That's your trouble, you try to please too many people. Live a little, Dave.'

'I just thought I'd pop back down to the canal and see how Rix's idea of the drunken wanderer accidentally falling in holds up in daylight.'

'It'll all still be there in an hour,' she said, laying her hands on a vital part of my anatomy.

Some time later we set off to the Castlefields Canal Basin together. I didn't anticipate any danger, which shows how wrong you can be. I wanted Janine's insights about Meg's last journey.

I parked my car near a converted warehouse opposite the Bargee's Rest.

There were still signs of the previous evening's revels – smashed bottles, a couple asleep in the back of a Jag – but in the cold light of day, with most of the luxury cars gone and only the pigeons for company, the area appeared very mundane. The eighteenth-century brickwork was as grey and uncommunicative as the dark waters of the canals.

'That's actually the River Medlock,' Janine explained knowledgeably. She pointed across Deansgate. 'It's completely enclosed now, but that's why the Romans built their fort here on this sandstone outcropping above the river. It was a ford.'

'Are you sure it wasn't a Morris Minor?' I quipped.

'No, I'm into all this,' she insisted.

I looked at her with a surprised expression. She doesn't normally study history.

'I did a piece about it for the paper,' she confessed.

We walked away from the spot where Meg's body had been found, up past the pubs, along the cobbled street, and then to the crossing point on Deansgate before walking back down towards the car.

'That's quite a long way for a drunk to stagger,' Janine commented, 'particularly if she was trying to get to bed.'

'Yes, and how did she negotiate all those steps?' I asked. 'If she was just walking along expecting to turn into her luxury apartment at any moment why would she go down there?'

I pointed to the steep flight of steps leading to Grocers' Quay.

'But she might have just walked the way we've just come, along the cobbled road into La Venezia and down onto the bank from the beer garden.'

'Not according to the manager, a little weasel called Ted Cosgrove. He got quite offensive when I suggested that she could have walked past his security men.'

Just at that moment Cosgrove emerged from the front door of the La Venezia. He clocked me, scowled and scuttled back inside like a mouse spotting a lurking cat.

'Speak of the Devil, if I dare say it!' I exclaimed. 'That's him. Cosgrove, I mean.'

'Not very impressive, is he?' Janine commented.

'He's only the manager, not the owner.'

'Do you think he's hiding something?' Janine asked.

'He claims that all he's interested in is property values and the good reputation of this area.'

'Area! Twenty years ago this whole scene was ripe for demolition. Look at it now. You've got to admit that they've brought it back to life. Your weasel may be right to be concerned. I mean because you don't like him – '

'OK, maybe he's only doing his job,' I conceded.

Just then a tram rumbled overhead on one of the three railway viaducts that span the basin. We both looked up.

'You've got to admit it's a pretty atmospheric spot,' Janine said cheerfully. 'You can almost cut the history with a knife.'

'Ha-ha,' I muttered. 'Meg Hands was drowned.'

'Where's your soul?' my partner asked. 'Look at those bats flitting about up there under the arches. I bet they're the ghosts of the handloom weavers and dockers who worked here, returning to haunt the place.'

'Handloom weavers?'

'Yes, it was their last stand round here. They gathered to protest against the Duke of Wellington when he came to open the world's first passenger railway just across the road.'

'Any killed?'

'Only one of Wellington's mates.'

'Really. I thought there was a massacre.'

'No, that was at Peterloo a few years earlier, but a lot of those weavers must have starved to death as the new machines undercut their wages.'

Janine has a vivid imagination. Nevertheless, in the cathedral-like gloom under the immense pillars and vaults I did feel a certain chill creep up my spine. Janine held my hand. We walked all round the three pubs.

'She could have fallen into the water anywhere round

here,' Janine suggested as we continued along the bank. 'You could just walk in here,' she said, and then she demonstrated stepping off the stone quayside.

'Hold on,' I said, 'one fatality's quite enough. Meg was found in the main basin near La Venezia so the body must have gone in there.'

'Unless someone deliberately towed it up there.'

'And who might do that?'

'I don't know,' she said, waving her arms. 'A rival of this Ted Cosgrove wanting to do the dirty on him . . . someone from one of the other pubs perhaps?'

'Sound's a bit heavy for a business rival,' I said dubiously.

'But it might explain why no one saw Meg go in. If she walked past all the pubs and then fell in at the Potato Wharf, who would have noticed?'

'Love, I've seen the CCTV of Meg clinging to a lamp-post. That girl wasn't out for an evening stroll. The amazing thing is that she didn't end up face down in the gutter in Deansgate before she even crossed the road. One possibility is that she conked out with the booze and some passing hooligan thought it might be funny to see if she'd float and dumped her in the water, just for the hell of it.'

'And you think Cosgrove knows who it was?'

'He's been very shifty. It could have been one of his customers walking down here.'

'Oh, come on Dave! For Pete's sake! *Walking?* Don't you have to have a Porsche, or a Golf GTI at the very minimum to come here?'

'Lots of people walk. I did myself last night. There are plenty of posers in fancy cars but there's nowhere to park after the evening gets into its stride.'

'So, according to you, the quickest way to the canal from Deansgate is via the steps at Grocers' Quay? What about a little further on? You've got the slope to the water's edge near the weighbridge. There are no steps at all there.'

'But there are dozens of parked cars, people coming and going and a car park attendant. That's the last place an assailant would drag his victim to, whereas at Grocers' Quay there are plenty of dark corners.'

'Face it, Dave, there are dozens of different routes.'

'No,' I insisted, 'not for someone as drunk as Meg was.'

We walked back to Deansgate. The road was busy but we crossed and found ourselves outside the 'luxury' flats. The geography was rather complicated. One canal went to the left and the River Medlock to the right, but their presence had been suppressed. They were hidden from view. We followed the small street that led us around the back of the flats and would have given us a view of the Medlock if it hadn't been enclosed behind fences. It was only by scrambling up onto a bank by a car park facing the flats that I was able to look down at the river. I was trying to work out just how it connected with the canal system, when Janine tugged my sleeve.

'Someone's trying to get your attention,' she said.

I looked up.

Ruth Hands was waving at us from the balcony of one of the flats. She was wearing a similar safari-type outfit to that she'd worn yesterday. Jackets with turned-up collars and trousers with big pockets were her uniform.

'Come on up,' she yelled.

Heads turned on the other side of Deansgate.

'She's not shy, is she?' Janine asked, with raised eyebrows. Meanwhile Ruth was vigorously waving us on.

Whatever she had to say was too urgent to deliver in her apartment because she came down to the street, or maybe she didn't want a tradesman to cross her threshold.

'Dave, where've you been? I've been trying to get hold of you for hours,' she accused.

'Well, I won't say sorry because that'd upset you, but

my answering service should have put you in touch.'

'Oh, it did, some man called Snyder who didn't know what I was talking about.'

'Peter's my manager.'

'Manager! He didn't manage to contact you. Something urgent's come up.'

I took my mobile out of my pocket. It was switched off.

'Sorry,' I said with a smile.

'Is he always this irritating?' Ruth queried Janine.

'Yes,' Janine agreed, with a certain tone in her voice, 'but he's here now and I can tell you that he's been chewing over your problem for most of the last twenty-four hours.'

'Is that why you're walking round here,' Ruth asked, 'or are you just taking the air?' Her features had settled into that slightly menacing look I knew from our previous meeting.

'Yes, to both,' I said.

'We're not here for the sake of our health!' Janine protested. 'Dave, tell her!'

I shrugged.

'Mrs Hands,' Janine said, arms folded, ready for a verbal punch-up, 'it's a miracle Dave can walk at all – '

'That's all right, Janine, leave it . . . What's come up, Ruth?'

Ruth stared at Janine as if framing some cutting comment on the general uselessness of Englishmen, but then remembering her purpose, she turned to me. The angry look was exchanged for one of lip-biting anxiety.

'I had my solicitor on the phone first thing,' she said, and then paused as if uncertain.

'Yes?' I prompted. The tension was catching.

'The coroner's inquest into Meg's death has been moved to this Monday – something about an unexpected gap in his timetable.'

'Or a little arm-twisting by DCS Rix,' I said angrily. 'That bastard, I knew he was up to no good.'

Ruth looked at me quizzically and I briefly recounted my meeting with Rix.

'He can pressure you like that?' Ruth demanded incredulously.

'He just did,' I said.

'And he can pressure the coroner?'

'Probably.'

'Sweet suffering Jesus!' Ruth exclaimed. 'But the lawyer says that the inquest's certain to come up with an accidental death verdict unless we have new evidence to contradict what the police say and you haven't got any, have you?'

'To be blunt, nothing that would stand up in court,' I said. 'I can't accept that Meg just ambled down into the canal on her own. I'm certain there's someone else involved.'

'But you can't prove it!' Ruth exclaimed bitterly.

'Not yet,' I admitted.

'There must be some way to make them delay,' Janine said.

Ruth stared at her open-mouthed and then with no warning she was overcome by grief. Her face folded in on itself and she struggled and then failed to hold back the sobs.

'You don't understand, do you?' she said between gasps. 'I'd go anywhere, do anything, spend every last penny I own to catch whoever did this to my Meg. I know she was murdered.'

To my slight embarrassment Janine then wrapped her arms round her. 'I understand,' she said gently. 'I'm a mother. Dave will do everything he possibly can between now and Monday, and whatever the coroner does we'll make sure whoever did this doesn't get away with it.'

She signalled me to leave and I walked away back to

the canal side as my partner led Ruth back into her apartment. I phoned DCS Rix's office at Bootle Street. I was told that he'd 'gone fishing' for the weekend by someone who could hardly be bothered to disguise his lie.

5

Newsstand on Deansgate, Manchester: 'Serial Killer Fears'.
'Parents of four alleged serial-killer victims called today for
action to locate the alleged serial killer stalking the city. A
police spokesman said, "Everything that can be done is being
done, and any attempts to stoke up popular fears are unhelpful.
People should maintain normal vigilance and take the usual
precautions."'
Report in local paper

What to do next? One part of me wanted to storm into
Bootle Street and punch the face of the cynical underling who thought he could palm me off with lies, but I
was sufficiently rational not to want a weekend in the
cells.

There was no time, certainly no time for throwing a
wobbler in the cop shop.

What could I do between now and Monday? Rix had
been very clever and I was a fool to have expected less.
Yesterday he'd come sniffing round to see if I had new
information that might prevent him closing the case. I
had nothing then but he must have decided from the
sour way we'd parted that I might just be motivated to
come up with something. Hence the speeding up of the
coroner's inquest. Well, if he could speed things up, so
could I.

There was no one about on the wharfs and streets. So
far the only soul I'd seen stirring was Ted Cosgrove and
I didn't want to waste time with him. Things might not
be buzzing round here for hours but I needed to make
a start.

Back in front of the Bargee's Rest I phoned Peter.

'Boss,' he said immediately, 'do you know your mobile has an on switch? I've just been called every name in the dictionary –'

'Yeah, yeah, by a nice lady called Ruth Hands, I know,' I said, cutting him off. 'I've just been with her.'

'For a so-called Christian woman she has a fine collection of insults.'

'Listen, mate,' I suggested, before he got into top gear.

'No, Dave, I don't have to listen to that kind of stuff on a Saturday morning. I think you should tell her we're dropping the case.'

'Peter, listen! We're running a detective agency, not a church social.'

'It's not on, Dave. Besides it's not in the firm's interest to go raking up stuff against the police. What can we find that they haven't already covered?'

'Peter, I've taken her on and that's that!'

'If you say so,' he said grudgingly, after a lengthy pause.

'I do say so and now I want you to make up a handbill using the photo of Meg Hands you'll find on my desk. Something on the lines of "Did you see this girl on the night of Friday seventeenth of November". Then put our phone number. "Substantial cash reward for useful information" in big letters will do. Then get to a print shop and have twenty or thirty thousand copies made. Don't put Meg's or the firm's name on it. We're less likely to get bogus claims if they don't know what it's about.'

'Run that by me again,' he muttered.

It took another ten minutes before I'd dictated and checked the wording. I was in a frenzy of impatience but Peter was proceeding with solemn deliberation. At the back of my mind I remembered that Celeste Coe was keen on the case and that Peter tended to bridle at anything Celeste or her husband were in favour of. Keeping the crew of my little ship happy was a hard job.

'When do you want them for? Next week?' he eventually enquired. 'It'll probably be Tuesday or Wednesday.'

'I want them today!' I bellowed. The strain was getting to me.

'It'll cost,' he said cautiously. To give him his due, Peter always has one eye on our balance sheet like any good manager.

'Bugger that,' I snapped. 'Then I want you to find a good canvassing firm and ask them to supply a couple of dozen bodies to give the handbills out on Castlefields, this end of Deansgate, Whitworth Street and those streets near the Student Village.'

'Whoa! Dave, I'm your finance director and I'm telling you we can't run a business by spending every penny in the contingency fund on a whim.'

'Whim! Peter, I want those pictures on the streets by lunchtime and I want them there all evening and tomorrow as well.'

'You're joking!'

'Do the very best you can, then. We've already lost Friday night.'

'I take it everything's suddenly become very urgent.'

'You could say that,' I said, briefly explaining.

'I suppose it's worth a try,' he agreed cautiously, 'but if Rix is determined to close the case we'll have to come up with something good.'

'Great! You've finally got it, Peter, and listen, don't forget the CSWs. They're more likely to have noticed a lone female on their patch than anyone.'

'Prostitutes, Dave? I don't mind working Saturday and Sunday but what's Levonne going to say if I tell her the weekend's off because I'm talking to a load of streetwalkers? She'll go ballistic.'

It was on the tip of my tongue to ask 'Who the hell

cares?' or 'Why should she know?' but Peter Snyder is the most married man of my acquaintance so after a struggle I controlled my impatience.

'Will Levonne be worried that the ladies of the town'll want to get their claws into a handsome dude like you?' I taunted.

We have a joke that Peter resembles Denzel Washington.

I've never been quite able to work out what it is between Peter and Levonne. In their case the marriage bond appears to be set with super-glue. I do know that her name always comes up when Peter wants to apply the brakes to some business deal he doesn't like. He paints this grim picture of Levonne, a keen Seventh Day Adventist, as a domineering moral guardian, ever alert for any straying. But whenever I've spoken to Levonne in person she denies pulling Peter's strings.

'Don't joke about Levonne, Dave,' he cautioned. 'You don't have to live with her.'

'All right, leave the CSWs to me,' I replied.

'You're welcome to them, Dave,' he said with a giggle.

They say a good deed never goes unpunished, and it must be true because as soon as I turned off the phone, my elbow was firmly grasped from behind and I was roughly pushed against the wall of a warehouse at the end of the Rochdale Canal. To my left, across the cobbled street, was another warehouse, which had been converted into modern offices. No one was in sight.

Muggers! was the thought in my mind. I must have been so absorbed that I hadn't heard them approach, though I was in full view of the La Venezia. Then the penny dropped. Cosgrove!

I twisted violently to face my attackers. There were two of them.

'Oh, it's you,' grunted the one struggling with my arm. He let go of me.

82

'Go on, Nose, give the bastard a smack,' the other character urged in that nasal, twangy Manchester accent that can sound a bit like Liverpool to the uninitiated.

I faced the pair, fists clenched and adrenalin surging. They made a study in contrasts. The one who'd grabbed me was older than his mate. He was wearing a thin, ripped sweater over a tattered T-shirt, faded blue jeans and dirty white trainers. He came over in grainy monotone like a fifties kitchen sink drama but his companion was very much in technicolour, clad in local 'scally' uniform – an eye-catching striped Lacoste jumper and grey shellsuit bottoms, which were tucked into the tops of his Rockport boots. He flaunted a glittering range of accessories: sovereign rings, chopper necklace, and bracelets. A cap perched at an angle over cropped carroty hair topped off the rig.

I recognised the older man as No-Nose Nolan, to give him his full name. He's also known to his mother, and to almost no one else, as Tony.

'What's going on, Tony?' I asked, hoping that a touch of the Auld Lang Syne would jog his conscience more efficiently than a boot in the stomach. 'Has Bob asked you to do this?'

No-Nose, a thin scrap of a man, no taller than five foot three, who looks more like an accident victim than a practising criminal, used to be a member of my friend Bob Lane's 'gang'.

Bob doesn't put it like that. He claims that he employed No-Nose out of charity. Knowing Bob, that's possible.

The younger man, about twenty years old, was better nourished than No-Nose. The orange stubble under his baseball cap clashed with everything else he was wearing. Like No-Nose he was deficient in inches. If anything, he was even shorter than No-Nose. Regardless, he was keyed up for action.

No-Nose swung away from me to grab his colleague,

who was snorting like a pit bull terrier on a choke chain, pawing the ground in his eagerness.

'Leave it, you knob-head,' No-Nose ordered.

'Thinks he's hard, does he?' the youth snarled.

'What's all this about, Tony?' I asked. 'Are you going to introduce me to your girlfriend or are you just going to dance with her?'

This produced more fuming and cursing from Carrot-Top.

Looking at the duo, I didn't feel in any danger but these things are a matter of perception. My attackers obviously regarded themselves as very menacing.

No-Nose's face was so battered and flattened that it was hard to read any expression as he stared into the crazed blue eyes of his mate. He shook his head sadly and put a hand on his partner-in-crime's arm. He whispered something. The noisy macho-man routine came to a dead stop.

'Sorry, Mr Cunane,' No-Nose explained, 'we were both feeling a bit short of the readies and this guy phoned us and offered us money to do you over, like. Like, he didn't say it was *you*, I mean. He just said there was someone making a dick of himself down here that needed sorting, like. We were supposed to mug you and give you a good leathering. Like a robbery, like.'

'Oh, who is he?' I asked conversationally.

This request caused confusion.

'I mean the guy that phoned you, not the dick,' I added.

No-Nose glanced anxiously in the direction of La Venezia before shaking his head. 'You know I can't tell you that,' he said miserably.

'So, you'll beat me up but you won't tell me who wants it done? I'm surprised you're so particular.'

He looked at me blankly. Incomprehension is the one expression that comes naturally to No-Nose.

I almost felt sorry for him.

'Take me further away, Tony,' I said. 'Make it look as if you're dragging me off.'

They were as inept at acting as at enforcing, and in the end I had to lead them out of sight of La Venezia round the corner of the converted warehouse that fronted on to the Bridgewater Basin.

'Now you can tell Mr Cosgrove you've kicked the crap out of me and no one need be any the wiser,' I said.

Immediately both their faces lit up. Cheating an employer was up their street.

'Do you think so?' No-Nose asked hopefully.

Carrot-Top was equally pleased. I guessed they were on payment by results. He started miming blows and kicks.

'How did you know it was Cosgrove?' he asked between karate chops.

'I didn't until you just told me,' I said.

'Lee, you're a knob,' No-Nose said contemptuously. 'Now we'll get nothing.'

'No, you're all right, lads,' I offered generously. 'I'll not grass you up to that bugger.'

I suppose I was flattered that No-Nose assumed that I'd steam straight into La Venezia and give Cosgrove a smacking. Maybe that's what I should have done but I hoped the leaflet campaign would produce a witness and then I would confront Cosgrove.

'If you want we could give the geezer a few raps for you,' Carrot-Top volunteered, 'after he's paid us for doing you, like. The fucking wanker knocked us down to fifty.'

'Thanks for the offer, Lee,' I said. 'Mr Cosgrove will keep for another time as far as I'm concerned, but if I were you I should demand at least a hundred, even two. Tell him I put up a hell of a scrap,' I said.

'Yeah,' No-Nose agreed after a moment of consideration.

'Anyway,' I continued, 'I thought you were working for Bob Lane?'

'Bob cut me loose when he went into the timeshare business in Tenerife. He says I haven't got the languages, like, and he's no use for muscle.'

'I don't know about that,' I said encouragingly. 'You two certainly have the technique to be good timeshare salesmen, and isn't it mainly English people they sell to? I shall have a word with Bob next time he's in Manchester.'

'Will you?' No-Nose asked eagerly.

By this time, if I'd asked him to kiss my arse he'd have been on his knees quick as lightning.

'I will,' I agreed, 'and now before you claim your reward from Cosgrove you'd better have one or two bruises to convince him you did the job.'

'Yeah, fucking right,' Lee agreed, stroking his tattooed fist. He studied me as if measuring for a blow.

'No, not me, Lee,' I warned. 'Him. Nose, I mean, and yourself.'

Lee looked upset. Giving blows was his plan, not receiving them.

'Say you give him one and he gives you one,' I suggested to No-Nose.

'Are you sure you don't want to . . . er . . . do that yourself?' No-Nose asked. 'I mean I might feel better, like.'

'No, each to his own,' I said. 'Just give me a few minutes and then you two get on with it.'

I turned to walk away. I felt pleased with myself, almost ready to laugh out loud, but No-Nose Nolan wasn't quite finished with his surprises. He laid a hand on my sleeve.

'Mr Cunane,' he said humbly, 'we'd never have done you round here, you know.'

'You're right about that,' I said, raising my fists.

'No, you don't understand.'

He pointed upwards.

A CCTV camera was mounted on the warehouse wall opposite. It was focused directly on us.

'It's like a dead spot for cameras over there, like,' No-Nose explained obligingly. 'You can do what you like round that side. They've got the pub bouncers there, you see.'

It was my turn to give the blank look.

'They don't want them bastards on candid camera, do they?' he explained.

'Thanks, Tony,' I said gratefully. Intellectually challenged or not, he'd spotted something that I'd missed. If one, or several, of the La Venezia bouncers had decided to have a 'bit of fun' with a drunken student they could have performed right there, knowing that no record would be made. Was that what happened to Meg Hands?

Sensing that he'd said the right thing for once, No-Nose crumpled his face in the nearest approach to an ingratiating smile that he could manage. 'If you ever want me to sort anyone, you know where to phone, the club in Cheetham Hill.'

'I might just do that,' I promised. I was still slightly puzzled that No-Nose was so happy. 'But, Tony,' I said, 'won't your man over there know you haven't beaten me up when he sees what's on this camera?'

'Oh, no, he won't see that. This one's private,' he explained.

I wasn't anxious to see them knock holes in each other so I hurried around the side of the modernised warehouse looking for an open door. I went down some steps and came to one that said 'Wild Ride Studios'.

I went in. Perhaps their cameras had recorded Meg staggering towards what No-Nose chillingly called the 'dead spot' in front of La Venezia. If they had, then both Cosgrove and Rix would have to come up with explanations.

The room I entered was decorated like Madame Tussaud's chamber of horrors – very modern. Blacks and reds predominated. The walls were covered in pictures, some illuminated by tiny spotlights. Images of violence flickered across an outsized computer screen. I hadn't time to study any of them but they created unease. I half expected a Schwarzenegger lookalike to come bounding round the corner.

The feeling of insecurity wasn't lessened when I spotted the human occupant of this strange grotto. She was sitting so still at her desk, and the surface of her skin seemed so much like plastic, that I wondered if I was looking at an animatronic figure.

But no, she was flesh and blood. Her long, mascara-heavy eyelashes quivered in a way that no machine can yet replicate and her jaws were slowly moving up and down. She stared up at me from behind a high-tech console with a number of phones, switches and a small screen displaying a picture of the entrance. Still, she might well be an automaton. The way her shiny blonde hair moved as one piece was creepy. Her faced was rigid, presumably with boredom, as she was too young for Botox.

I felt I was getting warmer. Surely such a high-tech establishment, where even the human help resembled robots, must have a recording of Meg's last walk?

'Excuse me, miss,' I said deferentially, 'I'm a private detective and I'm inquiring into an incident that took place near here.'

She removed her chewing gum, quite a large wad, and gawped intently at me for a moment. I guessed she was in her early twenties, though she could have been a teenager trying to look sophisticated. She was out of place behind an office console. She should have been on a cat-walk. There was a name tag on her ample chest but the lettering was too small to be read without coming so close that my intentions would be mistaken. No doubt there was a panic button within reach of her dainty little fingers.

'If it's about Nana Akimbola's Ferrari getting scratched,' she said in a lazy, slow way of speaking she probably thought was very sexy, 'we've already told the club security that our cameras were switched off at that time of night.' Akimbola was an African footballer recently signed by the Reds for some improbable sum.

I injected maximum charm into my smile before continuing the conversation. Her response wasn't encouraging. She looked away from me as if I was of no further interest and studied her fingernails. I guessed she wanted me to know that she was well used to being gaped at by the opposite sex. I followed her gaze. Each fingernail was glazed with the colours of a different country. The Union Jack gleamed on the index finger of her right hand.

'That must take you quite a while,' I said admiringly.

The gum went back into her mouth. She nodded, as impervious to my chat as a china doll.

'I'm interested in any CCTV coverage you might have of the area along the canal there,' I said, while admiring her fascinating fingernails.

'I'm not allowed to say anything about our CCTV system. We're private here.'

'I see,' I said, nodding my head in agreement. 'You know, I've got a friend who works on the *Evening News*. She's called Janine White. You've probably read some of her articles. She does the "Woman About Town" column. I'm sure she'd be interested in doing a feature about your fingernails.'

This produced a flicker of interest.

I took out my notebook.

White teeth and red lips parted. The grey wad re-emerged and was parked on the edge of her counter.

'These cost me a fortune,' she confided. 'My name's Ariadne Witherspoon and I can give you my agent's name if your friend's really interested in an interview, but I can't tell you anything about our CCTV. Mr Hobby Dancer is very particular that we stay separate from the scheme they have in the city centre. He doesn't want clients getting nervous about having their faces on our recorders.'

'Why, what are they? The Walking Undead or something?'

'Don't be silly,' she giggled. 'They're international businessmen, and Mr Hobby Dancer doesn't want his rivals to know who he's dealing with.'

'Wise man,' I agreed, 'and what's that name again?'

With a smooth motion she took a business card out of the recesses of her well-developed cleavage. It was her agent's card. I tucked it carefully away in the flap of my notebook.

'And your boss, what did you say his name was?' I persisted.

'Haven't you heard of him?' she asked in astonishment. 'O.R.G. Hobby Dancer? He owns this building. You know, the computer games developer? That's what we do here. Wild Ride computer games, yes? Our games are on PC and every other games platform.'

'Oh yes, Wild Ride,' I agreed.

'I don't know if Hobby Dancer's his real name but Mr Hobby Dancer's very well known in computer games. They did a feature about him in the *Sunday Times* colour mag a couple of months ago. Apparently we're doing wonders for the balance of payments. His games are really big in the States and Europe.'

She indicated the framed pictures of heavily muscled male and female figures fighting against monsters. The effect was very Gothic.

'Oh, *that* Hobby Dancer,' I said, still none the wiser.

'Ariadne isn't my real name. I'm really Jane, but I think Ariadne's more memorable. You see, I'm hoping to break into modelling.'

'I know people in that field too,' I said, remembering Annie Aycliffe's neighbour. 'Is there anyone I could see about the CCTV?'

'Mr Hobby Dancer lives over there on Deansgate but he can be a bit hard to get hold of. He's a genius, you know. He doesn't work regular hours.'

'Could you phone him?' I wheedled.

'I don't think he's on the phone. He comes and goes when he pleases. You know when one of those City players smashed up Nana Akimbola's car Nana had half his team-mates down here slavering for blood but even they couldn't contact Mr Hobby Dancer. No, he's above all that sort of thing.'

'Suppose I wanted to commission a new computer game, how would I arrange a meet?'

She shrugged her shoulders. 'People don't get in touch with Mr Hobby Dancer. He gets in touch with them. If you were desperate to see him I suppose you could wait here,' she said, nodding in the direction of a hard-looking chair, 'but it might be days, weeks even.'

'Could I go to his house then? Knock on his door?'

'It doesn't have a door as such. It's like a sliding thingy. There's no knocker or bell or anything.'

This time she came out from behind her console, led me to the plate-glass window, and pointed. She was wearing enough scent to make my head swim. I looked out across to the other side of the Bridgewater Basin.

'It's only over there,' she said, pointing to a stainless-steel entrance in the base of a concrete shaft built between the bridge carrying the main road and the side of the Wharf Café. I'd wrongly imagined she'd been referring to one of the 'luxury flats' on the other side of the road. This concrete shaft extended upwards from canal level to a massive brick and concrete structure adjacent to the extension of Deansgate where it becomes Chester Road. I looked at this with fresh eyes. It resembled one of the fortifications with which the late unlamented Adolf had littered the coasts of Europe. I half expected to see a cannon or a machine gun poking out from one of the narrow concrete embrasures. The building pre-dated the restoration of the Canal Basin and belonged to the neo-brutalism era of the seventies when similar ugly pillboxes sprang up round the city like a rash.

'I thought that was a restaurant or something,' I said vaguely.

'It is, but Mr Hobby Dancer lives in the penthouse above. Very spacious, it is, I'm told, not that I've ever been there. They say he isn't interested in female company, if you know what I mean.'

'Really! Not even interested in you?'

'Well, I don't know if he's actually gay,' she simpered. 'He might be as camp as a row of tents for all I know, or he could be just the opposite. They say he spends all his spare time cuddled up with his computers. He must be good at it. The firm's worth millions.'

'Well, thanks very much for your help,' I said as I left. 'I'll give your card to my friend at the *Evening News*.'

She replaced her gum, by now surely hardened, and began chewing vigorously.

I took the steps at the side of the building down to the canal level, tramped over on the footbridge and walked along to Mr Hobby Dancer's front door. Ariadne was right. It was just a featureless sheet of steel. The elusive entrepreneur's privacy was safe from me, for the moment at any rate.

My friends Carrot-Top and No-Nose were nowhere to be seen but I didn't want to get involved with them again so I stayed on the bank opposite La Venezia and mooched along for a considerable distance, thinking about what Ted Cosgrove might have to hide. What with Ariadne's talk of rampaging footballers and the shy celebs in La Venezia, there was fuel for my suspicions. I knew that bribing or intimidating a pub full of witnesses was no problem for some of the citizenry.

Feeling that I was on the scent, I strode along the canal bank at a cracking pace. I needed exercise to get my brain working at speed. I soon left the renovated area behind. Railway arches parallel the canal bank for miles like so many abandoned cathedrals, or the fossilised spine of some gigantic prehistoric creature. From ground level the whole area's unbelievably compelling and impressive. Eerily, this secluded world is just a short walk away from the Saturday bustle of Deansgate.

I could imagine any number of sinister events taking place under those vaults. Nor has the stink of decay been entirely banished by restoration work. Instinct told me that this was a place where danger lurked. The fault line between the grimmest period of the industrial past and the bright new world of 'city living' and loft conversions was still jagged here, like a gaping wound.

I almost jumped out of my skin when someone stepped out from behind one of the arches directly into my path. It was a man and he was carrying two rucksacks, one on each shoulder, and a shopping basket in his hands. His grey hair was matted onto his head in irregular shapes like the horns of some rare breed of sheep.

He seemed as startled by my sudden appearance as I was by his. He spoke before I could. 'Have you got the price of a cup of coffee?' he asked bluntly.

'I might have,' I replied, patting my pockets for change. I took in his looks. His skin was as grey as his rank hair. He was a dosser and he looked as if this was a spot he slept in.

'Do you live round here?'

'What's it to you?' he demanded.

'Nothing, I'm just asking because I'm inquiring into the drowning of a girl back there in the Canal Basin.'

'Oh, that,' he said dismissively.

His reply came quickly, as if he was anxious not to remember the topic.

'Do you know anything?' I pressed.

'You the police?' he asked nervously. 'I'm doing no harm to anyone. Jed Eagles causes no trouble.'

'I'm not police, Mr Eagles, I'm a private investigator. Do you know anything about what happened to that girl?'

A knowing glint lit up his old and weary eyes. The optimism with which I'd set off to explore this benighted area was renewed.

'I saw them fishing her out,' he boasted.

I pulled a five-pound note out of my back pocket.

'Did you see anything unusual?' I asked eagerly.

'I might have but I've learned that it's best not to say too much about things that aren't my business. There's things going on round here that certain people want kept quiet.'

He didn't seem very interested in my money, which figured. If he'd wanted money he wouldn't be living rough. However, if he was on drugs cash flow might be as much of a necessity for him as for his loft-dwelling neighbours.

'Was there anything out of the ordinary?' I repeated. 'Did you see her fall in?'

'I didn't see that but I know something else,' he said.

'What?' I demanded.

'Depends on what's in it for me,' he said infuriatingly.

I took a tenner out of my back pocket and waved it at him.

He shook his head.

'Not worth my while,' he grunted. 'Some o' them security would break my neck as soon as look at me if they thought I was grassing. Hard cases, they are.'

I decided that I was wasting my time.

'Are you round here all the time?'

'Sometimes here,' he said, waving his hand towards the arches. 'Sometimes I find a bed.'

'Where do you eat?'

'I don't eat much.'

That seemed true. His grey, dirty face was as lean and gaunt as a Dürer etching.

'You must have something.'

'I go to Cornerstone in Denmark Road. They give me tea and a sandwich.'

'So to get there you'd pass through the Canal Basin?' I said, pointing back in the direction I'd come from.

'I've said enough. I'm not talking for a lousy ten quid.'

He brushed past me and I grabbed his arm. It was as thin as a broom handle. I immediately let him go.

'Here, what will fifty do for your memory?' I said. I felt a little guilty for grabbing him so I offered him more than I should have. He stopped in his tracks.

'I didn't *see* anything, like,' he said out of the corner of his mouth, 'but I *heard* them.'

'Who were they?'

'People,' he said vaguely. He spoke slowly as if every word was costing him ten pounds. 'Jed didn't see them.'

'Bouncers?'

'I'm not saying that. Could have been them but some of them sounded more posh than them, if you get my meaning.'

'OK, so what were they talking about? You'll have to do better than you've done so far for fifty.'

'Jed's telling you . . . "She's just what he wants, a perfect subject," that's what they said. They didn't know I was there but I'm sure it's that girl they were talking about.'

'Why?'

'They described her, like. Dirty talk like the dirty animals they are. It was that girl they fished out. Jed knows it. She was big, like they said. Long black hair. Jed heard them. They said, "Silly mare won't be a virgin much longer. She'll get the fright of her sweet young life." One of 'em said that afterwards she'd be the same as they were.'

'Was this girl with them?'

'No, they were talking about something they'd all just done. Excited, like, they were.'

'When did you hear this?'

'It was the Friday before they fished her out on the Sunday. I know that because it was raining and I came down here looking for a cardboard box in that skip at the back of the pub.'

'You're sure?'

'I'm not saying any more. You've had fifty pounds worth. Jed always gives good value.'

'Here take my card,' I said, offering it with the notes. 'Phone if you remember more. There'll be more money for you.'

'Money's no use to Jed Eagles,' he muttered.

Nevertheless, he grabbed the cash and my card and stuffed them in his basket and then hurried on.

I turned back then and walked some distance towards Deansgate. A cold wind was whipping across the canal, riffling the opaque surface. I was excited. Eagles' evidence sounded like a break in the case. It could have been Cosgrove and his platoon of security men that he'd overheard. Yes, maybe they were discussing what was going to happen to Meg at the hands of some oversexed soccer star.

An elderly couple were walking towards me. They had a golden retriever on an extending lead. The dog was sniffing around here and there and slowing their progress. They were a very proper pair, in marked contrast to Jed Eagles, who'd now disappeared. The man had neatly parted thinning grey hair, polished shoes, well-creased trousers and a warm, new Spray-Way jacket, which I envied as the wind penetrated my suit. His partner was also well protected against wind and weather.

They cautiously stood to one side and hauled the dog back under control while I passed. In my business suit, I must have looked like a strange person to come across on the canal bank.

'Good morning,' the man said with an Irish accent.

I whipped one of my cards out and handed it to him.

'Excuse me, but I'm inquiring into the drowning of a student in the canal up there.'

The senior citizen examined the card carefully without speaking but his wife was more forthcoming. She put her hand to her mouth. 'Oh God, I remember that. She was that jam family's daughter,' she said, also with an Irish accent. 'The poor thing must have had a few. We have a granddaughter, Sinead, who's a student and she knows how to put it away.'

'Don't they all?' her husband chimed in. 'I think some of them go to university to do research on how much alcohol the human body can tolerate.' He laughed at his own joke. 'Pat O'Carroll,' he continued, extending his hand, 'and this is my wife, Nuala. You're in a fine line of business, Mr Cunane. I bet you don't get your hands dirty in your job. Me, I worked on Salford Docks for thirty-odd years.'

'You look well off it,' I commented. It was true. He had a sprightly figure, and if he was seventy or so he looked set for another twenty years at least.

He laughed again. 'I can see that you haven't just got an Irish name, Mr Cunane. You must have kissed the Blarney Stone, right enough.'

'Maybe,' I agreed, 'but do you know anything about this tragedy that hasn't appeared in the papers. The girl's mother is desperate to find out everything she can.'

'That poor woman, what she must be going through!' Nuala exclaimed sympathetically. 'We didn't see anything but we were both surprised that someone drowned there, weren't we, Pat?'

'Yes, we live in those flats just down there,' he agreed. He pointed to the flats on the other side of the Merchant's Bridge over the Canal Basin. 'We like it there. It's dead quiet on our side of the canal. The slamming of a car door will wake us up but then we do go to bed at nine o'clock.'

They both laughed at their own eccentricity.

'Well, there's nothing worth watching on telly,' Nuala explained.

'I was surprised about the drowning because the water's quite shallow there,' Pat continued. 'It's not like the Ship Canal or the Pomona Dock. Hellish deep and cold it is there. You wouldn't have much chance if you took a swim there on a dark night.'

'You said "she must have had a few",' I commented, turning to his wife. 'Have you any definite reason to think that?'

'We didn't see it, but it's what they said at the pub across the canal. Pat says he's going over the water when he wants a drink, and that's what they were saying in there. How else would the girl drown there unless someone held her under and I've not heard that they're looking for anyone.'

'No, they're not,' I agreed. 'Was it La Venezia you went "over the water" to, Pat?'

He nodded.

'You don't happen to remember just when they were claiming she was drunk?'

'That'd be the day they found the poor soul. Lunchtime on Sunday. It's not my local but it's handy when I'm with the dog. I can drink at those tables outside.'

'Thanks,' I said. 'You don't happen to know a local character called Jed Eagles, do you?'

'Jed! Of course we know him,' Nuala said, clapping her hands. 'Local character, that's just what he is.'

'Hold on? You haven't been talking to him, have you?' Pat asked. 'Spin you a yarn, will Jed Eagles. Talk the hind leg off a rhinoceros, he can, when he's in the mood.'

'He's in mortal terror of the security men at the pubs,' Nuala added. 'I'll bet a pound to a penny that he's tried to pin this girl's death on them.'

I nodded sheepishly. Suddenly my back pocket felt very light.

'Well, Mr Cunane,' Pat O'Carroll said jovially, 'they say there's one born every minute. I'll not say that Jed's a liar but you have to be prepared to discount ninety-nine per cent of what he tells you.'

'Oh, you're too harsh, Pat!' Nuala commented. 'He's just saying that because Jed gave him a cert for the Derby and it came last. I'll say this for Jed Eagles, he ought to know what's going on round here. He comes and goes like a ghost. You don't know he's there half the time, until he pops out on you.'

I thanked them and resumed my walk, going back towards Deansgate on the other side of the canal. This took me past La Venezia. There was no sign of Cosgrove or of anyone lying in wait for me. I avoided the site of No-Nose's attempted ambush by going through the reconstructed entrance gate of the Roman fort and into the narrow roads beyond.

My meeting with the O'Carrolls had cast doubt on Jed Eagles' story. It was interesting that the clientele of La Venezia were saying Meg must have been drunk well before the post-mortem disclosed that fact. How could they know, unless one of the bouncers had seen her? Did she call in for a drink? Did Cosgrove turn her away? Was that what he was hiding? Perhaps the bouncers had marched her off the premises and dumped her on the canal bank.

A jogger overtook me. Stencilled across the back of his tracksuit were the words 'O. R. G. Hobby Dancer'. A small black boy was running alongside him.

I yelled to him but he was plugged into a Walkman so I had to run along the Potato Wharf to catch up, and it was impossible to get his attention without laying a hand on his shoulder. He recoiled as if I'd shot him. He slowed down but didn't stop. I noticed with a shock that the person loping alongside him, who I'd taken to be a boy, was a very small adult whose creased and lined face suggested that he was fifty, if not older. He had a startlingly bulbous nose, a real conk of a proboscis, and positioned himself between Dancer and myself.

'Mr Hobby Dancer,' I gasped. I was sadly out of condition. My knees were already advertising their sad state by sending shooting pains up my legs.

'How do – you know – who I – am?' he rasped, pacing his words to match his strides.

'Well, if you're not Hobby Dancer you're wearing his tracksuit,' I pointed out.

'Oh, – very – well,' he admitted.

I'm used to the aggressive ways of joggers when forced to slow down so I decided not to take his gruffness personally.

Struggling to get my breath, I explained myself and thrust one of my cards into his hand. 'I wanted to ask if you'd got any CCTV recordings for the weekend when Miss Hands was drowned?'

'CC – TV?' Dancer repeated as if I was asking about a flying saucer landing on the Canal Basin. I was surprised at his youthfulness. Somehow I'd expected the entrepreneur to be in his forties. He was actually in his late twenties and fairly nondescript in appearance, with mousy brown hair, blue eyes, beaky nose and thin face and such a light build that if he'd flapped his arms I'm sure he could have flown into the air.

We were approaching the steps leading out of the redeveloped canal-side area and onto Liverpool Road. Hobby Dancer was fresh but I was wilting. He seemed to be considering his answer . . . He paused for a moment, bending with his hands resting on his bony knees.

He got his breath back quickly.

'We do have CCTV cameras on the side of the warehouse where my studio is situated but they're just for show. I've already told the police this. I don't like CCTV. My cameras are dummies so if you were hoping for a quick solution to your inquiries you can forget it.'

That was a lie as I knew from my encounter with Ariadne Witherspoon, but before I could follow through, he was on his way again. His courtly way of speaking didn't extend to his manners in general.

'Spare me another minute!' I pleaded. I wanted to ask him about Cosgrove.

'Must – get on,' he rasped.

I'd no intention of letting him go but Hobby Dancer kept dodging round me and, by accident or design, his black friend was getting under my feet. My battered knees were about to give way and short of bringing him down with a rugby tackle I just couldn't keep up. So, when he reached the steps at the Castlefields Visitor Centre and bounded up with springs in his heels, my efforts to question him ended.

'Just one minute!' I shouted.

'Timed – run. Must – keep up,' he panted over his shoulder.

He tucked my card into his back pocket and plugged himself back into his music. I sat on the steps and considered what I'd found out so far. It didn't come to much.

When I was breathing normally again, I set off slowly, retracing my steps along the Potato Wharf and round the bend of the River Medlock to the spot where Meg's body was found. If Cosgrove was observing from La Venezia he could hardly have missed me as I walked right through his beer garden and down the steps to the waterside. I didn't much care if he was observing me. My abortive meeting with Hobby Dancer had left me ready for violence. If Cosgrove had emerged with the bald dome of his thuggish bouncer gleaming behind him I think I'd have smashed a chair and offered resistance with a chair leg, but it was not to be.

For one thing, all the chairs were screwed to the ground. For another, as always with me, aggressive intentions quickly faded.

I gazed at the blank windows of the bar. Nothing stirred.

I took my time, willing Cosgrove to emerge for another confrontation. It seemed that would be the only way I'd get a break in the case.

Eventually I sauntered back past the entrance of the bar and then under the threefold viaducts and turned to walk up the middle of the sloping street that cuts through what had been the Roman soldiers' bakery and as I did, as if choreographed by an unseen director, a red Range Rover, tyres screaming as it cornered, hurtled towards me. The driver must have seen me in the centre of the road but he made no effort to slow or turn. I leaped for the pavement but he whipped the vehicle towards me. Fear lent me speed and I vaulted up onto the low wall round the Roman excavations and the Range Rover swung away to avoid smashing into the brickwork. The projecting wing mirror passed so close that I felt disturbed air flick across my face.

This all happened in the span of seconds. One moment the massive ATV was on top of me, the next it was screeching under the low arch of the brick viaduct and off towards Castle Street. I had no time to get the number and the windows were tinted so I couldn't see the driver.

I looked around. There was no one else in sight, no witness to verify a clear attempt at murder. The only things moving were the clouds beyond the reconstructed Roman battlements. As I stood to catch my breath, a mainline train from Liverpool rumbled over the viaduct on its way to Oxford Road station. Normal life resumed, but if the driver of the Range Rover had had his way I would have been lying in the middle of the road as dead and departed as any hostile tribesman with a Roman javelin through his guts.

For a moment I considered going back down to canal level and shaking Cosgrove by the throat but I realised that I had no evidence that he'd anything to do with it. I'd been walking in the middle of the road and there were lots of wealthy drivers who frequent this secluded spot, but there was one thing: the driver had never sounded his horn.

It could have been a coincidence. People do get killed by joy riders, but still it must have been Cosgrove. If he could summon No-Nose Nolan to 'sort' me, why not some ape with a Range Rover?

Shaken, I retraced my steps and crossed Deansgate, heading for Ruth Hands' flat.

6

'A Chamber of Commerce spokesman described as "nonsense" claims that takings are down in inner-city stores and that some nightclubs popular with young people are facing a meltdown situation as parents encourage their offspring to shun the city centre during the current panic over an alleged Mangler. "This story is all down to the heated imaginations of a few overpaid tabloid journalists," the spokesman continued. "Next thing you know they'll be staging interviews with this so-called Mangler. It's anything to sell their sheets." '
Report on BBC local radio

In the inconvenient way that things happen my mobile phone rang just as I reached the entrance to Ruth Hands' flat and saw Janine emerge with a face like thunder. She had her head down and she bumped into me but kept on going.

'Janine,' I shouted, 'wait!' but she didn't.

I answered the phone while walking swiftly after my loved one.

'Mr Cunane? It's O.R.G. Hobby Dancer here. I'm afraid I'm feeling a little guilty about our brief encounter. I have your number off the business card and so I thought I'd call.'

'Oh, yes,' I said. I was more than slightly gob-smacked. What was new that he couldn't have told me before dashing away up those steps? He hadn't shown much sign of guilt when I was begging and pleading with him to answer a few questions.

With furrowed brow I tried to work out what he was phoning me for while, to my dismay, Janine receded into the distance. It seemed all my contacts with the jogging millionaire were doomed to be frustrated by someone running faster than I could. She reached the end of the short street and turned the corner without a backward glance. She was moving like a runaway horse with a thistle under its saddle. There was no way I could catch up with her and find out what Hobby Dancer wanted.

'Can I call you back?' I asked him desperately. 'I'm just in the middle of something.'

'Sorry,' he said firmly, 'I've got a taxi at the door waiting to take me to the airport. I'm afraid it's now or never for my little confession.'

'Fire away then,' I snapped, thinking the man must be one of the world's movers and shakers because he'd been in a tracksuit not fifteen minutes before.

'I misled you. In point of fact my CCTV cameras aren't dummies but I've no idea if your client's daughter was recorded on the day in question.'

I scratched my head and tried to remember if I'd told him Meg was my client's daughter. I hadn't. I'd just mentioned Meg's name.

'Mr Dancer, do you think you could find out?'

'Hobby Dancer,' he corrected. 'I'm afraid that's why I feel guilty. We don't keep the tapes. We're not as up to date as the Manchester CCTV centre. All our stuff's analogue, miles and miles of tape, and I think it's likely that the day in question's been recycled by now.'

'Could you check? It's pretty urgent.'

'I'll get a technician onto it when I come back from overseas but I can't do anything now.'

I wanted to ask him why he hadn't said all this to the police when they asked for the CCTV evidence but there didn't seem to be time.

'Listen, Mr Cunane, I must dash now but I feel I need to make a gesture.'

'You weren't ready to make a gesture when I was trying to get you to wait for minute.'

'I'm sure you know how it is when one's running against the clock. One loses perspective, but let me put my cards on the table. I have property interests that can be adversely affected by the wrong sort of publicity. It's worth a very great deal to me to have advanced warning if something very bad is going to explode onto the media. I'm sure you get my drift?'

'Sort of,' I said guardedly. I could only think that he was up to some sort of double-dealing, though what he thought I might uncover that would affect property values was beyond me.

'How about if I put a cheque for ten thousand or so in the post for you? Would it help you to give me first call on any bad news you may uncover? It would also make up for me being so unhelpful today? You must know what it's like when the endorphins are bubbling through the jolly old blood stream.'

My eyes bulged in surprise. I took a deep breath.

'I'm sorry Mr Hobby Dancer – '

'Just Hobby Dancer – '

'But I can only accept payment from one client at a time.'

'I see . . . professional ethics, eh? Well, you mustn't feel that my offer's meant to deflect you from your enquiries. I only want to help. I feel horrible about this happening right outside my own front door, as it were.'

'Thanks anyway,' I said awkwardly.

'No, look. I'll write the cheque now. You don't need to be so scrupulous. What did I say? Twenty thousand? Listen, look on this as a perfectly normal business trans-action. After all, anything you found out for Mrs Hands would have to be reported to the police anyway. It's not as if murder or accidental death are purely private affairs like a divorce case.'

'But – '

'I'm a businessman with valuable investments in the Castlefields area. If anything's going down there I need to know what it is.'

'Hobby Dancer!' I bellowed, 'I can't accept your money under any circumstances.'

'I could go as high as twenty-five.'

'No!'

'This is just business. I can put the cheque in the post made out to you or I can open an account for you in a Channel Islands bank. No one need know. This'll be strictly between us.'

'No!'

'Stubborn lad, aren't you? Well, that's what they say about you. No harm done, least said soonest mended, what?'

'All right,' I murmured, 'but what about those tapes?'

'Oh, I must go now. I'll check back with you about the tapes when I return and I want you to feel that my offer's open at any time you feel in need of cash.'

'When . . .?' I started, hoping to ask when he would be back but the phone went dead.

I was rooted to the spot for a whole second while I tried to work out why I'd just been offered a bribe before I remembered Janine. I pressed the speed button to call her and then set off at a trot. There was no answer. I pocketed the mobile and accelerated round the corner.

As I hobbled along at the best speed I could muster, it struck me that Hobby Dancer must be on the point of doing some deal. If the value of the property was in the millions maybe a tip-off about what was going to be in tomorrow's news was worth a fortune. Whatever he was up to, I was a total amateur when it came to such wheeler-dealing and I wanted no part of his game.

Janine was halfway down Deansgate before I caught up with her.

'Oh, it's you, Dave,' she snorted bitterly when I tried to fall into step alongside her. She implied that I was the source of her troubles.

'What's the matter?'

'That Hands woman's impossible,' she snapped. 'I've had to come away from there. I can't bear to have the woman close to me.'

'Oh God!' I muttered.

'Why do you take on these hopeless cases? I don't want you going anywhere near her again. Phone her now and tell you're backing out of her case.'

'But, Janine – '

'Phone her,' she continued relentlessly, her head bobbing up and down as she steamed away. I wanted her to stop but she ploughed straight ahead. It was my day for hopeless chases.

'I can't just drop out without further explanation. I've got to check out the flat. I haven't even seen Meg's room yet,' I protested. 'If nothing turns up this weekend I'll think about telling her to accept the inevitable.'

'Forget it!' she snorted through gritted teeth.

I'll swear that her hair was crackling with electricity. She pressed on through the crowds, which instinctively parted to let her pass. I meekly followed.

I wondered where she was headed. The *Evening News* offices were on the other side of the street but she made no move to cross. I realised she was going nowhere in particular. Blind fury was in the driving seat. Her face was set and her teeth clenched. Short of wrestling her to the ground there was nothing I could do.

Living with Janine has helped me to recognise those occasions when discretion is the better part of valour. Like summer storms, her rages gradually moderate themselves after the initial violent cloudburst. Eventually, she slowed down enough to allow me to fall into step alongside and we walked together for a few minutes. Without speaking, I gestured towards the Starbucks sign a few yards ahead of us. She allowed me to steer her into it and then to an empty seat. I left her for a moment while I ordered for both of us. I reflected that a bar and one of Jack Rix's special cold cures would have been more appropriate but it's coffee only on that side of the street.

Janine gave a rueful stare at me when I placed the cup in front of her, her mood changing as unpredictably as the Manchester weather.

I was determined not to demand an explanation. I just treated her to one of my nicest, kindest, most understanding smiles.

'You're impossible, Dave Cunane,' she exploded in exasperation. 'I don't want to be humoured. I'll never understand how I managed to get hooked up with you. You cling like . . . like poison ivy, but I know that in a minute you'll go straight back to that incredible creature and carry on trying to do her bidding.'

'Well, what am I supposed to do?' I complained. 'She's the client. I can't keep up with you, Janine. Last night you were all for me trying to solve the case, now you spend an hour with the woman and you've changed your mind. What's she done that's so bad?' I took out my mobile and laid it on the table. 'Tell me and I'll phone this instant and tell her to get stuffed.'

'Please spare me the dramatic gestures, Dave. I know you've never jacked a case in and you'll not start now.'

Janine shook her head, lost for words for a moment. Then she said, 'She's awful. When she wasn't on about religion and the Devil and all that nonsense, she was on about how bad the police are and how everyone here is useless.'

'She's recently lost her only daughter. You can't expect her to be making polite conversation about the Manchester weather.'

'Do you think I don't know that?' Janine rapped. 'It's

just that I'm certain someone else will be hurt before this thing's finished. I don't know who's more menacing, American fundamentalists like Hands, or Osama bin Laden and his crew. They're both so sure they're right that it's God help anyone that comes between them and their precious convictions. She may claim to be a big Christian charity worker but she talks as if she's got a cut-throat razor for a tongue. No one's safe from her.'

I must have stared open-mouthed at this.

'Don't you dare look at me like that, Dave Cunane!' she groaned. 'Someone's got to stick up for the rest of us against these nutters.'

'I'd no idea you felt so strongly.'

'Neither had I until she started up her rant.'

'I see,' I muttered.

'No, you don't!' she snapped. 'You don't see a damn thing. You're always asking me to settle down with you for a "normal" existence, whatever that is, yet you think you can swan off to your office and take on work for a real crazy like Ruth Hands without a word to me. Don't you see that you can't do "normal" and "weird" at the same time?'

'What's brought all this heart-searching on?' I asked mildly.

'Oh, it's you . . .' she said.

I shook my head in bewilderment.

'And your insane idea of what constitutes a job.'

'I'm only trying to find some evidence.'

'No, you're not, Dave. You're doing what you always do – pleasing yourself. You're trying to go up against the whole system like a one-man crusade and it's only a matter of time before you get smashed to pieces. That thing with your knees was just a taster. See if your darling Ruth Hands gives a damn when they're scraping you up from the pavement. She'll be off to the States without so much as a backward glance. She only cares about herself.'

Ruth must be harder for a woman to take; much, much harder. With me the big boobs, the shapely figure and the whole lady-in-distress syndrome that's the curse of the Cunanes produced a different chemical reaction. I guessed that was what Ruth's odd comment about wanting to get into her pants was all about. She wasn't cautioning me, she was cleverly tweaking my libido.

Still, Janine was completely wrong. Hands was hiring me to take on her concerns, not the other way round. I'd no right to expect her to show consideration of anything apart from my ability to do the job she was paying me for.

'Tell me this!' Janine barked, bringing me back to earth. 'Have you found a single scrap of evidence that that girl's death was anything other than an accident?'

'I've only been looking for a few hours.'

'So, you've found precisely nothing. Dave, haven't you learned from your dozens of nonvoluntary visits to the hospital that when you turn over stones some very nasty creepy-crawlies may emerge?'

'So what?'

'"So what?" he says. This is what I'm now finding I can't take about you any more, Dave. Last night I had to mop the blood off you before we could make love. Is that normal?'

'I didn't notice you complaining.'

'It didn't strike me then, but it hit me like a sledge-hammer when I spoke to the bloody woman! She expects you to be hurt or badly injured! I wouldn't be surprised if she's looking forward to it. To her mind, a few injuries, and maybe the odd bullet wound, are par for the course. Beneath that pious exterior she's violent.'

'Oh, come on! She's hardly threatening anyone.'

'By my definition somebody who sees another person as just a tool to be used *is* violent; and that's what she sees you as: a stick to be poked into the faces of the

111

courts, the police, and for all I know, the criminal underworld, on the remote chance that her daughter was murdered.'

'It's up to me to look out for myself,' I mumbled. Against my better judgement Janine was persuading me to throw in the job.

'Dave, some things are best left alone. DCS Rix has the right idea. The woman's obsessed and dangerous. It's better to let things take their course. Let the coroner close the case and then we can all hope she'll leave the country, seeing as she hates us so much. If her daughter really was murdered it's bound to come out eventually.'

I shook my head. It would be nice if all my clients were politically correct *Guardian*-reading liberals but it was never going to happen. Whatever was wrong with Ruth Hands – and the list of her failings was fairly long even if you only started with A for Anglophobia and got as far as D for Diabolism – she was still a client and as entitled to hire my services as anyone else.

I tried to argue but I could see that my words were having no effect. 'So we wait until we're old and grey and then some TV documentary reveals all?'

'It would be nice if we could live to be old and grey, you especially.'

'Janine, I've already found a few hints that not everything down in Castlefields is hunky-dory. The manager of that bar hired a couple of goons to sort me out when he saw me back down there.'

Telling her about the near miss with the Range Rover would only send her into orbit so I left that detail out.

'Dave!' Janine gasped, putting her hand to her mouth. 'Are you stupid or what? Can't you see that this is just what I'm saying?'

'Don't worry. They were nothing,' I said confidently. 'I persuaded them to sort each other out.'

'Really, what did I just say about violence? Do you

112

suppose whoever put that manager up to giving you a smack will leave it at that? Do you think a pipsqueak like him decides these things on his own? Listen, you big fool. I'm telling you Ruth Hands means more trouble than you've ever handled before and I don't want you to have anything to do with her. Call it woman's intuition. Call it what the hell you like! But get off this case.'

'Unless she told you that she's planning a murder on her own account I can't just back away from her problems,' I said miserably. Even to my own ears I didn't sound too convincing.

'I wouldn't put that past her but she didn't say anything like that.'

'Well?' I said.

'Right, now listen to this very carefully, Dave,' she instructed, folding her arms and fixing me with her firmest gaze. I loved her when she was in this mood. I'd have cheerfully jumped into the Ship Canal if she asked.

'Things have been going very well for us lately,' she announced.

'Except that a certain person won't – '

'Shut up! I'm coming to that. You're wonderful with the children and I'm sure they regard you as more of a father to them than their real father is or ever could be. I know some of the things I've said in the past have been wrong . . . you know, about relationships, and that . . . and I've been thinking that it might be a good idea if we formalised our connection.'

'Marriage?' I asked, hardly daring to believe my ears.

'Yes,' she said in a whisper. 'Dave, I don't want it to sound as if I'm blackmailing you but I really do believe Ruth Hands will go on thirsting for revenge whatever happens and that she doesn't care if you or the whole of Manchester goes up in smoke until she gets it.'

'But, Janine, are you saying she's clinically insane, or what?'

113

She shook her head.

'Then until I find out something different I've got to treat her like any other client. Part of that is accepting that her belief that Meg's death wasn't an accident is evidence that she was murdered. Nine times out of ten in these cases that kind of belief's the only evidence we have to go on.'

'Dave, you're an idiot! What if the next piece of evidence is another body floating in that blasted canal . . . yours, for instance?'

'Janine,' I said after a long pause,'what you said about us getting on well is true. The firm's doing OK. There's a steady income coming in, something I've never had before, but if that was all there was I think I'd blow my brains out.'

She grimaced and then reached across the table and squeezed my hand tightly. 'Don't exaggerate, Dave,' she said quietly. 'But if you go on with this case someone might spare you the trouble of killing yourself.'

I stared at her for a moment after these words. It's possible that I frowned.

'I'm only telling you what I feel,' she insisted. 'Dave, what is wrong with you? You're the only man I know who thinks sky-diving without a parachute is dull. Ninety-nine out of a hundred men would say that you already have a pretty interesting life, running your own business. You're independent. Why should you tie yourself to the likes of Ruth Hands?'

'Janine, this is what I do,' I said. 'I can't just leave the case up in the air.'

'You mean you want to prove that Rix is wrong.'

'That too.'

'And where will it leave me, Dave, if some scum-bag decides to dispose of you?' Janine said softly. 'Think about what I've said about us. You say, "This is what I do," but I'm telling you this is what men with families do – they put their families first.'

'That's so unfair, Janine,' I said in a whisper. 'Why do you think I have a successful detective agency? It's because I have a reputation for not letting tough cases go.'

'Do they have to be so tough that you get killed?'

'It's not like that and you know it. I'm a private detective, obviously people are going to come to me with the cases the police have given up on, or say aren't cases at all, like this Hands business. You're asking me to give up the best part of my job.'

'You admit that you've almost been killed several times on these cases?'

'There's a risk in every job. Even nursery nurses get assaulted by lunatics these days.'

'Oh yes, but on this case you nearly had both your legs broken on the very first day.'

'That was my own fault.'

'Fair enough. You take choices that result in you getting hurt. You do what you want, Dave, just as long as you accept that I don't want the role of grieving widow at your funeral. I love you too much to want to see you in a coffin.'

That was a conversation stopper.

We left the café and slowly walked back along Deansgate in silence until we reached the corner of Whitworth Street. This was the parting of the ways. I could go on to Ruth's flat or turn right to collect the car from where I'd parked it on Liverpool Road and then go home to sort out our wedding plans.

'You'd better do what you've got to do,' Janine said with a sigh when I made no move to turn right and cross Deansgate. 'But don't count me in.'

I gave her the car keys and she hurried off without a backward look. I carried on across Whitworth Street.

I could feel the blood pounding in the veins in my neck. I told myself that things would blow over. Janine had thrown wobblers before. I gave up trying to put the thoughts that were rushing through my brain into any sort of order. All I knew was that I had to do what I'd agreed to do. An overheated little neuron at the back of my brain was screaming about the injustice of it all. Men with families put their families first but what did women like Janine put first?

When I was admitted to the Hands flat I was met by a tall, grave-looking young man.

'This is my son, Arthur, Mr Cunane,' Ruth said. 'He's Meg's only brother.'

'I'm sorry for your loss, Arthur,' I said woodenly. I think I was shell-shocked after my conversation with Janine.

'Thanks, it's been awful recently but we're hoping things will eventually get back to normal,' he said.

As he spoke each word came out smoothly and well polished but lacking in something. His accent was English but not regional. I recognised the stamp of a certain type of public school education. The personal feeling I'd have expected from an 'ordinary' person in his situation was missing. It was as if everything too 'tacky' was being filtered out, repression being nine points of the law.

His mother gave him a sharp look.

Arthur shook my hand with a firm grip and uttered a sad little sigh, which seemed to indicate that he was of a more accepting temperament than his formidable mother. He was wearing fawn cord trousers, a navy-blue cashmere pullover over a cream silk shirt, open sandals over white socks, and a pair of thick-lensed Gant specs. He shared his dark hair colour and pale blue eyes with his mother but his thin features didn't convey her frightening 'full speed ahead and damn the torpedoes' tenacity.

'Can we get you some coffee?' Ruth suggested. 'But before we offer you hospitality I owe you an explanation. I've just been engaged in hand-to-hand combat with your partner, Ms White.'

116

I tried to keep my face blank.

'It was verbal combat actually,' she added. It was the first time I'd heard her qualify a remark so maybe Janine had stood her ground well. 'It was unfortunate, Mr Cunane, but I've no intention of being offered sympathy by anyone and that made things rocky from the get-go. My daughter was the victim, not me. I want action, not words.'

'Right, well, I've made a start,' I said, intending to tell her about the canvassing but she ignored my interruption.

'I expect Ms White thinks I'm very odd, a throwback to the Stone Age,' she continued, 'but I haven't much time for modern women. Feminism is wrecking our civilisation.'

'Janine's entitled to her views,' I said curtly.

'Yes, she is, and so am I.'

'That's right,' I agreed quietly, striving to keep the temperature low.

'OK, I suppose your loyalty to her has some value. Have you come to tell me that you're dropping the investigation?'

'To be honest, and I know you object to me saying that, I've already invested too much time and effort for that. Janine and I have agreed to differ.'

'How very sad,' she said with a trace of a smile, 'but then she isn't your wife, is she? I suppose in these modern unions you have to give each other space, as they say. Thomas and I never felt any need to pretend we lived on opposite sides of the planet.'

'Can we get on?' I asked impatiently.

She nodded and I related an edited version of the morning's events. Arthur listened intently. I described the mission I'd given to Peter Snyder.

'CSWs?'

'Commercial sex workers.'

'Arthur, go and make the coffee,' Ruth ordered.

'Mother, I'm not a child,' he asserted in chilling tones and remained where he was. Perhaps he did have some of his mother's determination. He was proof that the cliché that domineering women produce cowed and timid offspring is untrue. I found myself admiring him, and then I wondered what effect Ruth had had on poor Meg. Did she totally dominate her or was there a secret rebellion? They were a family of only three members, yet the inner workings of the Hands family were as baffling to me as the hidden byways of a Chinese tong. I told myself that I was here to find things out.

I looked at Arthur. His smooth young face was as inscrutable as a slab of alabaster.

'This man Cosgrove,' Ruth said when I'd finished describing events, 'could he be the killer?'

'Mother!' Arthur said sharply.

'What's up?' I interjected before Ruth could order him to the kitchen again.

He opened his mouth to speak but Ruth quelled him with a withering glance. 'My son's been exposed to your English ways more than I have.'

'Mother, I am English!' he protested.

'So you claim!' she snapped before turning back to me.

I kept my eyes on Arthur. He was a cool character. His expression never changed while his mother was putting him back in his box.

'Mr Cunane, like the rest of you, Arthur, can't believe that there are evil things hiding out there in the long grass. He thinks everything's peachy-peachy. Everything coming up roses as far as the eye can see. He's inclined to accept that Meg's death was just an accident – '

'We don't know that,' I interjected as she paused for breath.

'You don't know it. I'll never believe it but Arthur's

inclined to. That's an English education for you. He's so fair to people who mean him nothing but harm that he'd pass them the knife while they stab him in the back.'

A flicker of annoyance crossed Arthur's face at this.

'You were saying about this saloon-keeper, Cosgrove,' she continued, addressing me.

She was the client and I was the employee and I'd burned my boats with Janine for the sake of the employee/client relationship so I had to go on taking her drips of venom but I couldn't let her get away without correction.

'It's not a saloon and Cosgrove doesn't wear a black hat,' I said firmly. 'It's a highfalutin bar-restaurant that's packed with celebs night after night, but I do think he's hiding something. It may not be anything to do with what happened to Meg.'

'Hmm,' she muttered. 'If you need a bodyguard while you're finding out what this grubby little man's up to I can arrange for someone to come over from the States. I know several ex-marines and FBI men.'

A vision of the US Marine Corps deploying on the cobbled streets of Castlefields flashed across my mind.

'I can get someone from the firm if I need help,' I countered.

'Does this get us any closer to stopping the coroner bringing in an accidental death verdict?'

'No, I'm afraid until we get a witness –'

'And we've got to keep on waiting.'

'No, there is something we do right away. I'd like your lawyer to demand a copy of the CCTV footage of Meg walking down Whitworth Street West.'

'I'll get that coffee, Mother,' Arthur said, springing to his feet. I noticed that he was holding a mobile.

'If you've any idea how reluctant the police have been to release material you wouldn't ask,' Ruth replied.

'He can only try,' I suggested. 'Tell him to threaten to

hold the inquest up if he doesn't get it. I've seen it already, but I'd like another look.'

Ruth picked up the phone and started giving her lawyer a series of rapid-fire commands.

'If I offered him money for information,' she said as soon as she put the phone down, 'how do you think this Cosgrove person would respond?'

'He'd bite your hand off, I should think,' I told her. 'If you offered enough he'd probably find you the names and addresses of half a dozen likely murderers but once you start bribing people their evidence becomes useless. Rix would find out as well.'

'Why is Rix doing this to me?'

'He thinks he's right and you're wrong,' I said bluntly. 'He's been known to bend the evidence slightly when it was a matter of putting some notorious villain away but you've got to face it, he's an honest cop.'

'Who bends evidence and twists coroners' arms,' she commented acidly.

'Mother, you've got to realise that there are just as many shades of grey in this country as there are in America,' Arthur murmured enigmatically from the kitchen doorway.

'Arthur thinks I see things only in black and white,' Ruth said. 'Maybe he's right. He thinks I should resign myself.'

'Mother, I never said that,' he grumbled. 'I'm as willing to see Mr Cunane try to catch whoever did this to Meg as you are.'

'Except you don't believe that he will,' Ruth said crossly as her son served the coffee.

'We've got to be prepared for that,' he replied sensibly enough. Ruth's face clouded over. She clenched her chin and I prepared for anguished sobs but she composed herself.

'I've got some things to get on with,' I interjected,

before the family discussion became too tragedy laden. 'I need to search Meg's room and I need to interview Arthur . . . on his own.'

'The police have already turned Meg's room upside down,' Ruth objected. 'What can you hope to find?'

'It's not simply a matter of finding anything. I need to form an impression of what Meg was like.'

'Don't you believe what I told you?'

'Mother,' Arthur implored, 'there's no point in employing a detective and then stopping him from doing his job.'

'Well, as long as everything's put back just as you find it,' she allowed grudgingly. She got up off the hard chair she was sitting on and led me to Meg's study bedroom.

A hermit's cell might have been a better description of the room we entered. A battered old office desk bearing a laptop computer, a metal chair with canvas seat up against the desk, a wardrobe that had seen better days and a bookcase were among the sparse furnishings. They were nothing like those the average student demands nowadays. A second-hand furniture dealer might have offered five pounds for the lot.

An expensive pinkish-mauve blown-vinyl wallpaper contrasted sharply with the furniture. I ran my hand over the raised pattern. I knew it was costly because I'd recently paid fifteen pounds a roll for paper that didn't look as luxurious as this. Heavy cream damask curtains also conveyed the impression that there'd been money available for spending if the occupant had so desired it.

A bed took up one corner. It was unusually narrow, nothing like the normal size of a single bed. A small wooden cross was pinned to the wall above the pillow. There was no figure on the cross. A black leather-covered Bible lay on the bedside table. It looked well thumbed.

A red page marker was visible so I picked up the book and opened it. The page was Jeremiah, Chapter 37 to

38, with an illustration of the prophet being cast into the well. I hastily closed the book. Jeremiah had survived his troubles. Had something similar, but with more fatal consequences, befallen Meg? It was rather spooky that she'd been reading those chapters just before her death.

As if reading my thoughts Ruth commented, 'Meg was seeking a simple uncomplicated life. She took the troubles of the world's poor very personally. She was preparing for a life of service. She chose this furniture herself.'

'Austere is the word that springs to mind,' I replied, looking at the sheets and pillowcase. They were made from some rough substandard material that looked grey in the brilliant sunlight flooding the room from the full-length window that took up most of one wall. I noticed that there was a splendid view of the whole Castlefields area. Even if she'd never walked down there Meg must have been well acquainted with the layout of the Canal Basin.

'Meg took her commitment too seriously at times. I tried to get her to moderate her attitude to some degree. Perhaps you can see why I'm so shocked that anyone should say the girl who lived in this room went off for a sex romp and drinking session before she met her death?'

I looked at her, eyebrows raised.

'Oh yes, I know all about that,' she said. 'Did you think your precious Superintendent Rix spared me anything? He so carefully left that out of his report but he couldn't resist dropping some heavy hints and I made him tell me everything.'

I said nothing. I could well imagine the scene. What struck me was the sly way in his account to me that Rix had cast himself as a kindly censor of unpleasant news.

When Ruth had gone I set about searching methodically. I took the books out of the bookshelf one at a time and leafed through each. They were mostly on religion, the environment and English literature. The English books seemed to be course materials rather than personal choices, with the date of purchase written in a neat girlish hand on the inside cover. Most were bought on the same date. Apparently, Meg had no shelf space for a single novel printed after 1900, not even a children's story. Nothing appeared to have been chosen for anything so trivial as pleasure. There were no hidden letters or billets-doux in her desk, just neatly filed lecture notes and a completed but unmarked essay on the Metaphysical Poets.

A search of her wardrobe was equally unproductive. She had only four pairs of shoes, all sensible and sturdy. Her principal ensemble seemed to be jeans and sweatshirts. There was one black dress and no hair shirt. I began to wonder if this girl was for real. There were no pink things in the room, no fluffy white sheepskin rugs, no little ornaments, soft toys, or full-sized mirror. There was no mirror of any description. The only decoration, if you could call it that, was a map of the world in Peters' projection, showing the true relative size of the continents, pinned to the wall above her desk. Red pins in various places in Southern Africa presumably marked her mother's travels. There were also several Friends of the Earth posters rolled up under the bed.

I took my time and went through everything carefully. The image that I was forming was of a girl who was not so much austere, as fanatical. I turned down the bed and checked underneath. She wasn't using a proper interior sprung mattress but a lumpy palliasse on wooden slats of a type that you might find in a Third World village.

The one area where she seemed to have indulged herself was personal cleaning products. I pulled out a large box of them from under the bed. There were four or five types of soap, washing gels, skin cleansers, moisturisers, and bath additives. Mostly Boots' own brands. There were at least forty or fifty items. I wasn't quite sure what that meant. Obsessive behaviour syndrome? Or merely skin problems?

I sat down on the very uncomfortable chair and thought for a minute. Someone was trying to pull a con trick here. But who? And for what purpose? All I knew was that this wasn't the room of any girl born and brought up in late twentieth-century England. It was more like a reconstruction of the living quarters of a seventeenth-century Carmelite nun. All it lacked was a whip for self-chastisement, or broken walnut shells inserted between the sheets to prevent a comfortable night's sleep.

I tried to recall the rooms of 'normal' students. The walls should be covered in pictures of one sort or another. Where were Gareth Gates and Will Young? More to the point, where were Mum and Dad? Lack of a picture of Arthur was understandable as she was living with him, but surely there should be dozens of photos of parties, events, family gatherings, etc., particularly as Meg didn't see all that much of her mother. Also female students often had birthday greetings or congratulations cards all over the place. Come to think of it, there wasn't one letter from a friend.

What kind of girl was Meg Hands? Even prisoners were allowed more personal touches.

I kneeled in the corner and looked obliquely at the dazzlingly illuminated wall by the window. There were dozens of tiny holes made by drawing pins. I ran my hand over the surface. Someone had also used an adhesive such as Blu-Tack to stick up posters.

So that was one lie this room was trying to tell me. There'd been plenty of pictures in here, but not now.

The walls had been stripped bare.

But why and by whom?

I tapped all the surfaces for hidden compartments. There was nothing. There was no electronic or audio equipment of any sort apart from the laptop computer.

I switched it on and then summoned Arthur for the password.

'Meg was a very, very clean person,' he said, pointing to the opened box of skin-care products. 'Those were in the bathroom originally but I put them in here when Mother arrived. It's bad enough keeping the flat on without being reminded of Meg every time we use the bathroom.'

'I see.'

'The password is 'MANUS' in capitals. That means "a hand" in Latin,' he explained for my benefit.

I didn't enlighten him that I'd had Latin banged into me at school until my head ached, or that 'MANI', meaning 'hands', would have been a better password. He showed no urge to leave but settled on the bed while I accessed Meg's emails.

'Did you often come in here, Arthur?' I asked quietly.

He looked at me strangely. 'Funny you should ask that. The policeman Rix asked me the same thing, and the answer is no. Meg was insistent on her privacy. She yelled at me to clear off if I even knocked on her door.'

'So you wouldn't know if there were pictures and such stuck up in here?'

'I hope you're not implying anything?' he said, ignoring my question.

'Such as?'

'My relationship with Meg was entirely normal.'

'I'm sure it was, but do you mind telling me how you knew her password if you never came in here?'

'She asked me for a password and I gave her that one.'

'Although you say Meg was fanatical at defending her privacy she allowed you to choose the password for her computer?'

This query produced a lengthy silence. I decided not to make an issue of it. There was no point in antagonising Arthur at this stage and I might need his help with Ruth.

'I don't know what was going through her mind. Maybe she thought it was a good idea if someone else knew her password.'

'Yes,' I agreed. 'That's likely.'

'Look, she knew I'd never dare to come in here without her permission. That's why she trusted me with the password,' he argued vehemently.

'That's OK, Arthur. It's just a minor point,' I assured him. 'I'm only trying to build up an image of Meg.'

'Just as long as you don't get the idea that you're fucking Hercule Poirot,' he said sourly.

I laughed and turned to the emails.

Sure enough, the last three messages to Ruth mentioned premonitions about hidden evil and a feeling that she was being followed. I flicked through some of the earlier messages. They were mainly practical questions about Ruth's work with Aids victims, availability of anti-retroviral drugs, fundraising activities etc. There were very few personal comments of any sort. They were more like branch office reports to headquarters than letters from a daughter to a mother.

The thought struck me that emails don't have any identity checks. It's not like a phone call or a handwritten letter. Ruth Hands had no way of knowing that these rather spare communications really emanated from Meg. I looked at Arthur speculatively. If they were fakes it was hard to imagine what possible motive he could have had for sending them.

'So, how are you getting on?' I asked Arthur when I finished.

'You can see how it is here,' he replied with a rueful smile. 'Mother's taking this so hard.'

'And you aren't?'

'No, I was completely shattered for the first month but it's as if Mother thinks that if you catch this imaginary killer it'll somehow bring Meg back. I can't accept that.'

'You're sure the killer's imaginary?'

'Pretty well, but I'll be delighted if you do come up with something.'

'Did Meg tell you that she thought someone was following her?'

'Yes, but the first time she said it I thought she'd been overdoing the carrot juice. Meg was so intense. She often had nightmares, you know.'

'About being followed?'

'No, they were about our father mainly. He was working in Uganda when he was killed by Hutu guerrillas who'd crossed the border from Zaire – Congo, as they call it now. It was a pure tragedy, a needless and senseless crime. They took him and two other white men off a bus and shot them.'

'I'm sorry.'

'Mother was in Kampala. She saw to it that justice was done. The Ugandan army crossed the border and killed all the guerrillas.'

'It must have been a hard time for you.'

'Yes, it was hell. I'd just come here to university, and Meg was still at boarding school, a Quaker place in Yorkshire, and now this has happened.'

'Did Meg resent her father being killed like that? I mean . . .'

'I know what you mean. Did she resent him being in harm's way in Africa when he could have had a comfortable life in England? The answer is no. She revered the work that he and Mother have dedicated themselves to. If anything, the murder strengthened Meg's wish to solve all the problems of the world.'

'What about you, Arthur?'

'I've never had that feeling,' he said emphatically. 'Do you know that this is one of the longest times I've spent in my mother's company since I was a small child? I don't think it's right to sacrifice your children to the cause of doing good to others. For God's sake, though, don't tell the Old Queen I said that.'

'The Old Queen?' I repeated with a smile.

'Distancing, I think the shrinks call it. It's what we used to call our mothers, though most of the others saw a lot more of their parents than I did.'

'Anything you tell me is confidential,' I assured him.

'I thought it might be. Seal of the confessional and all that?'

'Not exactly. Tell me about this student party,' I said to change the subject slightly. The interview, with him lolling on the bed, reminded me uncomfortably of a psychoanalysis session.

'I have friends in the Student Village. It's a bit of a swamp in there because there's no supervision. You can do what you like, within limits. Well, there was this party on that Friday. You know the sort of thing? Bring your own booze. Meg had been going on and on about being followed so I persuaded her to come. I don't know everything that happened at that party but I think someone must have spiked her orange juice or something,' he said lamely.

.'What about the day before? Did she spend it with her boyfriend?'

'Boyfriend?' he echoed with a hollow laugh. 'You must be joking. Meg never had a boyfriend.'

I scratched my head.

'Look, I know what you're on about. Mother's told me. Meg had a life of her own. I wasn't on her case twenty-four hours a day. I was away on the Wednesday, Thursday and Friday of that week. It was a field trip. I'm doing urban development studies and I was in London for those three days. We only got back at six in the evening. You can check with Dr Bledsoe – he's my supervisor.'

'So what's your theory about what happened?'

'Listen, I've had this question five times a day from the OQ. This is how it went down. Meg and I walked to the party, OK? I thought it might put her fears to rest. Crazy or what? But the Student Village is only a short distance from here. Meg was nervous right enough. There may well have been someone stalking her but I saw no one and I put her nerves down to it being the wrong time of the month and Meg missing her mother, you know?'

'OK,' I agreed.

'I didn't take the mysterious stalker seriously then and I'm not sure if I do now.'

'Fair enough, Arthur. No one's blaming you.'

'Except myself and my mother!' he said forcefully, slightly losing his cool for the first time.

'Calm down and tell me the rest.'

'All right,' he said. His eyes were closed and the interview wasn't going as I wanted it to. I'm used to studying the body language when I talk to someone in this kind of situation. A prone subject is hard to read.

'When we got there she started to come out of her shell a little . . . talking to one or two people. I went in another room with a couple of mates . . . Oh God!' he groaned.

'You were smoking pot,' I said.

'How the fuck do you know?' he shouted angrily, sitting up on the bed. 'Have you been checking on me? Am I the obvious suspect?'

'Arthur, there are three things the student population of this fair city do on a Friday night and one of them is smoking weed until their eyes pop out.'

'Yes,' he agreed, 'I know what the other two are:

boozing and bonking. Anyway, Meg came in and saw us and virtually went into hysterics. She was way over the top, in a real paddy. If you've seen Mother in full cry, imagine something ten times worse. What was I doing? Drinking, using drugs? Didn't I know that I was letting our father, Saint Thomas Hands who art in heaven, down? Not to speak of the Old Queen herself.'

'I see,' I murmured sympathetically.

'I'm sure you don't. You can't unless you're a member of my crazy family. Christ, Mr Cunane, I swear I'd only had a couple of cans of lager and shared a single spliff, more of a roach really, but to hear Meg go on you'd think I was up to the eyeballs in crack cocaine and heroin.'

'She overreacted.'

'You could say that, if you like understatement. To say she hit the bloody roof and went completely off her trolley would be nearer the truth.'

'Go on,' I prompted.

'There were these girls, they were really great. They calmed her down. One of them gave her a drink of camomile tea and it seemed to soothe her. I went back with my mates. God Almighty, I swear that was the last time I saw her.'

He covered his face with his hands. 'It's not my fault,' he insisted. 'Meg was nineteen, at university attending a party with people of her own age group. Was I supposed to watch over her every minute? Honestly, Mr Cunane, she was the one who usually watched over me. My guardian angel, she called herself. More like a mother hen, I used to say. How was I to know that someone would spike her orange juice, although they all deny it? Either that or she drank a glass of vodka by mistake for water. How was I to guess that she'd take it into her head to walk home on a cold, wet night when she had a sack-load of money to pay for a taxi?'

'You know she had money?'

'Of course. Who do you think was paying for my night out? I always spend my allowance before the end of the month but she's a hoarder . . . was a hoarder, I mean. She probably walked to save the planet from that little bit of hydrocarbon pollution.'

'I'm sorry if this sounds brutal, but what's your theory on how she came to end up in the canal?'

He stood up and paced the room for a moment and then stopped and stared out of the window. I joined him and followed his line of sight. Beyond the ugly fortress-like Hobby Dancer residence on the viaduct you could see the Basin clearly. It was gleaming now in the bright winter sunshine and looked almost inviting.

'I don't have a theory,' he exclaimed. 'Maybe it was this man she must have met if we're to believe the police. Knowing her, he's probably a religious eco-nut like herself. Perhaps he called her mobile and asked her to meet him down there. She certainly knew the layout of the streets. Even pissed out of her mind she must have known where the Canal Basin was. God! She looked at it every morning.'

'She had a mobile? It wasn't mentioned in the police report.'

'It's not in here,' he said when I turned towards the desk. 'I looked.'

'Did you?' I asked.

He blushed a little. 'She was my sister, you know.'

'I wasn't implying anything.'

'Oh, I'm sure you weren't.'

'There's one more thing, Arthur. I'd like the names of the people who were at your party.'

'So you can check up on me?' he asked hotly.

'No, they might have noticed something that you missed. Now can you tell me who they were?'

'I'll have to think about this. I'm already in the shit with my mates,' he muttered almost inaudibly.

Just then there was a rap on the door and Ruth came in.

'My solicitor has just delivered this,' she said, holding a disc in her hand, 'but if you think that by watching this you're going to persuade me that Meg was crazy or drunk, you're very wrong.'

'Mother, I'm sure that Mr Cunane has no such intention,' Arthur said wearily. 'I think I'll go out for a walk.'

I wanted to press Arthur but the moment had passed.

'One last thing, Arthur. When was this room decorated?'

He gave me a blank look and shrugged his shoulders, then left with a surprising turn of speed.

'I had it done when I bought the apartment. That was just under two years ago,' Ruth Hands answered on her son's behalf.

'And, Ruth, did you see this room before Meg died?'

'Why do you ask?'

'It's just that I thought you might have been a little startled at the Spartan standard of living Meg apparently set for herself.'

'The first time I've been in this room was after Meg's death. You may call this Spartan but I've already told you that Meg was dedicated.'

I raised my eyebrows but made no further comment. Dedicated to what, was what I wanted to ask.

I also wanted to ask her about Meg's missing pictures but I held my tongue. The way Arthur had scooted off when I mentioned the décor in his sister's room suggested that he was hiding something. Or possibly not; there could be some perfectly innocent explanation for the blank walls. Perhaps he was trying to spare his mother's feelings in some way. But how? Meg wasn't likely to have had male pin-ups – or was she?

It would keep. It would be better to spring a question on Arthur at some future point rather than giving him time to prepare an answer that would suit his mother.

She handed me the disc.

'Ruth,' I said earnestly, 'I've already studied Meg's last walk once and I felt there were some odd features. I want you to help me pinpoint what they were, that's all.'

'All right, but I'm doing this under protest.'

She strode back to the living room, inserted the disc in a DVD player and then almost flung herself into an armchair and sat with her arms wrapped round her knees.

Heritage had included all the material showing Meg so the first extract we saw was her walking down Deansgate and looking over her shoulder. There were people behind her but after a moment most of them crossed the road at a pelican crossing. Meg continued to look behind her. The pavement was deserted except for people at a considerable distance. It was too much for Ruth. Tears began rolling down her face and then she buried her head against her knees and slumped over in a foetus-like position. I switched off the DVD player.

'I'm sorry. It was very insensitive of me to subject you to this,' I said by way of apology. 'I'll take it and view it in my office. I'll let you know if I come up with anything.'

'Go ahead,' she said brokenly. She was weeping silently. 'We both know you'll find nothing. It's obvious that whoever was following her was visible only to Meg and no one else.'

'I'm sorry, I don't understand,' I said.

'An African would know what I meant right away,' she said grimly.

'Ruth, I was married to an African girl, a medical student who came to Manchester from West Africa. What is it that an African would understand that I'm incapable of?'

'So, you've been divorced?' she stated with her usual tact. I wondered just what it was she'd said to Janine.

'No, I've never been divorced,' I said patiently. 'Elenki

133

died of sickle-cell anaemia. We'd been married less than three years. She was training so that she could return to Africa and use her skills to help her people but that wasn't to be.'

'I'm a fool,' she said, putting her hand to her mouth. 'I'm so wrapped up in my own grief that I can't see that other people have problems. Can you let me off the hook?'

I shrugged. 'That doesn't arise. You couldn't be expected to know my background, but I'd like to know what it is you suspect – juju, witchcraft, or what?'

'And I've insulted your partner too. You must think I'm losing it.'

'Can you just tell me what you believe happened?'

'I don't know!' she shouted, holding her head in her hands. 'I'm saying crazy things. Maybe, I'm going the same way as my daughter. Maybe it was the Devil stalking her, maybe someone's put a curse on our family. They believe in these things in Africa.'

'I'll let you know what I find,' I said.

She sat back in the armchair and curled herself up. I was expected to leave.

My thoughts kept going back to Meg's room.

'Er, Ruth, there's just one more question, if you don't mind.'

She looked bleary-eyed but wasn't so sunk in grief that she'd lost the power of speech. I guessed that would never happen to Ruth Hands.

'Ask away,' she said listlessly, 'though I can't imagine what you hope to find in this apartment. Meg's killer's out there somewhere.'

'Yes,' I agreed, 'but if you don't mind me asking, how did Meg and Arthur keep the flat clean?'

'I don't know whether I'm going crazy or you are. What in the name of creation does that have to do with anything?'

'Think of the need to know these details as an eccentric quirk of mine. Did they have a cleaner?'

She roused herself and went over to the roll-top desk in the corner. She retrieved a sheaf of bills.

'Here you are. We have a maintenance contract with the firm that owns the building. They own the public spaces but we have to pay our share of the cleaning costs. Then if one pays extra the same company will arrange to valet the apartment. You can see I've made payments by standing order for a cleaner to come in here three times a week.'

I took the bills off her and noted the name of the firm of contract cleaners: Twin City Valeting Services, with an address in Regent Road, Salford.

'Let me forestall your next question,' she said with a grim attempt at a smile. 'I never saw the woman who cleaned for Meg and Arthur. She stopped coming immediately after Meg's death. I had to phone the firm to send us another woman. I believe she was an Indian national, from Goa. The one we've got now's Irish.'

'Do you know the Goan woman's name?'

'Why would I know that?' she asked in surprise.

'Surely Meg or Arthur mentioned it. You know she's from Goa.'

'Oh, our Irish biddy mentioned that. My children wouldn't have discussed a cleaner with me.'

'I see.'

'Now tell me why you need this information? Fair exchange is no robbery.'

'I'm trying to establish if Meg's room's always looked the way it does now. I just wonder if it was altered in the period before her death.'

That wasn't quite the whole truth but it was enough for Ruth to be going on with. In a gesture I recognised from our first meeting she pouted her lower lip and blew air upwards. Presumably it was a sign of relief.

'You know,' she said earnestly, 'I think that stale cheese Rix was trying to imply that there was something sexual going on between Meg and Arthur. I thought . . . well, I'm glad that you're not going down the same dead end.'

7

'Hildegard Hughes, 34, professor of contemporary media studies at the University of South Lancashire compared the current scare about an alleged Mangler with the fears of a witch cult in the Middle Ages. The high-flying academic, whose recently published book, *Moral Panic and Penal Policy in Modern Britain*, was highly praised by the Lord Chief Justice in a recent speech, was speaking at a conference organised by the Greater Manchester Police to discuss issues arising from the tabloid-induced panic in Manchester, which now appears to be on the decline . . .'
Report in the *Guardian*

Walking back to the office canvassers collared me twice. The fliers they were dishing out contained a recognisable picture of Meg Hands, but such is the power of suggestion that to my eyes she looked like Joan of Arc waiting for the bonfire to be lit.

To distract myself I bought an early edition of the *Evening News* and glanced through it as I strolled. The catalogue of crime contained nothing relating to my immediate problems. The wounds on my knees seemed to be healing. The pain had settled down to a dull pinching sensation.

I was certain that there was a rational explanation for what had happened to Meg Hands. It was sad about Ruth, but the best chance of saving her sanity was to come up with that explanation a.s.a.p.

When I arrived the office was buzzing. Celeste was at her desk with her baby in a pushchair at her side. As if to stress that she was busy she didn't bother to speak.

She gave me a look of saintly resignation. She was dividing up bundles of leaflets into small stacks and Peter Snyder was passing them to an oddly assorted group of individuals who formed a line that snaked out through the door into the street.

'Any response yet?' I asked eagerly.

Peter stared at me blankly. I sensed a certain air of disapproval in his attitude. He took his time before speaking.

'Oh, you mean replies,' he said finally. 'No, nothing yet.'

'I want to interview them myself.'

'This'll cost, Boss,' he said. 'Best part of three grand for the emergency printing and then hiring all these canvassers.'

'Peter, that'll be cheap at the price if we get a result,' I said dismissively. 'Don't forget the client's paying.'

'Dave, you're a lovely man, and a great person to work for, but you're no businessman,' he replied.

It was hard to keep a note of irritation out of my voice. I knew he meant well, but what did he think we were? A building society?

'The client'll pay,' I repeated.

'She'd better or there'll be a hole in our budget big enough to sink the *Titanic*. And, of course, you were aware before you started this caper that the police have already circulated fliers with Miss Hands' picture?'

I wasn't aware of that but I wasn't about to admit it. I could feel the blood pounding through the veins in my neck.

'Listen, mate, if there's one person out there who saw Meg Hands being led away by some evil-minded pus-bag then we've cracked the case.'

'As the police have already canvassed the area and appealed through the media that's quite a big if, isn't it?'

'Some people may have their reasons for not to talking to the police and we're offering a reward.'

'Hmm,' he murmured sceptically.

'We only need to throw doubt on the police story about an accident and then the coroner will force Rix to put more resources into investigating what really happened,' I insisted.

'And that's another thing. We can't afford to offend Rix. He's "The Man" in this town.'

'Sod Rix!' I yelled.

This outburst produced a momentary silence in the office.

I leaned over Peter's desk. My facial expression must have signalled imminent violence, because he backed away.

Then the noises resumed and I subsided. I felt as if I was burning up. I loosened my tie. It had been a bitch of a day so far and I didn't need to crown it by sending my office manager home with a black eye.

'Keep your hair on, Dave,' Peter said mildly. 'Everything you asked for is happening.'

'How are you making sure these people don't just take our money and then dump the fliers in the nearest bin?' I demanded, just to throw him off his stride.

'Thought of that,' he bragged. 'Michael Coe's keeping an eye on them in the street and as soon as I finish here I'm taking over so Michael can get something to eat.'

That reminded me that I was ravenous.

'Tell him to pick up a couple of BLT sarnies for me on his way back,' I said.

Peter picked up the phone and I went into my inner office. I pulled out the Oasis disc someone had left in the DVD player and inserted the CCTV copy.

As I settled down to study every bit and byte it contained I felt spooked. Ruth's talk about a satanic stalker must have been producing an effect because my palms were sweaty. As the images, some jerky, some smooth, flickered across the screen I told myself that this kind of surveillance was enough to throw a scare into the boldest. Talk about Big Brother, but almost everybody seems to accept surveillance as perfectly normal. If you've nothing to hide, why bother objecting?

It was harder to pick Meg out of a crowd than I'd expected. Her clothing was the standard student uniform – there were dozens of similarly dressed young women. But someone at the control centre must have done their work thoroughly because Meg was among the crowds in most frames. What I was watching was a series of extracts collected over many days showing Meg coming and going along the major streets.

As I viewed I realised that there was a strong similarity to her mother. Meg bowled along with a firmness of purpose that made most of her fellow pedestrians look like hesitant wimps. There was nothing casual about this girl. Her dark hair marked her out, bobbing along the streets, frequently overtaking slower walkers.

Then in the more recent clips there was a change. She became more hesitant, often pausing and looking behind her. I felt a chill along my spine. It was eerie. What was I witnessing? Mental deterioration, or the presence of the invisible stalker? Because, though I scanned until my eyes ached, I couldn't pick out a single person following her.

Now I could understand Jack Rix's confidence. Seeing this, the coroner was likely to offer Ruth nothing but his sympathy on her daughter's sad decline. We'd be lucky to leave the court with any verdict other than suicide. What was going on here? If only there was a camera able to record thoughts.

The champion of technology arrived with the sandwiches before I reached Meg's final appearance.

'So nerds have their uses,' Michael said when he saw what I was watching. His words penetrated my defeated mood. I paused the image.

'They may have,' I admitted reluctantly. 'Sit down and

have a drink,' I prompted. I needed his insight. I took out a bottle of Lagavulin malt and two glasses.

'What's this?' he asked cheerfully. 'Have we won the Lotto?'

'No,' I muttered. 'I just need something to restore me after the day I've had so far.'

I filled him in on Ruth's suspicions of satanic intervention.

'Dave, she sounds as if her brain's curdled. Some of Celeste's family think in the same way. Nothing's ever simple with them. It's always the Devil or some other bogeyman who gets the blame.'

'You don't subscribe to that?'

'What, me?' he asked with an easy laugh. 'I'm good old C of E myself – at least I was when I was in the army. Our lads don't even mention Old Nick these days.'

'Good,' I said.

'But, Dave, if this old trout's more than halfway round the U-bend should we be doing this investigation?'

'I don't know. Your wife was mad for it,' I said waspishly, 'and it pays your salary. Have we got to ask our clients for a certificate of sanity before we take their money? . . . And she's not an old trout.'

At this he sat up straight like a squaddie waiting to be bawled out by a particularly coarse sergeant. I was embarrassed both by my own touchiness and his reaction. At the back of my mind, I knew the real cause: my troubles with Janine.

'Damn it, Michael, stop being so bloody sensitive!' I snapped. 'If anyone else in this office starts giving me disapproving looks I'm going to deck them!'

'It's not me!' he retorted with a grin. 'It's you! This case is getting to you.'

'You can say that again,' I muttered with a painful smile.

'So where are we up to?'

'I don't think Meg's death was a simple accident,' I said after taking a deep breath. 'There are just too many coincidences.'

That sounded weak, even to my own ears.

'Sometimes things look like coincidences when it's just the operation of probability. When I was in the army – '

'No,' I said, holding up my hand. 'Don't try to talk me out of it. I'm having a hard enough time trying to convince myself there was something sinister going down without that. Janine thinks that the whole hullabaloo is due to Ruth Hands being crazy and dangerous to know. I'm struggling to keep a firm grip on normality.'

'Dave,' he laughed, 'you and normality, they don't exactly go together like ham and eggs.'

I grimaced.

'On the subject of normality have you ever seen a female student's room without a single picture of family or friends?'

He shook his head.

'It's almost as if someone's set out to create the impression that she was very odd.'

I told him about the pinholes and the absence of pictures.

'So you think there's a sinister explanation?'

'The brother denies that there was a boyfriend. Maybe he's telling the truth. It's hard to say, but suppose there was a boyfriend who removed any photographs featuring himself.'

'You think the brother's tied up with this boyfriend?'

'He could be. I don't know.'

'How are we going to check?'

'There was a cleaner who did for them three days a week. She must have seen any pictures, even eyeballed this very discreet boyfriend herself. If I could establish that then I could go after Brother Arthur in a big way.'

142

'What's holding you back?'

'This cleaner just happens to have jacked the job in when Meg was killed.'

'What a coincidence!'

'I thought you didn't believe in coincidences?'

'You've got me bang to rights there, guv,' he squeaked in a comical cockney accent. 'What's the punishment? Five days' bog-cleaning duties?'

'I thought you might like to check the firm where this woman worked. She was an Indian national, from Goa. Locate her.'

I passed him a slip of paper with the address of Twin City Valeting Services.

'A Goan, eh? She certainly sounds like a goer. Any name?'

'The Hands family don't get familiar with the hired help.'

'Like that, eh?' he asked, giving me an old-fashioned look.

'Yep!' I muttered.

We munched our sandwiches and drank in silence. In addition to my knees, I felt bruised and battered in other ways. I do wonder why I take some cases on. I ached to find irrefutable proof that Meg had been murdered. I switched on the DVD player with the remote and this time it was showing Meg's final walk down Whitworth Street West after she'd fled from her brother's party.

'Do you spot anything?' I asked Michael.

He shook his head.

I played the disc again.

'There, look how much more drunk she appears when she gets as far as Deansgate,' I suggested.

'I'll grant you that,' he said hesitantly after a second viewing, 'but if she'd a skinful the effects might not have kicked in until she was out in the street.'

I couldn't argue with that.

I felt a powerful need to puncture the layer of scepticism that was thickening around me like the ice on an Arctic trawler. I played the disc again, stopping every few seconds.

'Boss,' Michael said gently, 'I've done some research on your idea that someone tampered with these images. It's just not technically feasible at the moment and anyway the security round the control centre's pretty tight.'

'Not that tight,' I commented.

'All right, you were able to bluff your way in there but would you have been able to feed something into the computer? I don't think so.'

I picked up the edited file that Rix had given Ruth. There was an A4-sized shot of Meg's corpse lying on the canal bank. I hadn't studied the picture before. It was the sort of gruesome item that an amateur in pathology, such as myself, is inclined to pass over. Gritting my teeth, I took out a powerful magnifying glass and pored over it.

Thick tresses of black hair splayed out beneath her head. Sightless eyes gazed upwards. The sharp, clear photo caught the streaks of torrential rain splashing on the body. It was as if the weeping skies were trying to reclaim what the waters had given up. Pools of rainwater veiled the face, covering it like a shroud.

'Oh, come on, Sherlock!' Michael mocked. 'Admit it, the police haven't missed anything.'

I ignored him and carried on. He whiled away the time by picking bits of bacon out of his teeth with the sharpened end of a matchstick.

Then it happened.

There wasn't a clear chiming note going 'Bong' and echoing round my head but suddenly my throat and chest tightened as if a giant hand was squeezing me.

'Look at this,' I gasped excitedly. 'See the belt buckle on this photo? It's on the right side, but it's on the left on the CCTV image.'

144

Michael came to my side of the desk with a tolerant expression on his face. He studied the photo and then the TV screen. The final CCTV image showed Meg wearing a dark coat. The coat was loosely draped over her shoulders. Her sweatshirt and jeans were quite visible. The belt buckle of the jeans was clearly pointing to the left.

While Michael cleaned his glasses and took another look at the TV screen, this time going down on his hands and knees, I buzzed Celeste on the intercom and told her to call Ruth to find out whether Meg was right- or left-handed. It was better for her to phone than me. I didn't want any false hopes raised.

'It can't be,' Michael said wonderingly. 'There must be some mistake. The photo must be a reversed negative or something.'

'No, you don't,' I said. 'The writing on that manhole cover is legible. The belt buckle shown on this photo is definitely pointing right.'

Michael scratched the stubble on his chin, took his glasses off for another wipe and turned the photo in every possible direction.

'There's something deeply weird going on here,' he eventually acknowledged.

'Yes, such as that between the last image on the CCTV and turning up drowned, poor Meg was stripped and then dressed again and whoever dressed her put the belt on the wrong way round.'

'It can't be,' Michael insisted. He scratched his chin hard enough to leave a mark. 'Oh, Christ, Dave, somebody did kill her. Are you going to phone Rix?'

'He can stew in his own juice,' I said vindictively. 'He brought the inquest forward, so he can find out then like everyone else. Anyway, he's supposed to have gone fishing.'

'Peter's not going to like that, Boss. He has nightmares about us getting on the wrong side of the local fuzz.'

145

I shrugged my shoulders and pressed on. 'We're going to need several blow-ups of this photo and of the computer images.'

'No problem, I've got a DVD player on my own computer and a high-grade printer.'

I was so excited that I could hardly breathe. I poured us both a stiff measure of Lagavulin. Even at forty pounds a bottle it was worth it.

'Dave, I'm really sorry I didn't believe you,' Michael began. 'It was because you were taking the piss out of us nerds.'

'No problem, Michael,' I said, not paying much attention. 'That was meant as a joke, you know.'

Celeste put her head round the door. 'Mrs Hands says Meg was right-handed,' she announced. Celeste looked at her husband, still furiously polishing his specs and looking uncomfortable, and then at me. Her face was ablaze with curiosity. 'She sounded pretty rough, Dave? Have you something to tell her?'

I made no reply and after a second glance at Michael and a shake of her head in the direction of the Lagavulin she departed.

My mind was racing ahead. I drained the whisky at a gulp and my lack of respect for the famous malt was repaid by a coughing fit.

The coroner would be sure to ask for additional information about how the body was raised from the water and if anyone had removed the belt at that stage.

When my coughing subsided I picked up the phone and dialled Dr Ashley Gribbin's number.

The ringing tones went on for ever and then the voice of her answerphone came on. However, I hardly had time to get the words 'Dave Cunane' out of my mouth before Ashley picked up the phone.

'Dave, you call at the oddest times. Don't you know this is Saturday afternoon?'

I felt a surge of relief at hearing her voice.

'Ashley, I'm so sorry to break into the sacred weekend.'

'It's OK, Dave, I'm always prepared to make an exception for you. You know you've a standing invitation to come for a meal. My jerked chicken's to die for.'

Ashley's been divorced for about two years, and when I was briefly in her employ, she'd made it clear that the experience hadn't put her off marriage. The problem I helped to sort involved her fifteen-year-old son, Basil. He'd been on the point of getting himself seriously involved with the Law in a way that might have harmed his mother's career prospects. Like others, the lad had become a slave to the dreaded weed and, according to his mother, his black skin made him more vulnerable than a white contemporary would have been. She felt that the police would come down more harshly on him, particularly as he was buying the stuff for others as well as himself. Naturally, he'd ended up owing hundreds to various unsavoury characters who were pressuring him. I was able to straighten things out, though not cure his attachment to the weed.

'How's Basil?' I enquired. I was still wheezing.

'Oh, he's fine. He's still smoking pot like it's going out of fashion and not doing a tap of work at that expensive school I try to send him to. Every morning except Saturday and Sunday I have a battle royal to get him out of bed and this is supposed to be his exam year.'

'You sound tired,' I sympathised.

'I could do with a break. You know Basil's nickname's Weed, and that's not because his daft father insisted on calling him after a herb, or because he smokes grass, but because he just keeps on growing. The boy's enormous. But you didn't call to talk about him. What's all this soft soap for, Dave?' she demanded with all the directness with which she applied the scalpel to her customers.

'It's about the Hands case,' I said.

'I take it you've been retained by the family?'

'Correct.'

'Dave, you're wheezing so much that I thought you were going to ask me to come round and rub your manly chest with Vick's VapoRub, and of course I'd do that like a shot, but I'm giving evidence on behalf of the police on Monday and it would be quite unethical of me to discuss the case with you.'

'I thought you might like to look at another little piece of the jigsaw that's just come to light. You wouldn't want to look silly in court.'

'Ouch, Dave! Are you saying I missed something? Sorry, but if I get egg on my face, so be it. You'd better not tell me. Now about your chest, has Janine given you some time off?'

'Not exactly,' I said.

'But you're not a married man yet, are you?' she asked with a roguish chuckle.

'Not exactly,' I repeated gloomily. Nor likely to be, I thought to myself.

'Then a girl can still have her hopes.'

It was obvious that Ashley wasn't going to say a word about the case so after a little more banter I rang off.

The rest of that weekend was an anticlimax.

I arranged a rota with Peter and Michael to cover phoned replies to my poster campaign. That ended up with me sleeping on a camp bed in the office while the married men were tucked up with their wives. I spent some time during both evenings trying to interest the local sex workers in Meg's case. That was pretty much of a disaster. Once they heard I wasn't interested in 'business' most of them didn't want to know and the ones that did listen treated my questions as a joke.

I went home several times to change clothes and pick up some food. Janine was very cool. Lacking the energy for further disputes, I said nothing.

A clerk came round from Ruth's solicitor to collect my new evidence on Sunday afternoon. When he'd gone I sat in the office waiting for the phone calls to pour in. They weren't pouring in. All I got were crank calls. Several punters thought I was offering Meg's services as an escort.

The solicitor's clerk had agreed that my hunches weren't going to make the coroner jump out of his seat, nor was the news that the manager of a local tavern had hired a couple of thugs to sort me out, or that Meg's room had pinholes but no pictures, but he was impressed by the blow-ups Michael supplied.

So was Mr Kropotkin, the coroner.

Against police objections he returned an open verdict.

'Dave, that was wonderful,' Ashley Gribbin said as she came out with me. 'I've been waiting to see Rix get his comeuppance for years, but watch your back from now on.'

I was conscious of flashing cameras.

8

'Prison chaplains killed in freak accident. Two chaplains at the Manchester Prison, formerly known as Strangeways, were crushed to death when a lorry overturned and fell onto the car they were travelling in.'
Report in the *Daily Sport*

'Has the Mangler widened his scope?' asks the *Daily Sport* in an editorial following the above report. A spokesman for the Salford Roman Catholic diocese condemned the article as a crude attempt to exploit a tragedy.

If Ruth Hands was delighted with the result she was certainly very clever at hiding her feelings. She came up to me on the pavement outside. 'So it looks like your so-delightful *British bobbies* pitched us a curve ball,' she said. Her lips were twisted into a sneer.

'What do you mean?' I snarled. Lack of sleep over the weekend and the stress of waiting for the coroner's decision had eroded my patience.

'My solicitor tells me that this means that the police will do no further investigation unless significant new evidence comes up. We're back at first base.'

'But surely they've got significant new evidence. What do they want? A signed statement from the killer?'

'Apparently your Mr Rix claims that without witnesses or forensic evidence the belt must be regarded merely as an anomaly. Meg could have rethreaded the belt herself for whatever reason.'

'I wish you'd stop calling him *my* Mr Rix,' I said angrily.

'Mother, come away,' Arthur said soothingly. 'I'm sure

150

Mr Cunane's done his best.' He steered Ruth towards a waiting taxi. She shot me a parting glance that was full of reproaches.

As I pounded the pavements en route to my office my indignation didn't subside, despite my stretching the journey out with a long diversion. I brushed past Peter, marched into my room and flung myself into my chair.

The internal phone buzzed but I left it alone.

It took some time before I was ready to speak to anyone. When eventually Celeste came in and put coffee and two dark chocolate digestive biscuits on the desk in front of me she had the tact not to speak.

I emitted a long-drawn-out sigh and snapped a pencil in two.

'Like that was it?' she asked.

'Not really. I did what I set out to do but it seems there's no pleasing some people.'

We then discussed minor details of office routine for half an hour.

I ordered Celeste to draw up an itemised bill for Pimpernel Investigations' services and send it to Ruth Hands by courier. If I was going to be insulted I might as well be paid for the privilege.

'Dave, I'll swear the veins on your head were standing up like hydraulic cables when you came in,' Celeste said as she was leaving. 'You want to be careful with these rages. They can be dangerous for a man of your age.'

I mimed throwing an ashtray at her and she ducked out quickly.

A moment later the door was flung open with a terrific crash and like the Demon King in an opera Detective Chief Superintendent Rix was standing before me.

Now, *he* was in a rage.

He threw the early edition of the *Manchester Evening News* down in front of me. There was a picture of myself and Ashley Gribbin. She was grinning at me. I looked

151

bemused but triumphant. The headline read 'Open Verdict shock for Police'.

'That's what all this fucking bullshit was about this morning, publicity seeking!' he roared, reaching many decibels louder than the sound of a space shuttle launch. 'You shitty little moron! Call yourself a detective? You're not fit to wipe the arse of a real detective, you bum hole!'

By this time I was out from behind my desk ready for violent action. I could see flecks of foam on Rix's lips as he squared up to me and I raised my fists. I was within an inch of decking him when a tiny little warning bell went off somewhere in the inflamed bunch of nerve-endings I call a brain. This was 'Smiling' Jack Rix I was dealing with. What was he up to now?

'You're not even an arsehole,' he taunted. 'An arse-hole at least serves a useful purpose, whereas you do nothing at all.'

'So you want me to hit you?' I said calmly, lowering my fists and retreating behind my desk. 'And then you arrest me, right?'

'Listen, arse wipe,' he fulminated.

'No, you listen, Rix,' I shouted. 'I've been insulted by experts but with you, we always end up in the toilet, don't we? What's your problem? Was your mammy too harsh with the old potty training? Did she make you wipe up your own mess?'

For some reason that seemed to hit home. His eyes sparkled dangerously and I could see that I was right to suspect his motives. The rage was feigned. No doubt he had backup out on the street, waiting to rush in and drag me off to the pokey.

'Leave my dear mother out of it, you pathetic shite hawk,' he said menacingly, not ham-acting this time. 'My problem is this, Cunane, you've been screwing that fat tart Gribbin and she's given you forensic information she should have revealed to me first.'

I calculated what would cause greatest annoyance.

I started laughing. It was a little forced but not bad in the circumstances. Then I took the Lagavulin out of the desk drawer.

'You're a joke,' I muttered as I poured myself a glass. I could see his tongue hanging out but I made no move to offer him refreshment.

'Your squeeze won't be laughing when I make an official complaint to the Home Office about her unprofessional behaviour.'

'Peevish sod, aren't you?' I commented. I picked up my large magnifying lens which was still on the desktop. 'Seen one of these before? The belt was news to Ashley Gribbin just as it was to you. I found it myself.'

'You couldn't find your own way out of a wet paper bag,' he snarled.

'I tried to tell Ashley, over the phone I might add, but she didn't want to know. You were incommunicado.'

He grunted.

His eyes were on the malt whisky. I suspected that displaying expensive whisky in front of a man with Rix's tastes was like inviting a pyromaniac to start a bonfire and then hiding the matches.

I laughed at him again.

'I'll not forget this,' he whined.

'Oh, sit down and have a drink,' I relented. 'All this hysteria's wearing me out.'

He complied with speed. What a change – from raging Rottweiler to hurt spaniel in one millisecond! He drained the shot of Lagavulin and then shoved the tumbler back under my nose. I poured us both another stiff one. My own nerves were twanging as if the entire string section of the Hallé Orchestra was playing pizzicato.

'We'll have to stop meeting like this,' I said after a long interval. 'It's costing me a fortune.'

'Go on, gloat,' he muttered self-pityingly. 'You're

entitled to, but this morning's little caper has cost me a lot more than the price of a few lousy drinks. I'm up for deputy chief constable next month. Well, that's gone up the Swanee.'

'Why don't you collar whoever killed Meg Hands? The Chief will think you're the dog's bollocks then,' I suggested.

'Typical civilian comment,' he grizzled. 'Have you any idea how many police man hours have gone into this case already? At the CCTV centre alone I've gone through half a year's overtime budget sifting VCR footage . . . No, don't say it! I can see the words forming on your lips. *The belt! It's the belt!*' he brayed.

'I wasn't going to say a thing.'

'Well, wipe that clever smirk off your face then.'

I wiped the smile. Rix's very comical when he sets his mind to it.

'OK, so we missed the belt, but what does it prove? Thanks to that woman's insistence this case has been treated as a murder inquiry practically from day one and yet we've come up with nothing.'

'Jack, the fact that the belt was on the wrong side suggests that her clothing was rearranged before she went in the water.'

'Not necessarily by someone else. She may have had a jimmy down by the canal bank.'

'What about the hostile reception at La Venezia when I tried to ask a few questions?'

'Oh, grow up. That whole area is a rich kiddies' playpen. The last thing the proprietors want is outsiders questioning the paying customers. We tried it and they were barely co-operative. A private eye's got no chance.'

'There's one of the bouncers called Neville, I haven't got his other name. He looks like Central Casting's idea of a professional criminal, you know – shaven head, hyped to the eyeballs with steroids. You could check him out again.'

'I'm sorry, Dave, excellent though your whisky is, I can't reopen the case.'

'I still think you're making light of the belt.'

'So the belt was the wrong way round. Did someone take advantage of a drunken girl and give her a bonk before she fell into the water? I don't think we'll ever know. I can't restart a major investigation just because of this belt business. It raises a doubt, I'll admit that, but where does it take us? You tell me, genius . . . Nowhere, that's where.'

'There you are. You've said it yourself, someone from La Venezia could have interfered with her, which would explain the aggro I got down there, and I'm telling you, this Neville looked like a prime candidate to me.'

'That's a hunch, is it?' he said scornfully.

'Look, Jack, why do people keep pit bull terriers? Because they bite, that's why. I'm telling you this Neville's got to be in the frame if you accept that somebody replaced Meg's belt.'

'Description?' he said reluctantly.

'Shiny bald head, well over six feet, brick shithouse.'

'But for the haircut you could be talking about yourself.'

'I don't use steroids. The aggression was pouring out of this guy.'

'And you're as sweet as a nut, I suppose? You were ready to knock my head off ten minutes ago.'

'Jack!'

'All right, all right! I'll get someone to pull the bugger's record if he has one, but I'm not promising anything.'

'Brilliant, so there's someone walking around who knows how to drown students and get away with it.'

'That's assuming this Neville drowned her.'

'Someone did.'

'You're thinking of this nonexistent Mangler, I suppose?'

155

I shrugged.

'Let me tell you something in confidence, and I mean in strict confidence. The tabloids have been warned that they'll get the full works . . . editors jailed, massive fines, etc. – if they reveal this before any trial occurs.'

'Perhaps you'd better not tell me then.'

'I'm telling you so that you'll ditch your obsession.'

'Gee, thanks.'

'Three young women have been atrociously murdered. Despite what the tabloids claim, the killings were not linked.'

'Yes, I think we've all got the message about that.'

'Spare me the sarcasm! We know they weren't linked because each had a different crime signature – completely different MO, different traces of unidentified DNA, but there was a single similarity which one officer – now reduced in rank from detective inspector to plain old constable, I might add – incautiously revealed to the press. Each of the corpses lacked a different internal body part.'

'Ugh!'

'That's why they're harping on about a Mangler but we know from the circumstances that it's a complete coincidence.'

'All right, not very nice to know, but why tell me?'

'Because, unlike them, your client's daughter's remains were unmolested. So even if we hypothesise that there *is* a Mangler, which I don't for a moment, she wouldn't be one of his victims.'

'I see.'

'Do you? I hope for your sake that you do. But, whatever's going on inside that tiny twisted brain of yours, remember, what I've just told you is secret. We don't want to start a panic.'

'That would never do! People might start defending themselves!'

'Cunane, *old boy*, there are dozens of people walking

round out there knocking people off, half of 'em carrying guns. We have to *prioritise* our time. We'll act if there's evidence. Thanks to you the Hands case is still open but this isn't the nineteen fifties with about ten murders a year max. Have you heard about these clerics?' he said, pointing out the headline in the paper.

Once again Rix was speaking in that cogent, half comical 'I must be believed' tone of voice that complemented his Irish accent. The musical quality put me in mind of a mountain stream gushing over smooth pebbles.

'Have you ever been up the wee lane at the side of Strangeways? The press got it all wrong as usual. It's a steep hill with a truck hire place at the top. The clerics were in their car, doing what clerics do, at the bottom of this incline and somehow the brakes failed on this fully loaded ten-tonner parked halfway up. They never knew what hit them.'

He demonstrated the finality of the collision by smacking his hands together.

'Are you saying someone deliberately let the brakes off?'

'Deliberate, shmeliberate. I don't know. It could be, but we've had so many freak accidents and fires lately, not to speak of the nonsense about these so-called Mangler killings that it's beginning to look as if the Man Up There's got it in for us.'

'What were these clergymen doing then?'

'Oh, nothing. I only said that to wind you up. One of them was helping the other to start his car.'

I pondered why Rix thought implying the dead clerics were queer would wind me up.

'Were they Catholics then?' I asked eventually.

'Yeah,' he muttered as he pushed his empty glass across the desk at me.

He must have detected something in my expression because he felt that further explanation was necessary.

'Dave, I didn't tell you that to annoy you. I told you because it's an example of the way this Mangler hysteria is being whipped up. One paper's even suggested that this one-in-a-million accident is down to the Mangler. It sells papers, you see.'

Responding with a thin smile, I poured another hefty tot for him and a smaller one for myself. I needed to be sober enough to rebuild my bridges with Janine this evening and didn't have Rix's sponge-like capacity.

'Jack, I don't know where you get this idea that I'm the head of the local branch of the Legion of Mary. I haven't been in church . . . well, for quite some time.'

'Maybe you ought to go more often,' he responded. 'Maybe your new playmate Ruth Hands will bring you round to her way of thinking. She's built the way you like them. A big girl.'

'Hah, some playmate!' I echoed, ignoring the innuendo. 'I've just sent her my bill and I expect that's the last I'll hear from her.'

'Good man!' he crowed approvingly. 'So, despite all this bellyaching about belts and bonking bouncers, you're backing out of the case?'

'Maybe.'

'Are you or are you not, you argumentative prat?'

'The ball's in her court. I'm sick of being insulted every time she opens her mouth.'

'Ooh, aren't you the sensitive one?'

'Well, she never lets up.'

'She's like that, isn't she?' he said, smiling warmly, 'a human angle grinder with all the safeties off.'

At last I'd said something to make him happy. I felt a certain glow, or perhaps that was just the whisky.

Peter Snyder poked his head round the door at that point.

'Everything OK?' he asked nervously.

'Why do you ask?' I quizzed mischievously.

'It's just . . . er . . . just that everything's been quiet for a while,' he admitted hesitantly.

'And you wanted to check if he'd murdered me?' Rix demanded, roaring with laughter as he spoke. 'Dave, old son, you'd never have hit me, would you?'

'I might have,' I said with an equally jolly laugh.

'And I might just have a Black Maria waiting round the corner,' he said, slapping me on the shoulder.

On that happy note we parted. Rix walked out none the worse for having downed about a third of a litre of malt whisky.

'Nip out and check if he does have a Black Maria with him,' I said to Peter as soon as Rix was out of the door.

I was trying to work out just what the agenda had been for Rix's unexpected visit. First he'd try to provoke me. The reason for that was obvious enough. Then he'd confided about the recent spate of murders and unexplained accidents. I was worried. If anything, Jack Rix trying to be friendly was much more menacing than Jack Rix sour and nasty. It meant that he considered that I could affect his meteoric rise to the top in some way. But how?

It's difficult for Peter to look stealthy but he gave a passable imitation as he slipped out after the detective. It's also hard for a black man to look pale but he did when he returned.

'There's a rhino round the corner,' he gasped. 'I could hardly believe my eyes, six coppers in the van. He got in the back with them.'

I laughed almost until I cried. Peter gaped at me as if I'd gone mad.

'At least you parted on good terms,' he suggested hopefully.

'Oh, yes, good until the next time I do something he doesn't like.'

'Boss, Jack Rix can do us a lot of harm.'

159

'I think you'll find that DCS Rix came round here because he was worried that we can do him a lot of harm. If we'd solved a case he closed he could kiss his career goodbye.'

'So we're not on the Hands case any more?'

'That depends,' I said. 'Have any more phone calls come in?'

Peter whipped out a notebook.

'Up to now we've had two hundred and seventy-three calls, including those you took. Some were nuisance calls, some were trying to find out how much of a reward we were offering. Several seemed promising but were just hoaxers. Michael's followed one up but it turns out the caller's in prison and has been for the last three years. I'm afraid there's been nothing positive,' he concluded apologetically.

'It's not your fault,' I said.

'No,' he agreed. 'So far, the cost, including staff overtime, comes to three thousand seven hundred and ninety-one pounds and sixty-two pence. I got us a reduction on printing charges by promising that our next office stationery printing will be done by the same firm.'

'Thanks,' I muttered. 'Thousands of leaflets and not one firm sighting of Meg Hands.'

'That's about the size of it,' he said.

When Peter returned to his calculations I phoned Janine.

'I suppose you're pleased with yourself,' were her first words. 'That's a lovely photo of you and your pet pathologist on the front page and, by the way, which of your various organs was she squeezing to make you smile so broadly? I know which one she wants to get her hands on!'

'Janine!' I squeaked. 'There's only ever been you.'

'Can it, Dave! I've had it with you. I don't need twenty questions to work out where you spent the weekend.

160

First, you kick me into touch when I offer what you've been yelping about for years like a love-lorn tomcat; then, you insist on carrying out the wishes of a madwoman despite –'

'I'm not . . .' I started to protest, but she hung up.

I slumped back in my chair and considered the remaining contents of the whisky bottle standing on my desk. There was another in the cupboard. I sat for a long time just looking at that bottle and its promise of oblivion. Outside I could hear the normal sounds of office routine: phones ringing, doors banging, printers chattering. In the end I put the bottle away and phoned Janine again. There was no answer.

I was thinking of getting the unopened whisky bottle out for an inspection when Celeste came in and plonked a coffee pot and cup down.

'You need to drink all this before you go home,' she advised.

'Thanks, Mother,' I quipped.

She giggled.

An hour later I drove home, taking much longer than usual, courtesy of the city council's road-narrowing schemes. When I reached my flat there was a cardboard box standing outside. It contained pots and pans and various other domestic articles and clothing that I'd left in Janine's flat. There was a note stuck to it.

> Dave,
>   I was owed a few days' leave so I've taken the children out of school and booked a short holiday with my mother.
>   I'll see you when I get back,
>   Janine.

I could feel my heart thudding as I read this. It looked like I'd really blown it.

I let myself in. My mobile rang. I snatched it out of my pocket, hoping against hope that Janine was having second thoughts but it was an angry American voice that I heard.

'Mr Cunane!'

'It's Dave,' I said wearily.

'Dave, then, I want to see you at once!'

'If it's about the bill –'

'It is about the bill. If you think I've any intention of paying you before you complete the investigation you can have no idea of how the Hands family has made its money.'

'From what you said outside the court I thought you'd terminated my employment with you.'

'You're scared, aren't you?' she drawled harshly. 'I should have known there was no one on this rain-sodden island with enough sand in their craw to find out what happened to my Meg.'

'No, I'm not frightened! I'm just sick of listening to your rubbish about this country. Your husband was murdered in Africa but I haven't noticed you organising a boycott of that continent!'

'You're shooting wild there, cowboy! The President of Uganda had a regiment on the road within an hour of hearing the news about Thomas. Inside of a week they'd caught up with the Hutu thugs who killed him and dealt with them.'

'By "dealt with" them, you mean shot them?'

'I don't imagine they invited them for afternoon tea. What do you think they should have done? Those guys killed eight hundred thousand Tutsis in the summer of 'ninety-four.'

'That was Africa, this is England.'

'Don't I just know it? . . . So are you just another flabby-faced coward with a nice line in chat or are you prepared to find out what happened to my girl?'

162

'Flabby-faced coward?' I spluttered. 'I'll be round at your place to get this sorted in ten minutes.'

I think if she'd said flabby-faced *limey* coward I'd have told her to forget the bill and written the cost off to expenses but she didn't.

Arthur let me in. He didn't say anything but raised his eyebrows evocatively as he led me to the living room.

Ruth was holding a cheque.

'Oh my!' she exclaimed sarcastically. 'You look as if you've just had root canal work without anaesthetic.'

'That's exactly how I feel.'

'Here, this is what I owe you,' she said, passing me the cheque. The figure was considerably more than I'd asked for.

'This is too much. I can't accept it.'

'According to Arthur, I owe you a great deal more. He's just finished explaining to me that without your efforts over the weekend the case would have been officially closed and what would I have done then? I was going to chain myself to the railings outside ten Downing Street.'

I looked at her. I'd no doubt that she was serious.

'Look, I'm not going to apologise, if that's what you're expecting,' she said. 'There are a lot of cowards in this country, but then there are everywhere, and I suppose it's no worse here than in America. So I was out of line about ye little Olde England. If you're still mad at me you can take the cheque as a final payment, or you can carry on with what you set out to do.'

'I can't guarantee to imitate the Ugandan army,' I said, 'but I don't seem to have anything else to distract me at the moment.'

'Good,' she said eagerly, 'I'll take that as a yes.'

'OK, take this cheque back and write me another for the amount requested. It'll make things easier at the office. Peter Snyder likes to keep his books straight.'

She wrote me another cheque. 'Now tell me what you found out with all those fliers,' she said as she handed it over.

'Nothing at all,' I answered bleakly, carefully tucking the slip of paper in my wallet.

'But surely someone must have seen Meg?'

'There wasn't one positive sighting.'

I could sense storm clouds gathering so I hurriedly carried on. 'But that in itself's an important clue. We don't even know that she was on the street.'

'Mr Cunane,' Arthur intervened hotly, 'we know she left the party and walked down Whitworth Street. The CCTV images are timed and dated.'

'The CCTV for that Friday certainly shows a young woman closely resembling your sister going down Whitworth Street West towards Deansgate. As she reaches Deansgate where the CCTV coverage ends she suddenly seems a lot more drunk than before. Then on Sunday morning her body was pulled out of the canal.'

'I saw the pictures,' Arthur protested. 'It was her.'

'Why must we always rely on technology? Your mother will tell you that they do things differently in Africa.'

Ruth nodded but looked mystified.

'For once, let's not give technology the benefit of the doubt,' I argued. 'Let's assume that there was a full-blown conspiracy and that someone set out to convince us that Meg, against all her beliefs, got blind drunk and staggered into a canal that she didn't know was there although she saw it every morning when she drew back her bedroom curtains.'

'How could that have been done?' Ruth asked. 'What possible motive could there be?'

'How?' I repeated. 'The person we saw on CCTV could have been a body double. They use them in Hollywood all the time. Why? Well, you tell me. Have you got any deadly enemies?'

'I've quarrelled with a few people in Africa,' Ruth said slowly. Arthur raised his eyebrows energetically. 'The South African health minister ... drug companies ... But that's nonsense. Why would anyone come to England and kill my daughter?'

'Point taken, but there's the alcohol to explain. Meg had three times the legal limit for driving in her blood-stream. Now she either drank it herself, knowingly or unknowingly, or someone forced it down her throat. No one at the party's confessed to giving her booze and the last time Arthur saw her she was drinking camomile tea.'

We both looked at Arthur, who blushed flaming crimson.

I assumed that was because he was afraid I was going to reveal why Meg came to be drinking camomile. 'That's right, isn't it, Arthur? You were in another room but you did see Meg drinking a cup of camomile?'

'Y-y-es,' he stuttered.

'Whatever's the matter?' Ruth asked him.

'Er ... er ... it's just that ... er ... you don't know the hassle I've had over what Meg's supposed to have drunk at the party. Besides interrogating me for days, the police questioned all my friends about giving Meg alcohol.'

'Ruth, knowing DCS Rix, it's safe to say that if he couldn't get a confession it's because there was nothing to confess. So we have to accept what Arthur and his friends are telling us – Meg was stone-cold sober when she left that party. So how come she was falling down drunk when the CCTV picked her up? Rix believes that Meg was making a break from her old life.'

'No! That didn't happen,' Ruth said firmly.

I looked her in the eye and took a deep breath. Was this how lion tamers made a living?

'Whatever ... I've persuaded Rix to check out one of the club bouncers down at the La Venezia pub. There's just a chance that he was the one who interfered with her before the drowning.'

'It was rape!'

'Not in the sense you mean. This isn't a very nice thing to discuss.'

'I'm paying you to give me information,' she said nastily.

'I know you are. It's just that some of it might not be welcome.'

'Oh, for the love of Mike, get on with it!'

'Right! Meg lost her virginity a day or two before she died and there was no sign of rape. It was consensual sex. While a street thug might have had his way with her when she was drunk, he wasn't the man she lost her virginity with.'

'No!' Ruth interrupted. 'Don't go on. Meg would have told me if there was anything like that.'

'You'll have to accept the scientific evidence that there was a man in Meg's life.'

Ruth shook her head again.

'You haven't a shred of evidence. I wish I'd had my own pathologist to verify these mad stories put about by the Gribbin woman. A woman's no business to be in that profession anyway.'

'Ashley Gribbin's a highly reputable pathologist. She was naturally looking for evidence of unlawful sexual intercourse and all she found was evidence of lawful intercourse. If she stakes her reputation on that you have to believe her.'

'Hmmph, I don't have to believe anything.'

'The other thing is her room. The walls are full of pinholes where someone's made a clean sweep of all the pictures she must've had pinned up. My guess is that this boyfriend did it.'

Ruth fixed her gaze on her son.

'Don't look at me!' he said angrily. 'I never went in

the damned room. As for a boyfriend, if there was one she must have arranged for him to come in when I wasn't around because I never laid eyes on him.'

Despite myself, I had to admire Ruth Hands' self-possession. She got up and went into Meg's room. I remained in the living room with Arthur. He shot an intent look at me first, as if trying to read something written in the lines on my forehead, and then studied the pattern on the carpet.

'I'll admit there could have been pictures stuck up on the walls,' Ruth said grimly. 'But it doesn't prove anything. Is this why you made all that fuss about whether there was a cleaner?'

'Don't you think it's interesting that this cleaner failed to turn up the day after Meg's body was found?'

Ruth looked thoughtful.

'And you think . . .?'

'I don't think anything yet. I'm trying to trace her.'

'Arthur, did you speak to this woman? Did you tell her to leave?'

'Of course not, Mother. Why on earth would I do that?'

'Did you know her?'

'Listen, I only saw her a couple of times. She was an ugly bat, with a face like a stewed prune. Why would I talk to her? I wasn't that desperate for company.'

'So,' she said sharply, 'my son's so observant of the comings and going in his own apartment that he can tell us nothing about a person who was here three days a week. I guess that means I have to accept that there could have been a boyfriend. For all you know or care, Arthur, there could have been an endless procession of men going in and out of Meg's room.'

'Mother! That's rubbish and you know it,' Arthur shouted.

'I apologise if this is causing a rift in the family,' I commented, 'but I have to be frank.'

167

'Let me worry about my family,' she said crossly, giving Arthur a very dirty look. 'You get on with what you're being paid for. Tell me what you guess about this squalid, seducing boyfriend, if I have to accept that he exists.'

'My best guess is that this character met Meg when she left the Student Village, that she went with him and then something went tragically wrong, i.e., the drowning, which I don't think happened in the Canal Basin because somebody would have seen it.'

'Meg would've told me if there was a man in her life. I wasn't opposed to her meeting someone. I was only eighteen when I got married myself.'

'Which suggests she had a good reason not to tell you.'

'What reason could there be?'

'I'm saying someone's staged an elaborate cover-up. Why, is what I'm trying to find out.'

'Mr Cunane, your theory's brilliant but for one flaw,' Arthur chided, enunciating his words carefully in case I didn't understand English, 'the police accept that Meg drowned immediately after the party so, unless he had a time machine how could your mystery man a) spirit Meg away from the Student Village, and b) arrange for a body double of her to walk down Whitworth Street?'

'But did she drown immediately after the party with your so-discreet friends? Or does everyone just assume that?' I said. Picking up the police report, which lay on the coffee table, I opened it at the relevant page. '"Water-soddening of the skin, while present, was not extensive. It is consistent with the body having been in the water from twelve to thirty-six hours." The body was found on Sunday morning so if we take twelve hours as our bench-mark that means Meg was alive for most of Saturday.'

Ruth clapped her hand to her mouth in horror.

'But the CCTV pictures are dated and timed,' Arthur asserted. 'Going along with your idea of a body double means that this man acted with malice aforethought. He must have planned everything.'

'Maybe they both planned it!' I countered.

'Mother, this is pure fantasy. What motive could Meg have had for such a weird trick? Anyway, there's no one rich enough or clever enough to organise a deception on that scale. Meg's friends were students!'

'How do you know?'

'I lived with her.'

'Meg lived in this apartment about a hundred yards away from the watering hole where some of the richest footballers, TV soap stars, and God knows what else congregate, and you're saying it's impossible that she met one of them down there?'

'Mother, this is ridiculous,' Arthur said flatly. 'If Meg was simply going to spend the weekend with some fictional footballer why pull an incredible stunt like this?'

'Is it so incredible? Meg wore similar clothes day in and day out, ideal for a body double, and as for the whys and wherefores, we just don't know. It could have been a fake kidnapping that went wrong, some high-minded scheme on the part of Meg's friends to make Hands Jam pay a ransom. It could be like the Patti Hearst case or the Stockholm Syndrome. It could be that the man involved was cheating on his wife. Until we find him we'll never know.'

'This is such incredible rubbish!' Arthur snapped. He got up and walked to the window.

'Let me see if I've got this right,' Ruth said slowly. 'You think Meg left the party to meet this . . . man, who'd previously arranged for a lookalike of Meg to simultaneously stagger off towards this flat. He had to do that to cover his tracks because he already intended to kill her and he knew that CCTV would record everything?'

'Something like that,' I muttered. 'I know it's not very credible but it's the best I can come up with.'

'No, it's believable. It's just what you'd do if you were abducting someone under TV cameras. You must find this man,' Ruth said urgently as if expecting me to dash out like the Ugandan army, 'and the woman too.'

'The problem is, how? I'd like to check out Meg's friends. She must have told someone who he was.'

'She didn't have any friends,' Arthur said quickly.

'Oh, come on!' I argued. 'She was into ecology and saving the Earth – there must have been someone.'

'Not that I know of,' Arthur said gloomily. 'She stayed in most of the time.'

9

'Another victim for the Mangler?'
Headline story in the *Mirror*
'Police in Stockport denied that the young woman (name with-
held) who was sexually assaulted and left for dead in the
Offerton area last night is a victim of the so-called Mangler.
"The case is unrelated to any previous cases," a police
spokesperson announced.'

I was in a contemplative mood as I drove home. Arthur
was happy enough for the investigation to moulder where
Rix had left it. He definitely intended that sleeping dogs
should be ignored. Well, if he wouldn't help me then I'd
have to work round him.

When I arrived at the car park of Thornleigh Court I
found Naomi Carter loading suitcases into the back of an
old Peugeot 504 estate.

'What's going on, Naomi?' I asked politely.

'It's nothing to do with you, Mr Cunane,' she crowed
in a surly, sing-song voice.

'Oh, it was "Dave" when you wanted me to lug vacuum
cleaners round,' I commented.

'I'm not going to speak to you,' she said primly. 'I'm
just collecting these things for Ms White.'

'Where is she?' I asked, again trying to keep my cool.
'Surely I'm entitled to know?'

'Janine's warned me that you're very persuasive.'

'Just tell me where they are,' I pleaded.

The words were scarcely out of my mouth before my
shoulder was grabbed from behind and I was spun round
to face a formidable female.

171

'Annie Aycliffe, I presume,' I said facetiously, though I could see from the grim set of her features that humour was wasted. Annie was least as tall as I was, and better built across the shoulders. Her massive log-like limbs were swathed in a dirty old tracksuit. Naomi's description of Annie's method of dealing with perverts flashed through my mind.

'Get your hands off Naomi,' she bawled, startling pigeons into the air. The expression on her plump, pasty white face was close to the edge of hysterical fury.

'I haven't touched her.'

'Smack the bastard,' a youth shouted. Whether the invitation was for me to hit Annie or vice versa wasn't clear. We'd already attracted an audience of about seven local teenage lads. They gathered on the car park wall to witness the developing scene. Like bluebottles to a muck heap, others were coming all the time.

'Annie,' I said in my most reasonable tones. 'Why don't you back off while I have a private word with Naomi?'

'No, you back off, mister,' she barked. 'I've heard all about you and your sly tricks.'

Before I could say another word she laid a meaty hand on my chest and pushed.

I couldn't say that I lost it but I was so surprised at Naomi's hostile attitude and at being manhandled by her friend that I did the wrong thing. I should have given up and gone inside. Instead I grabbed Annie's right wrist and batted her hand away from my chest.

A chorus of whistles and jeers greeted this manoeuvre.

Annie had unusual upper body strength. She clawed at me with her left hand, red fingernails extended like talons, and I did what I should have done before. I jumped back but not in time to stop her little finger raking across my chin. It stung like hell.

I whipped out a handkerchief and dabbed my wound.

'That was completely out of order,' I scolded mildly.

'I'll give you more of the same if you don't clear off,' Annie spouted, licking her lips in anticipation.

'This is nothing to do with you!' I snapped. I was careful not to raise my hands.

'It's everything to do with me,' she answered wittily. 'Get in the car, Naomi.'

Naomi did as she was told.

'And just in case you're thinking of following us,' Annie said, taking out a large penknife, 'you're going nowhere.' As she spoke she plunged the blade into the offside front tyre of my Mondeo.

'Hellfire!' I swore.

'Come near me and you'll be going to hell quicker than you expected,' she snarled.

There was a squeal of brakes and a police car pulled into the car park.

Annie piled head first into the Peugeot, revealing an enormous backside, which I resisted the urge to kick. At the same moment a petite police person hopped out of the jam sandwich. Someone from the flats must have phoned. I hadn't thought our voices were that loud, but they must have been. At least, Annie's was.

'What's going on? We've had a report of an incident,' the slightly built officer asked with her hand clenched on her baton. Meanwhile, the last of the air was whistling out of my ruined tyre.

'Nothing,' I said. 'These ladies are just leaving.'

'Do you want to make a complaint?' she asked, peering at my bloodstained chin.

'It was just a domestic argument that got a little heated,' I explained.

Annie drove towards the car park entrance. The officer considered stopping her but then waved her on as Annie gave a cheery thumbs-up sign. I cleared off. Over my shoulder I saw the police woman heading towards the spectators.

173

Back in my flat I waited for a few minutes. No police fists pounded on my door and so I poured myself a whisky and then studied the blemish inflicted by Mad Annie. It was just a scratch on the underside of my chin, not too visible. I dabbed it with disinfectant and then went in the kitchen and looked in the cupboards. There was plenty of food but somehow I didn't feel hungry enough to bother. Instead, I took out a pan-scrub and began scouring the inside of my oven. It was some time since I'd cleaned it, and I also tackled a build-up of burned-on grease on the bars of the oven shelves.

I laboured on those bars for a long while. I kept trying to focus on the Hands case and Arthur's curious evasiveness but, burning with a sense of injustice, my thoughts insistently returned to Janine. Why had she set Mad Annie on me? I felt as if a hot needle was pressing into my head.

The full vileness of my situation began to weigh on me. I felt tears beginning to form but shook my head angrily instead. It was Janine's fault! I'd built my life round her and round Jenny and Lloyd and then suddenly it's up sticks and away because I wouldn't change instantly into a nine-to-five salary earner. She must have known what I was like when she met me. How dare she imagine that she'd change me into something I didn't want to be? Perhaps that was the problem with both of us. I'd wanted to domesticate her . . . but was that right? I'd never expected her to turn into a little *hausfrau* filling our home with poker-work mottoes and cosy chintz.

Slowly, as the bars began to gleam, I achieved a state of calm. I admitted to myself that I couldn't make sense of anything tonight, and took myself off to my lonely bed. I missed Jenny and Lloyd as much as I did Janine. Somehow having them around had given my life a sense of purpose.

Next morning I woke up in the dark. It was six a.m. I didn't feel rested but I didn't feel like staying in bed either. I went downstairs and changed the tyre on the Mondeo. Then just as the first tinge of light was diluting the surrounding gloom I took my bike off the pegs where it was stored in my garage. It was months since I'd moved it. It was covered in cobwebs and the tyres were soft.

I pumped the tyres up, dusted it down and set off across the road and out onto the Meadows bordering the River Mersey. Either my muscles were unused to the exercise, or the bike needed oiling, but at first I found it hard cycling along the rutted track leading to the Mersey banks. At last I managed to get into a rhythm. I could feel sweat trickling down my back. I rode along the bumpy track for half an hour until I halted at a stile.

I remained there for a long time, watching the brown foam swirling along above swiftly flowing waters. All these waters eventually reached the sea where they mixed with all the other waters of the earth. It seemed that Janine and I were failing to blend though we'd got along well enough for years. I couldn't believe that our relationship had ended with the finality of a bereavement. There had to be a reunion. I couldn't let everything slip through my fingers as if it had never happened.

On my way back I noticed the cormorant colony silhouetted against the dawn sky on an electricity pylon. They were patiently waiting for the fish to rise.

Good for them, I thought, but however much I needed to do the same, both with the mystery man in the Meg Hands case, and with Janine, patience has never been my defining characteristic. The flier campaign and the coroner's verdict were rattling the bars of the mystery man's cage. For the moment there was no way I could influence Janine, but I was confident that something would turn up in the case.

175

Back at home I showered and then ate a large breakfast. After carefully restoring my kitchen to pristine condition I put in a call to Jack Rix. He wasn't in but I left a message asking him to phone.

He rang while I was dropping Annie Aycliffe's handiwork off at a tyre repair centre.

'Jack,' I said pleasantly, 'the report you gave Mrs Hands didn't have the names of the students who were at that party.'

'Naturally,' he grunted. 'Do you think I'm in the business of handing over the names of innocent members of the public to a headcase like Ruth Hands? She'd probably have had them kidnapped to somewhere she could safely torture them.'

'Oh, come on. She's not that bad.'

'It's what the CIA do. Didn't you know that? They send any unfortunate Arab terrorist who won't spill the beans off to Egypt where the secret police are perfectly happy to burn his balls off with a blowtorch.'

'Jack, please, Ruth's not the CIA.'

'I take it that this means that you're back on the jam factory payroll?'

'Yes.'

'In that case, Boy Wonder, you're getting no names from me.'

'Just one name, Jack,' I coaxed.

'Sorry, Chief, no can do,' he said brusquely. 'You're the ace investigator with his picture in the papers, not me, and you'll have to do your own legwork, just like we did.'

'Can't you give me just one name?' I pleaded.

'No way, José!' he answered cheerfully. 'What's up? Is the sulky brother proving less than helpful?'

'You could say that.'

'Well, *old boy*, the mother's darling was the same with us. You'll just have to extend your leaflet campaign to the whole student body. There were about eighty-five

176

thousand of them at the last count.'

'What about Neville at La Venezia? Have you come up with anything about him?'

'Same difference, Dave. I can't tell you anything that's going back to Ruthie baby. Suppose she has this geezer bumped off? What do you think his family would rightfully say if they heard I'd passed his details on to a shady private eye?'

'Shady private eye, Jack? It's only the other day you were telling me I'd be taking over the police force.'

'In my eyes, Dave, *old boy*, while you're working for Hands you're as shady as a half-price knocking shop with the lights out.'

'I'm the only person she's employing to look into this case.'

'And how do you know that?'

'Are you trying to tell me something?'

'I don't know that she *is* employing any muscle apart from a boneheaded PI, just as I don't know that Neville Fraser *has* a record of sex offences,' he said infuriatingly.

'Is she?' I demanded. 'I mean, has he?'

'Could be.'

'Oh, cut out the back-talk, Jack. Which one could be, her or him?'

'Hmm, could be both of 'em.'

He chuckled. 'Got you confused, have I? You ought to be worried.'

'What about the other bouncers? There aren't many of them. Couldn't you at least run their names through criminal records and check for sex offenders?'

'Dave, you sweet, naïve wee man, wouldn't the agency that employs them just love me to do that? Then they'd be able to say all their men were vetted by the police and charge double.'

'Just the ones who were there on the Friday Meg went missing,' I protested.

'No, the agency's bonded and it's up to them to check. Ta-ta.'

So much for co-operation from the police, I thought.

If Jack Rix had been setting out to wind me up he'd done an excellent job of it. I mentally subjected his sly back-cant to textual analysis. The clue was the mention of Neville's surname – Fraser. That detail could only have come from criminal records, so Neville probably was a sex offender. How surprising! Still, that didn't make Fraser Meg's rapist, but the knowledge that the Tale from the Riverbank included at least one rat with a record of sexual assault did make one of my scenarios more credible. Neville Fraser might offer me another track to Meg's elusive boyfriend.

I reasoned that the other comment, deliberately planting suspicion about Ruth, was a typical Jack Rix ploy. There was all the difference in the world between *is* and *has*, or so I told myself. If he'd had any evidence he'd have been delighted to tell me. I'd had no hint that Ruth was employing anyone else. Then I remembered her offer to supply me with a Marine Corps bodyguard.

Was she secretly mustering her forces somewhere?

Uneasily, I concluded that despite Rix's words, I had to trust my employer.

Charlie Brown's garage on Chester Road decided that Annie's handiwork on my tyre had damaged it irreparably so I needed a new spare. I had to wait for delivery from another garage and that took the best part of an hour, ensuring that I'd make a late start at work. I used the minutes sitting in the grimy waiting room to work out my next move.

Enquiries among the party people were out unless I could persuade Arthur to give me their names. He seemed about as likely to do that as he was to cut his throat with a blunt bread knife. Further questions at Castlefields were likely to produce painful bruises, if not something worse.

178

I didn't like having to steer clear but I wouldn't be able to do much investigating from a hospital bed, or Manchester Southern Cemetery.

I considered briefly what they might write on my gravestone. Jack Rix would probably insist on something in eighteenth-century style:

Ne'er ask a question, where e'er thou be,
It was asking questions that did for me.
Here lies Dave Cunane, RIP.

Thinking on those lines led me to muse about literature. What poem offered insight on my situation? Something about fog and shimmering mists.

One thing I knew for certain about Meg was that, in whatever restricted way she'd gone about it, she was studying English literature. I wondered if she'd ever read *Hamlet* and had a presentiment that she going to end up playing Ophelia for real. Perhaps she had. The poor girl was into prophecy.

I decided to visit the English department at MMU to see if I could turn up anything there, but first I had to check in at the office.

When I arrived at Pimpernel Investigations the first thing I saw was Peter Snyder, wearing glasses and studying a balance sheet. He gave me a cool stare over the top of his lenses. I guessed that he and Levonne had been having a discussion about my spendthrift ways. My office manager was studying me as a phenomenon, waiting for something juicy to report back to HQ. There was no flicker of movement. His face might have been carved out of teak. I got the clear impression that the next office reform he'd introduce would be clocking-in cards for everyone.

'Here you go, me old pal, me old beauty!' I quipped with a cheerfulness I didn't feel. 'A cheque from Ruth Hands for everything she owes us to date.'

'Wow! Does this mean you've dropped the case?' he asked, grabbing the cheque eagerly.

''Fraid not! You know the motto of the firm, "Onwards and Upwards"?'

'I didn't know we had a motto,' he said, deadpan.

'Get a life, mate,' I joked as I passed into the inner office.

'What's got into you?' Celeste asked when she followed me in with my morning coffee.

'Nothing. I'm doing exactly what you want me to do, trying to get justice in the case of Meg Hands.'

'Great!' she enthused.

'Pity everyone round here doesn't feel the same,' I muttered.

'Peter's a born worrier, Dave. His heart's in the right place.'

'Are you sure he's got a heart? I think Levonne's probably locked it up somewhere.'

'Dave!' she scolded. 'Michael's just down the street buying something for lunch. He's getting underfoot round here. Why don't you give him something to do?'

Michael had finished the surveillance job he'd been doing in Angel Meadow and he'd also completed the little project I'd set him. A few minutes later he poked his head round the door, or rather his arm came first, clutching the trademark granny glasses and then, after a delay, the rest of him followed.

I was pleased to see almost any part of him.

'Michael, what part of your military training taught you to give onlookers a trailer of yourself before putting on the main feature?' I asked.

'Reconnaissance and concealment, Dave. They're the secret of surprise in warfare,' he answered without batting an eyelid.

'I must try that myself. I'm certainly not having too much success at the moment.'

'Bad news, Dave,' he continued. 'Your Goan lady, name of Teresa Menezes, is actually a goner.'

'Dead?'

'No, gone back to Goa and the valeting firm has no forwarding address for her.'

'You mean she was working as a cleaner and then she just upped sticks, back to Goa?'

'Pretty much. The theory down at Regent Road is that she must have come into some money, possibly a lottery win, because she was always pleading poverty and appeared to be boracic the whole time. Sent half of the pittance she earned here to her relatives in Goa. The firm got a phone call from her when she was at London Airport on the Monday after Meg died. She said she was going home to India and wouldn't be coming back.'

I scratched my head while considering possibilities in my nasty suspicious way. Meg is bumped off by a person or persons unknown. Her room is stripped of photographic evidence leading to the killer or killers and then someone remembers the cleaner. They arrange for her to disappear too.

QED.

'Who took the call? Was it someone who knew her?'

'I thought you'd ask that. The answer is no. Staff turnover's high in the cleaning business and it was an office temp who logged the call. So short of going to Goa there's no way of discovering whether Teresa Menezes is still in the land of the living.'

'Ha! I suppose you've got your bag packed.'

'Well, as you mention it, I hear they've got some wonderful beaches in Goa.'

'There are a few things you can do before you go swanning off east of Suez,' I said coldly. 'For instance, you could check with the airlines that Menezes actually boarded a flight to Goa.'

181

'Oh, well, Boss. I was just joking. Do you think you should take this to Rix?'

'Rix as good as told me that he doesn't give a flying fuck what we uncover. He kindly invited me to do my own legwork.'

'What a sweet man.'

'I suppose he's right, in a way, and it might come down to you going to Goa but we can check if there are any private detective agencies there first.'

'Do you want me to get on to that? Peter won't like it.'

'What!'

'He was telling Celeste that I'm bringing in a lot of repeat business with the stock leakage investigations.'

I studied his face. Just what was he up to? Was he trying to drop Peter in it with the boss, or was he genuinely stating an objection? Office politics was one of the things I'd started a one-man business to avoid, now it was rearing its fevered face. I could have joined the police force if I'd wanted internal feuding and turf wars.

I kept my face completely blank and pressed the intercom switch.

'Peter, can I have a word?' I asked mildly.

After half an hour in which there was a 'full and frank exchange of views', as the politicians would put it – in other words a major row – it was decided that Peter would get out of the office more and take on some of the surveillance work while Michael would devote half of his time to 'research' into the Hands case.

We didn't come to blows, and no one resigned, so I suppose the meeting was a success, but there was something in Peter's expression as he split that told me I hadn't heard the last word.

'As I was saying,' I continued, nothing daunted, 'there's too much for me to do on my own. I'm going to check out Meg Hands' contacts at the university, but I'd like you to try to locate Teresa Menezes and make discreet enquiries about Ted Cosgrove and the people he works for. He may be concealing our perp. And when I say discreet, I mean it. Use the Internet as much as you can. Cosgrove paid for me to be beaten up and he may have tried to run me down with a Range Rover. See if you can find who owns a red Range Rover down there.'

'OK, Boss,' he muttered, throwing a snappy salute. 'If I go to Castlefields shall I disguise myself as a bargee?'

'You can disguise yourself as an onion bhaji if you like, but until we know what's going on, keep your distance. Cosgrove plays rough.'

A few minutes later I was glad to take the car and set off for the university, where I got nowhere.

'The girl's dead!' I complained to the secretary of the Humanities Faculty in the Geoffrey Manton building, who was refusing to release the names of any of Meg's fellow English students. 'How can she object?'

'It's not the unfortunate Miss Hands' objections that I'm worried about,' she answered. 'Don't you read the papers?'

A well-formed woman in her early fifties, verging on plumpness and now leaning forward on her boat-shaped desk, elbows out and hands clasped, she radiated authority from behind a sign that announced her name and position – Greta Armstrong, Faculty Secretary. She wasn't exactly a Gorgon. No, Greta was quite presentable if you like big-busted ladies in tight bras wearing clothes about ten years too young for them. Experience has taught me that ladies who dress to show that they're still up for it may be susceptible but my battle with Peter had drained my battery and I wasn't able to exert the full power of my charm on her.

I felt my heels sinking into the plush carpet of Armstrong's office as if I was about to disappear into a pool of quicksand.

She pulled a copy of the free morning newspaper out of her drawer.

'Man sought after Stockport attack,' the subheading read. 'Don't you realise that if anything happened to a student after I'd given you her name the University would be liable?' she said, smiling over her half-moon glasses at me.

It was the same argument Rix had hit me with.

'It's only through the exchange of information that people like that will be caught,' I muttered. I noticed a lack of conviction creeping into my words as I spoke. I'm as brainwashed as everyone else. We're rapidly reaching the stage where no one will talk to anyone unless they've been previously vetted by a remote bureaucracy.

'Much as I'm thrilled to receive a visit from a real private eye, and I love crime novels, it's more than my job's worth to give you a name.'

I thought of a lot of answers to that but decided to be cautious. These faculty secretaries are powerful figures. Perhaps I do look like a potential rapist. In the prevailing atmosphere of panic it wasn't a good time to be demanding the addresses of vulnerable young women.

On my way out of the university building I studied one of the notice boards. Security-conscious hands had been at work here also. The usual lists of names were completely absent. The only thing of any relevance to my quest was a reading list for first-year English students. I hastily ripped it off the wall when no one was looking and pocketed it.

At the bookshop in the university precinct the manager was much less fastidious than Greta Armstrong. I introduced myself as a private investigator.

'Makes a change from publishers' reps,' he said with a smile.

'I'm working for an insurance company,' I announced, which normally was the truth. 'This young lady has put in a claim for hundreds of pounds' worth of brand-new books stolen from her flat and we think she's pulling a fast one. We want to stamp on this before it becomes the next fashion in insurance fraud. I mean, when did you last hear about one of the local scallies making off with a load of literature? Could you check if she actually purchased the books? She claims she bought them all at the same time and from here.'

'What's her name?' he asked. He was very willing to display his expertise with a computer terminal.

'Janine White,' I said, without a second's hesitation. 'She claims to be studying English literature.'

I fed him the titles.

'There's only three female students who bought half a dozen or more of these titles,' he said eventually, 'and your Janine White wasn't one of them.'

'Just as I thought,' I said smugly.

'Yes, terrible thieves some of these kids. *Buying* course books is the last thing some of them think of. You wouldn't believe the shoplifting that goes on in here.'

'In my job, I would,' I assured him, 'but how am I going to nail Ms White? She's claiming six hundred for stolen books.'

'Cheeky mare,' he laughed. 'Most of the lecturers spend a lot less than that.'

'We prosecute in cases of serious fraud. I don't suppose I can coax you to come round to a solicitor's office and sign an affidavit? It'll have to be today.'

He seemed to lose interest after this suggestion.

'Where is this place?' he asked doubtfully.

'Middleton,' I replied.

His enthusiasm for law and order waned rapidly.

'How about if I just print out a complete list of the students who've bought any of these books?' he suggested helpfully. 'Then as her name isn't there she'll have to come up with an explanation. I know some of these titles

185

can only be found in this shop and nowhere else in Manchester. The faculties tell us what to stock. They'd have to be on special order anywhere else.'

I left clutching the print-out.

I knew from comments by friends about their offspring that university policy was to house first-year students in halls of residence. Only students like Meg, who already had a local address, were likely to be in private houses or flats. Once again the problem of making contact loomed. There are university halls, and other halls owned by housing associations. Not having the number of legmen available that Jack Rix had, it crossed my mind to roust out the entire staff of Pimpernel Investigations and give them all one name each to track down, but remembering Peter's reaction when I detailed one person to work with me on the Hands case I reconsidered.

In the end I decided on honesty as the best policy. I found the address of the university accommodation office in the phone book and took myself there and threw myself on their mercies.

'You want me to supply you with the addresses of all these students?' the male administrator, Abe Greenglass, asked. 'And you're not the police, but you're private?'

'That's right.'

Greenglass nervously combed his fingers through the few remaining strands on his almost bald head.

'I don't know,' he muttered.

'I'd like to point out that Ms Hands was also one of your students and that her mother is paying me for this investigation and that all I want is to get a bit of background on Ms Hands' pitifully brief life as a student.'

'Hands Jam, eh?' he asked. He went to an inner office for a moment, then came back and asked for Ruth's phone number. Ten minutes later I had a print-out of the addresses.

Jam or not, I spent the rest of the afternoon in a fruitless search. Students weren't in. If in, they didn't wish to speak about Meg Hands or claimed that they didn't know her. By two o'clock in the afternoon I was beginning to doubt that Meg Hands had ever existed.

My search took me in a full circle and I finally came back to Chatham Hall, which was the nearest hall to the accommodation office. The only person on my list living there was a girl called Patricia Manningham. Expecting to fail yet again I went into the courtyard and approached. The staff I met at reception were being harassed by a group of Chinese students asking about holiday jobs. They didn't appear to understand English. Determined to drain the chalice of failure of my afternoon's search to the last dregs, I waited patiently behind them until they finally made some sense of what they were being told.

Then a calm middle-aged lady in a navy suit consented to listen to my enquiries.

'Yes, she's here. She called in earlier for a parcel.'

The relief must have shown on my face.

'I can phone her and ask her to come down but it's up to her whether she admits you,' she said, pointing to the massive iron gates that protected the interior of the hall.

'Perhaps if I can explain over the phone it'll save time,' I suggested.

She agreed and when I told Manningham – 'Trish, to my friends' – what my mission was she agreed to see me. The student had to come down, sign me in, and usher me through the fortified entrance.

As I followed Ms Manningham to her study bedroom I noted that the building, although new, was already showing signs of wear and tear from the attentions of eight hundred students. Ms Manningham, however, looked like the last person in the world to indulge in vandalism. Sweet and innocent were the words that came to mind, as we walked along the corridors past some very mature-looking young people. Looking into their jaded faces made me feel quite youthful.

'Trish' herself seemed impossibly young to me, more like thirteen than nineteen. A slight figure, she was wearing the universal jeans and sweater with a single note of individuality provided by a scarf tied round her brown hair. A cross on a gold chain round her neck gave me a slight hope that she had some affinity for Meg Hands.

Her room was liberally sprinkled with photos of family and friends.

'You haven't got a picture of Meg amongst these?' I asked hopefully. 'Perhaps one with some of her friends?'

'No, I ought to have but somehow I never had the opportunity.' She spoke with a strong Yorkshire accent.

'But you knew her?'

'I knew her, of course,' she agreed as she poured me a cup of instant coffee.

I must have looked grateful for this information because she immediately qualified her answer: 'Not that Meg was easy to get to know. She was very stand-offish.'

'Did she ever talk about her other friends?'

'You mean, was there a boyfriend?' Trish asked with a laugh. 'I don't think she was interested in anything apart from her work and her mission.'

'Mission?' I repeated hopefully.

'Yes, she was intending to save Africa from Aids when she left university. Now don't get me wrong, I think that was a wonderful idea but I believed that poor Meg needed to get herself a life before she went saving other people's.'

'Was there a man, possibly a student or lecturer, who expressed interest in her mission?'

'Not that I heard, and I'd say that I was about the closest friend she had on the course. I used to sit next to her in lectures and we went to meetings and things.'

'No recreational events?'

'I go to those, chaplaincy events, trips and the Union, but I couldn't persuade Meg to come.'

'What about the other meetings then?'

'They were mostly related to her work. We went to all the meetings laid on by the English Department. Meg was specially interested in Elizabethan literature and mythology – you know, Mallory and his later imitators, and, of course, Spenser.'

'I'll take your word for that.'

'She went to Professor Carver's house more than once. He's absolutely fascinating when it comes to Elizabethan literature and all these references that people ignore these days.'

'References?' I queried.

'You know, magic and spells and things. Shakespeare's full of it. The prof has the plants growing in his garden, you know, henbane and hellebore and things like that.'

'Really? Where does this professor hang out?'

'I don't know. I didn't go. My main field is nineteenth-century women's writing. Meg's brother should be able to tell you. He went with her at least once.'

'I see,' I murmured, 'and Meg never mentioned any boyfriend or even expressed an interest in the opposite sex?'

'No. I'm not being funny, but if you ask me that brother of hers was creepy.' She illustrated her opinion with a reflexive shudder. 'He put people off with his public school ways. Most of the people here are from ordinary back-grounds like me.'

I laughed at this.

'Well, I mean my dad's only a lorry driver in Bradford. But without a word of a lie, Arthur used to follow Meg around like a sheepdog. I remember thinking it was funny he went with her to Professor Carver's Hermetic after-noons although he was supposed to be doing town plan-ning or something.'

'What?' I muttered, ''*Ermetic afternoons*?' fearing her broad Yorkshire vowels were obscuring some revolting practice.

'Hermetics,' she explained tolerantly. 'It's the study of ancient magical lore.'

'You learn something new every day in this job. Next thing you'll be telling me Jane Austen was a French spy.'

She gave a tinkling laugh. 'Don't be silly. Hermetics was very big in Elizabethan England. You know, John Dee and Simon Forman – they were both alchemists and mages.'

I made a show of writing the names down in my notebook.

'You won't be able to talk to them,' she explained. 'They've been dead hundreds of years.'

'I thought I might get out my crystal ball. Apart from you, that seems to be the only way I'm going to get information in this case.'

She laughed again. 'It's funny you should mention crystal balls. John Dee had a crystal ball through which he claimed to be able to talk to angels and it's still kept in the British Museum.'

'And Meg was into this stuff?'

'Not really, but she did mention that Carver had talked about it and that Arthur actually wanted them to go to the British Museum and try it out. Crazy or what?'

I felt a first faint tingle of interest. The vein in my neck throbbed slightly. I tried to keep my voice neutral and avoid leading Trish in any particular direction.

'You mentioned that Arthur was creepy. I wonder if you could tell me in what way? Naturally I've met him, and he seems normal enough to me.'

'That's because you're a man. He always tries to put me down in some subtle way. I think he's got a raving inferiority complex.'

'You complained about his public school ways.'

'I know, what I mean is that, although we all know he comes from a wealthy family, he seems envious of ordinary folk. He asked me about my parents several times. Then when you tell him something about them he comes over all offhand and pretends that he doesn't want to know.'

'And his interest in Meg? That was just brotherly affection?'

'I suppose so, but how many students have a relative following them around? I think she'd have found a lot more friends if Arthur hadn't been fussing round her the whole time. He treated Meg as if she was made of glass. That's what I meant by creepy. As for brotherly affection, he could be quite domineering with her. He bossed her about and I think that's why she was so keen to go to Africa, to get away from him.'

According to Trish Manningham, Meg Hands didn't quite come across as the determined young woman described by her mother. Maybe I looked gob-smacked as I tried to make sense of all this because Trish felt she had to offer further explanation.

'I'm not saying there was anything unnatural about Meg's relationship with Arthur, anything . . . er . . . incestuous, that is, it was just that Arthur couldn't bear to let her out of his sight for long. I put it down to their difficult childhood, with their parents on another continent most of the time and then their father being murdered.'

'Right,' I said, letting out a sigh. 'About the party . . .'

'That was unusual,' said Trish, without prompting. 'She didn't want to go, it was mostly Arthur's friends. She told me that he'd insisted that she go.'

I had a lot to think about when Trish Manningham signed me out of the hall. Ruth Hands had wanted this investigation. Was it going to uncover something best left swept under the carpet?

By association of ideas the thought of carpet brought

me back to Greta Armstrong and her two-inch shagpile. A visit with Professor Carver might be productive.

I walked back to Armstrong's office. My car was parked close to there anyway.

She was just putting her coat on when I knocked. My arrival seemed to fluster her.

'Oh, it's you again,' she muttered, checking her face in the mirror at the side of her coat stand.

'Persistent, that's us private eyes,' I quipped.

'Persistent you may be, but too late. I'm off.'

I lounged back against the door and looked at my watch. It just after three. I raised my eyes ever so slightly.

'Don't say a word,' she huffed. 'I've started at half seven every morning this week.'

'Far be it from me to criticise academic hours.'

'Precisely. Now do you mind getting out of my way while I catch my bus before the schools let out? The position's just the same. I can't give you names of students.'

'Oh, it wasn't that. I wonder if you could tell me where I can find Professor Carver.'

'That makes sense,' she said briskly. 'First you try students, then the staff. Same answer.'

'Sorry, Mrs Armstrong. you don't understand.'

'It's Ms.'

'Yes, Ms Armstrong. I've spent the day interviewing Meg Hands' fellow students,' I said with only a slight inaccuracy. 'One of them mentioned that Meg showed great interest in the courses Carver teaches. I wondered if I could speak to him.'

'Look, the MMU's not paying me to stand here answering questions like this,' she said, retreating back to her desk. 'You're making me late. If you don't go I'm going to call security and have you removed.'

'OK,' I said, holding up my arms in surrender, 'but I wouldn't have thought this Professor Carver's in any danger of being raped, certainly not by me, and God knows what Mrs Hands will say about the university English Department next time she's interviewed on the BBC. She's already lambasted the police.'

'You're persistent, aren't you?' she said, finally raising a smile. 'I suppose Carver can look after himself, anyway you don't look like his sort.'

'Why, is he that way inclined? Confirmed bachelor, like?'

'No, of course not! He's a married man. You'll be getting me sacked! I meant that you don't look as if your inclinations extend to other men,' she said with a grimace. 'Not that I'd have anything against you if they did,' she added hastily. Then she looked at me and laughed. 'Oh dear, I'm getting myself into a muddle, aren't I? All this correctness – one has to mind what one says.'

'Nothing will pass my lips,' I said, grabbing her hand and raising her fingers to my lips, 'but can you tell me where his room is?'

She withdrew her hand slowly, with an embarrassed grin.

'I can see that I'll have to watch you, but you're wasting your time with Professor Carver. He won't be in the university now. He's a morning person like me. He enjoys an early start and an early finish to his day. He has a lovely house in Hale Barns and a narrow boat on the canal near Dunham Massey. He goes there to think and write.'

'Would that be the Bridgewater Canal?' I asked. I was unable to keep eagerness out of my tone.

'Of course it is,' she replied, gazing at me speculatively and then she thought for a minute before speaking. 'Oooh! You detectives. Your eyes lit up when I said "canal" and I had to think for a minute what I'd said that was so interesting. That poor Hands girl was drowned in the Bridgewater Canal Basin, wasn't she? Well, if you're putting two and two together and making four about Doug

Carver, I can tell you that you're getting your sums very, very wrong.'

'I'm sure, but can you give me Carver's home address?'

'You're at it again! Trying to get me sacked. If I was to give out the home addresses of staff they'd have me out of here in a heartbeat. You'll have to come in the morning and I'll ask him if he wants to see you.'

'Couldn't you phone him?'

'Listen, dearie, I haven't achieved my present status by annoying senior academic staff in their homes.'

It was on the tip of my tongue to ask her exactly how she had achieved her status but I restrained myself.

'Now look what you've done,' she continued, looking at her watch. 'I'll have missed the bus and I'll have to travel with a gang of noisy school kids.'

'I can give you a lift.'

'Now you're talking daft!'

'Why, what do you think's going to happen?'

'I don't know you from Adam.'

I took out my ID and showed it to her for the second time. She looked at her watch, then she stamped her foot. 'No, Mr Cunane, that won't work. You're thinking that you'll get me in your car and then find some way to wheedle his address out of me. Well, it's not on and it's not necessary. His name's in the phone book. There can't be all that many Carvers in Hale Barns.'

'Thanks,' I muttered, trying to hide my shame at being so transparent.

Maybe my forlorn look stirred some almost extinguished maternal instinct in Armstrong's generous breast because she continued, 'Listen, I can tell you now you'd be wasting your time trying to talk to Professor Carver about one of his students. If there's anyone on the staff who's more tight-lipped than him on anything like that, including his own personal details, I don't know who it is. Why, updating his entry for the departmental

194

brochure's like doing dental extraction on a crocodile. He wouldn't give you the time of day if he was standing in front of the Town Hall clock.'

'So he's some kind of oddball?'

'You said that, not me,' she said with a broad smile, 'but how many men do you know who bake their own bread, cut their own hair, dress in cloth made from wool they've spun and woven, and speak in Elizabethan English?'

She followed me out of her room.

I walked back to my car and felt that I was making progress.

Meg and Arthur had attended sessions at this eccentric professor's home. Had Meg also met the mystery man who drowned her there? Was Carver the man? She didn't seem to have had many other opportunities to meet people. Approaching this tight-lipped Carver directly wasn't too clever. If he'd had anything to say, why hadn't he come forward before now? Possibly there was a simple explanation but I was being paid to be suspicious. The best approach would be to stake him out and find out who shared his interest in crystal balls and alchemy.

That raised a problem – Peter Snyder. I didn't feel in the mood for another head-to-head with him. But where there are needs, there are also ways, so I phoned Harry Sirpells, a private detective of my acquaintance who has an office in Rochdale. Ruth Hands would pay.

'Eeeh! Dave, lad! Manchester's leading private eye coming to a little one-man-and-his-dog outfit like mine, I can't quite grasp it,' Harry said when I laid the job out for him. He speaks in a Lancashire accent with vowels as broad as the Pennine Moors.

'Come on, mate,' I muttered.

'No, t'concept takes some grasping.'

195

'I just want you to do a simple surveillance job, not an impression of Peter Kay.'

'It's the hours, though. I'll need someone to spell me.'

'Get someone to help you. It won't be round the clock because you won't be able to watch him when he's at the university. I just want to know who his associates are – you know, photos, long-lens cameras, that kind of thing. I particularly want to know if he moves his barge to Manchester.'

'Eeeh, lad! I were doing this job when thi still had thi rear end in short pants.'

'Not quite, Harry. Are you up for it?'

'Aye, aw reet. It'll cost you, though, but I suppose you titans of t'crime industry aren't worried about that.'

'No, Harry, we're not,' I said patiently.

'There'll be no trouble, like, rough stuff?'

'For Pete's sake! The man's a university professor, a doctor of literature.'

'Aye, and that bugger Shipman were a doctor and look what he got up to. I know you, Dave. You mix with some rum customers.'

'There'll be nothing like that, Harry! I just need to know what he does and who he knows.'

'All you wanted to know about that Brandon Carlyle was his family names on tombstones and look what happened to him, roasted alive in his own home like a Guy Fawkes on a bonfire. Aye, and you had t' fireworks an' all.'

Brandon Carlyle was the head of a massive local criminal enterprise who came to grief in a complicated series of events after I got entangled with his daughter-in-law. The memory of the time I'd spent in hospital during that little investigation wasn't pleasant.

'Look, Harry,' I said, losing patience, 'I can probably find someone else if you don't want the job.'

'Nar, hold on, owd lad. It'll make a change from infidelity cases. I'll start tomorrow.'

There were two messages waiting for me at the office. One asked me to phone Ruth and the other was an invitation to call round at Mr Hobby Dancer's residence above the Wharf Café on the Bridgewater Viaduct at any convenient time this evening. A technician had some information for me.

I put my feet up on the desk for a few minutes and tried to make sense of the day's meagre discoveries. It was difficult. Trish Manningham supported Arthur's claim that there was no man in Meg's life, but in my job I'd known many cases of successful concealment of an intimate relationship. Maybe she'd met someone at Professor Carver's 'Hermetic afternoons'. Maybe Carver was the man in her life. I suddenly regretted not asking how old the professor was. Not that age made any difference.

I was in the midst of these ruminations when the gleaming granny glasses of Michael Coe appeared round the doorway, followed by their wearer.

'Here you are, M!' he quipped. 'You ought to have one of those coat stands that you can throw your hat at.'

'You're not wearing a hat,' I pointed out, 'and you're not James Bond.'

'Yeah, that makes things more difficult,' he agreed.

'Anyway, you look more like Harry Potter with those specs.'

'Well, he comes up with a trick or two when he needs them, which is more than I do. There's a little puzzle about your mate Ted Cosgrove that could be called magic.'

'What's that?'

'Friend Cosgrove appears to be receiving far more stock, food, drink, and everything down at that bar than could be consumed by a place five times the size. I sat on a bench by the Roman fort and there's one long procession of delivery vans going down to him. It's possible he's pulling some kind of scam. That would explain why he's not particularly happy to have detectives nosing about.'

'Maybe trade's very good.'

'Stock leakage is one of my specialities,' Michael reminded me. 'I shall be able to check discreetly with some of his wholesalers.'

I related all my day's doings to him apart from the fact that I'd employed another investigator.

'This Manningham piece sounds a bit on the spiteful side to me,' he commented. 'Maybe she fancied Arthur of Hands Jam for herself and he wasn't having any of it.'

'That's possible, anything's possible in this case,' I muttered gloomily.

'Another thing I didn't mention,' he added.

'Yes?'

'Guess where your friend DCS Jack Rix spends a lot of his spare time?'

'Go on.'

'Yeah, apparently he's in La Venezia most nights and half the weekend. Seems that he fancies himself as a bit of a local celeb.'

I phoned Ruth.

10

What do you think, George? Is this yet another victim for the Mangler?

Come on, Mavis, the poor woman's not dead for a start. The Stockport police have denied that she's a victim of your so-called Mangler. God help us, he's an urban myth. They've withheld her name for obvious reasons . . . For listeners who've just joined us, we're discussing the unfortunate woman who was assaulted and left for dead in the Offerton area yesterday. The police have released a statement that the case is 'unrelated to other events'.

They would say that though, wouldn't they? Panic, panic, they want to avoid panic.

Do I detect a note of cynicism creeping in there, Mavis?

Say what you like, George, it's not men he's after. All I know is that I'm not going anywhere without my two hungry German Shepherd dogs until this creep is caught. Hear that, out there? . . . Grrrrr . . . Grrrrr . . .

Early evening news programme on Key 103 radio

Ruth was her usual easy-going self when I attempted to pass on an edited account of the day's findings.

'I told you that there was no man in Meg's life but you wouldn't listen,' she barked.

'No, that's not what I said,' I insisted. 'I'm trying to tell you that we haven't yet managed to find this man but he's definitely out there.'

'You don't need to look at me like that, Dave,' she said. 'I'm not an idiot. I know what you're hinting at in your delicate way . . . that slimy s.o.b. Rix as good as told me.'

'What?'

'That you think Arthur had sexual relations with Meg and that's why she killed herself. It's completely ridiculous.'

My jaw dropped.

'Ruth,' I said firmly, 'the one witness who's prepared to talk about Meg's private life entirely agrees with you.'

'So?'

'So, I go on looking for this man, whoever he is. There's nothing to throw suspicion on Arthur, whatever Rix has implied to you, but if evidence emerges that he was somehow involved in her death – '

'You'll do your duty. Yes, if that's the way the bagel bounces I'll be the first in line to help you, but believe me, it'll never happen.'

'Right, now to get back to this mystery man.'

'Your mystery man.'

'OK, *my* mystery man. I've put someone on to tracking down a possible lead. You're going to have pay top whack for him, he's good.'

'Money's not a problem,' she said in the careless way that only very rich people can bring off convincingly, 'but I want to know what's going on.'

'I can't give you the details at this moment.'

'That means it's Arthur again.'

'Not in the way you think.'

She folded her arms and I prepared for an outburst but nothing happened. Instead she cradled her head in her arms for a moment.

'All I know is that my daughter's dead. I can't believe Arthur had anything to do with it,' she said in an anguished voice.

'If it's any help it's not Arthur that I'm putting under surveillance.'

'One of his friends, then?' she wailed.

'I've told you enough. It's better if you don't know.'

'Because you don't trust me? Because you think I might let something slip to my own son?'

I shrugged. If I told her any more I might as well put an advert in the local paper. She put her head between her arms again and sobbed bitterly.

'This is all my own fault,' she moaned. 'If I'd been a proper mother to them both this wouldn't have happened.'

'There's no point in reproaching yourself,' I commented uneasily.

She looked at me. The tears had stopped. That fierce determination was back in her face. 'I don't need you to tell me that!' she snapped. 'Just catch the bastard who did this. I don't care who it is. Just catch him.'

'That's what I'm trying to do,' I murmured.

'OK, what's next?'

'I've had a message from Hobby Dancer, the guy who owns the building overlooking the canal where Meg's body was recovered. He has some information for me.'

'Isn't he the idiot with the dummy CCTV system?'

'That's what he told me at first, but apparently it's for real.'

'So what's he playing at?'

'He tried to brush me off by saying that his system was a dummy but later he owned up that it's for real.'

I didn't feel that I knew Ruth well enough to tell her that I'd turned down a hefty bribe from Hobby Dancer.

'Why the change of heart?'

'I don't know – remorse or something. Possibly he tells people that it's a dummy because he doesn't want the hassle that goes with a functioning system. If we're in luck he may have material that the police haven't seen.'

'Can I come with you?'

'It's not advisable,' I demurred. If there were going to be more offers of money it might not be wise to have my customer with me. On the other hand her presence

201

might act as a deterrent. I decided to let myself be persuaded.

'You don't know what it's like being cooped up in here and sitting by the phone waiting for news.'

'I'm sorry, but it's not a good idea to take a client on an investigation. You're too involved.'

'There you go again, Dave. I've travelled the length and breadth of Africa. I've seen people in every stage of distress and terror. I've been in vehicles that have been shot at. I've been threatened by powerful men and governments. I've probably seen more people on the point of death than you can imagine but I'm still here. Let me come with you.'

I stared back at her and remained silent.

'Fuck you! That's what you want to say, isn't it?' she asked. For the first time in our brief acquaintance there was a trace of a smile on her careworn face. 'That's what you'd say if I was a man.'

It wasn't what I'd have said but I kept quiet.

'There, I've shocked you,' she said. 'Well, I say, Fuck you too, Dave Cunane! All I want is just to take a tiny part in this investigation.'

'Why hire me if you want to do the job yourself?' I asked with a smile. Against my instincts I felt a trace of liking for the woman's determination. She knew in her heart of hearts that I might uncover something that would destroy her relationship with her remaining child but she wanted to press on.

'I need you,' she confessed. 'I was stupid to keep mouthing off about England and everything but I'm so shell-shocked by what happened to Meg that I need to lash out at someone. You've been great at putting up with me and so has poor Arthur.'

'Get your coat,' I ordered.

We walked the short distance from her home to the Bridgewater Viaduct at the end of Deansgate. The fortified structure that housed the upper storey of the Wharf Café and also Hobby Dancer's penthouse, towered above the roadway. When we arrived we quickly discovered that gate-crashing a maximum security prison was child's play compared with gaining access to the eccentric computer genius's quarters.

We descended to the glass-fronted restaurant. There, a sour-faced female bar attendant was detailed to check my ID. When she was satisfied that I was who I claimed to be she withdrew to an inner room, presumably to organise our visit.

Despite her boast about visiting the grimmer picnic spots on the 'Dark Continent' without turning a hair, Ruth seemed ill at ease in this ultramodern Manchester bar-restaurant. She goggled at people quietly sipping like a Victorian sightseer in a Whitechapel opium den. I decided it might not be a clever idea to offer her a drink so we stood in awkward silence. Eventually the bar attendant emerged, accompanied by a stockily built steward.

'Outside,' the muscle grunted, and then he and the female accompanied us to the base of the concrete shaft that paralleled the staircase we'd just passed down and led up to Hobby Dancer's apartment. We walked up to the stainless-steel door, expecting to be admitted, but that wasn't to be.

'Spread 'em,' the chatty minder ordered.

'You've been watching too many American films,' I countered, but this drew no response, so I raised my arms and let him pat me down for concealed weapons. The female did the same with Ruth.

When he was satisfied, our minder spoke into a lapel mike and the door opened like the entrance to Aladdin's cave. The guard waved us forward and we entered. There were no controls for passenger use. Only a faint whirring sound and the slightest possible vibration betrayed that we were moving once the door had shut.

'Who is this guy?' Ruth muttered. 'It's easier to get in to see the President of the United States.'

'They say he likes his privacy,' I replied.

With a click, the door opened and we entered what appeared to be the main living room of Hobby Dancer's apartment. There was no sign of him. Instead his small African jogging companion greeted us with a broad smile and an elaborate bow. Dressed in a long shimmering gold robe and a small red skull cap, he looked as if he'd just been auditioning for the part of one of the Three Kings in a school Nativity play.

Not wishing to seem overawed I nodded to him and then checked out the room. I peered through the narrow window to make sure that I was still in Manchester and hadn't been beamed to some remote location. The window was made of thick, tinted material but it revealed the familiar terrain of the Canal Basin. There was no sound of any sort and I guessed that the glass would probably stop a tank shell, let alone traffic noises.

My eye was caught by the array of clocks along one wall. Something strange about the labels caught my eye. I looked again. The clocks didn't have the familiar names of capital cities. Instead, they read Mount Rushmore, Kathmandu, Great Zimbabwe, Machu Picchu, Stonehenge, Easter Island, Borobudur and Angkor Wat.

Turning to Ruth, I was surprised to see that she was eyeing our host with keen interest. Admittedly, he resembled a very cuddly, animated soft toy, and the winsome smile playing across his face was very fetching.

I looked away.

The apartment was furnished in a severe minimalist style with lots of complementary 'natural' colours: oatmeal, sand, white wood. It might have been designed as a deliberate contrast with the gorgeous robe of the African.

Thinking about how much the private lift must have cost, I realised that it probably was.

There was no sign of Hobby Dancer.

'You must be Mrs Hands,' the African said, rubbing his hands together and smiling warmly.

'Why must I?' Ruth asked bluntly.

I winced but the African's smile merely broadened.

'Because I know that Mr Cunane is inquiring into your daughter's tragic destiny,' he replied with a flourish of his wrist, 'and because your fame has preceded you in other ways. I am one of the many who have heard about your sterling work among Aids sufferers. I am Ariel Ngwena. I am one of the forest people.'

His voice belied his size. It was so deep that he could have sung bass with a Russian church choir.

Ruth changed completely. It was as if someone had switched a light on inside her head. She smiled and nodded and looked to be on the point of crossing the room and giving Ngwena a warm hug.

I intervened before things got too cosy.

'I was told there was information,' I said.

'Yes, it is not good, I am afraid,' he said gravely.

'I was expecting to see a technician,' I persisted.

'Yes, that is me. Cannot a mere African be a technician?'

'Ariel, you're one of the forest people?' Ruth intervened.

'Yes, I am what people in the West call a pygmy. Sadly, we are a dying breed.' Each word was carefully enunciated. 'Our neighbours in Africa treat us very badly. My friend Hobby Dancer has trained me as a technician. I hope that many more of my people will be able to find refuge and work in this country and in America.'

'How wonderful!' Ruth enthused. 'And your lovely name, Ariel, how did you come by that?'

'It is mentioned in the Holy Bible, Isaiah chapter

twenty-nine. It means "the lion of God". The missionaries . . .' he said, extending his hands in an open gesture.

If Ngwena had casually informed her that he was actually the Holy Spirit himself I don't think it could have had a more powerful effect on Ruth. I laid a hand on her sleeve to prevent her rushing forward to hug the diminutive African.

'But what's the information?' I persisted.

'Among my people it is the custom to come to such news by a roundabout path,' Ngwena said in a gravely rebuking tone.

'I see,' I muttered, although I didn't.

Ruth was harder to put off. Bringing her back to the purpose of our visit changed her manner.

'Why did your friend tell Mr Cunane that his cameras were dummies?' she demanded.

'It is a matter of convenience. There are so many fights among the profane people and revellers down on the quayside that we would have to employ someone to run the tapes full time. It's easier to say we aren't operative.'

'But you are?'

'Yes, the insurance people insist but it has taken me many hours to find the relevant tapes that Hobby Dancer promised Mr Cunane.'

'That was very good of him,' I muttered.

'He phoned me from Nepal and ordered me to make it my top priority.'

'Nepal? What's he doing in Nepal?' Ruth asked brusquely. 'I thought he was in the computer games business.'

'Hobby Dancer seeks enlightenment and does similar work to your own in Africa. He's a great benefactor. My own people owe him much.'

'That's very righteous of him,' Ruth commented. She wasn't being sarcastic. 'But now you've found something about my daughter's death?'

'Hobby Dancer has great regrets about all this,' Ngwena said, walking up and down with his hands joined as if in prayer and pressed against his lips. 'We have had much discussion. His satellite phone bill will be extreme.'

'I'll meet any expenses,' Ruth volunteered.

'That's not necessary. I only mentioned it to stress that we don't speak without careful thought. Hobby Dancer is worried that what I've found may make a problem for you, Mr Cunane.'

He picked up a copy of the *Evening News* opened at a report of Meg's inquest. 'An open verdict, I believe.'

'That's right,' Ruth agreed.

'Believe me, Mrs Hands, Hobby Dancer greatly admires your struggle against the obtuse legal and criminal authorities, and the last thing he wants is to weaken your efforts to find the full truth,' he enunciated. 'Hobby Dancer thought you were the sort of person who wouldn't want to be shielded from contradictory evidence.'

'Contradictory?' I said.

Beside me, Ruth drew in breath sharply.

'The tape shows Miss Hands negotiating her way down the steps at the Grocers' Warehouse.'

'And that's all?' I asked.

'That's all. The camera's programmed to cover different angles. The next shot in that area a few moments later shows the quayside at the Grocers' Quay and Miss Hands is no longer in sight, nor is anyone else.'

He stared at Ruth as he said this and she seemed to shrink under his gaze. Though small, he seemed a very powerful figure. I could feel the emotion flowing out of him. Like his friend Hobby Dancer, he had charisma to spare and something else. I just caught a faint impression that he was enjoying the whole scene. I don't know why but there was just that feeling . . . regrettable duty to be done . . . perhaps it was the way he continued to rub his hands together. The action conveyed a certain amount of relish.

'I'm so sorry, Mrs Hands,' he continued gently, 'but it would appear that – '

'Perhaps if you just show us the tape we could form our own impression,' I suggested.

'Of course. In our frequent discussions Hobby Dancer has suggested that Mrs Hands might prefer to be spared this last glimpse of her daughter. Possibly, you could . . .'

Again I caught that faint suggestion of gloating that underlay his front of deep concern. Perhaps I was hyper-sensitive, or prejudiced, as he'd suggested earlier.

'No, I must see it too,' Ruth retorted.

'It doesn't show Miss Hands entering the canal waters but I'm afraid it confirms the police assumption that she wandered down to the canal side unwittingly, and there is something else.'

'Just show us the tape,' I commanded.

'Very well,' he said in a more-in-sorrow-than-in-anger tone. He inserted the cassette into the recorder and pressed play.

After a moment of flickering movement the picture on the screen settled down. It showed a young woman dressed like Meg Hands staggering down the steep steps at the Grocers' Quay, considered a marvel in its day. The visual quality was much poorer than in the digital images from the CCTV Centre. There were patches of darkness and no clear view of the woman's face.

What was clear, though, was that the woman was swinging a belt in her hands. She wasn't wearing a belt in her jeans, she was holding it in her right hand.

The tape sequence only lasted a few seconds.

'That's not Meg!' Ruth said immediately.

'Could you run it again?' I requested.

Ngwena complied.

The date and time on the images matched those on

the CCTV centre's. There was one strange feature. The woman never once looked down to see where the steps were. She moved as if in a trance.

'Again?' Ngwena enquired.

The woman might be drugged, possibly with Rohypnol, the 'date-rape' drug. I became so absorbed in the tape that I didn't notice that Ruth was unwell.

Ngwena interrupted my studies with a cough. He was bending over Ruth and handing her a glass of water when I turned round.

'It could be Meg but it could be anyone,' she said tearfully.

'I'm so sorry,' Ngwena reiterated. 'It's just that the time marked on the tape is approximately the same as the police thought that your daughter met with her accident.'

'It wasn't an accident!' Ruth exclaimed. 'If that was Meg, what was she doing in that dreadful state? Why was she holding her belt like that?'

'As you say,' Ngwena agreed unctuously, 'there are indeed questions to ask.' He seemed on the point of tears.

'You mustn't blame yourself, Mr Ngwena. You're only trying to help. I understand that, but if that woman is Meg then I'm as crazy as –' She broke off and gestured angrily at the image frozen on the screen. 'I'm still going to find out exactly how she came to be in such a dreadful state.'

'Hobby Dancer appreciates that,' the African commiserated, 'as do I.' He moved towards the door to indicate that our meeting was over.

'Can I keep the tape?' I asked as we were leaving.

'I'm afraid that won't be possible,' he said with every appearance of genuine regret. 'I've not yet been able to rerecord the relevant tape and what you were just watching is the original. The firm is required by the terms of our insurance to retain the tapes for four months so it will be some time before we could let you have this cassette.' I remembered Hobby Dancer telling me that Wild Ride didn't keep the tapes at all, but possibly knowledge of such details was beneath him.

'It doesn't matter,' Ruth said sadly.

'Hobby Dancer's perfectly willing to suppress knowledge of this tape if you wish. He owes the police no favours and would prefer that they remain in ignorance of his system.'

'That's up to him,' I said. 'I wouldn't want him to do anything illegal.'

Ngwena nodded at this and then turned and retreated to an inner room. The lift door opened.

He descended with us.

As we finally parted he had literally one last trick up his sleeve. He turned back the sleeve on his golden robe and withdrew a cheque from a concealed pocket.

'Mrs Hands, your work in Africa is often in Hobby Dancer's thoughts and he'd like to make a contribution to it.'

He handed the folded cheque to Ruth, who took it without a murmur. Then he clasped both her hands in his and gave them a gentle squeeze. 'I shall be praying for you,' he concluded.

He then popped back into the room and the lift door closed immediately.

Ruth unfolded the cheque. 'Twenty thousand,' she said. 'Well, this Hobby Dancer certainly puts his money where his mouth is. I must meet him.'

'What did you think of that performance?'

'Performance?' she echoed. 'Ngwena, you mean? A charming man, but his boss is outstanding. Have you any idea how many doses of antiretroviral drugs this will buy?'

'No,' I said. 'He's very kind.'

There was obviously no point in launching into a bout of criticism of man or master, but I was uneasy. Twenty thousand was the same sum that Hobby Dancer offered me to betray Ruth. Was there some kind of subtle message implied?

'What will you do now?' she whispered. 'What's your next move? Does the fact that she was holding the belt alter things?'

I shrugged my shoulders.

'Not really. There's still the question, why? I'll carry on with what I was doing. There must be someone who knows more about Meg's last hours.'

'That tape doesn't alter anything, does it? It was so blurred it could have been that body double you spoke of.'

'It could have,' I agreed, wondering about my own sincerity. 'By the way,' I asked as she turned to walk to her apartment, 'was Meg a good swimmer?'

'Oh yes, excellent. That's another thing that makes accidental drowning so unlikely.'

On the way home I considered my options.

The tape from Wild Ride made it ninety per cent certain that the official version of the final events in Meg's life was correct. There were cases in the pathology literature where strong swimmers intent on drowning themselves had tied themselves up before plunging into the water. Maybe Meg stood at the canal side, having previously removed her belt intending to tie her hands, and then in her confused state replaced it on the other side of her body.

As I turned into Seymour Grove I noticed a grey car following me. I thought nothing of it. The route I was taking is the main route from Deansgate to Chorlton. The grey car stayed two or three cars behind at every junction. Then when I turned into Wilbraham Road to go towards my flat it followed. I guessed that DCS Rix was keeping an eye on me. It doesn't do to make waves for the police in this town.

If Rix had something to hide, whether it was about

Meg Hands or some dodgy relationship with Ted Cosgrove and whatever he was up to, then he was going the right way to make sure that I followed it up. The speed with which Rix appeared down at La Venezia after my first meeting with Cosgrove now seemed highly suspicious in the light of Michael's findings. Was he connected there? Was he on his way to that meeting in the upper room when he chanced across me?

I slowed down as I approached Thornleigh Court and the car, a grey Vauxhall Senator swept on past. Perhaps I was becoming a little paranoid.

It was just as well that I'd slowed. I was able to avoid the furniture van that blocked most of the entrance to the car park. I recognised the furniture that was being loaded. Some of it was mine.

I dashed upstairs to find Annie Aycliffe propping open my door while two removal men struggled out with my sofa.

She gave me a toothy smile but before she could speak Naomi Carter popped out of Janine's flat.

'What's going on?' I demanded.

'We're moving Janine's furniture into storage,' Naomi explained. 'The flat's going on sale. There are one or two things which you shared which were kept in your flat and so I used this key to get in.'

Brandishing Janine's key for my flat in front of my face, she gave me a cheeky and defiant stare. I wondered once again what I'd ever done to deserve Naomi's hatred, because that's how I read the expression on her face. I put out my hand for the key.

'Not so fast, you,' Mad Annie interjected.

'Oh, no, not the minder,' I groaned, moving out of her reach.

'You get those back when we're done and when you return your keys to Janine's flat,' Annie said in triumph. She was really enjoying herself.

'But that sofa doesn't belong to Janine,' I objected as it disappeared down the staircase.

'Janine said you'd moan,' Naomi chortled, 'but she told us to remind you of the wear and tear you've put her furniture through, especially the bed.'

Both she and Mad Annie cackled at this witticism.

'Where is she? Has she gone completely crazy?' I exclaimed.

'You're not going to find out where she is,' Annie warned. 'I'm here to stop you.'

'Oh, no you don't!' I said, dashing downstairs to my car before she could puncture another tyre.

I locked my Mondeo in the garage and turned round just in time to see my bed disappear into the back of the van. I could hardly believe my eyes. Janine was being so vengeful. I've had my share of hard times. After my wife died I thought I'd lost the capacity for further grief but now I couldn't get my head round the thought that it was Janine White who was doing this to me. I've seen enough marriage break-ups to know that nobody comes well out of these things. I tried to square my shoulders and put a brave smile on my face. After all, this wasn't even a matrimonial dispute, just a spat between friends.

I must have failed completely.

'Cheer up, mate!' one of the removal men said as he paused to roll up a fag. He was wearing glasses with Coca-Cola bottle lenses. 'Wife giving you the boot, eh? It's not the worst thing in the world, believe me. I've never felt better since the old slapper I was married to gave me my freedom.' He let out a self-congratulatory whinny at this.

I looked at him. He was massively overweight with his gut straining over a taut belt. His face was full of nasty-looking pimples or incipient boils. The dirty pullover he was wearing was holed at the elbows and his trouser flies were tied up with string.

213

He was hardly an advert for male independence.

Rather than argue, I nodded weakly.

'Right tartar, that big lass, if you ask me you're well rid of her. Tell me, is she your wife and the other one your daughter?' Even the glasses he was wearing didn't stop him clocking the look of shock on my face but before I could put him straight he wittered on, 'Pardon me for asking if it's a sore point with you, but that bloke over there wanted to know.'

'What bloke?' I snorted.

We both looked in the direction he was pointing.

There was no one there.

'Bloke in a big grey car,' he muttered.

Before I could press for further explanation, or put him straight about my marital status, one of his colleagues gripped him by the forearm and pointed him back upstairs to my flat.

I decided to remain by the van. No more of my possessions came down, just the familiar pieces that had been part of my life with Janine and her children for so long.

Eventually the removal men descended for the last time and slammed shut the doors of their pantechnicon. Naomi and Mad Annie followed. I gazed at Annie. She was in exactly the same clothes as yesterday, and although I was keeping my distance that didn't prevent a mingled aroma of sweat and cat pee from invading my sensitive nostrils. Even wearing thick lenses and seeing her in a poor light, how could that removal man think she was my wife?

She came right into my space and shoved her ugly face close enough for a kiss. I noticed the tide line round her neck.

'Sorted!' she said gleefully as we exchanged keys.

As I tucked myself up in my spare bed that night I told myself that I wasn't heartbroken. It was probably time that Janine and I went our separate ways. No, that wasn't true. It was the exact opposite of the truth. All my thoughts for the future involved Janine, Jenny and Lloyd. Now suddenly I had no future, just a chequered past. I just kept churning the situation over and over in my mind.

It was the realisation that I now had no part whatever in the children's lives that made me physically sick. I rushed into the bathroom to part company with dinner, but the self-pitying emotions still played in my head like a dissonant tune even as I rammed my head down the white porcelain maw. That was an added horror. It brought back the death of my wife, the last occasion I'd reached such a low point.

A divorced father has some rights but as a mere 'boyfriend' I'd none at all. It was so desperately unfair. I'd put as much effort into child rearing as Janine had. More really. I was the one who entertained them at weekends. She'd admitted that I was a good father to them. I wondered how my parents would take the news. They'd become quite accustomed to regarding Jenny and Lloyd as their own.

I had to get up and pour myself a stiff drink to steady my nerves and take the taste of nausea out of my mouth. Then I flung myself into an armchair.

How could Janine be so determined to make a break? Was it so terrible of me to want to finish a job I'd started? Couldn't she have given me a deadline: come up with a solution to the Hands case in a week or jack it in? No, there hadn't been a trace of compromise on her part. From the back of my mind the ugly thought now loomed that she'd found someone else. But who could he be? He could only be someone from her work because that was the only time we spent apart.

If there wasn't somebody else did she expect that I'd cave in on all fronts? Was I supposed to run up the white flag and come out with my hands up? No, that wasn't likely either. She'd hardly have made off with my furniture if she'd intended a future reconciliation.

Well, if she could be stubborn, so could I.

I decided that I'd pursue the Hands case to whatever bitter end it led me. I'd give Ruth's theories the benefit of every possible doubt. What would Janine think when she found out that someone was being arrested for Meg's murder? Would she care? Would she come crawling back? Knowing her, that was hard to believe. I kept imagining various unpleasant fates befalling Janine but then thoughts of the children immediately surfaced. How could I get them back without her? Anything that affected Janine – unemployment, illness, an unhappy relationship with another man, etc. etc. – would only make their lives miserable.

The situation was intolerable. I went to pour myself another large Scotch, but as I reached for the bottle my hand stopped. I'd tried the telescopic view of the world from the wrong end of a whisky bottle when my dear, faithful, loving wife Elenki died. I knew all about the danger of risk takers such as myself drifting into alcoholism and suicide when things went badly wrong. Flooded with an angry determination, I decided I wouldn't give Janine, or anyone else, that satisfaction.

I went back to bed and eventually exhaustion kicked in and I slept.

Next morning I went through the motions. I got out my bike and went down onto the Meadows. I was so self-absorbed that I almost ran into a milkman while crossing Edge Lane. Exercise didn't chase away the mood of depression. Ruth Hands and her troubles seemed very far away.

When I got back to my flat I phoned in sick. What's the point of having your own business if you can't play hooky when you want to? I soon found out my mistake.

After nine o'clock the phone didn't stop ringing.

'Are we still on this job, or what?' Michael Coe queried. He sounded as if he'd just swallowed a lemon.

'Get yourself down to Castlefields and suss out what's going on that shouldn't be.'

'It's a small place. I'll be spotted,' he said.

'Well, make sure you aren't,' I snapped. 'Go in the old van with the mirror windows and film all these extra deliveries you were on about. Hire a helicopter or even a bloody submarine if you like.'

'No need to be sarcastic, Dave. I get the message.'

'Sorry!'

'Is there something I should know?' he asked. I couldn't fault him for persistence.

'Such as?'

'Has somebody given you a going-over? It's not like you to take time out.'

The more he probed the more determined I was that he wouldn't find out from me that Janine and I had split up.

My bad news couldn't remain a secret for long. I could imagine the speculation down at the office only too well.

Celeste phoned with the excuse that she needed my approval for one of our agency worker's expenses. 'By the way, Dave,' she said slyly, 'I've phoned you on Janine's number several times but the line seems to have been disconnected. Is there something wrong?'

I made my hand into a fist and bit my knuckles but I didn't tell her anything. Perhaps that was superstition – if I didn't say the words then the event wouldn't be finalised. Whatever the reason, I kept my mouth shut. Celeste would find out all she needed to know soon enough, but not from me. I cut her off with a few mono-syllabic words.

In the end I gave up. Staying in the flat I'd only end up brooding or hitting the sauce. I went down to the car, fixed the bike carrier on the back, loaded the bike

217

and set off for my parents' cottage on the moors above Bolton to see if a change of scene would improve my temper.

11

Police statement: 'After prolonged forensic investigation the Greater Manchester Police have now concluded that the assault on the Offerton woman who has since died of her injuries was in fact the work of the killer whom the Press are referring to as the Mangler. . . . However, panic should be avoided. An arrest is expected "very soon" according to police sources.'
BBC Radio 4 announcement

Any fleeting hope of sympathy from my parents over my personal problems was dashed as soon as I told them that Janine had left. I could see that they were badly hurt by the news but they put up a brave front.

'You're a fool to yourself, you are, David,' Dad stated flatly. 'I told you right from the start, things would have been all right if you'd laid down the ground rules. It's a man's place to do that in any relationship.'

'Hark at him,' my mother said wryly. 'He's known me since we were in school together, never been out with another woman, and now he's an expert on love and romance.'

'I've had my moments,' he said.

'Ooooh!' Eileen exclaimed.

'No, listen, David,' Paddy countered. He never let my mother best him in argument without putting up a futile struggle. 'If you'd insisted that Janine marry you, right from day one, that is; if you'd told her to give up that daft job of rewriting a load of stale gossip and settle down, then it's fifty to one that she'd still be with you.'

'Right,' I muttered, too dispirited to argue.

'I shall miss the little ones,' my mother said sadly.

'Me too,' I murmured. I struggled to maintain my composure. Blubbing in front of my parents was something I couldn't bear.

She put her arm round me and then with the capacity for making the best of a bad job that's seen her through so many years with Paddy Cunane she remarked, 'I was speaking to Kate Mackenzie's mother outside church last week. She's back in England after nursing in Saudi Arabia for five years.'

'Mother, who is Kate Mackenzie?' I asked patiently.

'Kate Mackenzie! You were at primary school with her. A lovely girl with long dark hair!'

A faint recollection of Kate registered in some dim corner of my brain. I'd last seen her when I went to secondary school at age eleven. Even as the memory surfaced I started laughing madly. My mother was priceless. She saw Janine's departure as a final chance to fix me up with 'the right sort of girl'. Well, maybe I needed a girl with lots of nursing experience.

I laughed so much that I doubled up. My parents looked at me in alarm. I went out to the car and took my bike off the back and then changed for cycling.

'At least he can still laugh,' Paddy said when I prepared to leave.

'Are you staying for the evening meal?' my mother asked. 'Because I'll do a hot-pot if you are.'

'Mmm,' I answered, 'sounds good. Mother, was Kate doing psychiatric nursing?'

'Well, what if she was? Don't be cheeky. Though you'd do well to get some medical attention for your idiotic behaviour.'

'I was just wondering about Kate's qualifications.'

'You could go a lot further and fare worse than Kate Mackenzie, David – not that any nice girl in her right mind would look twice at you.'

'I don't know,' Paddy chipped in. 'He's got his own business, you know.'

I started laughing again. Paddy's sense of solidarity with the male sex even extended to his errant son.

I cycled down to the end of the lane that meandered past their eighteenth-century weaver's cottage. I chose a route to avoid the chaotic farm that adjoins their property. There were other weavers' cottages and then I was out onto the main road. The manic mood that I'd experienced with my parents didn't last very long. I came to a fork in the road. One branch led to a steep climb over the hills, the other offered an easy route along by the reservoirs.

I took the steep road and toiled at the pedals almost to the point of heart failure. The punishment did me good. When I could go no further I got off and pushed until I reached the summit with views over Bolton and South Lancashire. It was a fine day, visibility extended all the way to Manchester. But I had no time to stand and stare. I started pounding the pedals again until I reached a dangerous speed on the downhill slope that leads towards Horwich. There were many bends in the road and I could have come off at any one of them but I didn't. Eventually I eased up. Despite myself, I was thinking about the Hands case rather than my troubles with Janine.

I tried listing the things that I didn't know and the clues that I hadn't followed up. I tried to make my head into an incident room with reports from different departments. There was nothing glaringly obvious that I'd missed. I could go to Yorkshire and get more background from Meg's school but I had a feeling that it would only be more of the same. I was no nearer finding what had happened to her.

It was almost dark when I got back to the cottage and Eileen had already run a hot bath for me. She was used to my ways. As I soaked I knew that whatever happened with Janine I couldn't ever become a 'confirmed' bachelor. Women were just too much a part of my life. Perhaps Janine was only trying to give me a jolt, a shock to make me come round to her way of thinking. If so she was doing a hell of a good job.

No, my life with Janine was over. It was no use dwelling on the past.

I thought about Paddy and Eileen.

Eileen had had her ups and downs with Paddy. He'd been a dedicated copper. Twelve-hour shifts were nothing. When he was on an important case lasting weeks we often only caught glimpses of him when he called to collect clean shirts. But to my knowledge there'd never been any ultimatums from Eileen. She accepted him for what he was, and God help me, as I got older I realised more and more how like him I was. Eileen had never demanded that Paddy become a postal worker or a bank clerk.

I sighed.

Unfortunately that kind of relationship isn't on offer these days. Everything comes with strings. I giggled at the thought of Kate Mackenzie. My only memory was of her and other 'big' girls chasing boys screaming round the playground. Probably she was a fully paid-up member of the women's movement now with incredibly stringent requirements for potential male companions, and bookshelves packed with well-thumbed works of the major feminist authors.

'I've turned down your bed, if you want to stay the night, David,' Eileen shouted through the bathroom door. She was really checking that I hadn't fallen asleep.

Over the meal we talked about my brother and his two daughters. They at least were a consolation for Paddy and Eileen.

I was pleasantly exhausted and not in a challenging mood when unexpectedly the conversation turned back to Kate Mackenzie. She was a widow, whose husband and two children had been killed in a car crash. After that trauma she'd gone back to nursing . . .

'Completely normal, then?' I said sarcastically.

Eileen ignored the sarcasm.

'She's got a good head on her shoulders, like her mother,' she said. 'Kate's put her life back together and that's more than you can say for some who use a tragedy as an excuse for never straightening themselves out.'

Paddy smiled at me benignly while I absorbed this message.

I suddenly remembered the problems I had to sort out in Manchester.

'You'll have a cup of tea before you go?' Eileen said when I announced that I was leaving. 'We've got ordinary tea, Earl Grey or even camomile if you want to soothe your nerves.'

I looked at her.

'David, whatever's the matter?' she asked, as I continued to stare. 'I was only teasing you about Kate Mackenzie, though she is a lovely woman. Your father and I know quite well that we can't make you do anything you don't want to.'

'Camomile tea,' I said. 'Can I see the packet?'

She looked at me strangely but hurried to the kitchen and brought me the packet.

'There's nothing odd about it. We get it at Sainsbury's. I give it to Paddy when he starts babbling,' she said.

'Here!' Paddy interjected. 'Less of that!'

I snatched the packet off her and opened it. There was a strong scent of apples.

'It's only medicinal,' Eileen protested as if I was about to accuse her of possessing a kilo of heroin.

'Can I take it with me?' I asked. I could hardly get out of the door quickly enough. Eileen looked shocked as I ran to my car.

'But your bike!' Paddy roared. 'It's still in the garage.'

'I'll come back for it,' I shouted, giving them a wave.

I drove off up the narrow lane from their cottage at dangerous speed. Fortunately there were no stray cows or half-starved sheepdogs to impede my progress.

I waited until I was on the M61 heading towards Manchester before I phoned Ashley Gribbin at her home.

She answered immediately, 'Dave, lovely man,' she said, 'is what a little bird told me true?'

'What little bird?' I replied suspiciously.

'That you and Janine are no longer *à deux*, of course. What else would be of interest to me?'

'Actually, I wanted to ask you something about pathology,' I said with a certain grumpiness.

'Blow that!' she said jollily. 'Is it true that you're now on the open market of life, a free agent at last?'

'I suppose so,' I muttered cautiously.

'Speak up!' she shouted. 'I can't hear you.'

'Yes!' I bellowed.

'Music to my ears,' she said. 'Say it again.'

'Ashley, I wanted to ask you a question about Meg Hands' stomach contents.'

'How banal!' she snapped. 'And I thought you wanted me for myself!' Then there was a lengthy pause. 'Go on then,' she said finally, 'what is it this time?'

'Ashley,' I said soothingly, 'you know I'm very fond of you but this is a difficult time for me. I've just had my parents trying to marry me off to someone I last met twenty-odd years ago . . .'

'But you met me a lot more recently than that,' she said quietly.

'Ye-es,' I agreed.

'And if it's difficult for you, what do you think it's like for me, working on cadavers all day and then coming home to this rambling house with only a teenager who speaks in grunts to talk to?'

'Not easy,' I murmured.

'Oh well, they say the road to a man's heart is through his stomach. In your case I'll have to accept that it's through someone else's! What is it you want?'

'Was there any trace of camomile tea in Meg's stomach?'

'Tea?'

'According to her brother she drank camomile tea before leaving the party and then, according to CCTV evidence, she drowned a couple of hours or less later. Was there evidence of camomile tea in her stomach?'

'I can't say definitely. Liquids metabolise more rapidly than solids. I'd have to check, maybe run a sample through the gas chromatograph. Of course alcohol was definitely present. A single malt whisky, by my guess.'

'But wouldn't there have been a trace?'

'I'd expect traces if she'd drunk it within such a short time of her death, even if she'd vomited extensively, though there wasn't much sign of that. There ought to be traces.'

'Could we check that?' I asked eagerly.

'What now?'

'It's urgent.'

'Everything always is with you, Dave, except when it's not. Like when I invite you to dinner.'

'That's not fair. Janine and I were practically hitched.'

'Oh no, there's all the difference in the world between living together and being married.'

I had a mental image of lottery balls jiggling about in my head. Ashley was implying that it was time her number came up.

'You're right,' I agreed.

'So there's a chance for us?'

'Of course. I've always found you very attractive.'

'Right, where are you now?' she asked in businesslike fashion.

I told her.

'Meet me at the Path Lab behind the MRI.'

It was eight o'clock in the evening when I met Ashley on the doorstep of the MRI Path Lab. She was waiting for me and must have really stepped on it to get there so fast from Hale Barns.

'You're looking well,' I said, and kissed her on the cheek.

'And you're looking more like the late Oliver Reed every day. You'll have to do something about getting rid of that paunch,' she replied, chucking me under the chin.

'What!' I snapped.

'Just joking, Dave. You're as glamorous as ever,' she said with a laugh.

She was wearing a three-quarter-length black and white check coat over a white blouse and black skirt, with her hair gathered in a bun at the back of her head. Her eyes were a particularly melting and luminous shade of brown and her café-au-lait skin seemed to radiate a certain kind of heat.

'Dave, you're hopeless,' she gently mocked as she watched me studying her. 'You're supposed to say something like, "Darling, this is wonderful of you turning up like this and you look even more beautiful than last time I saw you." Living with that feminist has spoiled your manners. You can be as chauvinist as you like with me.'

'And what was the last romantic novel you read?' I countered.

'Well, a woman's got to do something. As far as I'm concerned romance might as well be dead. All the men I meet are either lying on a slab, stiff as Christmas turkeys – or might as well be – stuffy and pompous policemen and judges and such.'

She took me into her office, which adjoined her lab.

'Look the other way, Dave,' she warned as she slipped out of her coat.

I wondered what she meant until she began to remove her blouse and skirt. Her shape was as I remembered it, voluptuous.

'You don't need to look away if you don't want to,' she said with a laugh as she put on a lab coat. 'I never wear day clothes in the lab. Basil says I stink of formalin as it is.'

'And how is Basil?'

'Flourishing as ever. He drinks milk by the gallon and he's now over six foot five. I'm thinking of putting him in for a basketball scholarship to one of these American universities. He's sleeping over with a friend tonight.'

'Right,' I murmured.

'You'd better put a lab coat on too,' she said as we went into the lab. 'In case anyone comes in, it saves explanations if they think you're a colleague. Not that there's anything unusual about me working late, what with the amount of sudden violent deaths we have round here. It's getting more like Dodge City every day with the number of gunshot wounds I see.'

'Stomach contents,' I reminded.

'Yep, no prob!' she said. 'I kept all forensic samples.' She then led me to a stool and busied herself round the lab. It was a pleasure to see the competent methodical way she set about her work. A floppy plastic bag contained the liquid contents of Meg Hands' stomach. She used a pipette to draw off a small extract, which she then centrifuged. For the next half-hour she worked at the computer, retrieving data about the trace elements contained in the leaves of *Anthemis nobilis*, used to make camomile tea.

An hour later she completed the final analysis.

'Well, the conclusion is negative,' she announced.

'Damn!' I swore.

'No! Negative means that it's highly unlikely that Meg drank camomile tea within five hours of her death.'

227

'So Arthur was lying?'

'It would take at least five hours for all the trace elements to be metabolised. That means that death took place more than five hours after the brother claimed she had the tea.'

'Or that all the tapes have been faked in some way.'

'That's about the size of it,' Ashley agreed.

The memory of Hobby Dancer's African friend showing Ruth and myself the tape of that woman, allegedly Meg, going down the steps of the Grocers' Warehouse clutching a belt, flashed into my mind. The time registered on that was ten forty-five Friday p.m. There had been an almost gloating, triumphant expression on Ngwena's knobbly face. Was he aware that the tape was a fake? Had he even produced it himself?

'What is it, Dave? What were you expecting?' Ashley asked.

'I was hoping you'd find the tea and then at least we could reconstruct a logical sequence of events leading to Meg's death and I could be shut of this case. It's brought me nothing but trouble.'

'All I can say is that she definitely didn't drink any of that tea before her death. God, Dave! Am I glad that you have to do the detection and not me! Finding cause of death is child's play.'

'No, it's not. You know the immediate cause, water in the lungs, alcohol and so on, but there must be some way of finding out what happened before. Was she forced to drink? Was she held under the water? The more I find out, the further certainty recedes.'

'Dave, don't discuss that here. Do you want to come back to my place? We can talk over a bottle of wine. Maybe something will emerge from the fog.'

I smiled.

'Dave, I'm not pressuring you. I didn't do all this analysis in the hope of a return. You don't need to come if you don't want to, but just tell me that there's some hope of us having a relationship.'

'You know there is,' I said.

'Good,' she murmured, and then turned to take off her lab coat.

I slipped my hands under her breasts and she pressed her back against me and shuddered.

'Not here, Dave,' she whispered.

We disengaged gradually and then I followed her back to Hale Barns. She drove very carefully. It was half ten when we arrived at her house in a cul-de-sac backing down to the main road. As always with me there were at least two things on my mind. I considered phoning Harry Sirpells to see how his surveillance, also in Hale Barns, was going on, but when I parked on the gravel behind Ashley she came out of her car towards me and it was obvious that the time for second thoughts had passed.

We made love very gently and slowly in a big four-poster bed. The room was decorated with William Morris wallpaper and reproductions of Burne-Jones paintings. I felt as if I was in a waking dream and when we finished Ashley lay on her side and said, 'You've not got yourself free from that woman yet, have you?'

'It's not just her. It was the children, the whole situation. I can't just switch off a major part of my life and chalk it up to experience. I'm not eighteen any more.'

'No, neither am I. Look, let's just take this a step at a time . . . You do love me, don't you? This isn't just a one-night stand?'

'I'm getting there. I told you, I need to draw back from what's happened.'

'Still, there is hope?'

'Yes.'

'Dave, I could give you a good life. You've got me really buzzing.'

'Ashley, my life's complicated at the moment . . . the job . . .'

'Don't worry about that, Dave. I'm telling you I've been so lonely . . . I wouldn't be demanding.'

'You aren't.'

'You wouldn't have a hard time with me. I'm not as flighty as you might think. I was really impressed by the way you sorted out Basil. I think you could get on well with him. Half his trouble is that he doesn't have a good role model.'

I felt a painful lump in my throat. I was embarrassed that Ashley thought she had to bargain for my affection. What was I worth to anyone? We made love again. Much more passionately this time.

We woke with slabs of coloured light streaming onto the bed from the stained-glass windows.

'It's like sleeping in a church,' I commented.

'Yes, I often think I'm the last stop before the Chapel of Repose.'

'What do you mean?'

'My job. It can be a bit grim at times . . . horrific accidents . . . murders . . . dead children, you know – I see them all. That's why I need a good man to look after me.'

'Ashley, I should think you're strong enough for anything.'

'Maybe I am, but I need to be with someone. I'm sick of being on my own or fending off married men who have the idea that being black makes me an easy lay . . . which I'm not.' She squeezed my hand. 'Dave, tell me this isn't a one-night stand,' she said again softly.

I luxuriated in the comfort of Ashley's lovely bed for a long time. I knew I was on an emotional roller coaster. Ashley deserved an answer but I didn't trust myself to speak. I was experienced enough to know that 'rebound' relationships rarely last long and I didn't want this to be one of those.

230

'You're sure that we aren't a pair of psychological basket cases?' I asked.

'Well, if I am, and you are, then we've each found the right person, haven't we?'

'Could be,' I agreed cautiously.

We lay quietly for a while. It was pleasant listening to her steady breathing.

Finally, I said, 'Ashley, I'm ready to let things develop if you are, but don't rush your fences. It'll take me a long while to get over what Janine's done to me and you might not like me when that's finished.'

'What did she do? Two-time you?'

'No, I can't talk about her, but it wasn't that . . . I don't think. God! Ashley, I don't know! It was all probably as much my fault as hers.'

'Dave, I promise I won't get clingy but I'll be happy if you'll just say there's a chance for us. I know that's a cliché but when you've had nothing for so long you grab out when you see something good. Is there a chance?'

I kissed her by way of answer.

'Yes, there's every chance,' I said.

'That Janine is a pure fool,' Ashley murmured.

I put my finger on her lips.

I felt surging confidence and hope for the future lifting me out of the clouded valley where Janine's departure had left me. Yes, life in Hale Barns with Ashley would be very agreeable.

One thing led to another and it was almost an hour later before we got out of bed.

When I reached the Pimpernel Investigations office at nine that morning I was arrested on suspicion of the murder of Annie Aycliffe.

Bookshops are groaning with books by top coppers relating how they arrested various major villains. It's also a favourite topic on TV but for obvious reasons there are very few accounts from the other side. I suppose, having been arrested for murder twice I should consider myself an expert, but I don't.

It's an incredible process, particularly when, as in my case, one is completely innocent of the charge.

The police arrived at the Pimpernel Investigations office soon after I did. They obviously had the place staked out. There was no preamble of any sort. They just came in, arrested me for the murder of Annie Aycliffe, an event of which, having listened to Radio 2 on the way in rather than local radio, I was in complete ignorance, handcuffed me and hauled me out to a waiting vehicle. My heart rate doubled. All my senses were at full pitch. I seemed able to hear my watch ticking. My brain was racing from one possibility to another. As a private detective I know the danger of getting involved in a murder investigation. Let's face it, although the police usually get things right in the end, they're under immense pressure for early results. I strained to think how they could connect me with Annie Aycliffe's death.

I soon found out when interrogation started at Stretford Police Station.

Fortunately, as my arrest took place at the office, Celeste was able to send her solicitor cousin, Marvin Desailles, to give what counsel he could. Marvin, who is both black and gay, already has two strikes against him in the eyes of Manchester's finest, and he caps those by being fiercely anti-police.

'I don't like this,' Marvin said in the break after the first interview session. 'They're being far too polite.'

'You'd rather they were knocking me about?'

'In a word, yes, because it would mean that they weren't sure of their evidence but these two are just leading you through the events. They must think they've got a rock-solid case.'

'Thanks, Marvin,' I murmured.

232

I was being questioned by an unlikely-looking pair, a female detective sergeant called Leighton and a very youthful male detective constable called, Rayburn. He looked as if he should still be in school. I suspected that Rix had chosen them from among the sixty or so detectives under his command with the intention of knocking me off balance in some way. Leighton was a bosomy blonde with a winning smile and Rayburn looked ready to burst into tears when I couldn't bring myself to agree with his line of argument.

'Just agree to what you can't deny but volunteer nothing,' was Marvin's advice. It was good advice because I was still badly shocked by the sudden arrest. Meanwhile my mind and imagination were in hyperactive mode. Every nuance of the questioning raised a fresh surmise.

The story they laid out was a weird mixture of fact and imagination.

A witness had established that I'd gone cycling on the Mersey Meadows early yesterday.

Had I turned west towards Barfoot Bridge and Sale or east towards Didsbury?

'They wouldn't be asking you if they hadn't got another witness,' Marvin whispered.

I agreed that I'd turned west.

Was I aware that Annie Aycliffe was on the early shift at the animal sanctuary in Sale close to the Barfoot Aqueduct, which carries the Bridgewater Canal over the River Mersey?

I wasn't aware. I knew nothing at all about Annie Aycliffe's movements.

Leighton and Rayburn then suggested that I'd cycled the extra quarter-mile from where I claimed to have turned back and paid her a visit with murder in mind.

Someone had entered the sanctuary, brained Annie with an iron bar and then stabbed her repeatedly.

Being told by the two serious young detectives that I

233

was suspected of stabbing a woman repeatedly produced a strange sensation. I wanted to scream denial from the rooftops.

Marvin cautioned me against any show of emotion until they laid out more of their case against me.

I couldn't deny that I was in the vicinity at the time but I'd turned right at the aqueduct and come home through Stretford, not left towards Sale and the canal towpath. There were no witnesses to that. Nor could I deny that for the first time in several years I'd phoned in sick to my office, or that I'd previously had a violent altercation with Annie Aycliffe at my home.

DS Leighton suggested that the motive for my crime was that I'd called to intimidate Annie into giving me the address of Janine White, and then killed her in rage when she refused to play ball. I'd hoped to use the panic over the so-called Mangler to cover up my crime.

Again, I couldn't deny that there'd been a clash with Annie Aycliffe in front of many witnesses.

All the suggestions were put to me with unfailing, but sceptical politeness, like a bank manager discussing an overdraft application. Marvin never once had occasion to yell 'police brutality'.

Part of my mind was telling me how strange all this was. I remembered my grandfather telling me that in his young day the police rarely questioned suspects, just arrested them and charged them when they had enough evidence. The courts dealt with the questions. Now, two people who knew nothing about me were gently persuading me to accept that I was a violent murderer.

I'd no personal feelings towards Leighton and Rayburn except that listening to them painstakingly lay out their completely false case was a subtle form of torture. I knew who was feeding them their lines. I knew who was glued to his CCTV monitor studying my every reaction. 'Smiling' Jack Rix remained unseen but I didn't doubt for a second that he was supervising each step in the process that would leave me facing life imprisonment.

To help me to keep my cool I imagined Rix as a child catching insects and slowly pulling their wings off. I tried to put myself into his twisted mind and work out the next move.

Meanwhile, when the regulation lunch break arrived, Marvin decided that he had to lodge a protest.

'You only have vague circumstantial evidence against my client. I demand you release him,' he declared.

'I'm afraid not, Mr Gaye,' Detective Constable Rayburn began, before turning bright red with embarrassment when he realised what he'd said.

Having caught the opposition on the wrong foot Marvin was all for taking things to the police complaints authority. 'Homophobia!' he shrieked. It may or may not be true that the police are prejudiced against blacks and gays, but that is Marvin's perception. Now that Rayburn's slip of the tongue had given him a handle on the issue he looked ready to go over the top with it.

I'm afraid I laughed. After being bombarded with accusations for hours it was a relief to see someone else under fire.

'Sorry, Marvin,' I muttered when he shot me an accusing look. 'Constable Rayburn's probably a fan of soul music.'

Rayburn's colleague apologised profusely and answered Marvin's original question.

Her response swiftly deflated any humorous feelings. 'We're awaiting the results of various forensic tests which we believe will provide substantive evidence against Mr Cunane. We're going to hold him for the full thirty-six hours allowed and then apply for an extension if necessary.'

Forensic tests? I thought. They'd already taken a swab

from my mouth for DNA profiling, but what could they hope to find?

'They've got nothing on you, Dave,' Marvin tried to reassure me. 'You've been treading on some important toes, that's all. We'll have you out in no time.' Marvin has given up his dreadlocks, his tam and his purple track-suit. He now wears five-hundred-pound suits and works in an office in St John Street. I could only hope his opinion was as correct as his pinstripe suit.

When I was led away to be locked up I got a foretaste of what was to come. The entire uniformed staff of the station were lining the entrance to the cells and peering at me with obvious loathing and when I entered the confinement area the inmates began banging on the doors of their cells and screaming abuse.

So far, my mild inquisitors had only suggested that I'd used the existence of the Mangler as a cover for my crime against Annie. These good people had obviously been told that I *was* the legendary Mangler.

Things went steadily downhill from there.

The hours passed relentlessly.

There was a mass of forensic detail connecting me with Annie Aycliffe.

For a start she had my DNA under her fingernail. That was enough to get them an extension of my time in custody.

My blood was found on a tissue in her flat, as were fibres from my corduroy trousers on her carpet.

Annie's hair was found both in my car and in my flat.

The implication of this was that before finally killing Mad Annie, I'd made repeated visits to her flat. The elderly pornographer who lived on the floor below claimed to have heard loud shouting from above.

An iron bar was recovered from the canal near the sanctuary and it was found to be stained with paint matching stains found in my garage. It was regarded as the likely implement I'd used to stun the formidable Annie before stabbing her seventeen times and piercing every major organ of her body.

The knife used for that hadn't yet turned up but searches of the canal and River Mersey were ongoing.

Under consideration also was the violent struggle I'd put up at the Manchester CCTV centre and the fact that I'd threatened a senior police officer. My emotional state after the break-up with Janine White was regarded as a factor tipping a violent man towards murder.

'Dave, it's this Nanny Carter: she's cooked your goat, I'm afraid,' Marvin explained. 'We can only hope that if we get a top brief for your trial he'll take her apart on the witness stand.'

'But what's she saying?' I asked.

'Man, your explanation about the leaky vacuum cleaner was great but Carter isn't backing you up. If she had done, you'd have walked long ago. It's not *what* she's saying that's hurting you, so much as what she's *not* saying. Unfortunately she's the only witness for the visit to Annie's flat.'

'This is just pure malice.'

'Listen up, Dave. I don't know anything about Naomi except that her best friend's been killed and she's been told that the police think you did it.'

'Can't you approach her? She must know that I never met Annie before she brought her round to my place as her minder.'

'Dave, if I go within a mile of her I'll end up sitting in here with you.'

'Janine?'

'Apparently she's abroad,' he said bitterly. 'The press found her. There's talk of some tabloid paying her for her story. Think yourself lucky they didn't charge you with her murder.'

'Why?'

'She didn't come forward when they arrested you so naturally – '

'Great! But she can confirm that I took Naomi round to Annie's flat.'

'She can't or won't. You didn't mention the side trip to Urmston to her.'

I might have felt bad about that if I hadn't already been at rock bottom.

'There's something you're not telling me, isn't there?' I asked. Being questioned for hours with nerves at full stretch makes you sensitive to the most cryptic hint.

'I suppose you'd better know,' he said gloomily. 'The Five-Oh are lining you up as the Mangler.'

'I already know that from the reception I get every time I go downstairs.'

'No, Dave, it's worse than a load of cons jumping to conclusions. After denying that this Mangler existed for so long the Babylon is now fitting you up for the role. Their only problem is that they haven't found any evidence yet but they're tearing the town apart to do just that.'

'I've never even been in Offerton,' I said in a daze.

'You've used the M60 motorway, haven't you?'

'Along with millions of other people.'

'Dave, they're saying this so-called Mangler is forensically sophisticated. Right? He really knows his stuff. He changes his *modus operandi* after every killing, and uses the motorway to commit his crimes in widely separated locations. That's why the giant brains of the boys in blue were confused for so long.'

'So?'

'So, you own a whole library full of forensic science textbooks and you have a car.'

'That's not much, is it?'

'It's enough for them. Listen, Dave, I don't like to tell you this but you're famous. This is the biggest case since

Shipman. There's TV vans parked two deep outside of here. They've had to divert traffic.'

I groaned and put my head in my hands.

'It's hangin, man,' Marvin muttered sympathetically.

I got proof of the public reaction next day, after being formally charged and remanded to Strangeways.

I was led out to a van with my head covered in a blanket. I'd have preferred to walk out proud and erect. I feel this blanket routine brands you as a guilty man far more surely than if they plastered your picture all over town. Anyway, there it was. No sooner did the van leave the police station than I could hear the shouts and screams of a lynch mob. I had no feelings about that. The press had kept people on a raw edge about the Mangler murders for weeks so what was happening was only natural.

The only unnatural thing was the willingness of everyone, from the police downwards, to believe that a successful private detective in his mid-thirties would go on a murder spree just for the hell of it. Rix was probably consulting forensic psychiatrists to come up with a plausible explanation. Fatalistically, I knew they would.

Full-throated roars of hatred rose in intensity as we turned a corner. Something a lot heavier than a rotten egg struck the vehicle.

The officers handcuffed to me on either side, and that's how I preferred to think about it, were ashen-faced but I kept my features neutral. I'm too nice. I couldn't believe that people had gone out of their way to bay for my blood.

That was played back to me when we arrived at Strangeways.

'He's a cool bastard,' I overheard one of them telling a prison officer. 'You want to watch him. He'll do you as soon as look at you.'

So now I was Hannibal Lecter as well as the Manchester Mangler.

Prison wasn't as stressful as the interrogation phase of my arrest. I didn't speak for the first three days as my tangled nerves unwound.

My first meeting with my fellow prisoners had its moments. They mostly kept their distance but I saw one face that I knew. It was No-nose Nolan and he appeared to be smiling at me. I walked over to him and he suddenly spat in my face with sickening force and accuracy.

Perhaps there's something in my background that's always been preparing me for unjust imprisonment – all those stories about suffering saints and martyrs that had been banged at me from infant school right into sixth form. One particular picture stayed in my mind. Hanging outside the infants' classroom in my primary school, it showed the Holy Souls in Purgatory with their arms raised and flames flickering all around them as they pleaded for eventual release.

It was that prospect of eventual release that kept me going.

I must have looked pretty grim because I was on twenty-four-hour suicide watch for the first month. After the way Fred West cheated the system, great care was being taken that high-profile offenders didn't take the same escape route. One of my problems is that I can't sustain a mood of unrelieved gloom for long. I'd be no good at claiming compensation for hurt feelings. I had to see the funny side of things. The more the headlines shrieked about my iniquity the greater the amount of egg that would eventually be landing on certain faces.

I took some pleasure in teasing the grim-faced, wary guards by smiling at them and telling them feeble jokes. When I started singing 'Always Look On The Bright Side Of Life' in my cell the Prison Service finally decided I wasn't a risk but I was still under close observation and didn't follow normal prison routine. For one thing I wasn't sharing a cell.

I can't say that upset me.

As I hadn't actually been charged with any of the Mangler Murders, and the murder of Annie Aycliffe didn't appear to be a sex crime, the authorities were in a quandary about whether to put me in with the pervs. They solved the problem by leaving me in a cell in the normal prison with a vacant cell on either side of me, and then escorting me to the perv section for my limited social time. I'm a big bloke and they reasoned that I'd be able to fend for myself among the rapists and sex offenders, whereas the 'common criminals' just might save the court system a job.

Playing ping-pong with a pack of paedophiles wasn't the way I thought I'd end up passing my time but when you're between four walls you take your recreation where you can.

Surprisingly enough, my notoriety seemed to win me a certain number of friends. Contact with the Mangler apparently had glamour. I never had any trouble finding an opponent, but then that's never been a problem.

241

12

'Trial by Tabloid?
'The unanimous verdict of a section of the press that the man
being held in custody in connection with a recent murder in
Manchester is also responsible for the series of previously
unlinked killings, which the tabloids themselves have dubbed
the Mangler Killings, is only the most recent example of trial
by tabloid. It will render the choosing of a jury and the trial
of this individual extremely difficult and illustrates the difficulties created by the stampede to justice led by the red-top
press and certain irresponsible left-wing politicians.'
Editorial in the *Daily Telegraph*

One advantage of being remanded in custody was that I
was allowed visits to divert me.

My first visit was not at all to my liking. The visitor
was a solicitor from a Manchester practice representing
Ashley Gribbin, a tall, thin, young, bespectacled individual with a prominent Adam's apple, who was apparently having difficulty in shaving, judging by the number
of small cuts on his face. I knew from his expression that
he was not the bearer of glad tidings.

However, he had at least had the grace to look embarrassed as he began to explain.

'Mr Cunane, I've had permission of the High Court to
speak to you on behalf of Dr Gribbin about a private
matter,' he said.

Seated behind a prison table that was screwed to the
floor, I must have looked harmless enough because he
turned and spoke to the officers who withdrew out of
earshot.

'I don't wish to create a public spectacle, Mr Cunane, and in view of what I have to communicate it would be an advantage if you could keep your voice down.'

I nodded agreement.

'Your recent intimacy with my client has had an unfortunate result,' he continued in a low voice. 'She is pregnant. But because of recent events she now finds that she intends to seek a termination. She knows your likely views on this – '

'Which are?' I interrupted hotly.

'She believes that you're likely to be opposed.'

'She's damn right.'

'As you know, she does not need to consult you in any way before proceeding but . . .'

'She's nervous about any publicity which might be generated at my end.'

'. . . she wishes to ensure that you will respect her right to privacy and to have the comfort of knowing that you understand the situation which necessity has placed her in.'

'If she wants my blessing she can forget it.'

He paused for a moment and mopped his brow. 'Really, this is so difficult,' he murmured through pursed lips. 'She assumed that this would be your likely attitude. Apparently, you're already paying child support to one woman and have children by another . . .'

Something about the way I drew in breath must have reminded him that he was alone in a room with an alleged violent killer because he paused at that point and looked nervously at the door.

Rallying himself, he continued, 'Dr Gribbin was aware that this would be your likely reaction so she recorded a message for you.'

He bent down and took a mini-recorder out of his briefcase, placed it on the table and subjected me to an owlish stare.

I stared back.

'Will you listen to what she has to say?' he asked. 'Dr Gribbin wants to explain the reasons for her decision and to ask you for something.'

I nodded and he switched the recorder on.

'*Dave, so much has happened so quickly that I don't know where to begin talking to you,*' the familiar voice intoned. Then, of course, she did begin, speaking jerkily with many pauses for breath.

'*I know I came on to you something strong . . . but you're not the man to kick a woman out of your bed and I think I was feeling vulnerable at that time. One or two things were upsetting me and I don't regret . . . that is, I do regret . . . but I didn't know then what I know now. So, at the time, I didn't regret being with you. Dave, whatever you've done is between you and your conscience. I'm sure you never meant to go that far . . .*' The tape was interrupted by the sound of sobbing.

I felt as if the room had suddenly become stiflingly hot.

'*Anyway,*' she went on, '*that horrible man Rix has been to see me. I don't know why, but he may have heard a whisper that we were together that night, or maybe he just guessed. Of course, you and I know that it was the night after that poor girl was butchered and that I had nothing to do with that, but Rix wouldn't take much to tie me in to the killing and there's all this about you having forensic knowledge, which they'll say came from me. At the very least Rix will report me to the Home Office and make sure I get fired from the Government pathology service. Please, you mustn't mention that you were with me that night. It would ruin not just me, but also Basil, who'll have to leave his school, and my ex, who I'm still supporting. I know I can count on you for that. Whatever you may have done, I'm sure you're still a gentleman.*

'*Now comes the really hard part. Two weeks after you were arrested I realised that I am carrying your child. It is your child. I swear I've not been with another man for over two years.*

Anyway, that's irrelevant. I'd have loved to keep this baby but it would be unfair to any child to bring it into the world with all this hanging round its neck. Can you imagine what the tabloids would make of it and Rix is sure to find out? I'm not sure when you'll hear this but I've made an appointment at a private clinic . . . well, the solicitor will explain. I hope you can understand.

'We should have met in another time, in another life.

'Please remember that you've got not just my future but Basil's and his father's in your hands. I know you'll do the right thing.'

The solicitor clicked the tape recorder off.

'Well,' he said aggressively, 'is there anything I can tell Dr Gribbin?'

I rested my elbows on the table and thought for a moment. This had to be absolutely right.

'You can tell Dr Gribbin this,' I said slowly. 'If she can think that I'd sleep with her hours after allegedly murdering another woman she must know a lot more about how dead people work than she does about live ones.'

'Right,' he said briskly, replacing the recorder in his case. 'As you heard, what concerns her now is that a word from you can wreck her career.'

'Her career!' I repeated. 'That's safe from me. What does she think I'm going to do? Summon a press conference?'

'Er, er . . . to be blunt she fears that you'll bring up the relationship in your defence case.'

'Dr Gribbin is the only other person who knew about it, until she decided to tell you. The police think I was roving the highways and byways that night, no doubt scouting for my next victim.'

'So Dr Gribbin has gathered but it will be a relief to her that you've confirmed it. You must realise that the birth of a child would have made it hard for her to deny . . . that there was intimacy.'

'Hah!' I snorted. 'Poor inconvenient child.'

He made no reply and I managed to control myself.

'Was she involved in building up the forensic case against me?'

'No, in view of your known relationship the police used another pathologist.'

'Well then, her secret's safe me.'

'So I can tell her – '

Something in his smug manner now that he was leaving inflamed my temper.

'You can tell Dr Gribbin this,' I said quietly. 'I'm completely innocent of the charge against me and whatever the court finds, I'll be coming out of here one day, whether it'll damage her career or not.'

'Do I take that as a threat against my client?'

'As a lawyer, you should know that despite already being tried by the media and found guilty, apparently to Dr Ashley Gribbin's complete satisfaction, I'm innocent until proven guilty. If the court system has any integrity at all I'll be coming out of here a free man and very soon. That's all I meant.'

Sensing the rising tension, the two lurking screws moved forward like a pair of attack dogs. The solicitor took his leave.

My parents' visits were less gut-wrenching but painful enough in their way.

The first time I saw them I felt ashamed. They looked old, coming towards me in the visiting room. Paddy was walking tall as he always did but he looked baffled. For once he didn't have a ready solution to the world's troubles. Eileen was studiously ignoring the stares and pointed comments of her fellow visitors. I told myself that I'd nothing to reproach myself with except choosing the wrong career but I couldn't help blaming myself for my parents being mocked and insulted.

Unlike Ashley Gribbin they gave no outward sign that they were in any way upset or doubted my innocence.

We talked about my health and the weather and Paddy's latest building scheme until we ran out of small talk.

'Dave,' Paddy said eventually, 'in nearly forty years in the police I can tell you that I've met some violent killers. Never once in my experience has a savage murderer gone home to his parents, laughed, joked and gone on a bike ride.'

'Don't tell me, tell Jack Rix.'

'I have done, and you know what? The bastard said that he's known IRA terrorists back in Northern Ireland who'd blow a police officer away in front of his kids before lunch and then sit down to a four-course meal.'

'Implying that I'm a ruthless killer?'

Paddy nodded. His face was flushed with anger. 'He's making you out to be a flaming psychopath.'

'The man's a bigot!' Eileen exclaimed. 'The IRA aren't the only sick killers over there.'

We sat in silence and considered that for a moment. Left-footers, Catholic priests, IRA terrorists, the man had a weird fixation about me that stemmed entirely from his own background. In fact, my latest actual connection with the land of foggy dew had left those shores permanently some time in the 1840s.

Then Eileen's face brightened.

'Here, David, I brought you these.'

She took a small leather pouch from the prison officer who was hovering about three feet away. I recognised the pouch. It contained a set of rosary beads given me by my grandmother at the time of my confirmation.

'You should use these every chance you get,' she admonished. 'Don't forget, no prayer ever goes unanswered.'

I suppose I was embarrassed. We covered up the remaining time with chat about my childhood.

Ruth Hands showed up on another occasion. She too had confidences.

'Dave, I wanted to explain something to you.'

'That you're sacking me as your investigator. I understand, but you didn't need to come here to tell me in person.'

'Stow it, chum!' she snapped. 'I like you better without the self-pity, and you don't need to worry about my sensitivities. I'll come and go where I please. I've been in a lot crummier prisons than this.'

'Right, sorry, ma'am,' I said, managing a grin, a rare enough event to be memorable. 'I was forgetting what a hard-baked cookie you are. Sorry!'

'Will you leave over saying that word! I'm not sacking you. I wanted you to know one or two things about myself that might help you to put the situation in perspective. Being in here will at least give you time to think.'

'There is that advantage,' I muttered. 'But it doesn't give me a chance to act.'

'That's where I come in,' she said eagerly. 'If you think this gets you out of finding out who killed Meg, you're mistaken,' she asserted in her pronounced American accent. Heads turned all round the room.

I thought this was intended as a joke at first, but she went on, 'I've always thought there was the smoke of Satan about Meg's case but this confirms it. Can you deny that there's an evil influence at work here?'

'What do you suggest I do about it? Exorcism?' I snapped. 'I'm here because a pile of circumstantial evidence has been deliberately misinterpreted.'

'Dave, weren't you ever taught that Satan is the father of lies?' she replied calmly. 'Lies brought you here and lies are stopping the truth coming out about my Megan's death.'

I looked at her. It was the first time I'd heard her give Meg her full name. I wondered if her brain had finally softened. Being in the slammer makes you hard and uncaring towards others, but then I considered that no one had forced her to come here and that she still believed in me. It also started me on a train of thought that hadn't occurred before. What if the killer of Annie Aycliffe really was the so-called Mangler, and what if Meg's death was down to him as well?

I decided that was too much of a stretch of the imagination. If I carried on thinking on those lines my destination really would be a hospital for the criminally insane.

'Your business seems to have gone down the tubes,' she commented.

'Yeah,' I muttered dispiritedly.

'That so-called manager of yours has taken all your current insurance cases and set up on his own.'

This piece of bad news had already been relayed to me on several occasions by the detectives who regularly visited me to seek a confession to the Mangler murders. Snyder Investigations had set up on the other side of the street from where my office was situated. The detectives had even brought me photos.

'While we're on about the Bible and Satan, Ruth, have you ever heard of the expression, "Job's Comforter"?'

'Don't be silly,' she countered. 'Your firm's still keeping its head above water. I'm paying Mr and Mrs Coe to keep the investigation into Meg's death going. Of course, I couldn't keep up that fancy office of yours with twelve phone lines. Master Snyder's taken over all that side of your business, anyway. The Coes have moved into a small office and I'm paying them enough to keep things turning over until these clowns let you go. They're a nice couple but I think they're going to need your help to make a breakthrough.'

'And how do you imagine I'm going to do that?'

'The Lord will provide,' Ruth intoned quietly. 'Never lose faith. The truth will prevail.'

'Oh sure, when I've served sixteen years for a murder I didn't commit.'

'No, no, long before then, Dave. I know that God sent you to me to find out what happened to my child.'

'Do you believe that?'

'Yes,' she said fiercely. 'I know it and I wouldn't have picked you for this job if I hadn't been prepared to go the whole nine yards with you.'

I felt I was seeing Ruth in her true colours for the first time. I didn't know whether to be heartened or depressed.

'There are people working for you. Michael Coe hasn't been to see you because I'm afraid that if he attracts attention something very bad will happen to him but he's keeping things moving. He's quietly researched all kinds of information about what's going on down at Castlefields.'

'Has he found anything significant?'

'He's found a lot of background information about everyone,' she said uncomfortably.

'So, nothing significant.'

'There's no need to be negative. If you're so resourceful what would you do?'

I thought for a moment.

'I was puzzled that Meg's mobile phone and door key weren't listed among the possessions found with her. I think you should look for them.'

'You mean you think she might have been mugged?'

'Not necessarily, but most students would rather run naked through the streets than be parted from their mobile.'

'So where should I start?'

'The canal.'

This seemed to satisfy her. She looked at her watch. There was plenty of time left and, apart from my parents, I hadn't spoken to a soul who didn't believe I was a ruthless killer for what seemed like weeks, so I wanted to make the most of her visit.

'Ruth, you said there were things you had to tell me.'

For the first time in my acquaintance of her she looked slightly fazed.

'This isn't easy,' she said. 'I was all keyed up to tell you this when I came but now I've gone off the boil.'

'Is it to do with the case?'

'In a way. You probably think I'm pretty nutty, with all this talk about Satan and the Demon Drink.'

I shook my head vigorously. When you've only got a single supporter who isn't a blood relation the last thing on your mind is giving offence.

'The thing is, I know that Satan exists, or at least that there's a spirit of pure evil that gets into people and takes them over.'

She spoke in an ordinary conversational tone of voice and I settled down to listen to her. There was no trace of hysteria, but perhaps the story itself was a sign of madness, delivered as it was in the gaily painted visiting room at Strangeways.

'When I was a child my stepfather, who was a heavy drinker, abused me, my mother and my sister, who was also called Meg. You just can't conceive of the beatings and sexual abuse he handed out. There are no words to describe what he put us through. Nobody who hasn't experienced something similar can believe that a "normal" man could do such things. That's why I get impatient with your Inspector Rix and his limited imagination. We couldn't tell anyone what Father was doing because he threatened he'd kill us if we did and we believed him. I used to pray every night that he'd die, but he didn't.

'Instead the attacks seemed to be coming more frequently. The slightest thing could send him into these murderous rages – a headline in the paper or a chance remark, but usually it was drink. When he was sober he could be charming. He had a very good job with an investment bank and a long list of satisfied clients, but they never saw his dark side. It was pure evil, what he did,

251

and I'm as sure as I know I'm sitting here that there was an outside force directing him at times, but that's something you can't prove, only believe. I'm sure he enjoyed torturing and violating us.

'Meg, who was three years older than me, considered suicide. She had a knife she used to cut herself with but she never got round to suicide. She used to say she wasn't brave enough. I think she knew it would only have made things worse for Mother and me, but she had the knife, a marine K-Bar and she kept it under her pillow. Anyway, one night he went into her room. I don't know exactly what happened but she stuck that knife in his chest. He then pulled it out and killed her with it. My mother rushed into the room and she must have seen what had happened. She tried to get Meg away from him but he stabbed her and then he came for me. He must have known that he was dying but he kept saying, "If I'm going to hell, I'm going to take all of you bitches with me."

'I managed to run out of the house and he collapsed and died while chasing me.

'His last words as he lay dying were, "I'm putting a curse on you. You can run but you can't escape. We'll get you."

'So you can see why I don't believe in so-called "natural causes" so much.

'After his death the bank didn't want any bad publicity. He was a senior vice-president, after all, with some of the biggest corporations in the country on his client list. They hushed everything up with the Westchester County police. It was a domestic tragedy and everyone was dead except me, so why rake it over? I remember the inquest took fifteen minutes and in the statement they left it unclear whether it was Meg or my father who was primarily to blame. There was nothing I could do. I was too young. Whatever I said was conveniently ignored.

'So they sent me on a tour of Europe to see my long-lost Swiss relatives and while I was in Davos with them I met this nice young Englishman, Thomas Hands, who'd just qualified as a doctor. He was a total abstainer, which impressed me a great deal, and we fell in love.

'You'll laugh when I tell you that I thought that coming to England would be like walking into a storybook where everyone was courteous and chivalrous. Ha! How green can you get! But Thomas was all those things I'd read about, even if no one else was. I couldn't believe how rude everyone was, shop assistants were unbelievably surly and my neighbours never spoke to me at all. It was only Thomas that made my life bearable, and when he suggested that we both went abroad to work I jumped at the chance. Perhaps I should have stuck it out and stayed with the children. Well, he's been taken from me in circumstances which can only be described as evil and now my Meg . . .

'Perhaps I'm being punished for not being a good mother, but every time I think of Meg's death I think of my stepfather and his last words.'

After she'd finished we sat in silence for a while but eventually I had to say something. I was conscious that whatever I said was bound to sound trite and unfeeling but I wasn't willing to give up my commitment to rational investigation even to be sympathetic.

'Ruth, that's a terrible story and to be honest, which of course I am all the time,' I said, trying to inject a note of humour, 'certain things do slot into place but I don't think it explains your daughter's death. That's not down to any supernatural agency. I know there are real flesh-and-blood people who've been lying and I'm not just saying that. I can back it up with proof.'

'Tell me,' she commanded.

'I can't,' I said flatly. 'Why do you think I'm here? It's because I've found out more than somebody wants me to. It's best if you know nothing.'

253

'Don't you trust me?'

'It's dangerous to speak to me. I think you're only safe as long as whoever it is believes you know nothing.'

'But who is it?'

'That's what I was trying to find out.'

'And now, when they find you guilty, you'll never know.'

'Thanks! I was hoping the justice system having chewed me up, will spit me straight back out!'

'You and me both!' she said bitterly. 'But is that realistic? Dave, it's all right for you to talk about real flesh-and-blood people, but how do you explain those CCTV recordings? Meg was clearly terrified of someone behind her but there was no one there. That's got to be something satanic.'

'Not necessarily.'

She gave me a pitying look.

'There's more. I hired a man to do some surveillance work for me. I told you about him . . .'

'Surveillance on Arthur.'

'No, someone else. He's probably stopped now he thinks he won't be paid.'

'Give me his number.'

I gave her Harry Sirpells' name and number.

'Just pay him and ask him to carry on with the job, maybe a couple of days a week only, if money's tight. Don't ask for any details. Tell him to get a report ready for when I get out of here.'

'And when might that be?'

'Soon,' I said bravely. 'The police have ruined their case by linking me with this so-called Mangler. When he does his next crime they'll have to release me.'

'I see. So we're waiting for some other poor girl to be murdered?'

I shrugged. It didn't sound very heroic when you put it that way but how else was I going to get out?

254

'And another thing, Ruth, don't tell anyone else about Sirpells.'

'Surely Michael Coe and his wife –'

'Tell no one, not Arthur, not Michael Coe, not Celeste.'

'You don't suspect one of your own staff?'

'I don't know who I suspect but I do know I'm in here and that someone had a very complete knowledge of my movements.'

'Surely this manager, Peter whatever his name is, he's more likely –'

'I don't know that,' I said coldly, but after hearing Ruth's story and then thinking of my own position, with the whole tabloid press baying for my blood, I wasn't exactly feeling warm towards most of the human race.

Ruth looked very doubtful but nodded agreement.

When she'd gone I realised that it wasn't Castlefields that Michael ought to be researching, but the murder of Annie Aycliffe. Suddenly, for the first time since arriving among the lowlife inhabitants of Strangeways I wanted to communicate with people on the outside again.

13

'Saving the Expense of a Trial?
'Peter Critchlow, the head of the Prison Service, denied reports that the only suspect in the Mangler case had been so badly beaten by other prisoners that he is unlikely to survive long enough to appear in court. "My officers have this remanded suspect under constant watch. In the incident referred to it was not a case of a mob seeking justice. In fact the man concerned attacked another prisoner and will be disciplined under normal procedure when he has recovered from quite minor injuries." Critchlow refused to confirm that the Mangler suspect is being held in isolation.'
Report in *The Times*

However, before I could get in touch with Michael, fate intervened.

I saw someone I recognised. My stomach lurched. Neville Fraser, the grotesquely ugly bouncer from Castlefields, was leaning against the wall and watching me with vacant eyes. He gave no sign that he knew me. Should I go up to him and ask if he was the man who'd raped and drowned Meg Hands?

Looking at him across the common room, already a brooding presence and surrounded by a crowd of sycophants, a casual chat seemed above and beyond the call of duty.

Although this charmer had only arrived the day before he was reckoned to be the 'cock' of the section, largely because of his overdeveloped physique. He was on remand for indecent exposure, which seemed appropriate, given his appearance. He resembled a caricature of a

Michelangelo sculpture, weirdly taut flesh straining at all points of the compass.

Although he didn't look at me directly I knew he'd clocked me because one of the creeps, who was trying to ingratiate himself with him, was nodding in my direction. I tried to look unconcerned though my heart was pounding.

Our first clash came the next day when he was bullying a small black man. I've no doubt it was carefully staged for my benefit. There comes a point in prison life where you have to decide whether you're going to carry on living on your terms or to allow the scum to impose their own standards on you.

Any pretence that the prison authorities control the prisons is just that – a pretence. Once inside the grim prison walls violent criminals are free to impose their will on fellow inmates and that's exactly what they do. So you ignore the likes of Neville Fraser making life hell for someone else at your peril. Let him detect that you haven't the bottle to oppose him and his next victim will be you.

I watched everyone in the room, officers included, trying to ignore what Fraser was doing. The peripheral vision of my fellow prisoners was marvellous. They carried on with their own games and conversations as if unconcerned, but were scanning every move.

It was all standard stuff.

Neville first knocked over the draughts game that the guy was playing and then ordered his victim to pick it up. While the cowering man, who was doing time for rape, was on his knees Neville ordered him to lick his shoes clean.

That was too much for me to stomach.

'Can't you read?' I said, pointing to the placard on the wall titled 'Are you a bully?'.

'Me, I can't read,' Neville said proudly. He took a step away from his victim.

'Get up,' I said to the Afro-Caribbean.

'I told him to clean my shoes,' Neville drawled.

'And I'm telling him to get up,' I repeated.

'He's knocked all them draughts pieces over my feet.'

'No, you did that.'

'What's this nigger to you? Is he your bum boy?'

Neville put his hand on my arm. I roughly brushed him off. There was a collective intake of breath. All eyes were now focused on us.

'Get up,' I ordered the cowering man and pulled him to his feet. He scuttled away to a corner.

'You're a bender. I can tell,' Neville said conversationally.

By this time the prisoner officer positioned by the door was whispering urgently into his lapel microphone.

'I don't want a quarrel, but why don't you get stuffed?' I said.

'You East Ender!' Neville snarled, glancing towards the door where two officers had joined the first. 'I'll sort you out later.'

He gave me a wolfish grin, revealing teeth that could have kept an orthodontist busy for years.

'No you won't. I've got another engagement!' I rapped. 'I'm booked up all evening.'

'Funny man,' he said cleverly, glaring at me and trying to scare me with his ugly looks, an easy thing for him to do. His head was as bald as a beach pebble and I'll swear the muscles in his narrow little brow were more developed than most people's biceps.

I stared back and looked him up and down. Big, thick and stupid was the impression I formed, though his dark little eyes had an unpleasantly cunning look to them. The way his arms dangled from his massive shoulders was very simian. I noticed that he had the letters NF tattooed in blue biro ink on the backs of each huge paw.

I pointed at his hand. 'What does that stand for?' I

demanded for the sake of something to say. 'National Front?'

'What do you mean, National Front?' the brute snarled. There was a movement of the muscles on his ugly mug that approximated to a grin. 'Those are my initials. My name's Neville Fraser.'

I risked a scornful laugh at that. 'Yeah, we haven't been formally introduced but I knew that.'

'Yeah, and I know you too. You're that pillock that was bothering Mr Cosgrove.'

'That's me!' I laughed. 'What're you in for, Nev? Get your zipper stuck, did you?'

To my surprise he flushed angrily. 'I'll be out of here before you will, you murdering bastard. I shouldn't be in here at all. It's just a misunderstanding.'

'Not what I heard,' I taunted. 'Caught you with your kecks down outside a girls' school, didn't they?'

'Piss off!' he snarled.

'I'd be delighted to but they seem to want to keep us together. Perhaps they want us to be friends.'

He struggled to overcome his embarrassment and to reclaim the respect in the eyes of our audience that he felt entitled to. 'I know just who you are, Cunane, and I know everything about you,' were his parting words.

'Enigmatic, or what?' I replied, the words bouncing off his grisly back.

I understood that our confrontation was only post-poned, not ended.

Round Two took place in the phone queue on the evening following Ruth's visit when I wanted to call Michael Coe. Predators like Fraser can sense when a potential victim is at his most vulnerable. He must have noticed me anxiously joining the line early to be sure of a place.

He elbowed me in the back and shoved me to one side. The officer on duty looked up from where he'd been checking another inmate's phone card. 'He pushed in!' Fraser shouted. He then made the mistake of turning for acclaim to his racist clique.

I launched myself at him. It was a suicidal attack. Fraser was at least twice my weight but I was past caring. I clamped my arms round his neck and hung on while he pummelled my ribs and back. I did my best to pull his head off his shoulders. He tried to get at my face with his hands and, failing that, to bite my arm.

As a spectacle I imagine our struggle was similar to bull wrestling as practised in American rodeos. Heedless of the damage he was doing to me I twisted his fat neck for dear life. He tried to shake me off but I clung to him like a boa constrictor until he bent at the knees and crashed to the floor. Alarms went off and it took eight screws to separate us. They dragged me away and flung me into a cell.

Some time later I found myself under heavy guard in the prison hospital. As the aggressor in the fray I was placed in a partitioned-off cubicle on my own. Fraser had broken two of my ribs and cracked others. I was stuffed with painkillers and drowsing when I heard someone whispering. I couldn't make it out at first but what I was hearing was being repeated over and over. 'Cunane, your mother's a whore . . . Cunane, your mother's a whore . . . Cunane your mother's a whore.'

I tried to shut it out and sleep but it was no use. The repetition was maddening and I couldn't make out where the sound was coming from . . . 'Cunane, your mother's a whore . . . Cunane, your mother's a whore . . . Cunane, your mother's a whore.'

The mindless repetition began to get to me and I lost my cool.

Painfully, I levered myself up on my pillow and put my ear against the room divider. Immediately the sound became louder and I realised that it was coming through the thin plywood that made up the wall of my prison within a prison.

Such was the overcrowding, that the beds for 'normal' sick prisoners backed right up to my cubicle and some comedian on the staff had put Fraser in the bed separated from mine by half an inch of plywood.

There were three officers in the dimly lit room. They were there to guard me, the dangerous murderer, not Fraser. I guessed that it had to be him, not some other lag. The others had all kept their distance. Now he was scratching the wood with his fingernails. The officers gave no sign that they'd heard anything though my feeling at the time was that they must have. In that silent place even quiet whispers were audible.

If my ribs hadn't hurt so much I'd have tried to smash my way through the plywood and get at Fraser but I couldn't move without wincing.

Waves of pain, frustration and bitter anger washed through me.

The tormentor just went on mindlessly repeating the same phrase: 'Cunane, your mother's a whore ... Cunane, your mother's a whore ... Cunane, your mother's a whore.'

I banged the wooden partition with my head. That was enough for Fraser to guess that he'd got my full attention.

'You broke my collarbone, you bastard,' he whispered.
'It should have been your bloody neck,' I murmured.
The guards didn't stir.
My reply produced a moment of silence.
'I'll get you back,' he muttered.
I made no reply.
'I know all about you, Cunane,' he continued.
I persuaded myself that not answering would annoy him more than argument. It worked for a while. He went back to mumbling his limited vocabulary of swear words

261

until I was once more on the point of sleep, but then he said something that opened my eyes with a start.

'Hell of a piece to kill,' he muttered. 'Hey, she had red fingernails, didn't she?'

It took me a second to work out that he was referring to Annie Aycliffe. How could he know anything about Annie's fingernails? Nothing like that had been released to the media.

'So what?' I croaked breathlessly.

'Ha, so bloody ha!' he chuckled. 'Wouldn't you like to know?'

One of the screws got to his feet and took a walk down the ward to stretch his legs. Fraser's whispering stopped long enough for the sedatives washing round my system to take effect.

Despite my curiosity, I slept.

Next morning there was no sign of Neville Fraser and I spent the entire day mulling over his words. Was that just a guess about Annie's fingernails? I convinced myself that it was. It must be. The alternative was that he had information about the victim that could only have come from a police officer or the murderer.

During the night the whispering campaign resumed.

First it was the swearing, then when I made no response he got on to Annie Aycliffe.

'You were stupid with that iron bar, Cunane,' he taunted.

'What iron bar?' I couldn't stop myself asking. 'You're making up bed-time stories.'

'Th'iron bar with the red and blue paint from your garage on it,' he said. 'That was careless, like. You might as well have left your fucking name and address on t'corpse.'

To say I was gob-smacked doesn't cover it. My head was hot and my feet were cold. I wanted to smash my way through the partition and get him by the throat but

I couldn't do a thing. I thought of summoning the guards to listen in but I couldn't get off the bed. Anyway, Fraser would certainly shut up if he thought someone else could hear him.

I tried to sleep, but with the pain from my ribs, and my mind racing from explanation to explanation, it was dawn before I shut my eyes.

There were no further whispered insults for the remaining four days I spent in the hospital and then I had an interview with the governor, who wanted to put me in total isolation. That would have been fine when I was first jailed but now I was desperate to resume my acquaintance with Neville Fraser.

I considered revealing what Fraser had said but kept quiet because I didn't want to end up being measured for a strait-jacket.

I pleaded. I appealed to the governor's humanitarian instincts, reminded him of my previous good behaviour, insisted that there'd been provocation, and did everything I could apart from going on bended knee.

None of my words had the slightest effect. A bureaucratic decision had been made and it was set in concrete.

I then stated that as my chance of a fair trial was being compromised by the harsh treatment I was receiving in prison I was instructing my solicitor to prepare an appeal to a High Court judge. My trial date was too soon because, due to the barbarous treatment I'd received, I was in no state to defend myself. This threat had an effect.

I was marched out but was able to overhear an angry telephone conversation between the governor and the national prison authorities.

In the end the Prison Service gave way, but with the warning that further violence would land me in solitary.

I met Fraser some days later in the recreation room.

'I'll smash your fucking face in for you,' was his pleasant greeting. His right arm was in a sling, which is

263

probably what stalled an immediate attack. I was conscious that dozens of pairs of eyes were watching Neville a little more boldly than previously. It seemed that his prestige had been damaged as much as his collarbone.

'Yeah, sure,' I agreed, 'but later, eh? Sit down, Neville.' I indicated the chair beside me.

His sloping forehead rippled as he thought this one out. Did he lose status by doing my bidding or gain it by showing he wasn't frightened of the Mangler?

In the end, he sat.

'You're a mad bugger, you are,' he muttered. 'I'll rip your privates off next time we have a do.'

'OK, fine, but tell me, Nev, be frank: why do you set out to wind people up?'

'What other bloody amusement is there in here?' he asked, reasonably enough. 'It beats playing tiddlywinks with these shites.'

We sat and watched our fellow inmates at their various board games for a while. They seemed curiously attentive to their activities.

'It takes all sorts,' I said evenly.

'You're soft, you! Don't try and take the piss.'

'No, I'm really interested. Why are you such a bastard?'

'Me!' he laughed. 'I know people who could tell you things that would make your eyes drop out.'

'Is that what happened to your hair?' I asked.

He took his time while he worked this one out. For some reason he decided that my question wasn't an insult.

'My hair fell out when I was kid,' he whined. 'I fell through t'roof of a factory on my head and next day I had no hair.'

'Tough!' I commiserated.

'Me talking to you changes nothing,' he warned. 'I'll still have you when I'm fixed up.'

'Sure you will,' I said complacently.

He squinted at me with his narrow little eyes. 'You think you're special, don't you?'

I shrugged.

'You think you've the right to stop me making that little wanker over there's life so shitty that he'll kill himself.' He nodded in the direction of his previous victim, the young Afro-Caribbean rapist who was playing pool and trying to pretend that he wasn't watching Fraser like a hawk.

'He's being punished by being in here.'

'Oh, spare me that crap! It's no punishment just *being* in jail,' he jeered. 'Bloody rest home for some, it is. But there is real punishment here, as you'll find out soon enough. Oh yes, I can tell you there's some as dishes out *punishment* in here and it's not the fucking screws.'

'You don't say,' I sneered.

'Yes, I'm one of the ones as dishes it out,' he said proudly.

'You mean, you and your mates?' I asked, pointing at his diminished band of admirers.

'You're trying to find summat out. Fishing, aren't you?' came his reply. The fathomless ignorance of his face was brightened by a flash of cunning. 'It doesn't matter what you know because you'll never walk out of this place. I'm going to really damage you, Cunane. There won't be enough left of you to put on trial.'

'What! You think a cockroach like you can cheat the massed ranks of the tabloid press out of their chance to see me in court? The screws are watching you. They'll transfer you to Parkhurst if you make a move.'

'Scared are you, Cunane?'

'No, just telling you the facts of life.'

'Well, here's a fact of life for you. There's a lot more corridors and nooks and crannies in this place than there are screws. I'll have you just when I want you.'

'Maybe so,' I admitted, 'but if you're going to do me in at least give me the satisfaction of knowing just what

265

I've done to get up your nose. What is it I'm supposed to know? Is it about Cosgrove?'

'Cosgrove! If I'm a cockroach, he isn't even a flea!'

'Well, give! Even executioners let the condemned man have his last request.'

The concept of last requests was absolutely mint to Neville. He pondered deeply. 'Condemned man,' he chuckled. 'Yeah, you're condemned right enough. There's them has seen to that.'

'Who are they?' I asked, a shade too anxiously.

'Not so cool now, are you? All right, let's just say that there's a group of people in Manchester who don't have your best interests at heart and they know every move you make except when you're in here. That's why I'm here – it wasn't me at that school – to make sure you don't have an easy ride. Get used to it, Cunane. It doesn't matter what these dickhead lawyers do to you, you've already had your trial.'

'By the press?'

'No, you fool, by the people who really matter. Nobody knows their names except a few of their friends like me.'

'You really are an expert at winding people up, Nev,' I said dismissively. 'I almost believed you knew all about how Annie Aycliffe got the chop.'

'Got the chop? She didn't get the chop, she took the point.'

He gave a slow irritating laugh at his own joke. I longed to get his head in a vice and turn the screw until he squealed. All I could do was keep winding him up in the hope of more information.

'But all that stuff came out of the papers or your own daft head.'

'Believe what you like, but I know how that fat tart got it.'

By this time my heart was pounding away like a runaway express.

'You're a kidder, you are, Nev,' I scoffed. 'You're funnier than Bernard Manning.'

He took that as a compliment.

'That's a wheeze, in't it?' I commented, pointing at the blue tattoos on his hands. 'I bet it drives the screws mad when you say your name's Neville Fraser.'

He laughed. 'Yeah, it gets the coons going too. Fraser isn't the name I started with but I changed it by deed poll.'

'Deed poll!' I repeated. I was startled that an ape like Neville had even heard of the term.

'Yeah, those friends of mine told me about it,' he said proudly.

'So, is it like a game with you?'

'You think I'm joking but I've done it before – made soft lads top themselves. They can't do you for talking to them. I love it when they fall out of their prams. Most of them aren't like you. They won't have a go. Scared shitless when they see my pretty face. They clam up and turn all sulky. Then if you keep at them some of them top themselves.'

'You've no chance there with me.'

'I wouldn't be so cocky, pal. There comes a point when you can't take no more. Suppose I was to say, you should have dumped that fat bitch's body in with the hungry dogs when you'd jabbed her, that'd get on your wick.'

'No, it wouldn't, because I didn't kill her.'

'You know that and I know it,' he muttered, 'but if I keep on saying it long enough you'll top yourself, believe me.'

My chest felt tight and that wasn't because of the healing ribs. The fact that the dogs had been barking for food when Annie was killed was another part of Rix's scenario known only to me, my interrogators and the killer. The police theory was that the racket had given me the opportunity to sneak up on my victim.

I gave a happy smile to show that I wasn't affected by his baiting but inside I was seething. I had to know more.

But then the screws were shepherding us out of the recreation area because association was over. I'd have given half the blood in my body to discover what Neville knew but I didn't get the chance.

The whole case against me was suddenly dropped.

I was preparing myself for the crown court appearance, transferred from Manchester to Nottingham because of the danger of riots, when I was summoned from my cell. I couldn't follow the rigmarole the governor reeled off but the gist was that microscopic traces of DNA had been removed from Annie's skin and enhanced using a new replication technique. The same DNA was found on two other Mangler victims.

It wasn't my DNA.

I was in the clear. Or was I? The expression on the governor's face told its own story. There were now insufficient grounds to proceed with the trial but that didn't mean that he thought I was innocent. I knew that I wouldn't be regarded as innocent until the real killer was found.

I left the governor's office in a daze.

'Are you crazy, Dave?' Marvin Desailles asked when I told him that I didn't want to leave prison.

I struggled for the words but my explanation didn't come out right. Even as I spoke I realised that I was gabbling. I was in an agony of frustration. Weeks in the company of Neville Fraser and his ilk had sapped my power of argument.

Marvin shook his head sadly. He thought I'd finally lost it.

'These lags make a hobby of readin' about murders,' he protested. 'That's what they do, man! They're entitled to study their own trial papers and they pass 'em round like library books.'

'I'm telling you he knew stuff that could only have come from the real murderer.'

'Dave, there's been another Mangler murder while you've been chattin' this scummer.'

That shut me up.

'You need a long, long rest, Dave,' he said gently, 'and believe me, someone is going to be paying very big bucks to make sure you get it.'

Then he led me away like a little lamb, took Polaroid snaps of my bruises, helped me to get dressed, and constantly murmured soft phrases to reassure me.

'You goin' Barbados, man, six weeks in the sun minimum.'

When I didn't respond he offered me my choice of Hawaii or anywhere in the Mediterranean.

'Man, you goin' to get yourself a tan,' he crooned. 'You need rest in the sunshine and a pretty lady to help you recover and I'm goin' to see you get them.'

He led me blinking into the thin early summer sunshine where a media mob was waiting to jab cameras and microphones at me.

Marvin was in his element.

'Mr Cunane will be demanding a full accounting from those responsible for this gross miscarriage of justice,' he said. I was forbidden to speak while he repeated the same message over and over for the cameras of different TV companies. Eventually he led me to a brand-new people carrier and opened the sliding door panel.

Both Coes were inside.

14

'Greater Manchester Police in a statement today admitted that the release of the man accused of the notorious Mangler murders had not been solely due to new forensic evidence. A murder in Swinton formerly ascribed to a domestic incident is now regarded as a "Mangler killing". The murder occurred while the arrested man was awaiting trial.'
Brief report in *The Times*

We pulled out onto Great Ducie Street and turned towards town. Immediately police cars with flashing lights closed in at front and rear.

'Do you want me to ram our way through?' Michael Coe asked when they signalled us to follow them.

Marvin spoke up immediately. 'Hell, no! I've got a video camera here. If they're thinking of hassling Dave some more it can add thousands to his damages.'

So we followed.

They led us through a maze of streets to a car park across the road from Collyhurst Police Station. A section had been coned off.

A familiar figure got out of a van and strode over to meet us. Rix was taking no chances this time. He was flanked by two burly detectives.

'Oh, man!' Marvin squealed in delight. 'See if you can get him to hit you.'

'Dave's already got broken ribs,' Celeste reminded.

Rix rapped on the window. He smiled politely, as well he might.

I got out.

His colleagues positioned themselves behind me,

270

blocking Marvin's view. Marvin tried to get out but one of them held the door shut.

'How are you, Cunane, old boy?' Rix asked.

'As if you haven't had daily reports,' I said.

I tried to classify my feelings towards him. For the moment curiosity dominated righteous anger, but Rix's well-fed face was irritating enough to provoke rage in a frozen corpse. A copper as cute as Jack Rix could have had the truth out of Naomi Carter but it had suited him to believe her fairy tales. How the pressure must have relaxed when he announced that he'd made an arrest!

'Oh, come on, Dave,' he coaxed in his familiar friendly way. He pulled his face in mockery of my sour looks. 'There was nothing personal. I had to go with the evidence. You know that.'

'Evidence? You were only looking for evidence that pointed at me,' I said coldly.

'That was all the evidence there was, believe me. But I didn't bring you here to argue. I want you to listen. You're out now, old son. If you want to stay out, go back to investigating insurance frauds and leave the murders to me, and that's good advice.'

'So I ignore the fact that someone went to the trouble and effort of murdering Annie Aycliffe just to fit me up?'

'That's police business.'

'The fact that my investigation into Meg Hands' death triggered some nut into trying to put me away for life makes it my business.'

'Be told, Dave. It's police business. You're a civilian.'

'Police business!' I exploded. 'Police business isn't about catching killers any more! It's about meeting targets and getting good vibes with the tabloids by leaking them a load of lies about an innocent man.'

'None of that's down to me.'

'Don't give me that, Rix. All those leaks were meant to make you look good.'

271

He shook his head. 'I've done no leaking to the press,' he muttered.

'If it wasn't you, who was it?'

'I don't know,' he shrugged, 'and I'm not here to answer your questions.'

'No,' I agreed. 'You should be back at Strangeways finding out why one of the prisoners knows details of the Aycliffe killing that he could only have got from the killer or one of your officers.'

'Now you're fantasising. I suppose we're discussing your little friend Neville Fraser? He's in the clear.'

I nearly hit him then but managed to hold myself back.

'If he's in the clear explain how he knew about the paint on the iron bar used to hit Annie. He even knew there were two colours.'

Rix's eyes widened.

'He also knew about the barking dog that allowed the killer to get close to Annie.'

'This is absolutely typical of the bloody civilian mentality' he said coldly. 'You should have become a lawyer. I'll check Fraser again because I don't want you screaming to the Police Complaints Authority, but don't hold your breath. Prisons are awash with gossip. I bet half of what Fraser knows came from yon wee lad,' he said, jerking his thumb at Marvin. 'He's got enough lip on him to spread the story all over Manchester.'

I heard a grating sound and realised with a start that it was me grinding my own teeth.

'All right, we'll do it now. I can see you're obsessed.'

'Thanks,' I muttered.

He turned to the taller of his two sidekicks, a lumpy-faced man with a slight cast to his eyes. They whispered for a moment and then the underling stood to one side and got to work on his mobile.

Rix whistled 'Danny Boy' through his teeth while we waited for a response.

Eventually Lumpy Face got an answer. He went into a huddle with Rix.

'Sorry, Dave,' Rix said in mock apology, 'but it won't wash. Fraser's name was on our data base and he was thoroughly checked out after his latest arrest. At the time of Meg Hands' accident Fraser was being held for questioning in connection with an offence in Derbyshire.'

I could feel rage bubbling up.

'You fed him information so he could wind me up. You thought he'd make me confess.'

'Now you're developing persecution mania,' he said with a condescending smile. 'Take a long rest.'

That was it.

I didn't actually hit him. With my ribs still strapped up I could hardly swing my arms without pain, but I barged forward and cannoned into him. Then I went out like a light when Lumpy Face rapped me over the skull with his baton.

I came round in the back of the people carrier with Celeste bathing my head.

'Dave, you're leaving Manchester,' Marvin said seriously. 'That bastard will pin something else on you if you stick around.'

'Did you video what just happened?'

He held up the broken camera.

'I'll make a formal complaint to the chief constable,' he fumed.

'Save it, Marvin,' I muttered, nursing my sore head. 'They'll arrest me for assault if you do.'

There was silence for a moment, then Celeste spoke. 'Janine phoned,' she said brightly. 'She wants to see you.'

'She knows where I live,' I replied sourly. 'Not a word for weeks and then when I come out of prison, she wants to see me. I don't think so.'

'Dave!' Celeste scolded.

I did a mental accounting of all my aches and pains.

My head was throbbing and my ribs were sore. I burned with the injustice of my false arrest, but the worst hurt of all came from the gap where Janine had wrenched herself out of my life.

'Where does she want to see me?' I asked wearily. Despite everything, I was curious to know what she'd told Jenny and Lloyd about their sudden move.

'She said she'd see you at your flat.'

Michael took an indirect route to Chorlton, hoping to mislead anyone who might be following, but when we arrived outside Thornleigh Court the car park was jammed and the press was in full cry.

I was desperate to get home. For one thing I wanted to soak in my own bathtub for at least a week. Although I was clean enough by the standards of Strangeways, I felt tarnished. In the end, flanked by Michael and Marvin, I forced my way through the baying mob and up to my flat. The key was stiff in the lock and the rooms were like battlegrounds after the police searches but it was home and the hot water was still running.

I persuaded Michael and Marvin to leave.

Michael paused at the door . . .

'Er . . . Dave, there's never a good time to say these things . . .'

From the way he was twisting his hands like a curate in a Trollope novel I knew that what he was trying to say wasn't going to make good listening.

'Spit it out, Michael.'

'Celeste and I, you know she wants another baby soon, well . . .'

'Peter Snyder's offered you your old job back with him and you want to take it,' I said.

'How did you guess?' he asked incredulously.

'Michael, I don't have to be a genius to know that you were a pillar of strength at Pimpernel Investigations. Peter's bound to be missing you.'

'Yeah, well, it's more money for both of us.'

'You've done great sticking by me so far, don't worry about it.'

'We'll still be friends, won't we?'

'Michael, I haven't got so many friends that I can afford to take umbrage just when one of them looks out for his family.'

'No, that's right,' he agreed disconcertingly. 'Listen, I've made folders of all the stuff I found out about the merry folk down at the Canal Basin. There's a lot on that Hobby Dancer character. Did you know he has an African pygmy living with him?'

'I met him.'

He peered owlishly at me through his granny glasses.

'Right, well, Cosgrove seems to be clean as far as I can tell, but he definitely has underworld contacts. There's some right villains drink at La Venezia and that may be why he was so nervous about you, Dave.'

'I know one of the villains – Rix.'

'Yes,' he said uncomfortably, 'I suppose you would think that.'

'Did you do any work on Annie Aycliffe?'

'Sorry, Dave, but Celeste and me thought it might be too dangerous. I didn't want someone to turn round and decide you had an accomplice.'

'Michael, I didn't kill Annie Aycliffe.'

'That's right, Dave. Anyway, here's the key for your new office. It's above a Chinese takeaway near the *Evening News* Arena. It's dead handy for Trinity Way so you can reach anywhere in Manchester in five minutes, traffic permitting. Also it's great if you're feeling peckish.'

He dug in his pocket for the key and then handed it to me.

'No hard feelings, Dave?' he asked, squinting at me anxiously.

'Of course not,' I replied.

Oddly enough, I felt a certain amount of relief when he'd gone. I was now responsible only for myself.

I'd hardly had time to run the bath before my mobile chirruped.

'It's me,' Janine announced.

Moments later she was in my living room straightening up furniture.

I felt no particular emotion. Even anger was beyond me. I just stood and watched her as she restored the cushions to the armchair. It was like being with a stranger.

'Dave, I've not come here to say sorry, if that's what you're waiting for,' she began.

'No, Janine, I wouldn't have expected you to,' I commented.

'Don't get sarcastic. I only came because I thought you were owed an explanation.'

'Explanation? That didn't seem to bother you when you cleared off.'

'I needed to make a clean break. You made your choice and I made mine. You went on working for that mad woman and I didn't want to get dragged down with you.'

'Dragged down! Am I so horrible that you needed to send Naomi round to collect your stuff with Annie Aycliffe as her minder? Couldn't you have come yourself?'

'I knew you'd persuade me to stay. Naomi no longer works for me.'

'Oh, so that's all right then!'

'Dave, will you shut up and listen for a minute?'

I slumped down on the chair. I was aching all over and I needed this confrontation about as much as I needed another meeting with Smiling Jack Rix.

'I offered you what you always said you wanted – marriage and a family. But when they came up against your precious job, you threw them back in my face,' she said bitterly. 'I couldn't believe it when you walked off to that woman's flat. I may have said things to Naomi

276

that she misinterpreted. God knows I needed someone to talk to and, as usual, you weren't around.'

'Thanks! You managed to convince her that I was the worst thing in trousers since . . . who? . . . Jack the Ripper!'

'But Dave, don't you see I did the right thing by making a break? It was just as I told you: that Hands woman trails disaster behind her. Christ! Since she started working in Africa the whole continent's gone down the drain. She's lethal to know. Obviously someone was targeting her through you. Anyone seen in your company could have been killed. It could have been me.'

'Thank goodness your instinct for survival is so sharp.'

'That's unfair! Someone needs sharp instincts. You haven't any, and I've got two children to think of.'

'I never stopped thinking about them,' I muttered.

Janine gave me a thoughtful look and bit her lip.

'Have you told anyone else about this theory?'

'Dave, you do realise I'm one of the few people who really believe that you're innocent?'

'Thanks.'

'There you go again. You can't take anything seriously. For your own sake break away from Ruth Hands. I can lend you some money if you're short.'

'Great, but, Janine, when did you form this theory about the killer really being after Ruth?'

'I'm telling you now and don't say the thought hasn't crossed your mind. I know you too well.'

'Who do you think's after her then?'

'How do I know? She's American. It could be the Mafia, the CIA, Arab terrorists, anyone. All I know is that everything was going well for us until you got tangled with her and started making a splash in the papers, and then . . . whammy!'

I was about to ask how Jenny and Lloyd were getting

on when we were interrupted by a sharp rapping on the outside door. I stood up angrily and marched into the hall. If it had been a reporter he or she might have needed facial surgery but it wasn't.

Ruth Hands pushed past me and walked in.

When she reached the living room she faced Janine, who immediately stood up and started edging towards the door. I deliberately blocked her exit. There were lots of things I still wanted to say to her.

'I see you've got company,' Ruth observed.

'I'm just going!' Janine snapped.

'No, you're not!' I interjected.

'If you were man and wife I'd leave immediately,' Ruth started to say, 'but –'

'Don't you dare start that sanctimonious cant again,' Janine spat out in fury. 'Do you think I'm one of your hillbillies? I could tell that you had your eye on Dave. What do you want him to do: start preaching in Africa?'

'All I dropped by for was to remind Dave that there's still work to be done when he's ready. It's perfectly obvious that my Meg was murdered by a serial killer who's operating in this town with complete impunity.'

'Obvious to you but to no one else,' Janine flared.

'So there's more than one person going round Manchester killing young women in various inventive ways?' Ruth asked calmly.

Janine looked ready to explode. She hopped from foot to foot like a cat with haemorrhoids.

'Are you going to listen to this rubbish, Dave?' she asked angrily.

'It seems like I've no alternative. My business has been ruined and there's a man in Strangeways Prison who knows a lot more about the Aycliffe killing than I did before the police started giving me the third degree.'

'Who is he?' Ruth demanded.

'He's called Neville Fraser.'

'There, didn't I tell you?' Ruth crowed. 'It's not just one man. There's a whole gang of them.'

'Rubbish!' Janine snapped.

'If you're so certain it's rubbish, listen to this,' Ruth retorted. 'I've had a team of divers working in the Canal Basin for weeks and they've found all kinds of small objects – jewellery, guns and goodness knows what – but not Meg's mobile phone or door key.'

'So what?'

Ruth began to breathe deeply through her nostrils. 'So, you're very clever, but if you had an accident tomorrow your mobile and your door key would be found right alongside you unless someone abducted and robbed you first. But you're like the local police. I expect you've got another explanation.'

'I can't explain it. Why should I?' Janine protested. 'The canal's full of mud.'

She looked at me. I shrugged.

'Dave, can't you see what she's doing? Her daughter gets drowned, and because it's *her* daughter it's not enough that it's an accident. Oh no! The Devil himself has to be involved. Then she gets hold of the most wooden-headed detective in Manchester and sends him to butt and bash his way round town and, lo and behold, that idiotic man becomes a target for the criminals he's annoying. The next thing we know is that her daughter's death is part of a vast conspiracy. Where does it end?'

'It ends when I find out who killed my daughter,' Ruth said, 'and if Dave isn't man enough for the job I'll find someone who is.'

'John Wayne's been dead for years,' Janine said scornfully. 'Didn't the news reach you in Africa?'

'Janine,' I murmured, 'you said yourself that someone was targeting me. I have to find out who it was.'

'Do you?' she snapped fiercely. 'Does it have to be you? Isn't there a police force out there? Couldn't you move away from Manchester and let the whole thing die down? Or is it that you enjoy this mad life?'

I shook my head.

'You do, don't you?' she persisted. 'Well, I did have second thoughts about us but this has convinced me that I did the right thing in breaking with you.'

'Janine –'

'No, don't try and stop me. This is as much as I can take. You don't want a normal life, you just want to follow this crazy woman's whims.'

She stormed out. I didn't follow her.

'Do you think I'm crazy?' Ruth asked after a long pause.

'You're obsessed, but then so am I, according to Jack Rix.'

'What are you going to do?'

'At the moment I'm going to have a bath.'

'You do realise that your split with Mrs White has nothing to do with me, don't you? She was just looking for a pretext. If it hadn't been me, it would have been something else.'

'Possibly.'

I walked into the bathroom. I felt an overwhelming pressure building up in me. The break with Janine was final. I knew that. I think I hardened my heart against her during those weeks in Strangeways when no word came. Then she'd waited until after I was cleared of killing Annie Aycliffe to stage the big reconciliation scene. That was too calculated. I gloomily accepted that Ruth Hands was right about Janine.

I stayed in the bath until my skin was wrinkled but I still didn't feel clean.

When I emerged Ruth Hands had gone. She'd done some tidying up. I asked myself why I get entangled with women who want to smooth out the rough edges of my life.

I felt hungry but there was nothing in the kitchen so I went down to my garage. Of course, there was no car. The Mondeo belonged to Pimpernel Investigations. Fortunately, the press were taking a delivery of pizzas and I managed to slip out unnoticed. I set off walking and as I left Thornleigh Court two of my elderly neighbours were coming in. They both looked right past me when I spoke to them and hurried inside without a word. I felt like yelling, 'It wasn't me! I'm cleared!' But what was the use?

I don't know whether it was my imagination but as I walked up to the shopping area of Chorlton I noticed several people giving me sideways glances. Chorlton's the sort of place where you can't walk far without meeting someone you know, but as I approached people seemed to be hastily crossing the road in front of me.

So now, not only had I lost my business and Janine but most people thought I'd been released on a technicality. The Crown Prosecution statement that there was insufficient evidence to proceed with my trial was hardly a ringing endorsement of my innocence. At the supermarket, which was crowded with Asian shopkeepers stocking up on special offers, I didn't attract any attention and I bought as much as I could carry and retreated to my kitchen to lick my wounds.

On the way back it crossed my mind to wonder whether Chorlton was included in the CCTV network. Was Rix gleefully observing me creeping home with my tail between my legs?

I spent ages clumsily preparing a meal. It was as if I'd forgotten everything I knew.

Afterwards I lay on the narrow bed in my spare room staring at the ceiling for so long that I thought I could sense the motion of the planet beneath me.

What was I going to do?

Eventually I felt energetic enough to get up. It was quite dark.

I phoned Peter Snyder's home number.

Levonne answered.

'I see they let you out,' she said briskly. 'I thought you'd be in touch. Peter's not here.'

There was a defensive and hostile edge to the way she spoke that I wasn't used to with her.

'I was wondering – '

'I know what you're wondering,' she snapped, 'and the answer is no.'

'I haven't asked a question yet.'

'Oh yes, you have. You're phoning Peter because you want money. He owes you nothing. When you went and got yourself locked up . . .'

'I didn't.'

'. . . your firm collapsed. Peter had to liquidate it to meet your debts. He owes you nothing and if you start pestering him we'll put the Law on you.'

'Can I speak to Peter?' I insisted.

'He's in London and he won't be talking to a jail-bird like you anyway,' she said venomously, and then hung up.

This produced a momentary flare of anger but, as with my earlier meeting with Janine, I didn't seem able to muster the energy to hold on to any normal emotion for long. My parents were staying with my brother in Cornwall and I lacked the energy to go through my address book to see who might still be prepared to talk to me.

Some time later my phone rang. I grabbed it, hoping that Peter was calling, but it was Celeste.

'I just called to see how you are. We both feel really shitty about having to leave you but what can we do? We have to eat.'

'Yeah, I understand,' I muttered.

'Would you like to come to us for a meal?'

'Not at the moment. I've already eaten.'

'How did it go with Janine?' she asked, getting to the reason for her call.

'Things are just the same as they were,' I mumbled.

'Oh, Dave!' she squawked. 'Don't say you've blown it.'

I didn't reply. There was an awkward pause.

'Dave, I hate to think of you in that flat on your own. Michael and I are coming round. I'll get my mum to look after the baby.'

'No, I don't think that's a good idea.'

'It's not a good idea you stopping in that flat on your own and brooding.'

'Why, what are you worried about?'

'Oh, nothing, but you need some company.'

'No, I'm going out,' I said hastily. I wasn't in the mood for company and certainly not for persuasion to change my mind about Janine.

'Where?' she demanded.

'I'll go for a walk on the Meadows.'

'You sure you're not going poking round those canals again?'

'Certain.'

After a few more efforts to persuade me to join herself and Michael, she rang off.

The truth was that the walls of the flat began to seem ominously like the walls of my cell in Strangeways. I decided that I would do what I'd told Celeste. I dressed in dark jeans and a black leather jacket and then set off walking.

Getting out was a problem. The indefatigable sentries from the tabloid press were still on duty. I could see their cigarettes glowing. Fortunately, as I waited a party of visitors was leaving one of the downstairs flats. I tagged on behind them. They looked at me doubtfully. I pointed in the direction of the newsmen and shook my head. For a moment they were undecided but loathing of the press

283

was stronger than dislike of a suspicious character like myself. They went towards their cars, not to the newshounds. I dodged round the side of the building. Breathing heavily, I pressed myself against the wall and after a moment risked taking a peep.

The journalists remained where they were.

At ten o'clock I found myself looking at the dark pool of Chorlton Water Park. This former gravel pit, part of a land reclamation scheme, has been the scene of many suicides. The water's deep and bitterly cold. I stood watching the wind ripple the surface. There was a life belt mounted on a nearby post, presumably in case the suicide recanted in time to shout for help.

Rustling in the bushes, distant conversations carried on the still night air, and motorbikes occasionally revving across the meadows like the mating cries of lonely animals reminded me that I wasn't on a desert island. There were people about, people of a certain sort. Most likely some of them were the lurkers in the dark whose deeds filled the local papers, but I wasn't worried. Nothing could be worse than facing Neville Fraser.

My thoughts weren't on suicide, but on the death of Annie Aycliffe. I walked on, along the embankment above the river. It was horrible to think Annie'd been killed just so I could be framed as a murderer. Surely there was another explanation?

I tried to find one.

Suppose her death was just down to bad luck? She did work in a lonely spot down here on the riverbank.

That wouldn't wash.

I knew in my bones that the man in the grey Vauxhall Senator had targeted her after he'd wrongly identified her as my wife. If only I'd a fraction of the resources available to Jack Rix I'd have tracked that car down long ago. Rix could have done it but didn't care to believe me.

Baffled and bitter, I tried to think about Annie Aycliffe

in a more kindly way than I had during my months of imprisonment.

She was no prize specimen as a human being but she'd had her good points. I remembered that dingy top-floor flat smelling of cat pee, the loft apartment with a difference. No, Annie wasn't going anywhere fast in a worldly sense but she was a good friend to poor, daft Naomi Carter. She was even ready to risk fighting with a powerfully built man to protect her pal. I'd called her Mad Annie, but perhaps Brave Annie was fairer. Yes, she was certainly a friend of dumb animals, was Annie. She was even prepared to get up on freezing mornings to go and feed them.

I suddenly understood that Annie, aggressive and full of fight as she probably was, must have felt herself capable of dealing with any physical threat that might arise. But some malevolent power far stronger than she could cope with had seen her in my company and marked her out as a victim. It was weird, and Ruth Hands would say it was diabolical. Maybe she was more than half right.

I shivered.

A chill east wind blew along the river valley. I could see the outline of the distant Pennines, black against the night sky. Noise of traffic racing along the motorway echoed the wind sighing through the reed beds.

I wasn't near any CCTV cameras but it was hard to shake off the feeling that I was being watched. Was it some special squad Rix had assembled? Was he even now searching for the clue that would put me away for life? Or was it that malevolent force that had already shed so much blood?

I turned my collar up and walked quickly on.

They say there's a sixth sense that warns when one is being stalked. If there is it was operating at that moment. I felt the hairs on the back of my neck prickling against my T-shirt. I told myself that I was just jumpy after months

285

in prison expecting to meet Neville Fraser round any corner. Still, there was something. I looked over my shoulder and then hurried on.

Janine was wrong. How could I turn away from this? If I was ever to enjoy peace of mind I had to know who killed Annie. There was a connection with the death of Meg Hands. There must be. How could I throw Ruth Hands' job back in her face before I had an answer? Anyway, Ruth Hands was the only person offering me employment of any sort.

I walked along the Mersey bank and, because I know the paths so well, was able to find the turn towards Stretford even in the dark. This was the route I'd taken on the morning of Annie's death. I was close enough to the animal sanctuary to hear the dogs barking. If Rix's men were following me would they take it as a sign of the guilty man returning to the scene of his crime? I imagined Smiling Jack rubbing his hands at the news.

One maddening thought was that if the man in the grey Vauxhall was the killer then Janine was right. Only her urgent action in breaking the link with me had saved her from Annie's fate. I felt like screaming but I didn't. I kept on walking. When I reached the well-lit road at Stretford I didn't turn towards Manchester but kept on along towards Sale, and without any conscious decision I found myself at the motorway interchange.

It would have been better for Annie Aycliffe if I'd never been born. It might have been better for Janine if she'd never run into me.

My reverie was interrupted by the blaring of a horn and the squeal of brakes.

'What the bloody hell are you trying to do, mate?' the lorry driver screamed.

I was so absorbed in my troubles that I'd stepped out into the path of his leviathan, which was now slewed across both lanes of the M60 entry slip road.

Illuminated in the harsh glare of vehicle headlights, I had to jerk myself back into the real world. There was a queue forming behind the massive truck, whose wheels had so nearly crushed me to pulp.

'Are you after a lift?' the driver yelled.

'Yeah,' I muttered weakly.

'Get in,' he bellowed.

I hauled myself into the cab.

'Missed the last bus?' the driver asked, not unsympathetically. Perhaps he felt guilty about nearly running me down. He was a large, round-faced individual in blue overalls. 'Where are you going? I'm heading for the M6 and the Channel Ports if that's any use.'

'Could you drop me at Knutsford Services?'

'Sure, but you want to be careful how you try to get a lift. There's some drivers who'd run over you first and ask questions later, eh?'

I nodded agreement as he kept one eye on me and one on the road.

'Had a skinful, then?'

He must have been studying the rather glazed look my eyes had taken on.

'No, it's woman trouble,' I said carefully.

'Oh, that explains it!' he half shouted. 'I've had a bellyful of that, I can tell you. For a minute back there I thought you were trying to top yourself under my wheels.'

He then launched into a monologue about the troubles he'd had with women in every major city in Western Europe. I was only required to grunt affirmatively when he made generalisation after generalisation. In the warmth of the cab I found myself beginning to nod off.

He shook me awake.

We were at Knutsford Services.

'Here you go, mate,' the driver said, pulling to a halt. 'Look after yourself and don't let them grind you down.'

I let myself out and thanked him.

287

The truth was that I felt like death warmed up and made a grim sight. It took me some time to orient myself but eventually I staggered off towards the all-night café.

I sat there for two hours soaking up coffee. Part of the time I had my head in my hands, not because I was in the depths of despair but because I was trying to think my way out of my problems and wasn't getting answers. I was still totally baffled about the death of Meg Hands. Fraser had information about Annie's death but how was I going to approach him? The prospect of another stay in Strangeways to renew contact was deeply unappealing.

No thoughts occurred.

Suddenly I became aware that someone was observing me.

From the opposite corner of the café a man in a heavy black overcoat complete with fur collar was staring intently at me. I don't embarrass easily so I stared back. He made an exotic spectacle, like the villain in a Humphrey Bogart movie only far thinner than Sydney Greenstreet. I tried to work out what he was up to. He could have been an East European diplomat. It crossed my mind that he was looking for a pick-up but he didn't look that sort, however they're supposed to look.

He stood up and came towards me. The minor mystery was about to be solved. His collar was genuine astrakhan and his coat was cut from the finest cloth.

'May I join you?' he said courteously. 'I didn't mean to be rude. I couldn't help spotting that you're in some distress and I wondered if I could be of assistance.'

He wasn't an East European diplomat. He spoke with a quite broad Yorkshire accent. I wondered if he was a member of the Samaritans, perhaps heading for home after a gruelling night listening to the ramblings of the terminally depressed. If so, he was a glutton for punishment.

'I'm all right,' I muttered. Even to myself, my voice sounded miserable.

'Are you sure? You look really upset about something.'

'There's nothing you can help me with,' I said.

'Can I at least get you another coffee?' he asked.

Again the voice was courteous, there was nothing threatening about him. He was a small guy with an intense expression of concern on his narrow face. His jewelled signet ring caught the light as he gestured towards the coffee stand. I decided that I had nothing to lose by being a little courteous myself.

'OK, fine,' I said. 'I'm not going anywhere in a hurry.'

That was true enough. I was twenty miles from home with one pound in my pocket.

He came back a moment later with the coffees.

'It's a rough old world, isn't it?' he said calmly as he sat opposite me. I made no reply but he started to chat anyway.

As with the lorry driver, I held up my end of the conversation with nods and affirmative grunts where his tone indicated agreement was required. I wasn't really taking on board what he was talking about.

This went on for quite some time – the man in the black overcoat laying out his thoughts about life in general and me apparently lapping up his every word. My mind was almost entirely on Annie Aycliffe.

'Drink your coffee. It's getting cold,' he prompted.

I don't know to this day what the reason was, but I didn't drink the coffee. I think there was a faint edge to his words that I didn't like. I picked the coffee up, brought it to my lips but then put it down again. I'd had weeks of being ordered about by strangers and enough was enough.

Just then there was a tremendous crash as the waitress dropped a tray of cups. He turned to look and I took the opportunity to ditch his coffee in the fig plant on my right.

Turning back to me, he started talking again. I listened with half an ear.

It was only when the chat began to follow a particular line that I began to tune in. 'We're a bit like maggots crawling about on the surface of a piece of rotten flesh,' he opined.

That was a bit strong for four o'clock in the morning.

It was on the tip of my tongue to say that maggots serve a useful purpose but I was too tired and wasted to argue with a stranger.

I cradled my head in my hands again and tried to blank out his morbid musings but they went on and on. At first I thought that he was the one contemplating suicide and it was only when he started quoting *Hamlet* at me that I realised he was advising me that the best solution for my troubles was sudden death. He went on methodically listing the various methods of self-destruction and pointing out the advantages and disadvantages of each. There was a mainline railway track not far away. He felt that lying across the rails was the most decisive method of disposal.

It was only when he offered to drive me to a handy access point that I decided to put a stop to his rant.

I reached across the table and gripped his wrist with all my strength.

'Just what is your game?' I snarled.

I think prison had roughened me up to the extent that my normally pleasant features were twisted into a frightening grimace. Certainly the suicide counsellor thought so. He strained back in his seat and let out an involuntary yelp of fright. No one noticed. The place was so quiet that I could have pulled his head off without causing any disturbance. His stick-thin wrist didn't wake any feelings of compassion in me. I held on tightly and twisted his arm a little. Everything he'd been saying was so against the grain of what you'd expect that I guessed that he was pulling my leg, or trying some complicated scam.

Even under the artificial light of the restaurant I could see that his face had gone deathly white. His cheekbones stood out prominently. His tongue flickered out as he nervously licked his lips.

'What's it to you whether I do away with myself?' I growled.

He stared as if transfixed.

'I've got a gun in my pocket,' I bluffed, 'and I might just like to take someone with me if I do decide to leave this world.'

I was startled by the effect my words produced. I was grinning as I spoke but the man in the astrakhan coat went from wise counsellor to shrivelled wreck in two seconds. The change was too dramatic to be believable. I expected he'd suddenly say 'Fooled ya!' and break into a laugh.

He didn't.

Still not releasing his wrist, I stood up and pressed myself into the seat alongside him. Now he couldn't get out of the booth until I moved.

'Come on, talk!' I ordered, giving him a prod in the ribs with my fingers.

Incredibly, this scared him even more. Every trace of colour had by now left his face. Even his lips were bloodless. He must have thought I was poking him with the gun.

'My name is Geoffrey Wilmington,' he managed to blurt between chattering teeth.

'I asked you what your game is,' I said, 'not what your name is. What are you up to?'

For a moment I feared he was going to conk out on me. His head went back and his mouth opened wide as he sucked in air. I felt only curiosity, not pity. Seconds ago he'd been advising me how to catch the next London to Manchester express in the back of my neck.

'There's a group of us,' he said desperately. His eyes

291

wouldn't meet mine. They were roving everywhere, except to my face. He was scanning the whole restaurant. I looked around to see if there were more men in astrakhan coats hanging about but, apart from a waitress collecting trays and clattering them into a trolley, the place was as lonely as a pauper's grave.

'Talk sense,' I muttered. 'What do you advertise yourselves as, Suicides Anonymous?'

'You don't understand.'

'I understand that you were advising me to kill myself.'

'That's what we do. We get people to kill themselves.'

He groaned and scanned the room again. It was as if his eyes were beseeching some invisible person to intervene. The effect was frightening. I was already jumpy after my midnight stroll through the Meadows. Who was he expecting? It crossed my mind to chin him and drag him out into the car park but as he peered relentlessly round the room I followed his gaze.

In one corner a CCTV lens seemed to be winking in mockery at me. .

That was it. The neon lights suddenly seemed harsher. Shadows seemed deeper and there was a chill as if the stuffy chip-scented air had all been sucked into outer space.

The man was serious.

'I'm going to take you to the police,' I said, letting all the air out of my lungs suddenly.

'What for?' he asked. Taut, closely shaven skin and thin lips gave his face the appearance of a death's-head as he attempted a ghastly grin. 'There's no law against talking to people.'

As he drew on some inner reserve of courage a change came over his expression. Frantic fear was replaced by benign benevolence. His chalk-white face looked more normal for the early hour.

'The group I belong to believe that most people would

be better off dead than alive,' he said. 'We think it's our duty to give those who're hovering on the brink a helping hand. Why don't you admit it? You were making up your mind to kill yourself when I approached you.'

'Was I hell!' I barked. 'If I was to kill myself a lot of people would be very happy. I've no intention of giving them the satisfaction.'

'You shouldn't be like this,' he moaned.

'Like what?' I snarled.

He shook his head.

Light dawned. I put my hand in his pocket and pulled out a small enamel and gold pill box. I opened it and tiny square pills spilled across the table top.

'What are they?'

'Let me go and I'll tell you. You're hurting my wrist.'

I released him and he quickly gathered the pills up.

'Not so fast. You put one of these in my coffee, didn't you?'

He shook his head. 'I know who you are,' he gasped. 'I didn't want to say before. You're the one the tabloid rags thought was this so-called Mangler.'

'So what?'

'Are you sure you don't want to end it all? There are other ways . . .'

'Mate,' I grunted, 'I'll end you if you don't tell me what you're up to.'

His coffee cup was still full although the coffee was cold. I took one of the pills and stirred it well in. His eyes followed my every movement as if he was trying to slow down time.

For one who claimed to be helping others to shuffle off this mortal coil he was in an indecent terror of doing the same. Something was wrong, but I couldn't fathom it. He struggled to wet his lips and speak but all that came out was a sort of hoarse squawk. I pushed the coffee cup into his trembling lips.

'No, it's just a medication,' he groaned.

'In that case you won't mind drinking it.'

'No!'

'Drink it, or I'll kill you where you sit,' I ordered callously.

He gulped a mouthful down, but I realised that he was trying to retain the liquid in his mouth. To back up my threat I grabbed his throat. This time his eyes were imploringly fixed on me.

'Drink!' I ordered.

He swallowed, and, still clutching his neck, which was slippery with sweat, I made him down the whole cup.

Then I sat back and watched him with narrowed eyes.

I had to know more.

Nothing happened.

15

'Is he still out there?

'Speculation over the identity of the Mangler increased yesterday following a police statement that the Mangler may not be one man but several. "Intensive inquiries are continuing and more officers are being deployed," said a police spokesman. Asked why the police had initially denied the existence of the Mangler he stated, "At first incidents appeared to be unrelated. We now believe that this was a deliberate attempt to mislead our investigations and that more than one man must be involved."'

Report in local papers

'So what're the pills?' I asked after what seemed like an age. 'You'd better tell me, or I swear I'll make you swallow the whole box.'

'It's just a mild hypnotic.'

'And what is the effect you were so disappointed that I didn't show?'

'I said . . . it's hypnotic. It makes a person more open to suggestions.'

'And I was supposed to put my head on the railway track?'

He nodded.

'What's to stop me ordering you to do the same?'

'I wouldn't . . . It doesn't work like that. You have to be open to the suggestion.'

'I see, but I don't see,' I muttered. 'This group you belong to, the people who think we'd all be better off dead . . .'

'Some people call us Satanists,' he whined, 'but that isn't an accurate description.'

'Cut out the fine distinctions. Why the hell are you here in a motorway café at this unearthly hour persuading a total stranger to kill himself?'

'It's my mission. Our group try to have someone here at this time at least once a week. Tonight was my turn.'

He sounded like a double-glazing salesman describing a routine assignment. I knew he was lying. I tried to remember if he'd been seated in his corner when I came in. He hadn't been.

'You're lying, aren't you? You've already said you know who I am. Someone sent you here after me, didn't they?'

He shook his head. 'No, I told you. It's my turn to be here. Your face was in all the papers.'

That was believable enough, certainly about my face, but I still wasn't convinced.

'Are you telling me no one would notice a constant stream of suicides emerging from this service station?'

'My duty's not just here. I go to Leeds, Newcastle, all over. There are lots of places where lonely people need my advice.'

'And your pills –' I snarled – 'do they need them?'

He shook his head. 'No.'

This time his word had the ring of truth, but I still wasn't prepared to accept that our meeting was just chance. His caper sounded too much like Neville Fraser's bragging to be a coincidence.

'Give me your mobile,' I demanded.

'I haven't got one.'

My hand went towards his neck before he caved in.

'Here,' he cried, plucking it out of an inside pocket as if it was burning his fingers.

I took it. It was brand new. I clicked the call register. There was nothing in it except 'Number Erased', no other numbers. I tried 1471. 'Number Withheld.'

I thumped him hard. He groaned.

'Tell me the truth, you bastard!' I growled.

'Is this how you killed those women?' he whined. He looked ready to wet himself. His eyes were still searching the room for invisible helpers.

An angry answer was almost on my lips when I decided that I might get more information by going along with his fantasy.

'What if it is?' I leered. 'Someone like you should be happy in the company of a murderer.'

That seemed to get to him. He fixed his gaze on the CCTV camera.

'On your feet, Wilmington,' I snorted. 'We're going walkies.'

Once again there was a panic reaction.

'Oh, come on,' I muttered, trying to prise him out of his seat. 'I'm not really a murderer. Anyone who knows me will tell you I wouldn't hurt a fly.'

He shuddered again and clutched the edge of the table. I tried once more, but the more I tried to persuade him the more sinister I sounded. That's the trouble with threats: people tend to believe them.

'Listen, you idiot,' I snapped eventually, 'all I want is a lift home and some answers.'

Spookily, this reassurance seemed to work. His face lit up with hope.

'We'll go in my car?'

'Yeah, I left the hearse at home.'

I shepherded him into the car park where he led me towards a new Bentley. One new Bentley's like another, but this one was the same colour as the one I'd seen at La Venezia. Another coincidence? I felt a surge of hope that I might be on the point of getting a few relevant answers.

'There's still time,' Wilmington said expectantly. 'The London train's often late.'

I cringed. He didn't give up easily. Looking at the car I nervously wondered if his eagerness to get me in it meant it was fitted with some James Bond-type ejector seat that would fling me out into the cold night air once I'd settled into the passenger seat.

So when he'd zapped the car open I made him remove his overcoat, incidentally noting that it was of the finest mohair. I pulled the sleeves inside out and then made him put it on again, back to front. He made feeble protests while I buttoned him up.

'This isn't necessary,' he lamented, when I pushed him into the passenger seat and fastened his seat belt. 'I was only trying to help you.'

There was a rich scent of new leather inside the Bentley. There didn't seem to be any secret buttons, but would I recognise them if there were? I checked the mileage. There was less than five thousand miles on the clock. Wilmington's apparent wealth made his hobby even harder to explain. Was he involved in some kind of Faustian bargain – worldly wealth in exchange for evil deeds? Whatever, he was as sinister as a barrel-load of left-handed corkscrews.

'Please let me go,' he begged. There were tears streaming down his face.

I stared at him, racking my brain to decide what to do with him next. It's embarrassing to watch a grown man cry. I was at a loss. He looked like a turtle, with his scrawny neck and close-shaven head poking out of the reversed collar. My resolve to get information out of him at all costs was evaporating, he was so pathetic. Perhaps I ought to dump him in some lonely spot, but then I'd be accused of car-jacking.

There was no turning back.

How many sad individuals had he put his macabre proposal to? I tried to persuade myself that he deserved whatever was coming to him. How many more times would he use his drug on some sad unfortunate? Was it down to me to stop him? In Holland he'd probably be given a civic decoration.

There was one thing that was a little bit closer to home . . .

'So you knew who I was before you approached me?' I said.

'I thought I did, but your identity was unimportant. I would have approached anyone looking as sorry for himself as you did. It's a regular mission I have. There's a rota.'

'Rubbish!' I muttered.

'You looked suicidal and I wanted to help you.'

'Help me to kill myself?'

'Believe me, I know many painless ways. I can make it easy.'

'Shut it!' I yelled. 'The CCTV camera's part of your little game, isn't it? You wanted pictures.'

'No, no there was nothing like that,' he said unconvincingly.

'Who else was going to watch the charming scene? Do you have home movies of your suicide victims?'

'No, no, you can kill me but I can't tell you anything about my group.'

There was silence for a while. He looked very determined. Short of action that I wasn't prepared to take, such as roasting his feet over a slow fire, there was no way I could get him to spill the beans.

'I won't kill you, but I might thrill you,' I said as I started the car. 'Perhaps I ought to pop down to the track and tie you on it like one of those old silent film heroines and then you'll know what it's like, waiting for Virgin Rail to deliver you to the next world.'

This produced a whinny of fear.

'Just joking!'

Wilmington craned his neck to look back at the restaurant.

Wilmington may have been in a paroxysm of funk but I was getting the jitters too. Imagining a coven of angry

Satanists charging to his rescue, I decided it was time to make a hasty exit.

'Who are you expecting?' I asked as I slipped the luxury car into gear and turned towards the southbound M6.

'No one,' he insisted.

I put my foot down when we got onto the motorway and then cruised towards the nearest exit. There didn't seem be anyone following us, unless they really were on broomsticks.

'Talk!' I ordered.

It all came out in a rush – not that I could make much sense of his ravings. He seemed less nervous as we put miles between ourselves and the service area.

'The group I'm in, we don't worship spirits or anything. It's like an existential adventure, the ultimate in extreme sport.'

'You're barking mad.'

'No, it's all organised. For each person I persuade to commit suicide I get two hundred points.'

'Not on your reward card?' I quipped.

'No really, there's a league.'

'Names, let me have these people's names.'

'I've told you, kill me if you like but I'm not saying anything else.'

I felt a spurt of anger. What gave him the right to encourage people to kill themselves?

A bridge was coming up and I swung the Bentley onto the hard shoulder and accelerated towards the concrete pillars.

'How many points for a double suicide?' I cackled.

Wilmington put his head back and let out a full-blooded scream.

At the last possible second I swung the heavy car away from the bridge and cut the speed right down. His face was covered in sweat. For an extreme sport enthusiast he was pretty yellow.

'Talk, you wimp!' I prompted. 'What are you really up to? The truth this time.'

'We're post-modern,' he croaked. 'There is no reason for what we do that you could understand.'

I laughed aloud. 'Try me!' I snapped. If Wilmington was a liar, he was at least inventive.

'We don't believe in Satan, or a personal devil any more than many Christians believe in a personal deity. The Satan concept just gives us a convenient focus of unity.'

'Lovely,' I commented.

The scorn in my voice worked better than my previous threats.

'Why do people climb mountains?' he gabbled. 'Is it because they're there or because they're half in love with death? We're realists. We know that death is the ultimate thrill. You say I'm a wimp and maybe I am, but watching people go through with it, helping them to take that last step, well it gives you a wonderful buzz.'

I groaned.

'People in your position take up golf,' I said.

'Scoff if you like, but what are the most popular stories in newspapers? Crime stories! Some of us are drawn to the idea of perverse crime because we want to break out of our boring existence. Look at me for instance, I'm a banker . . . my card's in there.' He jerked his head at the glove compartment.

Leaning over, I opened it and took out a card.

'Ask yourself why you've committed crime.'

'I haven't!'

'But everyone perceives that you have, so it's the same as if you've done it,' he said angrily.

'No, it isn't. There's such a thing as objective truth.'

He greeted my words with a hollow laugh.

'You're simple, aren't you? OK, say you're innocent if you want to. Imagine you were a killer. That shouldn't be hard. Ask yourself why are you drawn to it? Isn't it because you want to experience the strange sensations of wickedness?'

'I'd like to experience the strange sensation of being in a nice warm bed.'

'So there!' he crowed. 'You do live for sensation, just like the rest of us. The only difference between you and me is that I prefer really refined sensations, like a gourmet who loves the finest food.'

I concentrated on the driving while he rambled on. I turned off the motorway towards Holmes Chapel.

'Won't you consider the possibility of ending your wretched existence?' he pleaded. 'What is there left for you now? You may have got away from the baying crowd for the time being but they'll catch you in their net eventually.'

'I told you, I'm innocent.'

'What does that matter? They perceive that you're guilty and they'll convict you. You'll spend the rest of your life penned up with sex murderers and paedophiles. Better to end it now. I can see you're a brave man. Make a clean break. I have sure ways, you don't need to feel any pain.'

'Thanks, but no thanks,' I said.

By now I was convinced that Wilmington believed every word he was saying. The only explanation that fitted was insanity.

We continued in silence for some miles. Dawn was breaking and there was a thick skein of mist across the road. The huge car cut through it in effortless silence.

We reached the A34 and cruised through Wilmslow and Cheadle, remorselessly on towards Manchester. I noticed that Wilmington now became more and more agitated. He squirmed against his bonds. I leaned across him and yanked his seat belt tight.

'If you haven't got the guts, let me end it myself,' he suggested.

'You want to kill yourself now?'

'The penalty for revealing the existence of our group is worse than death.'

'Oh dear,' I said.

'There's just one chance. Take me to a church. If I renounce what I've been doing I might be able to break away.'

'I thought you didn't really believe in Satan?'

'The symbolism is important.'

Wilmington had an answer for everything, that's what convinced me that he was a paranoid schizophrenic. The constant mood swings between elation and despair, the searching for an invisible companion, the recurrent fear, all suggested a mental patient who'd missed his medication.

'Is there someone at home?' I asked, wondering whether to drop him there or take him straight into a psychiatric unit.

'Take me to a church,' he stated. 'St Jude's in Old Trafford. There's a priest there who'll look after me.'

I considered the alternatives, including Jack Rix gleefully arresting me for kidnap, and decided to humour him.

I drove through Didsbury and Chorlton and on to Old Trafford. Wilmington was definitely suffering severe mental anguish. The backward glances continued. His eyes were rolling. He looked like a man on the point of a particularly painful death. I found my way to the church, near Ayres Road, easily enough and parked.

The sight of a raving schizophrenic in the company of a well-known murder suspect might be too much for the most stout-hearted clergyman so I decided to remain in the background while Wilmington approached the priest for sanctuary. I helped him out of the car and released him from his improvised strait-jacket. He offered no resistance. By this time he was making curious little mewing sounds to himself. I shuddered to think what was going on inside his head.

Having gained his freedom, he raced up to the presbytery door and began pounding away frantically. After a surprisingly short interval, lights came on, the door opened and a tall, solidly built figure, clad from neck to ankle in a black cassock, appeared. I couldn't make out his face against the bright light streaming from behind him, but there seemed to be a lot of hair and possibly a beard. However, he towered over the diminutive Wilmington, relieving me of any fear for the cleric's safety.

Words were exchanged and then the priest put his arm round the banker and scanned the street. As I was now on the other side I hoped he'd take me for a casual bypasser. He led the tormented man inside and shut the door.

I set off to leg it back to Chorlton through early morning calm disturbed only by rattling milk floats and racing newspaper vans. The night seemed like a dream or perhaps a nightmare. I put my hand in my pocket and touched the business card Wilmington had given me.

That was real.

I tried to rationalise the events. Neville Fraser had told a similar tale to Geoffrey Wilmington: that a gang was on the loose doing evil tricks just for the sheer hell of it. Perhaps Fraser had gleaned the story from the same source as Wilmington – the nearest large mental hospital.

I was on the edge of exhaustion when I eventually reached Thornleigh Court. It was outside my own front door that I discovered the truth of at least one remark that Wilmington had made: the most popular stories in newspapers are the crime stories. At least four reporters were lounging in their cars and keeping the entrance of my flat under their beady gaze. I doubled back. I was in despair until I came to a phone box.

This was one of those occasions when you begin to

reckon up how many friends you've got. It was too early for the Coes. That left Ruth Hands. I dialled her number.

Arthur answered and he didn't sound at all thrilled at being roused by my dulcet tones. He summoned his mother. I explained the circumstances.

'Get in a taxi,' she ordered firmly. 'Arthur will pay when you arrive.'

Half an hour later I found myself in the Hands' living room, nursing a cup of milk and recounting what Fraser and Wilmington had told me.

'Mother, the poor man's obviously off his gourd,' Arthur commented scornfully. 'His troubles have unbalanced him. Conspiracy theories are what every nut from Nutsville trades in. Mr Cunane can't find any evidence to keep you shelling out money to him so now he's inventing some.'

'It's not invented.'

'You don't have these pills that make you commit suicide, I suppose?'

I shook my head. Somehow Wilmington had got them back into his possession.

'Shush, Arthur!' Ruth said. 'There's no need to be so harsh. Dave's been through a lot.'

I pulled Wilmington's business card out of my pocket and slung it down on the coffee table. Arthur frowned. Ruth picked it up and studied it carefully before handing it back to me.

She looked at me as if trying to read what was going on inside my head.

'You need to rest, Dave. I don't know what's going on but I intend to find out. Do you mind sleeping in poor Meg's bed?'

'I couldn't . . .' I started to protest.

'No, it will comfort me to think that her room is being used by someone in need. I insist.'

I fell asleep as soon as my head hit that hard pillow.

305

I woke feeling grubby. My head was aching. I yawned. Almost at once the door opened and Ruth appeared.

'You've slept the clock round, I'm afraid. You must have been in a dreadful state after your stay in prison but I'm afraid Wilmington's trail will be cold by now.'

'Slept the clock round,' I repeated stupidly.

'Yes. There are clothes there,' she said, pointing at a pile of new clothes on Meg's desk, 'and there's shaving kit in the bathroom.'

I had to admire her efficiency.

Twenty minutes later, and feeling better than for days, I joined her in the living room. Arthur was there. He glared at me.

'Do you want to eat now or shall we go to this church?' Ruth asked.

'Perhaps we should try to contact Wilmington first,' I said cautiously. A full day's sleep had made the events of the night more distant. I could barely credit the story Geoffrey Wilmington had told me.

'There!' Arthur said triumphantly. 'He's bottling out. I told you his story was nonsense.'

'No, it's just that in broad daylight it all seems so weird.'

'Mother, this is nothing to do with us. Even if what Mr Cunane has told us is true it doesn't have any bearing on Meg's death.'

'I feel that it does,' Ruth said. 'I think that what happened to Meg was so well covered up that we're only going to find out more by indirect methods.'

'All right, let's go,' I agreed.

Arthur insisted on driving when we got out onto the street. 'It's a hire car and you're not insured for it,' he said peevishly. The sun was shining and as I gave Arthur directions to St Jude's the events of two nights ago seemed even more unlikely.

Ruth took the lead when we arrived at St Jude's. Everything was as it had been before: the door of the presbytery, the large red brick, mock-Gothic church along-side. Everything seemed the same but somehow different in bright sunshine. There was no sign of the Bentley.

Ruth knocked on the presbytery door.

We had a long wait and she had to knock several times.

The young man who eventually opened the door to us seemed to have stepped out of a different century from the tall, gaunt, almost aggressively clerical figure I'd seen previously. He was young and short and chubby with a fresh complexion and was wearing an open-neck grey shirt and slacks.

'Father Tim Flatley,' he said in an Irish accent when Ruth introduced herself. 'Wasn't I reading something in the *Catholic Herald* about you?'

'Could be,' Ruth said cryptically.

'Yes, I know you. You're the Ruth Hands who's done marvellous work for Aids sufferers. I'm honoured to meet you.'

For once Ruth was slightly at a loss for words.

Engrossed with the celebrity, Flatley barely noticed Arthur or myself, for which I was grateful.

Ruth explained why she'd come. I admired the way she put the questions. She suggested that there was cause for concern about an individual who'd called at the presbytery.

'Disturbed was he? Well, we get plenty of that sort round here. Sometimes I think I'm running a branch of Care in the Community instead of a parish. Not that I begrudge it,' he added quickly. 'Someone's got to help the poor souls, and when did this unfortunate friend of yours call?'

'The early hours of yesterday morning,' I said. 'The other priest spoke to him.'

He looked puzzled.

'What other priest? I'm here on my own.'

My heart thumped painfully.

307

'A tall man in a black cassock. He opened the door, spoke to Wilmington and let him in.'

'There was no one here last night or for the previous three nights. I was taking a short break in Ireland.' His eyes went to the golf clubs stacked in a corner. 'My daily masses were covered by another priest but he didn't stay here and St Jude's doesn't run to a housekeeper.'

Arthur exchanged a significant glance with his mother. To his credit Flatley wasn't discounting what I said. He was as puzzled as I felt. He led us into the hallway.

'There's my Ryanair ticket,' he said, pointing to the hall table.

I picked up the ticket. Sure enough he'd arrived in Manchester at ten this morning.

'You know,' he commented, 'it's funny you should say there was someone in the house. I had a feeling when I came in that someone had been here, doors left open that I thought I'd closed and vice versa, but there was nothing disturbed. For some reason, the local scallywags seem to imagine that the clergy keep large sums of money under their beds. Old Tom Makerfield over at Our Lady's was burgled so often that he gave out that he kept a loaded gun on his bedside table.'

'Did he?' Ruth asked.

'I don't think so, but he was an eccentric, God rest his soul, and the villains believed him.'

'Look,' I insisted. 'I definitely saw this person come into this house in the early hours of yesterday. Do you mind if we have a look round?'

'I'm sure that won't be necessary,' Arthur said. 'Mr Cunane's a student of the improbable.'

'No, it's fine,' the priest said. 'You'll put my mind at rest and I'll be able to have a chat with your mother. Feel free to go anywhere you like.'

Arthur followed me doggedly from room to room with a disdainful look on his face. I looked everywhere, even in the fridge. Father Flatley didn't have a very big store of food. Two sausages and a piece of cheese constituted his entire rations. There were no obvious signs of a break-in anywhere, nor was there a body tucked into a wardrobe.

Arthur Hands started tutting impatiently but I tried to keep my cool. It's usually just a tiny detail that provides a clue and when I came to the back door I found it. The Yale lock hadn't been jemmied but when I opened it and breathed on the edge of the door there was a faint mark just visible, two parallel lines.

'Someone's had plastic to this door,' I said.

'Where?' Arthur demanded. 'I can't see it.'

'Breathe on it,' I suggested.

Instead he whipped a handkerchief out of his pocket. I thought he was going to clean his glasses for a better look but he gave the door a good wipe before I could stop him.

'Sorry,' he said when I sprang forward to stop him. 'I was just trying to see the mark better.'

'It's not there now,' I snapped angrily.

'Really? Was it ever?'

We went back to the small room overlooking the street where Father Flatley was in an animated conversation with Ruth. He looked grim.

'Mr Cunane has seen an invisible mark of forced entry but like the invisible Wilmington and the invisible priest it wasn't there when I looked,' Arthur announced.

His mother frowned.

Flatley had a very serious expression. He took no notice of Arthur.

'I hear you think you've had a brush with Satanism,' he said to me.

Arthur snorted.

'I wouldn't like to go that far,' I said.

'He's backtracking now,' Arthur muttered.

'But that's what the man said and there was definitely someone here yesterday.'

Flatley had strikingly blue eyes and he seemed to be assessing me very carefully. I met his gaze.

'It doesn't do to take these things lightly. Mrs Hands and I are both agreed on that. Strange things happen.' He pointed to his bookshelves, crammed with theological tomes and saints' lives. 'You'll find plenty of references in there and the number of suicides has rocketed recently, especially among vulnerable young men.'

Arthur had a trick of raising his eyebrows to signal disbelief and now, out of the priest's line of sight, he was furiously semaphoring his scepticism to Ruth.

'We have the scriptural references, of course, and good old C. S. Lewis, who tells us that the Devil is at his happiest and most powerful when no one believes in him.'

'Mother, do we need to listen to this?' Arthur said impatiently.

Ruth stared coldly at him, and he rose from his chair and stalked out of the room in disgust. Flatley didn't turn a hair. 'There are some who believe and there are some who don't,' he commented drily.

The way Flatley was treating my story as if it was a normal, everyday occurrence chilled me. The sceptic in me found Arthur's unbelief much more reassuring than the priest's matter-of-fact acceptance.

'I think you ought to change your locks,' I said, to cover my embarrassment.

'After what you've told me, bell, book and candle might be more in order.'

'No, Father, you do need new locks.'

'I wouldn't quarrel with you but I don't think the Diocese can spare the funds,' Flatley answered with a laugh.

In an eye blink Ruth Hands was writing him a cheque. 'You need deadlocks back and front, and secure fasteners on all the windows,' I said. 'Also an alarm system might be handy.'

Flatley pocketed the cheque with an expression of thanks and showed us to the door. 'Take care,' he said as Ruth stepped outside. 'I'll pray that your troubles are soon resolved.'

I made to follow Ruth but he wasn't finished with me. He took hold of my arm.

'Do I detect a member of my own flock, Mr *Cunane*?' he asked.

'I suppose so,' I mumbled, 'but not a very practising one.'

'Well, man, just you be careful with what you're meddling in. These are deep waters. Remember to pray and remember that the Devil has no power in this world except through influencing people. Don't let him influence you.'

To me those words proved that he was the genuine article. It struck me that if I'd listened every time a priest passed on a warning I wouldn't be where I was now.

'Put a flea in your ear, did he?' Arthur sneered when I got in the car.

'Just a word of advice,' I said quietly.

'Mother,' Arthur began in that superior tone that was definitely beginning to grate on me, 'can we just consider the facts for a moment? Mr Cunane met this Wilmington by pure chance miles from Manchester. Amazingly enough, the man confirms the story a prisoner also told him. We go to check and not only has Wilmington vanished but also the priest Mr Cunane claims to have seen. It's just one improbability piled on another. I think you should dispense with Mr Cunane's services at once.'

Ruth looked thoughtful but said nothing.

Arthur drove us towards the university. He parked on Stretford Road.

'Well?' he asked turning to Ruth.

'These Satanists could have arranged that the fake priest was at the church just in case things went wrong for Wilmington,' she said stubbornly. 'I'm not giving up on this yet.'

Arthur got out of the car, slammed the door, and strode off towards the Metropolitan University without a backward look.

'Are you telling me the truth?' Ruth asked.

'If you don't believe that I might as well follow Arthur.'

'Don't worry about Arthur. He's always been headstrong. What shall we do next?'

'I want to see the material Michael Coe dug up.'

'Touch base at the office, but I want to check up on this Wilmington before he's had time to cover his tracks.'

16

'Police accused of cover-up!
'Yesterday Alexander Petrovic (41) father of the second Mangler
victim, Marisa Petrovic (19), and leader of the newly formed
Justice for Mangler Victims group accused the police of organising a cover-up. He said, "First there is no Mangler. Then there
is one Mangler and a man arrested but set free. Now there
are many Manglers. It is plain the police force are playing games
with us. They know who is responsible. It is someone in a high
place and the police are protecting him." Mr Petrovic, a refugee
from the former Yugoslavian republic of Bosnia, said also that
such things had happened in his former country when powerful officials protected their own. Asked if he believed the
killer was a politician in this country he replied, "Who knows?
It could even be one of your Royal Family. Death by firing
squad is too good for such people." '
Report in the *Sun*

My heart was in my boots as I walked through unfa-
miliar streets towards my new 'office'. It was the first
time in my working career that I was starting out in
premises that I didn't own or rent myself. I had to face
it. I was an employee.

The address on Dutton Street, behind a brewery, and
not very far from my previous address in Strangeways,
was no better and no worse than I'd imagined. The office
was up a narrow flight of stairs from the street and at
least had its own entrance. There were two quite large
rooms, a storeroom, small kitchen, and bathroom. Only
one of the rooms made any pretence to be described as
furnished. There were two upright chairs, a battered

313

second-hand desk with a word processor, an armchair and two filing cabinets. An electric kettle resided on a tray in the corner, with one chipped cup and a jar of cheap instant coffee for company.

At least Celeste had left me the means to supply myself with a drink.

The ambience was more or less the same as I'd started out with at Pimpernel Investigations except for the pungent smell of Chinese food wafting up from below. I didn't know whether to laugh or cry. There was a pile of my personal possessions from Pimpernel Investigations in one corner. I spotted the bottles of Lagavulin behind the forensic science textbooks.

I picked up a bottle and looked for a glass. I pulled open the desk drawer to discover a neat stack of files, including the original Meg Hands file. Why did everything in this case revolve around reading files? I hadn't even completely read that file, now there were half a dozen more. I flicked through them. One listed the complicated ownership of the pubs and restaurants at Castlefields. Another contained a profile of Hobby Dancer.

Later, I told myself, much later.

I went to the corner and picked up the chipped cup. I hadn't yet reached the stage of drinking whisky straight out of the bottle. I was bending down to pour myself a dram when Ruth knocked.

I was grateful for the knock.

I clumsily put the bottle back behind the books and switched the kettle on as she entered. Suddenly, I was all too well aware that she was paying the rent on this office. That was not at all like the early days of Pimpernel Investigations, when I'd been poor but independent.

'Are you ready?' she asked impatiently. She indicated the files. 'You can read those later. I think we need to get after this Wilmington right away.'

'So she who pays the piper calls the tune?'

'What do you mean?'

'Ruth, you hired me as an investigator not as your assistant.'

'You're in charge.'

'No, you're bustling me off in search of this Wilmington but he's nothing to do with the job you're supposed to be employing me for – finding out who killed Meg.'

She clenched her fists angrily and I prepared for a tirade, but nothing came.

'Stupid man!' she rasped in a barely audible voice. 'What do you propose to do? Sit here on your butt?'

'That might be a good idea as the indefatigable Michael Coe has supplied enough reading matter to keep me busy for a week.'

'Don't you see that Wilmington and Meg's death are all tied up together?'

'No,' I said coldly. 'I'm afraid I don't buy into Satanism, at least not in the way you and Father Flatley do. I think Wilmington was either mad or more likely was involved in some complicated scam. For all I know he was recruiting organ donors. There's money in that. The visit to St Jude's was his exit strategy.'

'I can't accept that,' she said awkwardly. 'He was doing the Devil's work.'

'Ruth, the big lead we've got now is Neville Fraser, not Wilmington. He was down at Castlefields.'

'But not on the weekend of Meg's death.'

'Yes, according to Rix he was in custody. Most people think that means safely under lock and key but it doesn't. They let them out on one excuse or another. Do you know how many crimes have been committed by people supposedly in custody? There are all kinds of ways he could have been released without Rix's knowledge.'

'So?'

'So I want to go through these files and see if Michael Coe turned up anything Rix might have missed about Fraser.'

I could see she wasn't about to give up on Satanism. She'd been sniffing sulphur from the first moment of Meg's disappearance.

'It can't do any harm for you to look up his address,' I conceded, 'but keep your distance. You're too well known.'

The address on Wilmington's card was an office in Fountain Street: Geoffrey Wilmington, Independent Financial and Banking Services, Floor 9, Adastral House.

When she'd gone I settled into the files. That wasn't easy. It took me a long time to concentrate. Prison doors kept slamming inside my head.

The security firm that supplied the bouncers to La Venezia was the oddly named Black Cat Services. Michael had found the names of some of the directors. They meant nothing to me but one was familiar: Professor Douglas Carver. What was a university professor doing in such a company? Presumably Carver was there to add respectability. There was information on the ownership of the various pubs and restaurants. None of the names rang any bells with me as far as criminal connections went. Michael had concluded the same. O. R. G. Hobby Dancer owned his own company. He'd produced several bestselling computer games and was reputed to be worth at least forty million. He spent much of his time travelling in search of ideas for his games.

Michael didn't think that Ted Cosgrove was involved in anything illegal. He explained the massive deliveries to La Venezia by the bar-restaurant's success.

My studies were interrupted after a couple of hours by the return of Ruth.

'There is no ninth floor at Adastral House. It stops at eight,' she explained despondently.

'So Arthur was right, I imagined everything.'

'No, you didn't imagine this,' she said, brandishing the business card. 'Someone went to the trouble of printing a fake card. Listen, Dave, honesty time. If this had been the genuine card of some man who knew nothing about your visitation in the motorway café I'd have believed Arthur's idea. But it's a complete fake. There's got to be some deviltry involved. Do you still think they're just some bunch of ordinary criminals? We've got to find out more.'

'Ruth, you can get business cards printed in any print shop. I could have done it.'

She laughed scornfully.

It was startling to see her intensely serious expression change suddenly. I was repelled by her fixation, almost ready to throw the whole thing up, retreat to my parents' home on the moors, and lick my wounds in solitude.

'But, if you'd done it just to keep yourself in work you'd have given the name of a person who existed but couldn't be traced, so then you could have spent weeks tracking him down. No, this is the Devil's work.'

Bile rose to my mouth. I realised that from within the depths of her obsession, which seemed to have grown during my time in prison, every scrap of evidence I produced would be twisted until it pointed back to Old Nick as the author of her troubles.

I looked round the threadbare office. Was it worth staying in business on these terms? It was a toss-up. I decided that I was more likely to find out who had set Neville Fraser on me if I stayed in Ruth's employ. Anyway, what right had I to meddle with my employer's religious beliefs?

By now it was late afternoon. I knew I wasn't going to settle with the files. They'd have to wait.

Being rich has certain advantages. Using her name as an introduction Ruth phoned all the independent financial consultants listed in the Yellow Pages and got an immediate hearing. No one knew Wilmington.

When we arrived at the Central Library to check the electoral rolls they were getting ready to close.

'This is hopeless,' Ruth muttered.

'There is one thing,' I suggested. 'He was driving a brand-new Bentley. Unless he stole it his name must be listed somewhere.'

'The dealers will have shut.'

'Listen Ruth, I'm starving. I've only had a glass of milk and a couple of sandwiches. I need to go home to eat and think.'

She frowned. Human frailties were not a big thing to Ruth but she drove me back to Chorlton. When we reached Thornleigh Court there were still two journalists staking out the flat.

'You'd better go,' I told Ruth. 'If they see me with you, God knows what they'll publish.'

She turned the car round in the road and headed back to her flat.

I made my way through the rhododendron bushes at the other side of the building, rapped on a window and persuaded a lady who'd known me all the years I'd lived in the block to let me in via the ground-floor fire door.

Preparing food and cleaning my kitchen utensils has always stimulated my meagre mental processes. Perhaps I only think properly on the prospect of a full stomach. Anyway, I was grating cheese and glancing out of my kitchen window over the Meadows when the thought struck.

Did I believe in the Devil?

Yes, I suppose I did, at least as a religious explanation of the inexplicable. If Conan Doyle, creator of the world's most logical literary detective, could believe in the existence of fairies, I could certainly entertain a proposal that almost everyone has believed in for centuries. But, still in religious vein, it was Father Flatley who'd implied that Old Nick relies on human agents.

318

I looked down at the lump of Cheddar in my hand. Thoughts of food receded. Was I losing my marbles? Did I need a long rest? Or did I need what Wilmington had kindly suggested, a nice lie-down on a railway track?

I felt that same chill and sense of oppression that had come over me in the motorway café when Wilmington calmly discussed the advantages of suicide as an answer to my problems. But it wasn't just Wilmington, was it? There was also the psychopath, Fraser. He shared Wilmington's weird hobby. I could accept the coincidence, say, of meeting two fanatical train spotters in completely unrelated circumstances, but Fraser and Wilmington, both keen on seeing me top myself? No, that couldn't be a coincidence.

So there was a bunch of crazies on the loose and they had me high on their list of items to be taken care of. But what did I know that could be a danger to anybody? Nothing.

I took out three eggs and began making an omelette. It was as I folded the grated cheese in that I realised that the gang must have been tipped that I was out on the Meadows the previous night. I'd evaded the press but not them. The sensation that someone was stalking me as I walked along the river bank, and then the meeting with Wilmington, weren't coincidences.

Moving mechanically, I turned my omelette out of the pan and arranged it on a plate. I buttered some bread and started looking for the tomato ketchup before I realised that I'd already done both of those things. The food tasted like cardboard when I started eating. There was only one person who'd known I was heading out to the Meadows that late in the evening. My appetite had left me but I forced myself to eat and tried to think about my next move.

I hated the thought of sitting around while strangers decided my fate. I had to do something. I had to strike out somewhere at somebody. But at who?

Despite what I'd said to Ruth, it all came back to Wilmington. He was my most recent contact with this mysterious mob. So where was he now?

Where had he been expecting to be?

I fixed the security switch for the living-room lights so they'd come on at irregular intervals during the night and then went down to the ground floor and exited through the fire door. When I reached the street I checked cautiously in each direction but there was no one about. I cursed the fact that I didn't have a car and began walking to Stretford to take the Metrolink into town. At the station I was the only person waiting on the platform so unless my mysterious persecutors could deploy a whole squad of radio-linked pursuers I was in the clear.

As the tram rattled over the rails into central Manchester I clung to the one fact I had. Wilmington, Satanist, suicide counsellor or simple criminal, was in mortal terror of his 'friends' when I saw him last.

Getting out to Ashley Gribbin's house in Hale Barns on public transport was hell but I finally arrived outside her front door just before eleven.

'Go away!' she screamed furiously when she identified me looming through her tasteful leaded lights.

'I just want to ask you something,' I shouted back. 'Does every conversation have to be through a solicitor?'

'Go away, I'm calling the police.'

'Go ahead,' I challenged. 'I'm sure Rix would love to know why you sheltered me the night after the Aycliffe murder.'

'Pig!' she screamed.

'And you're the one who told me to be as chauvinist as I liked!'

Dialogue was replaced by the sound of loud sobs.

'You've come to beat me up because of the abortion, haven't you?'

'Contrary to what you might think from reading the

papers, beating up women isn't part of my repertoire. I just want your technical expertise.'

'Oh no, you don't! That's what you said last time and I ended up carrying your child.'

Not for long, I thought bitterly.

'Look, let me in, Ashley,' I wheedled. 'You're going to rouse the neighbours, which is the last thing either of us needs. I'm not here to harm you, and as for what happened last time, well, I know you must have thought you had good enough reasons.'

There was much turning of keys and clinking of chains before the door eventually opened.

What a change in a few months! I tried to hide my shock but couldn't. Ashley's face was gaunt, eyes sunken in. Smooth curves and inviting roundness had been replaced by angularity. She looked as if she was being held together by willpower alone.

I must have stared at her oddly.

'I've been ill,' she gasped, 'very ill. Don't flatter yourself that I look like this because of you.'

'What was wrong? ... I mean, how are you? I've never wished you harm. You must know that. Nobody knows what happened between us. You didn't need to warn me off.'

'Christ, Dave! Spare me the code of the Woosters. Who do you think you are? Some sort of knight-errant out of a thirties detective story? I was unwell,' she continued sadly, putting her hand across her forehead as if to indicate the cause of her troubles. 'All right, it was a breakdown, if you like to use that word. I had to go away for a while.'

'Where's Basil?'

'His father's looking after him for a change. I'm free from encumbrances for the time being but I guess that doesn't matter to you any more. What a pair we'd have made: Mad Ashley and Convict Dave! – the couple from hell!'

321

I looked away. References to hell made me nervous.

Her face was screwed up with suppressed anger, though whether at me or her situation was hard to tell. She seemed to be struggling to stay on her feet and I wondered if she was on the sauce but the answer to that came in her next words.

'We both messed up big time, didn't we, Dave? But we're both still here. At least, I think I am. Although, with the muck I'm taking, I feel as if I'm floating about fifty miles above the earth.'

'Are you back at work?' I asked, thrashing around for a way to change the conversation.

'You bastard! You really did come round here for my technical expertise.'

'I only asked.'

'For your information I've been back at work for the last two weeks. I really think I'd prefer it if you'd come round to kick hell out of me. Maybe pain would make me feel real.'

'Not a chance, Ashley,' I said as my own anger flared. 'I wouldn't touch you with a barge pole. Your lawyer warned me off, remember? And as for the baby – '

'Don't you dare throw that in my face,' she said in a voice as cold as an Arctic winter. 'Was I supposed to bring the Manchester Mangler's child into the world? Can you imagine what the tabloids would've made of it? Besides, I have Basil to think of.'

I said nothing.

'Wipe that smug look off your face! What is it that you want?'

I sighed. What did I want? Certainly not sex. The urge that had once made me willing enough to leap into her bed was entirely dead.

'Oh, go on!' she said irritably. 'Ask me your stupid questions. They can't be any crazier than the ones I have to listen to all day long. I can't imagine why most people bother staying alive at all.' She shook her head from side to side. 'Day after day, same old thing . . . wait till your arteries fur up and then you snuff it, and for what? Better have done now.'

I couldn't recognise her voice. I remembered that suicide is the occupational disease of pathologists. By the sound of her Wilmington wouldn't have had to use much persuasion to get her head on the tracks. I felt sick.

'Ashley!' I said sharply, moving towards her. 'You're just a bit down. You need a long holiday.'

'Shut up!' she snorted, brushing my arm away. 'I can't take any more of that crap. I've been told to pull myself together so often that I feel like a contortionist.'

'Well, it's true. You need to go on a long holiday. Go back to Jamaica.'

'Are you offering to take me?'

'Ashley, you're not yourself. You need a long break away from everything. What does all this matter? I'm surprised they let you go back to work in this state.'

'Oh, now we're back to the truth. It's my job you're interested in, not me. For once in your life be honest enough to tell me the real reason you came and then get out.'

I gave up. She was right. My interest in her had died with the aborted child.

'I think someone I know might have turned up dead but I don't think the name I knew him by is his real name.'

'You do surprise me, Dave! A dead person, just up your street. Am I supposed to know the details of every sudden death in Greater Manchester?'

'I thought you might see the ones taken in for autopsy.'

'You don't change, do you?' she asked with a laugh. For a moment the atmosphere lightened a little. 'Maybe I do have the information you want. Come into my computer room.'

She led me into a small room off the entrance hall.

'I can access the departmental database from here. All recent cases will be listed.'

She logged on to her computer and told me to look away while she entered passwords.

'So what are we looking for? I've got all types of cadavers on offer here, some who wanted to land up in my little beauty parlour, and some who didn't.'

'This one didn't.'

'Little do you know.'

'He was a well-dressed, middle-aged white man, beautifully manicured hands, quite small with a bony face. He was wearing an astrakhan coat.'

'That narrows it down,' she commented scornfully. 'Only a hundred of those. When did your pixie pop off?'

'In the last two days.'

She studied the screen for some time.

'I've got a diabetic who dropped dead in a changing room at Selfridges, Exchange Square. He was struggling to get himself into a pair of designer jeans, small-sized ones. He was too big for his britches . . . but he can't be your man, he's only twenty-nine. Here's a myocardial infarction from Salford, right age, but sixteen stone so that rules him out. Oh, here we go! A drug overdose found stiff at the wheel of his Bentley.'

She must have clocked my expression.

'Wow! I've hit the jackpot, three cherries at once. Has my number come up again on the Dave Cunane wheel of fortune?'

'Stop it, Ashley,' I muttered.

'Show time!' she laughed. 'These days I take my humour where I find it.'

'Take your medication, you mean!'

'Ooooh, Dave's getting nasty! Right, the Bentley driving junkie it is! . . . Percy Pullman, an insurance and banking executive from Halifax. Address . . . thirty-six Park Drive,

Halifax, West Yorkshire, on his way home from a business meeting in Manchester. Enough tracks up his arms for Virgin Rail, but this time he was injecting between his toes for some reason. Heart stopped . . . bompity, bompity, bompity . . . *bomp*!' She clapped her hands to demonstrate. 'He must have got hold of some of the wrong stuff in Manchester because the heroin was pure. Poor bugger, he was so desperate for a fix that he picked a police observation point on the M62 to shoot up.'

'Do that a lot, do they? Junkies? Pull into a police lay-by for their fix?'

'They do it anywhere . . . Oh, I get it, we're back in the Dave Cunane school of morbid coincidences.'

'Is there any chance that I could see the body?'

'Don't want much, do you, Sherlock?'

'I need to confirm that your Percy Pullman is the person I think he was.'

'So, in for a penny, in for pound, is it? How's that for alliteration? Peter Piper picked . . . This is turning into a real adventure. I really feel like Dr Watson. Oh no, he was a man, wasn't he? And my troubles are of the female persuasion.'

'Ashley . . .'

'Let me check. This is elementary. I'll have to phone the mortuary chargehand to see if the body's been removed for disposal.'

She led me back to the hall after closing down the computer.

'Isn't it a bit late for phoning?' I asked.

'No, Albert's there all night. Can't leave our dear departed without a constant companion to see they don't get into bad ways. *Hey, nudge, nudge, wink, wink!* Necrophilia's absolutely rife in south central Manchester, horrific in the Chorlton area. A body's not safe for a moment. Albert'll welcome the chance to talk to someone.'

She spoke into the phone for some time. Looking at her back I realised that she was as mad as anyone can get. How flattering that I'd been the object of her affections for so long! Maybe she'd always been mad and I was just too thick to notice. I felt as if someone had walked over my grave. If things had gone another way I'd have been married to her months ago.

'Right, you're in luck,' she said. 'Better than the late Mr Pullman was, anyway. It's still there. They've had trouble getting rid. No next of kin to claim the remains. In the end his firm's had to step in. He was in insurance, after all. The corpse's due to be picked up by a Halifax undertaker for a private cremation over there next week. Identification was confirmed by an office junior.'

'Lovely.'

She shrugged. 'Sorry for him, are you? If he was mainlining, he probably got dumped by all his relations long ago.'

'But was still earning enough to be able to drive a Bentley?'

'Dave, the police aren't interested in this one, so stop stirring. And anyway, not every junkie's a human wreck. This one could afford his habit. He had the syringe in his hand. They figure he pulled into the police lay-by because there was a long jam on the M62 and he needed to top himself up. Only he topped himself up with the wrong stuff.'

She gave a peculiarly sinister giggle as she finished her explanation. I had to look away from her.

'I see,' I muttered.

'Dave, I know you well enough to know that you're imagining more illegalities than a Philadelphia lawyer working on piece rates could ever dream up. But you can forget it. I'm out of this and out of your life. Albert will let you into the mortuary. I told him to expect a human question mark built like a brick shithouse.'

326

'Thanks for the reference, but I was hoping you'd come with me and give chummy the once-over.'

She put her head in her hands and started laughing hysterically. Tears ran down her withered cheeks. 'You don't give up, do you? Charge straight ahead and take no prisoners.'

'But, Ashley, I know this one isn't an accidental death. He was with me two days ago in holy terror that his mates were going to do him in.'

We drove into Manchester in complete silence. Apart from Pullman, we seemed to have decided we'd nothing to talk about.

Business was surprisingly brisk at the MRI mortuary, with private ambulances lining up to take delivery. We slipped in through a side door. Albert didn't give me a second glance when he waved Ashley through to the examination room.

'He's in twenty-seven,' he shouted.

Walking with a very determined and exaggerated tread, Ashley crossed the room and pulling out the giant filing cabinet, removed the shroud from the occupant's face.

I've never been so pleased to see someone in my life. The elation was entirely genuine and owed nothing to the tension I was experiencing in Ashley Gribbin's company. I knew that when I'd been peacefully whipping up that omelette earlier the secret thought that had shaken me was that I'd imagined the whole Wilmington episode from start to finish. It was good to know that I wasn't as cracked as poor Ashley.

Wilmington's face was slightly bluish and waxy but what struck me was the relaxed, almost happy expression on his rigid features.

'I take it this is who you expected?' Ashley asked.

I nodded.

'You look as if you're about to kiss him.'

'It's nice to know that I'm not going mad.'

'All right for some!' she said, with a bitter giggle.

'He looks pleased with himself.'

'Dave,' she explained patiently, 'if someone knocks themselves off with a shot of medically pure morphine instead of street smack, this is how they look. Believe me, I've seen it before. He can't have known what he was taking, but for a second or two it must have felt as if he had a space shuttle booster strapped to his backside to take him up to junkie heaven.'

I thought about this for a moment. Had Wilmington/Pullman killed himself to order? I didn't think so. His fear of death had been too strong. He wasn't willing to go gentle into that good night.

'Even if he was forcibly injected?' I asked, remembering Meg Hands and her sudden acquaintance with single malt whisky.

'I didn't certify cause of death on this one myself – a locum pathologist, Dr Hernandez, did that – but I've no reason to believe he missed anything. It was routine. The tracks on his arms told their own story.'

'Just take a look.'

'I am looking. There are no defence injuries on the face.'

'There wouldn't be if someone was carefully faking an accidental death. They'd hardly give him a poke in the eye.'

'You never stop, do you?' she asked wearily, but she did roll back the shroud as far as the hips.

Wilmington/Pullman was a scrawny, narrow-chested individual but there was a certain wiry strength evident in his arms and shoulders. He made a healthy-looking corpse.

Ashley lifted the left arm, then she suddenly frowned and muttered, 'Oh God!' She took a pencil torch out of her pocket and shone it on the inner forearm. There were four shallow purple marks. She checked the right arm. Again there were four bruises.

'Well?' I muttered.

She took my hand and made me spread my fingers. Then she placed it over the marks. The span was just a little wider than mine.

'It looks as if he was restrained by a powerfully built man with big hands similar to your own – '

'Hold on,' I said sharply.

'Don't worry, the paws that did this were even larger than your mitts. Pullman was wearing a jacket and over-coat and the bruising only developed post mortem, which is probably why Hernandez missed it. We rush 'em through here these days. Targets, you know.'

She studied the tracks on the arms. Her attitude was entirely professional now. She rolled up the cloth and looked at the toes with a lens.

'He shouldn't have had any trouble raising a vein in his arms, despite the ectomorphic body type. He was well nourished and not at all wasted. So why, for the first time in his life, start shooting up between his toes?'

'Because the man with the big paws held him while someone else sat on his legs, took his shoe and sock off and injected him. Maybe he was making too much fuss for them to get him out of his overcoat.'

'Hmm,' she murmured. 'Say it as shouldn't, but I think you could be right for once. Well, they do say apes could write Shakespeare, given enough time.'

'Thanks, Ashley.'

'I'll have to inform the police that I'm not satisfied and we'll do a full PM this time but I don't think you should be within a mile of this building when the police get here.'

'I'm ahead of you there,' I muttered.

'I can say I had second thoughts about accidental OD because of where the car was found. Go out the side door. I'll tell Albert to forget about you.'

I turned to go.

329

Facing me in the corner of the room was a CCTV camera. My heart sank. There was another one by the exit.

'Are these linked to the city system?' I asked.

'Of course not!' she snapped. 'Do you think we want to be observed every time a cadaver's wheeled out of here? They're just there in case there's a break-in. Like private detectives, some of them are dummies.'

I didn't feel very reassured by that and she picked up my nervous expression.

'You're getting jumpy, aren't you?'

I shook my head.

'Dave, I'm going to do this PM and then I'm calling in sick and taking a holiday abroad just like you said. Seeing your face again's reminded me how sick I am. People you get involved with have a nasty habit of turning up dead.'

'It's not my fault,' I barked.

'Whatever, but I don't want to see you again. This makes us quits.'

'Thanks,' I said uncertainly, but she'd already turned her back. 'Ashley, are you going to be all right?'

'Worried about the little woman, are you?' she asked sarcastically. 'Frightened I'm going to do something I shouldn't? Don't worry, Dave. I'll stick around long enough to attend your funeral. I've still got a son who needs someone to supply him with money for his weed, don't forget.'

Once out on Oxford Road I pulled my coat up to cover as much of my face as possible. This main student route and site of innumerable muggings was bound to be covered by CCTV.

There were taxis shooting up and down the road but I decided to walk for a while to consider my next move. I walked away from the town centre, turning towards Moss Side along Moss Lane East.

I put thoughts of Ashley Gribbin out of my mind. She was a big girl now and the way things were going there was every chance that she'd be around long enough to dance on my grave.

The first idea that surfaced in my weary brain was to drag Rix along to the mortuary and shove Wilmington into his face. On second thoughts, that didn't seem such a classy idea. Those sinister marks were just a little too similar to ones my hands might have made for comfort.

Still, finding Wilmington was a break in the case. It gave me the chance to take things a little further without going to Rix. There was no way he would accept any findings from a 'civilian' unless he could somehow turn things to his own advantage.

17

'Day of Prayer: The Bishop of Manchester, the Roman Catholic
bishop of Salford, Free Church leaders and responsible figures
from the Muslim, Hindu, Sikh and Buddhist communities yesterday united in a call for a day of prayer. "We must ask the
Almighty to lift this cloud of evil which lies over our city like
a dark miasma," stated the Bishop.
'A spokesperson for Here and Now, the influential atheist
group, said, "Yapping to some vague figure in the sky won't
solve this problem. Only more police on the streets can do
that."'
Report in the *Guardian*

There was a problem if I was going to find out more
about Wilmington/Pullman.

The police would've already visited his address when
he turned up dead but when Ashley relayed the fresh
findings they'd arrive at 36 Park Drive in force. Most
likely it would be the West Yorkshire drug squad searching
for the connection that had led to the wretched insurance executive's assassination by overdose. There was no
way in the world they'd give a second's consideration to
the idea of a Satanic circle spending their evenings pro-
moting suicide and worse.

I laughed out loud at the thought of what Jack Rix
would say if I raised the issue with him. Then again, he
wouldn't say anything. He'd just summon the men in
white coats and have me sectioned as a raving loony.

So what should I do?

Stumble back home to Chorlton and forget the whole
thing?

Yes, that would be good. It would allow Neville Fraser and co. the opportunity to arrange for my demise at a time and place of their choosing. I had to act myself. I was still being paid to find the killer of Meg Hands. The method chosen to dispose of the unfortunate Wilmington bore enough similarity to Meg's death to suggest a connection.

I needed transport and the only person who could supply that was Ruth Hands. I phoned from the first call box. Even as I picked up the receiver it crossed my mind that if my comings and goings were under surveillance then so were hers.

The phone rang for several minutes before she answered. My chest felt tight.

'Ruth,' I said urgently, 'there's been a development. You were right about looking for Wilmington. I found him. He's dead.'

'I never expected anything else. Every time there's a lead – '

'No, listen. He lived in Yorkshire. I need to get to his house and turn it over for any clues before the police get there.'

There was a long pause.

'I know I'm just a foreigner but wouldn't that be illegal?'

'Yep!' I said cheerfully.

'Right,' she said briskly, 'where are you? I'll meet you.'

'Good,' I agreed. 'One more thing, is Arthur there?'

'No, he's visiting school friends in Oxford, but why ask?'

'Best not to involve him in anything illegal. OK?'

'I suppose so,' she muttered.

I gave her directions to pick me up on the Princess Parkway outside the brewery on the corner of Moss Lane East.

It wasn't much more than ten minutes later when the hired BMW cruised to a halt opposite the spot where I was lurking in the shadows. Ruth was wearing a black trouser suit and a black beret.

'Ruth, I'll drop you back at your flat,' I said as I slid in beside her.

She stopped the car in the centre of the Parkway and yanked the keys out of the ignition.

'You take me or you don't take the car,' she said laconically.

I was too tired to argue. I nodded. She started the car and did a U-turn right in the junction. A beat-up Jag with four Afro-Caribbean men shaking their fists in unison missed us by inches as she gunned the car away down the slope towards town. Horns blared. Even after midnight there's plenty of traffic at that location. Ruth hunched over the wheel. She seemed anxious to pass under the Hulme Arch at a hundred m.p.h.

'Er . . .'

'Yes, you drive,' she agreed before the words were out of my mouth.

She pulled over, we swapped positions and I took us out of central Manchester at a more sedate pace.

I thought I could easily get used to driving a BMW.

It didn't take us long to get onto the M62 eastbound. I stopped at the Birch Services and bought a street map of Halifax. Park Drive was just off Wilmington Avenue, so Pullman hadn't been original in his choice of false name. According to the map his address was a single row of houses facing a public park and backing onto a steep hillside.

'Are you going to confide, or am I just along for the ride?' Ruth asked when we turned off the motorway towards Halifax.

'Depends. Are you going to start giving me orders?'

'If you think I'll sit like a dead duck while you involve

me in a felony, you've picked the wrong woman. I've an international reputation to consider.'

'Of course, would you like me to leave you at a service area and pick you up on the way back?'

'You are, without exception, the most infuriating and difficult man I've ever met. Would I have come this far if I didn't intend to go through with whatever you have planned?'

'Maybe you would. How do I know?'

'Tell me what's going on. I've a right to know. I guess this is all about Arthur. He's the number-one suspect, isn't he?'

I said nothing.

'Oh, all right . . . sir! I'm sorry I told you to stop sitting on your butt. I promise not to order you around. But tell me what you've found out about Arthur. I'm frantic with worry.'

'I haven't found anything new about your son. I knew he was lying weeks ago.'

I explained about the absence of camomile tea in Meg's stomach.

'You knew this, yet you didn't tell me. You've let me imagine the worst possible scenario and all because your pet lady pathologist couldn't find some molecules in Meg's stomach. I suppose it didn't cross your mind that Arthur could've been mistaken about Meg drinking camomile? He didn't stand over her and pour it down her throat, did he? She might have only taken a sip and then put it to one side.'

I shrugged.

She looked as if she wanted to hit me.

Arthur had been definite that his sister had drunk camomile but it didn't seem worthwhile to argue the point.

'Can we get on?' I muttered.

'No! I want this sorted. He is my son.'

'Yes,' I agreed.

'Arthur's always been independent-minded,' she continued. 'I know he's sceptical about some things but that doesn't mean he's done anything wrong. I'll speak to him again. If he hears that Wilmington really existed –'

'That's not a good idea, Ruth. Don't tell him anything.'

'Oh, you want to spy on him? Or do you want me to do that for you?'

'It's not like that. You said you wanted to find the truth, however unpleasant it turns out to be.'

'I know the truth and so do you. There's a Satanic conspiracy which for reasons of their own the powers-that-be are ignoring. That's the only covering-up there's been.'

I sighed. I couldn't get through to her. My own position on the Satanic aspect was so fraught with ifs and buts that I hesitated explaining it to someone as forthright as Ruth Hands.

I decided to try.

'Ruth, there's some sort of group out there who're able to kill people and make it look like suicide or even to frame someone for murder.'

'Yes, and the Keystone Kops . . .'

' . . . won't believe us without a lot more evidence, which they're not even looking for. As soon as you say the word "Satanic" they switch off.'

'Stupid . . .'

'We need evidence, not folklore.'

'What's that supposed to mean?'

'If your son's tied up in this and these people think there's the slightest chance he might lead us to them . . .'

' . . . he'll get the same treatment as Wilmington,' she said, completing my words for me.

'And so might you.'

She shook her head angrily. 'There must be something. We could go back to the States.'

'Arthur may not be involved deeply. We don't know. He may think he's just keeping a friend out of trouble. It's safest to let him think you know nothing until we know everything.'

She made a noise in the back of her throat that I took as assent, before continuing, 'I haven't told you everything. There hasn't been time, what with one thing and another. Not everything's in those files at your office. Michael and Celeste had decided that they had to give up working for me and Michael didn't have time to write up everything he found. So I promised to tell you about the last thing he discovered. He'd managed to get in touch with that cleaning woman in Goa . . . Menezes, or whatever her name was. She confirmed that Meg's room was covered with photos.'

I felt a sharp feeling of satisfaction.

She looked at me uncertainly.

'Go on,' I prompted eagerly.

'It's not what you think. They weren't pin-ups of some stupid boy. They were group shots of a social gathering. According to the man Michael hired in Goa, Menezes was definite that Meg didn't have a boyfriend. She claimed she would have known if Meg had ever had a man in her room, which I could have told you without the privilege of paying nearly a thousand pounds for the information. The photos were of groups, mixed ages and sexes. Menezes thought they were something to do with the university.'

'You didn't think that was worth mentioning.'

'I would have, but a bunch of harmless snaps of Meg's college friends have nothing to do with the Satanist connection. I thought that was what you're interested in.'

'Ruth, those harmless snaps were removed after Meg's death. That must mean something.'

'Don't be so melodramatic!' she snapped. 'I'm sure there's a simple explanation. You're just trying to implicate Arthur again.'

'Did Menezes explain why she left Manchester in such a hurry?'

'Michael said she was vague about that part. She said nothing about Arthur!'

I drove on in silence, negotiating the steep hills of Halifax until we found ourselves driving slowly along Park Drive. It was made up of large detached Edwardian houses, the type with five or six bedrooms and rooms above for servants. Some had seen their best days and had been converted to flats. Others were still pristine behind their privets.

Wilmington/Pullman's house was one of the latter, gleaming under the streetlights in its fresh coats of black and white paint. There was no sign of police activity, no lights showing, and all curtains were drawn. I slowed to a halt outside. The house seemed as utterly silent and dead behind its hedge as its former occupant was.

I felt desperate to penetrate its secrets.

If the house was quiet, the street wasn't. Although it was almost one a.m. hoarse shouts and screams carried across the road from the park that faced the line of houses. Even as we watched a band of feral youths, male and female, emerged through a gap in the railings. They seemed in no hurry to leave. Shouting and cursing, pretending to fight, chasing each other up and down the pavement, and taking swigs out of bottles and cans, they seemed settled for the night.

'Where are the police when you need them?' Ruth muttered.

I broke the tension with a laugh.

We turned the corner and parked on Wilmington Avenue. There was no one stirring there.

'Now what?' Ruth asked aggressively.

'Now I walk past slowly and then I go in.'

'Gee!' she muttered scornfully. 'What about those kids?'

'I wait until they're not looking.'

'You're a master of your profession.'

'Before I do go, in case we get separated, is there anything else I should know?'

She considered for a moment.

'Sirpells. That man's been costing me a fortune. I got his reports.'

'And?'

'And what? They're still there at my flat, unopened, waiting for you.'

'Thanks.'

'Hey, you're the detective . . . so you claim. Now are we doing this thing, or are you all talk?'

'I'm going to do it and you're going to stay in the car.'

'No, I'm coming.'

I was starting to argue when a police car came round the corner. I froze. I felt like a complete fool. Even if the local fuzz didn't know yet that Wilmington had been murdered they'd know that the house of a wealthy junkie was unoccupied and they'd be keeping a close eye on it. I waited for discovery but then Ruth wrapped her arms round me and put her face against mine as police headlights illuminated us. Her acting skills were good. She had me in a serious clinch.

When I started breathing again the police car had driven on.

'Don't get any ideas,' she snapped, pushing me away as if I had leprosy. 'That was strictly business.'

In the end we both went, leaving the car on Wilmington Avenue and strolling down Park Drive hand in hand. We looked more natural that way and an empty car parked on a side street was less suspicious than one with a person in it.

The youths had gone, their cries echoing distantly along the deserted avenue. When we reached the house for the second time I made a quick scan in both directions. Apart from pigeons cooing on the roof, nothing was moving, so we opened the gates and went in. Ruth immediately snatched her hand away from mine. There was a substantial double-glazed porch, which looked resistant to forced entry, so I led Ruth round the back. Fortunately, the house wasn't overlooked by its neighbours. The back garden abutted open land and again there didn't seem much chance of being observed from that direction.

The curtains weren't drawn at the back. I could see into one of the living rooms. The room had been ransacked. Drawers were emptied, bookcases thrown onto the floor and generally the place looked as if an earthquake had just struck. Little though I usually appreciate their efforts, I realised that there was no way the police were responsible for this. I tried the patio door. It swung open.

'Don't go in!' Ruth whispered. 'We'll be blamed for all this wreckage if the police arrive.'

'We've got to find out who Wilmington's mates were. There must be something, a diary or a phone book that'll give us some names.'

'But what's happened here?'

'Burglary,' I muttered, thinking of the kids we'd seen. 'Wilmington's been away three days.'

'Oh, yes, highly likely. It's too much of a coincidence. I don't like it. What if it was the Satanists and they're still inside?'

'Let's find out.'

I went right in through the living room into a spacious hall and called out, 'Hello, anybody at home?' The words echoed emptily. We stood listening for several minutes. There was just the ticking of clocks. The place was empty. Although the house wasn't directly overlooked and the curtains had been left closed, presumably by Wilmington when he set off on his nocturnal suicide patrol, I couldn't risk switching a light on.

I started searching in the hall, the place where most people keep their telephone numbers. Headlights of cars passing along the road gave occasional illumination and my eyes were becoming accustomed to the gloom. Naturally, in my haste to pre-empt the police I'd forgotten to bring a torch but I found one in the old-fashioned fuse box by the front door.

There was nothing relevant, not the faintest hint that Wilmington was anything other than a normal middle-class businessman.

Yet I knew he wasn't, so I went on searching.

A big pile of *Yorkshire Life* magazines had been strewn over the carpeted floor. There were several pictures, hanging askew, of a heavily moustached version of Wilmington wearing 1940s RAF uniform. I puzzled over them for a moment. The martial figure was probably Wilmington's father. Ruth followed me from room to room as we sorted through the piles of once-treasured possessions flung all over the floors. The furniture had been badly savaged, almost as if the wrecker had been in a towering rage. A roll-top desk had been smashed to splinters. I fumbled through the scattered papers it had once contained. They were just bills going back years. No handy lists of acquaintances in Manchester. Chairs were broken, backs ripped off settees as if a person of unusual strength had been testing his muscle power.

I suppressed a nervous shiver.

Most of the stuff that could be dated seemed to be of

the same vintage as the photos of Wilmington père. Frustratingly, the son didn't seem to have had much of a life of his own . . . which I suppose figured. The guy was a heroin addict.

Then another explanation struck me.

Wilmington had had a life of his own.

'Ruth,' I whispered.

'What are you whispering for?' she asked irritably. She'd taken little part in my scavenging activities.

'You were right,' I muttered. 'This isn't a burglary. His friends, they've been here and removed anything that might lead us to them.'

'Let's get out of here right now,' she suggested urgently.

'No, there must be something they've missed,' I argued.

I hated the thought that I'd come on a wild-goose chase. I went back into the large back room that seemed to have been Wilmington's main living area; at least there was a television and armchairs in there. They were all overturned. The chairs had had their backs slashed open. There was stuffing and foam rubber everywhere. A clock was ticking particularly noisily. Possibly Wilmington had been obsessed with the passing of time.

I kicked at the pile of books and jumble. A book fell open, part of an illustrated history of the Great War in thirty volumes published in 1929. Soldiers posed amid scenes of destruction. The other stuff was of similar vintage. My eye was caught by a small red leather-backed book with a swastika on the cover.

'Bingo!' I muttered, hoping for a revelation of Wilmington's true interests.

I scooped it up. Disappointingly, it was part of the collected works of Rudyard Kipling in a 1917 edition, printed long before Hitler had claimed copyright on the ancient Indian symbol.

Whoever had collected these books, it wasn't Wilmington.

342

'Let's go!' Ruth said sharply.

'Let's just have a look upstairs,' I suggested half-heartedly.

'Go on then! Let's get this over with.'

Wilmington's bedroom held little of interest.

He must have had a mother but there was no trace of her, nor of a wife, nor of any companion. The room had been trashed like every other but held no clue to Wilmington's vices, unless copies of Wisden going back to the W. G. Grace era can be counted as evidence of an evil cast of mind. I don't know what I was expecting – pentagrams traced on the floor, images of Satan, books on witchcraft – but there was nothing like that. You'd have thought a man with such a keen interest in cricket would have steered clear of drugs and Satanism but, despite appearances, I knew he hadn't.

Still, he'd retained enough commitment to the normal world to keep his dark side well and truly hidden from view. It crossed my mind that in a house this size there might be secret panels, even hidden rooms, but I had no time to find them. If I was going to get any kind of lead it had to be in the next few minutes because Ruth was pointedly studying her watch.

I thought I'd hit pay dirt when I opened the next door on the landing. When it swung open it revealed a metal door, which the previous searchers had forced with a crowbar.

'Don't go in!' Ruth begged. 'There could be evil!'

I pointed to the thermostat on the lintel. 'I think the doors are for constant temperature,' I observed. 'Somehow I don't think the Devil needs that.'

'Stupid,' she muttered.

I slowly opened the inner door, I was just as strung up as Ruth was.

The white-painted room was windowless and bright strip lights came on automatically as we entered a scene of chaos. A large collection of butterflies and moths, once housed in narrow display cupboards fitted in special cabinets, had been utterly smashed. A bench had been overturned and a microscope flung into a corner.

Crunching over broken glass I looked at the labels, some said 'Lepidoptera', others 'Diptera'.

'Diptera?' I spoke the word aloud.

'Flies, you moron!' Ruth whispered. 'The guy collected dead flies. You know one of the names of Satan is Beelzebub . . . Lord of the Flies?'

'Ugh!' I grunted with a genuine feeling of repulsion.

She tugged my arm in her anxiety to leave the ento-mological charnel house but I held my ground. Wilmington must have been devoted to his insects, and there could be a clue to his other hobby.

Labels on some of the mounting cards had recent dates, proving that Wilmington was the collector, not his father. Every single case had been smashed and the pathetic con-tents liberated from its skewers, only to be trodden into the carpet.

Perhaps it was practice with the killing bottle that had led Wilmington into his other hobby. It figured in a way. I tried to put myself into his mind. Did he get perverted pleasure out of others' deaths? He'd claimed it was the ultimate thrill. I wondered briefly what emotions he'd experienced when his killers pinned him down like one of his own butterflies.

I surveyed the wrecked collection. It was hopeless. No clue was going to jump out at me.

'Come on!' Ruth urged, holding both the doors open for me, but I shook my head.

A pile of ripped-up books lay in a corner. I walked over. Possibly this collection had been assembled by Wilmington himself.

It had. They were mainly recent reference works on

insects. They'd all been trashed and ripped out of their covers.

I was on the point of giving up and leaving the jumble for the police to make what they could of it when I spotted one book. It stood out among the reference texts: *Elizabethan Fauna and Flora* by Douglas Carver.

My heart skipped a beat. 'This is it!' I said excitedly. 'This is what we came for.'

'What, a mouldy book about bugs?'

'No, look who it's written by,' I said excitedly. 'Douglas Carver, the Manchester professor who's also a director of Black Cat Services, which just happens to employ Neville Fraser.'

The words were hardly out of my mouth before a downstairs door slammed. Sound ricocheted through the silent building and seemed to magnify itself.

Ruth grabbed hold of me. I fended her off.

'They're here. They've come back,' she wailed. 'Lord, save us!'

'It's probably just the wind,' I said unconvincingly.

We both stood listening intently for a full minute. There was no further sound. I tried to convince myself that I'd hear a noise if someone was downstairs. We were both beginning to breathe again when the aching silence was broken by a dull concussive thud that shook the whole structure. Still clutching Carver's book, I ran through the double doors to the stairwell and looked down.

The hall was a sea of bright red and blue petrol flames. My throat was gripped by a powerful reek of petrol. An intense wave of heat drove me back at once.

'It's a bomb,' Ruth screamed.

I dashed to the landing window. It was a new double-glazed unit and it was firmly locked. I tried to kick it out with the sole of my foot. The frame didn't even quiver. We weren't going to get out that way.

'Don't just stand there,' I yelled, grabbing her.

We ran across the landing. Already the flames from below were shooting up with blast furnace intensity. To stay where we were another moment meant death. I remembered that there was another storey on the house. At the far corner of the landing there was a narrow latched door.

I flung it open, revealing a steep upward stairway. I pushed Ruth ahead and slammed the door behind us. The atmosphere here was still unpolluted by the deadly heat. We both gulped in cool air desperately but I knew this respite couldn't last because the noise of the conflagration was increasing all the time.

Ruth needed no pushing from me. We hurried on.

Two small attic bedrooms opened onto a narrow landing. Each was fitted with a new plastic window unit and each of those was locked. The windows were set low in the wall, just above floor level so I lay on my back and tried to bash one out of its frame by stamping my heels into in it with every ounce of my strength. It did no good. Whoever had double-glazed this place had had security firmly in mind.

By this time I could see that Ruth's lips were moving. Above the crackle of scorching timber I heard snatches of the Lord's Prayer.

I tried kicking out the window again. Dense black smoke was now coming up through gaps in the floor. Even as we watched the boards in one corner of the room began to buckle. Ruth held my arm tightly.

'Hold on to me,' she gasped, obviously feeling that her last seconds had arrived.

I pushed her away.

There was a trap in the ceiling. I dragged the upturned bed over, righted it and flung myself at the trap door. It burst open and I pulled myself through and upwards. I hauled Ruth after me into the rafter space.

'What are we going to do?' she asked. 'Wait for the fire department?'

As she spoke we both became aware that the roaring of the fire had slightly lessened. I tried to work out what could be happening to quench such a ferocious blaze and if it improved our slim chances of survival. I noticed that the dust cloud we'd raised wasn't moving upwards but down. It was being drawn into the fire beneath our feet. There was a powerful downdraft, air was being sucked from the roof space into the fire below.

'We've got seconds to get out before the windows give way and this place goes up like a volcano,' I told her. 'Our only chance is to smash out onto the roof and try to climb down.'

Fortunately there were no security or energy-saving features about the roof. It was just heavy tiles laid onto rafters. I started to make an opening. Ruth joined in. I helped her out through the gap we created.

Even as we clambered gingerly onto the steeply raked tiles there was a heavy crashing sound from below.

'That'll be the windows going,' I screeched at Ruth.

Sure enough renewed flames and thick smoke began licking up the sides of building as the increased oxygen improved combustion.

'Are we going to jump?' Ruth asked fatalistically. 'I'd rather do that than die in fire.'

I struggled to remember the geography of the building. Even if drainpipes were still attached, climbing down them through the flames gushing from the downstairs windows was the equivalent of lowering oneself into a red-hot furnace. We wouldn't even get over the edge to the roof without being roasted.

'We've got to crawl over there,' I croaked, pointing towards the side of the house which had only small windows.

It's amazing what you can do when you're pressed.

We both managed to negotiate the steep angle of the roof, the tiles of which were now rapidly becoming hot in spots as flames penetrated from beneath. I could see the top of a massive soil pipe and, sliding towards it head-first, I managed to grab it and somehow invert my body so that my feet were dangling along the side of the wall.

'I can't do that!' Ruth yelled. 'For Pete's sake! What are you? A trained acrobat?'

She remained perched on the angle of the roof like Guy Fawkes on top of a bonfire. She looked uncertainly at me and then at the flames licking up the side of the wall behind her. It could only be a matter of one or two minutes before the roof collapsed.

'Let yourself go!' I screamed. 'I'll grab you.'

With a despairing yell of 'Jesus, save me!' she slid towards me. I clung to the pipe with one hand and grabbed her as she slipped past me. My arm was almost jerked out of its socket by her weight and the pipe I was clinging to groaned alarmingly and began to move away from the wall as the stanchions were wrenched out of the brickwork. I braced myself to crash forty feet into the ground but the sickening forward motion mercifully ceased. For a second or two we were secure on the pipe.

Ruth released my arm. I thought she'd fallen but she'd got her feet into a Y-joint where a bathroom toilet outlet joined the main soil pipe.

She'd accused me of being an acrobat, but using the deep red glow of the still-mounting fire to find her footing, she swarmed down the remaining pipe like a practised performer. Gasping for breath, I followed more cautiously.

The relief when my feet touched solid ground was unbelievable.

Something thumped into the ground at my feet. I gazed at it stupidly. It was a dead pigeon. I looked up. The pigeons, which had inhabited the roof, were now wheeling above the blaze and occasionally flying into it.

Ruth had no time for sightseeing.

'Run, you fool!' she yelped, tugging at my arm.

We legged it past the billowing inferno, which the front of the house had turned into, and out onto Park Drive. Folk were gathering in the street but I took the lead and we charged right through them and round the corner to the BMW. No one made a move to halt us. All eyes were on the fire.

Our escape was not a second too soon. Fire vehicles and police cars were soon racing past in the opposite direction. I tried to think what I should do but connected thought was hampered by Ruth. Throwing her head well back, she began singing 'Amazing Grace' in a fine contralto voice. I listened for a second until she got to the part about 'saved a wretch like me' before telling her to belt up. I don't normally chide the paying customers but my nerves were at full stretch.

'Now do you believe in God?' she asked sharply.

'I believe my right arm's almost been torn out of its socket,' I answered crisply.

'That whole thing was the Devil's handiwork. They must have waited until they saw us go in.'

'Possibly,' I muttered. I thought it was more likely that a bomb had been set quite independently of us. That loud ticking in the living room could have been from the works. Whoever had set the bomb had seen us enter the building, leaving the door open behind us. He or she had come forward and slammed the door just before the bomb was due to go off. That had saved us by giving us those few seconds when the fire lacked oxygen.

Cold sweat broke out on my forehead when the realisation struck me that if we'd been downstairs at that precise moment the petrol went up there wouldn't have been enough of us left for identification.

I came to a junction and a sign for the M62 eastbound for Leeds and Hull. I decided on the spur of the moment to take that direction.

'Where are you taking me?' Ruth demanded shrilly. 'I've not escaped the flames of hell to go on a jaunt with you.'

'We're not taking a jaunt. This is a diversion in case they pick up the car on CCTV. We don't want anyone to think we're heading towards Manchester.'

'The ace investigator speaks,' Ruth said.

We drove in silence for some time before she put her hand on my arm. 'Turn back to Manchester,' she said. 'Much as I like your company I don't care to spend the night cruising round Yorkshire.'

I turned back, and after driving along minor roads for an hour I pulled up in a lay-by outside Holmfirth. I still had Carver's book. I'd stuck it in my belt during the struggle on the roof.

'So was it worth us both getting incinerated for?' Ruth enquired as I turned the pages.

'It's a lead,' I muttered.

'So?'

'I know why this was left,' I declared. 'It was left because the man who ripped that house apart couldn't read. Neville Fraser can't read. He ripped all those books up searching for something hidden in one of them, perhaps a list of contact addresses of Wilmington's playmates. He may have found that but he didn't realise that the book itself could be a clue.'

I didn't speak after that for some time as I studied the book by the dim light in the car. Despite its title, Carver's book wasn't a scientific work on botany and biology. It was a collection of references to the natural world in Elizabethan literature. It was signed by Carver on the title page. His handwriting was angular and jagged.

'As much as anything is worth getting roasted to death for I'd say this is,' I commented quietly. 'Wilmington's interest in nature was about as warm-hearted as his charity towards potential suicides. He was into dead specimens pinned on cards, and his taste in literature was limited to scientific texts and cricket, so why did he have this on his shelves? It's hardly the sort of thing a creep like him would be interested in. There are only two references to butterflies in the index. The only reason he had it was because he knew the author, who just happens to be Meg's English professor.'

'Praise the Lord!' Ruth sighed. 'We're getting there. This should put Inspector Rix's nose out of joint.'

'Hold on,' I cautioned. 'Arthur also knows Carver. He attended "Hermetic afternoons" at Carver's house and has a keen interest in Carver's pet theories about the occult.'

'No!' she moaned. 'This is what you've been hiding from me.'

'No, it still doesn't necessarily mean anything. Carver is a professor at the university Arthur attends. We shouldn't jump to conclusions.'

'You might not in your cold-blooded English way, but I will,' Ruth said fiercely. 'I want to know just what this so-called educator's been doing to my children.'

'Yes, so do I,' I murmured. 'He's the person Harry Sirpells has been watching.'

'You drag us all the way over here, and nearly get us killed all to confirm that this Carver was worth watching?'

'No, what we've confirmed is that there was a link between him and Wilmington/Pullman, the self-proclaimed expert in persuading folk they'd be better off dead.'

'Whatever! Let's get back to Manchester. Sirpells' reports must be burning a hole in my desk.'

We reached Ruth's flat at half four. She pulled a sheaf of envelopes with stickers on, labelled 'SCE' for

'Sirpells Confidential Inquiries' out of a locked desk drawer.

I tore open the first.

It contained blank sheets of typing paper, as did all the others.

18

'Aliens Blamed'
Headline in the *Daily Sport*
'Police discounted reports that asylum seekers or illegal immigrants were responsible for the spate of so-called Mangler killings, which now appears to have abated. They also said that it is possible that the killings were the work of some itinerant group that has now moved out of the city, but reports in the tabloid press that they are seeking aliens were described as "misleading".'
Report in the *Independent*

Despite the early hour, I phoned Sirpells. There was no reply. Suspicious thoughts went through my head. Had Arthur intercepted the reports?

Ruth read my mind.

'No one has touched them. I'd be able to tell, they're just as they were when they reached my mailbox. Besides, Arthur's never out of bed in time to collect the post. You know what he's like; if he'd known I was paying another detective as well as you he'd have hit the roof. By the way, the guy's invoices came monthly and I paid him by cheque. It adds up to a tidy sum for a stack of typing paper.'

She looked at me questioningly.

'No, I'm not going to Rochdale just yet,' I said wearily. 'Whatever scam Sirpells is pulling, it'll keep. I need sleep.'

'Poor you!' she mocked.

'Did you speak to Sirpells?'

'Only to tell him to send his reports care of this address. He was particularly anxious to make sure that he was going to be paid in your absence.'

'That sounds like Harry.'

'I told him that I'd hold on to the reports until you got out of jail, only we didn't know then that it was going to be so long.'

'It was lot longer for me than it was for you,' I said. 'Anyway, I need a soak and a comfortable bed.'

Ruth raised her eyebrows in that same irritating way Arthur had mastered.

'Since I got out of prison I've been assaulted by the police, almost poisoned and escaped from the Yorkshire version of the Towering Inferno by the skin of my teeth. Believe me, I'll do a better job on Sirpells and Carver when I've had a few zeds.'

'Wimp,' she said, but this time she laughed to show she was joking. 'This is what comes of not trusting in the Lord. Your energy flags.'

'I see.'

'You can sleep in Meg's room if you like,' she offered.

'No, thanks. I'll swear her mattress is more uncomfortable than sleeping on the floor. I'm for my own bed. Can you lend me the taxi fare?'

She went over to the roll-top desk and took out an envelope containing a thick wad of twenty-pound notes.

'Take what you need,' she offered. 'Just make a note on the envelope of how much and I'll deduct it from your fee.'

'Fine,' I said, counting out two hundred.

Maybe my mouth turned down a little, there was nothing deliberate on my part, but she detected something. 'Listen, Dave, I know I'm hard to get on with but I've been through a lot . . .' She spoke more hesitantly than her usual decisive bark.

'It's all right. No explanations needed.'

'There are. I know God preserved us tonight but in my case the method He chose was your strong right arm. I don't want you to go off on your own. I need you here,

354

or with me, or whatever, and don't think I'm proposi-
tioning you, but I'll just feel safer with you around. There,
I've said it.'

'Yes, ma'am,' I muttered in an American accent, 'you're
the boss, but I still need that bath and bed.'

'And you're clear that the word "bed" doesn't involve
me?'

'Never clearer.'

'How about if I book us adjoining rooms in a good
hotel? Would that do it?'

I nodded and then slumped on the sofa. I was almost
out on my feet. She got busy with the phone and then
packed a couple of bags.

'It looks better,' she explained.

Half an hour later we were checking into the Lowry
Hotel on the Salford side of the Irwell. It took us half an
hour because I insisted on following a roundabout route,
parking the BMW in a long-stay car park, and then taking
a black cab. Persecution induces paranoia in us all. At
my insistence, Ruth checked in under her maiden name
and she registered me as Smith, her personal assistant.
The clerk made no difficulties when she paid cash in
advance.

Before falling asleep I had to smile. Ruth thought I
was after her body. Nothing could be further from the
truth. Being in her company was like trying to pal up
with the Statue of Liberty, an exhausting process.
Although the bath and bed were all that could be desired
I slept restlessly, constantly jerking from deep sleep to
wakefulness until two p.m., when room service arrived
with coffee and sandwiches.

Sitting up at my bedside I had all the resilience of a limp
rag. I felt as if I'd been wrung out in an old-fashioned
mangle. Perhaps that was appropriate for the man suspected of being the Mangler.

I tried to analyse the reason for my lack of decent

355

sleep. After escaping from the inferno in Halifax anyone could expect jagged nerves, but it wasn't that.

It came down to one thing. I was used to having enemies but not to being let down by my friends. I tried to summon up rage against Celeste Williams-Coe and Harry Sirpells but I couldn't. My dominating emotion was despair and I sensed that it was clouding my judgement like a sudden descent of fog on the Pennines. I wanted to crawl back into bed until the mood lifted but instead I took a long cold shower, lingering as the water and the pain of the cold stripped away my depression.

When I emerged after twenty minutes, shaving kit, clean underwear, T-shirt, jeans and socks had been delivered with a note: 'Hope these fit, R.'

I considered Ruth for a minute. She must have entered through the adjoining door. Anyone else would have opened the door of the bathroom and shouted in, but not her. I guessed that the experience with her stepfather had left her permanently wary of men.

I looked out of the window. Bright sunshine was bouncing off the surface of the river. I watched for a moment. There was something hypnotic about the scene. The waters of the Irwell were oiling smoothly along like a gigantic conveyor belt. The sensation of motion and the bustling crowds on the gleaming new suspension bridge prompted me to action.

For the first time in days I checked my mobile. There were five messages, all from Celeste: 'Dave, please phone!'

This time I did feel a surge of anger but then caution prevailed. Nothing would be accomplished by a confrontation. Recalling Celeste's love of fine clothes and her need to break into the housing market I didn't doubt that she'd sold me out. But was it that simple? Had Peter Snyder insisted on reports of my movements as a condition of giving Michael and her their jobs back? Anything was possible. All I knew was that I had to turn her treachery to my advantage in some way.

But how? I was racking my wits when Ruth banged on the door between our rooms and barged in.

'Turn on the television!' she ordered, before dashing back to watch her own television. I followed.

There was a face I recognised on the screen. It was Pullman.

Then my own pretty face flicked on. At least it was a good photo, taken off a Pimpernel Investigations publicity brochure.

We were watching the BBC regional news. I just caught the final words of the package . . . 'Police are seeking the assistance of Manchester private detective, David Cunane, for information concerning the death of the Yorkshire-based insurance executive on the M62 motorway. Mr Cunane was recently released from Manchester Prison, Strangeways, following the collapse of the prosecution case against him in an unrelated murder. Detective Chief Superintendent Rix of the Greater Manchester Police said, "No comment," when asked if Mr Cunane was under suspicion in connection with the executive's death.'

'That rat!' Ruth raged. 'He's blaming it on you. How can he?'

I laughed, a bit hysterically maybe, but it was still a laugh.

'What's the matter with you? Are you insane?' Ruth shouted.

'No, it's funny. I've got to laugh.'

She looked at me with a strange expression.

'Don't you see? Rix has no one else to blame after months of investigating the Mangler killings when all he could come up with was a denial that the Mangler existed, then after the Aycliffe killing he tried to pin it all on me and ended up with egg on his face, but after all this he's still left with me as his only suspect.'

'And that's funny?' Ruth asked doubtfully.

'Yeah, it means we're further on in this case than he is. I know I'm not the murderer but unlike the police we do have a live suspect.'

'Carver!'

'Exactly. What a name for a murderer, by the way!' I was still laughing.

'So this is the famous British sense of humour?' Ruth asked again in a mystified tone. 'Hundreds of police must be scouring the city for you, and you laugh? How did they get on to you, anyway?'

'Ashley Gribbin may have told them.'

'I knew that woman was no good.'

'Or they could have found my fingerprints on the Bentley. Come to think of it, that's more likely.'

'What are you going to do? Will you turn yourself in?'

'Is that your famous American sense of humour? I've just spent months at the Strangeways Hotel and I've no intention of returning . . . ever!'

'Oh!'

'Yes, this puts you in a false position, so the first thing we must do is split up. If Rix asks, you haven't seen me. You know nothing.'

'I can't lie.'

'OK, then take a holiday somewhere. Don't let him find you. Go back to the States if you want.'

'I can't leave until this is settled.'

'But I'm going to sort out Carver and find out exactly what he and his pals have been up to.'

'That'll be dangerous, Dave. They've already killed this vile Pullman character just to keep their secrets. It's so ridiculous that we can't go to the official police.'

I shrugged.

'I hate to think of you going into harm's way on my behalf and my not being able to help you.'

'I'll get by,' I muttered. I hadn't a clue how, but I was determined enough.

'This is all my fault.'

'No, Ruth, this isn't just about Meg. It's personal now.'

'Would a gun help? Would it make you safer? I could get one delivered through the American Embassy. I have a Christian friend there who's the –'

'Ruth, a gun would help,' I said honestly, thinking about the inevitable next encounter with Neville Fraser. 'I have no fashionable prejudices against firearms – they're just ironmongery – but think of your work and the people who depend on you. Rix would be delighted to arrest you on a charge of arms smuggling. It's best if you make yourself scarce.'

'Money,' she said. 'You'll need money.'

Going over to the bed she retrieved her jacket and took out the large wad of notes I'd seen earlier. She started to count it, then thought better. 'Here, take the lot,' she exclaimed. 'No, scrap that! Give me a couple of hundred back. I'll get more.'

'Is this just an advance or is it my whole fee?' I humorously enquired.

'Come back safe and we'll talk about rewards then,' she protested.

The bundle held at least four grand. I tucked it into the inside pocket of my jacket. Ruth smiled nervously. It looked like the parting of the ways, but then a thought struck me.

'There is something else you could do for me,' I remarked.

'Name it.'

I ran my fingers through my curly locks. 'When you saw that picture of me on TV what struck you most about my ugly mug?'

'Oh, your hair. Do you want me to dye it for you?'

'No, that would probably make me stand out more. Could you nip down to the hotel shop and buy an electric hair clipper? I'll be less conspicuous with a shaven head.'

'Five minutes!' she answered, snatching up the notes I'd returned to her and dashing out. When she'd gone my own bravado drained away. Perhaps I'd be better taking my own advice and going to ground somewhere until the heat died down. That might be nice but there were too many people who had an interest in stopping me.

A few minutes later I was seated on a chair surrounded by newspapers spread on the carpet while Ruth patiently removed my beautiful locks.

'I hope this doesn't decrease your strength,' Ruth quipped.

'Like Samson?' I asked. 'Does that make you Delilah, Mrs Hands?'

'I don't think so,' she said quickly, drawing in breath sharply.

'And I don't think I'll end up "Eyeless in Gaza" either.'

'You know Milton?'

'Oh aye! I've got *Samson Agonistes* off by heart,' I boasted.

'Eyeless in Gaza at the mill with slaves,
Himself in bonds under Philistian yoke;'

I quoted. 'Actually Ruth, that's the only bit I know. I have a friend who bombards me with literary tags and I always have a few up my own sleeve as ammunition. It's quite appropriate if you think of DCS Rix as the Philistine yoke.'

'He's a yoke all right,' she agreed.

'And a Philistine,' I added.

'Now that's real English humour,' she commented approvingly, 'not this blue movie stuff you all do. It's what I expected when I first came over here. I thought you all'd be spouting Shakespeare and Shelley by the yard. Just as long as you remember that I'm not Delilah.'

For the first time in months I felt a quiver of arousal.

She brought up the Old Testament situation, not me. All those 'begats' get me going. I don't know if they put bromide in the tea at Strangeways but my thoughts hadn't gone in that direction for ages. Ruth was an attractive woman, physically at least, and she was performing an intimate action for me and there was a double bed handy.

Whatever the feeling that passed over me was – and with me, when I get the itch I like to scratch – Ruth felt it too. She knocked off barbering for a moment and took a deep breath.

'Whatever you're thinking, forget it!' she cautioned.

'How could I not forget?' I said. 'You warned me off at our first meeting, but you've got to admit that you're Ruth, "standing amid the alien corn" here in Manchester and didn't she –'

'Marry her master? Yes, but don't forget I'm *your* boss and that'll be quite enough corn from you, Mr Cunane.'

The moment, or whatever it was, passed. It took us ages to wrap up all the hair and to leave no tell-tale trace and then we went our separate ways, having made arrangements to keep in touch at various locations.

I crossed the Irwell on the new bridge. It was very strange to feel air on my scalp and I almost expected people to start pointing at me but no one gave me a second look. I noticed though. Men slightly younger than me, in their early thirties and below, were nearly all shaven-headed, or sported peculiar Mohican or other spiky crops. I certainly didn't stand out.

My route took me into the jumble of narrow streets behind Deansgate where the Pimpernel offices used to be. An estate agency roosted there now. I felt a degree of bitterness towards Peter Snyder when I saw the sign outside the new Snyder Investigations. There was going to be some investigating done into Peter Snyder when I got myself free and clear of my troubles. It hadn't taken Peter long to show me the door. I wondered if his move had been planned long before Ruth Hands walked into my life.

I continued until I reached Deansgate, crossed the street and positioned myself in the window of Starbucks. My intention wasn't just to watch the world go by. I stirred the large latte in front of me and considered how I was going to speak to Celeste.

Eventually I took out my mobile and called her number.

'Dave! Where've you been? Michael and I've been mad with worry. Where are you? I must see you.'

'Oh, I've been here and there, doing this and that,' I said noncommittally.

'Dave, when we didn't hear from you I feared the worst.'

'What? You thought I'd topped myself? Celeste, you should know me better than that. No, I'm fine and dandy.'

'But the police –'

'Have got the totally wrong end of the stick, as usual. I'll clear all that up.'

'It's great to know that you're well. Where are you speaking from? I'll come round.'

'No need. I'm on my way to see you. I'll be with you in two minutes. I thought I'd have a face-to-face with Peter and sort out one or two things.'

'Dave!'

'Don't worry, nothing violent. Now, don't you say a word to him. I want my visit to be a nice surprise. See you soon.'

I switched the phone off and dropped it into a litter bin on my way out of the café. I turned towards Market Street, intending to mingle with the crowds there and trawl the Arndale Centre for a change of clothes but I'd hardly reached St Ann's Square before my call produced the reaction I'd been more than half expecting. There was a blaring of police sirens heading in the direction of Snyder Investigations.

I cautiously made my way back, taking a vantage point in a window seat on the first floor of Waterstone's bookshop, from where I was able to see a police rhino hurtling round the corner of King Street West. It was all more conclusive than I'd dared hope. Fully armoured coppers carrying sub-machine guns closed off the end of the street. Police vehicles parked across Deansgate, blocking the traffic as they sealed off the whole area surrounding Snyder Investigations.

Crowds began to form at once but I slipped away, no doubt the CCTV cameras were focused on the scene.

So, I'd learned two things. Celeste was a traitor and Rix didn't just want me for a friendly chat. Judging by the number of police involved you might conclude that he wanted me dead or alive. I'd have to be careful not to be seen with anything that could be construed as a weapon in my hands. England is the one country in the Western world where police 'marksmen' routinely get away with executing the unwary.

As I entered the Arndale Centre I was conscious of the many CCTV cameras and could only hope that by mingling with such large numbers I was making individual surveillance impossible. I bought two new outfits and a small suitcase to carry them in, and then, leaving the Centre, walked up Market Street to the bus stop on the corner of Oldham Street.

I surveyed a number of destinations before choosing Ashton-under-Lyne. Who would look for a desperate man in Ashton-under-Lyne, I asked myself. I'd never had a case there and, to my knowledge, knew no one. The bus ride took forever, trundling up Ashton New Road past the new Man City football ground, the loudly trumpeted 'regenerated areas' of East Manchester, and then into Ashton itself. I wasn't pleased to see a massive new police station and magistrates' court on my left as we entered the old cotton town, but then I reflected that the police here were not so likely to have my features imprinted on their memories as the ones in central Manchester.

Still, the headquarters was depressingly large and I wondered whether to take another bus somewhere else. I tried to cheer myself with the thought that most of the blue-clad multitudes were seated in these and similar headquarters buildings, filling in PACE forms, or cruising in cars talking to their mates. The days of continual foot patrols and pounding the beat when a villain dreaded meeting an alert policeman round any corner were long gone, as my father had often lamented. Strangers to the streets themselves, how would the uniformed branch be able to spot a stranger? I might as well take advantage of the disappearance of the police from the streets as any other alleged law breaker.

I checked into a small hotel on Cavendish Street, the Mumbhai. The Asian proprietor, called Keki Mistry, a shy-looking, reserved individual, showed no surprise when I registered under the name of Constable and told him that my business as an insurance loss adjuster would take me out during the day and that I would be back late most nights. His eyes did gleam with a certain pecuniary pleasure when I paid cash in advance for two weeks while telling him I might stay longer if I liked the place.

The next vital piece of business was to get some wheels. I had to buy rather than hire because I had no documentation.

Mr Mistry told me that there were car sales showrooms a couple of streets away on Oldham Road and that his cousin Hermant worked in one of them.

'I only want a nice runner to keep me going for the next week. My BMW hit a kerb and the garage I took it to insisted that it needs a full check up and they wouldn't release it. The wife's taken the hump. She's got the courtesy car and I'm left with Shank's Pony,' I lamented.

'I can save you the trouble of walking round there if you want. Hermant will bring you one round. What kind of price were you thinking of?'

I told him.

It wasn't many minutes later that Mr Mistry's cousin turned up outside with a nice Nissan Micra in British racing green that 'only had thirty thousand on the clock and had been owned by an old lady who used it solely for driving to church on Sundays'. For cash the cousin was willing to knock down the price and send the registration document to the hotel on Cavendish Street.

When I mentioned that I'd lost my mobile it turned out that Mr Mistry had another cousin who'd be only too glad to supply me with one of those.

'Nice to do business with you, Mr Mistry,' I said as I left en route for Hale Barns.

'Anything you need,' he said obligingly, 'just ask.'

It was on the tip of my tongue to ask if he had a cousin who could supply me with a bullet-proof vest and a shooter but I thought that might be pushing my luck.

The M60, encircling Greater Manchester, isn't just convenient for serial killers as Jack Rix argued when he tried to have me banged up as the Manchester Mangler, it's also very handy for anyone wanting to travel to the outlying townships strung along it like beads on a necklace. After leaving Ashton I was at the M56 intersection and heading into the posh suburb of Hale Barns within thirty minutes.

I reflected on my past mistakes as I turned into Hale Road. I should have done this myself instead of subcontracting to Harry Sirpells. 'That's what prosperity does to you, makes you lose your edge,' I told myself as I looked up all the Carvers in the phone book.

It was simple enough. I said, 'Professor Carver?' when the phone was answered.

After only four wrong calls he replied, 'Yes, what is it?' in an irritable tone.

'Royal Mail here,' I said. 'We have a parcel for you. Can I check the first line of your address for security?'

'The Larches, Chapel Lane,' came the conditioned response.

'Sorry, must have got the wrong person,' I mumbled before hanging up.

Chapel Lane turned out to be a long winding road and The Larches was a large detached house in its own grounds not very far from the motorway. It had a double entrance and a semicircular driveway. I parked under trees about a hundred yards away and settled down to wait. I didn't know what I was waiting for. I was just following the maxim in the private detectives' handbook about putting oneself close to where the action was and hoping something would turn up. Only it didn't.

As the hours passed I speculated on what sort of game Harry Sirpells was up to. It's rare, but sadly not unheard of, for a private detective to switch employers in mid-case, and that's what I reasoned Harry must have done. He's always been keen on the shekels, as we all are, I supposed, but there's been a certain edge with Harry about how prosperous I was in comparison with himself, which I took as a joke. I thought it was possible that Harry had been paid off by Carver and then felt greedy enough to go on touching Ruth for payment.

After waiting three hours during which time no one went in or out of The Larches, the light was beginning to fade and darker explanations for Harry's lapse began to bob to the surface of my mind like unwanted corpses rising from a swamp. Had the old curmudgeon come to a sticky end?

I turned the car round and drove back to the motorways and took the route to Rochdale. The Micra was fitted with a radio and I tuned to a local station in time to get the travel report: 'Motorists are advised to avoid central Manchester. The blocking of Deansgate due to what police are describing as a "security incident" is now over but there is still severe congestion in the area. This incident, combined with a major accident on the inner ring road, has created conditions amounting to gridlock in Manchester and some motorists are complaining that they were trapped in their cars for more than four hours.'

Harry's office was in a back street off Yorkshire Street. To call it an office was something of a misnomer. He worked mainly from home but kept up this office as a refuge from his wife like some men have an allotment. There was no sign over the door or indication that it belonged to him and I only knew of its existence because he'd taken me there once, stressing what a great favour he was doing me by bringing me to what he called his 'inner sanctum'.

I rattled the handle. There was no one in.

I looked around. The main street was busy. There were shouts from packs of drunks shambling towards home, raucous arguments with minicab drivers and snatches of song but no sign of Mr Plod. The blue-coated lads and lasses were no doubt sitting in their vans at some central point leaving the streets to the drunks and the likes of me.

There was a lot of play in the door. It moved about a quarter of an inch when I shook it. I guessed it was only secured by a poorly fitting Yale lock. I leaned heavily and found myself inside. I scanned the room for an alarm but there was none and I guessed that Harry's resources hadn't stretched as far as a remote alarm connected to the police or a security firm.

He hadn't run to curtains either. The plate-glass window was coated with green paint to about three-quarters of the way up. I switched the light on. I had thought my new office on Dutton Street was fairly bare but it was luxurious compared with this. There was one filing cabinet, one hacked-up desk that looked as if someone had been trying to use it as firewood, and one rather large, comfortable-looking chaise longue. A small steel safe, vintage 1890, resided in one corner, but my detective instincts told me that commission, rather than detection of marital infidelity, had been what Harry had in mind when he set up this office.

There was a back room, empty apart from an ancient stone sink. Rear access was through a heavily barricaded back door and there was also a window with steel bars across it. Peering through the layered grime on the window I detected an outside loo in the small yard. The wall adjoining the back street was wreathed in barbed wire.

Further proof that Harry hadn't advertised his presence here was that there was no pile of junk mail behind the door. I went to the filing cabinet. It was empty, apart from a packet of condoms in the top drawer, also empty.

The safe door swung open when I turned the handle.

A single letter lay on the bottom shelf. There was a layer of fine dust on it. I blew it clean. My own name was written on the envelope. A chill ran up and down my spine. I ripped the letter open . . .

Dave,

Friend, and I still call you that, I guess you'll eventually find this one way or another so here goes . . . I'm dead sorry, honest mate. When you were arrested I thought this is the moment for Harry Sirpells to keep his nose clean and bail out like all your other friends were doing.

Look, I know I'm a soft bugger but I didn't, bail out, that is. I'd found nothing unusual about your professor so instead of jacking it in I went for one last look when your American lady asked me to stay with the job.

On that topic, talk about luck! Something

happened, I can't tell you what it was but certain parties paid me a very nice sum to keep my trap shut, so I suppose I should say thank you, Dave, except that they made it very clear that the alternative to taking their money was a swim in the Ship Canal wearing concrete boots.

Oh, well. If you're reading this you'll have found that the reports I sent in were just waste paper. Sorry about that but it was made clear that if I didn't do that I'd be making the acquaintance of the canal.

Right my old cock, that's enough for now. Me and the Mrs have taken early retirement in a nice warm spot and I'll be in touch about the money I took off you when I read that you're free and clear.

Best of luck (and you'll need it!). Keep your eyes open,

Harry T. Sirpells

The loose lock on the front door was just about closable, so I slammed it to and left. My feelings about Harry weren't much more charitable than they'd been before.

Just to make sure that Harry wasn't conning me I checked out his home in the Bamford district. Sure enough his house stood empty with a For Sale sign in the front garden.

I drove back to Ashton in a depressed mood. When I let myself into the Mumbhai with the key I'd been provided with, Mr Mistry was waiting behind his reception desk.

'Did you have a good day?' he asked.

'A frustrating one,' I replied. I suddenly realised that I was hungry. I hadn't eaten since two and it was now coming up to midnight. 'You haven't got anything to eat, have you?' I asked hopefully.

'No meals here but I have a cousin who has a restaurant and he won't be finished yet. Shall I phone him to expect you?'

I nodded agreement and took directions from him and remarked that he had many useful cousins.

'Oh yes, many useful cousins, many Mistrys in Ashton,' he said gravely.

'Yeah, many mysteries in my job too.'

'Yes,' he said interestedly. 'Who are they?'

'I'm afraid it's more a question of what are they and why won't they go away,' I said wearily.

'Oh, joke about name, I see,' he said solemnly. 'I hear that often but Mistry is a very common name here now, you know.'

'I know,' I assured him, 'no offence.'

When I reached the restaurant, also called Mumbhai, it was just closing but the cousins let me in and fed me well with a chicken korma, washed down with a pint of lager.

Later, I let myself back into the hotel and went to my room. The bed looked inviting but I wasn't really tired. I told myself I wasn't there for sleep or to admire the red flock wallpaper. I couldn't waste time on sleep while Professor Carver manipulated police and public opinion into accepting that I was responsible for his crimes. In my mind I saw him as a modern day Professor Moriarty, the Napoleon of crime. I suppose that with the police force and Neville Fraser on my trail it was understandable if I was feeling a little stressed. It could only be a matter of time before someone recognised me even here in the back streets of Ashton.

I stared gloomily at my bald pate in the mirror. I didn't like my own looks. Was the sacrifice worth it? I couldn't spend the rest of my life dealing with members of the Mistry clan who'd probably continue to suppress their curiosity only as long as I did business with cash in hand.

I was missing my kitchen, the scene of all my best thinking. I tried to imagine myself scouring the grill, but it did nothing for me. My inclination was to dash over to Hale Barns, take the wretched professor by the throat and wring the truth out of him. Instead, I clenched my fists in anger and tried to think of some other way to get out of my troubles.

I paced up and down, aware that I'd missed something somewhere along the line.

Harry Sirpells . . . his house was empty and up for sale, indicating a rapid move, yet his office was still there. He, or someone acting for him, must be paying rent unless he owned the place. But in that case, why not sell it too? And then, despite having made some kind of discovery at Carver's house, why was he still alive? What had he found that was worth Carver buying his silence? Why had a ruthless gang, who killed one of their own as casually as someone swatting a fly, left Harry trawling about the landscape?

No answers came for a while but then I remembered that in matters that concerned personal safety, Harry Sirpells was exceptionally crafty and cautious. He must have been caught red-handed while spying on Carver but had been able to strike a bargain. He must have said something that made them nervous about killing him. It would have had to be something more than the vague connection with Ruth Hands and myself. Mention of my name would have protected him for all of five minutes. These people knew a dozen ways to get rid of someone without suspicion arising. My discovery that Wilmington/Pullman's death was murder was pure luck. If I'd gone to the MRI mortuary a day later the corpse would have been in some inaccessible funeral home in Halifax, awaiting cremation.

The classic method of alerting the authorities to dirty work at the crossroads was to leave a letter with a solicitor, 'To Be Opened in the Event of My Death', but that wasn't Harry's style. For one thing he hated solicitors. He spent his life at their beck and call and had often told me that if he ever received the fees he was owed by numerous local shysters he'd be able to retire. Come to think of it, did I trust solicitors myself? Marvin was Celeste's cousin, after all.

I was wound up like a knocker-upper's alarm clock when the answer finally came. Harry had expected *me* to find and safeguard his discovery. Who else could he rely on? He was a one-man firm and working for me. There was no one else. After all, he'd gone to the trouble of leaving a letter where he knew I'd find it. He must also have known that he was putting the person to whom he passed on his info in mortal danger. He'd hardly do that to a relative or bosom buddy, but me, Dave Cunane, the big city detective, yes?

Thank you, Harry, I thought.

The recent attempts to ensure my silence, both during the prison spell and after, now made sense.

Why hadn't Harry already passed on the information? Why hadn't he just popped it in the post? He couldn't do that because I was in prison at the time and he didn't know who else to trust with such dangerous news. He'd hinted in the letter that he didn't trust my 'friends' at Pimpernel Investigations much.

I took the letter out of my jacket and studied it. At last my brain clicked into top gear. The first letters of each paragraph spelled FLOOR or FLOORB, if you counted the salutation. The incriminating evidence was under a floorboard in his office. God! I'd probably trodden on it a couple of times and now I'd left the office door loose for any passing vagrant to wander in and take up lodging.

I grabbed my jacket and headed for my bedroom door, pausing for a second to wonder if I ought to ask Mistry if he could supply me with a handy crowbar. No, that was too silly. I crept downstairs in my stocking feet and had just started to release the catch on the outer door when a soft voice spoke up from behind me.

'Leaving so soon, Mr Constable?' Mistry asked.

I whirled round.

'Actually, I decided I need to see a young lady, any young lady if you take my meaning. I can't sleep without it, you know.'

'Oh, naughty Mr Constable, now I've no cousins in that line of business but I can tell you where to go.'

I had to wait patiently while he gave directions on where to find commercial sex in Ashton-under-Lyne. There was a massage parlour above a cycle shop opposite the library that kept late hours.

Then I was off back to Rochdale like a shot.

19

There was a small cash box under a loose floorboard beneath his desk.

I opened it and took out a well-worn leather-covered notebook. Flipping through the pages I quickly realised that it had nothing to do with the Hands case. It contained the names and addresses of women in the Rochdale area with coded notations alongside each.

The cash box also held a spare key for the office, but nothing else.

I got down on the floor and peered into the gap. My eye was attracted by a hook with a piece of grey twine attached. I reeled in the twine, pulling up a cardboard envelope wrapped in plastic.

The first photo showed Neville Fraser seated on the bow of a canal barge named the *Virgin Queen*. He was holding a thick package, which he was handing over to Detective Chief Superintendent Jack Rix. The next showed Rix taking out bundles of notes with bank wrappers still on them. Finally, he was pushing the money into his pocket.

To say my eyes bulged doesn't cover the scene. This was completely unexpected. I've never found Rix particularly congenial, but dishonest? No, he seemed too full of his own importance to risk his position by taking bribes, especially from a lowlife like Fraser. I just stood there under the bare lightbulb in that tawdry office-cum-lovenest, trying to take in the implications of those photos.

Rix's irregular cash transfer must have taken place some time after I'd been remanded for the Annie Aycliffe murder. I couldn't grasp all the complexities. Was Fraser paying Rix for the details about the killing that he later used to taunt me? Or was he paying off Rix for doing the killing? Neither of those ideas could be right. I had Fraser pegged as the killer so why would he need to pay Rix for information? In that case what else could he be paying Rix for?

I groaned aloud.

Nothing seemed to fit.

Scumbag though he was now revealed as, Rix wasn't a killer. My theory of the motive for the Aycliffe killing was that she'd died because the man in the grey Vauxhall had thought she was my partner. Rix wouldn't have made that mistake. So was he being paid to keep the identity of the real killer from emerging? If only I'd taken the name of that removal man, he could have identified the driver.

I felt like tearing my hair out except that I had none to tear. At every stage in this case I kept getting more questions and a lot of wrong answers. I slumped onto the chaise longue to work out my next step.

I decided almost at once that I wasn't going to go public with the photos. I could email them to Janine White and within minutes every national newspaper and media outlet would be downloading them for publication. Rix would deny everything and I'd be back where I was before. No, I had to do what Harry had done and keep these as my security. I carefully returned them to Harry's hidey hole and put everything back as before.

For the rest it was back to Plan B: confront Carver and try to get the truth out of him. The barge was obviously his, who but an Elizabethan nut would name a barge *Virgin Queen*? I remembered that his faculty secretary, Greta Armstrong, had claimed that he liked to make an early start at the university. It was already Friday so if I wanted to catch him before he set off for whatever fiendish weekend entertainments he had lined up, I had to get myself back to his house and see him before he went out in the morning.

I took off my shoe and hammered and forced the battered Yale lock more or less back into place. The wood had splintered slightly but the door would hold against a casual rattle.

When I left Harry's office for the second time I felt much more vulnerable than previously. The streets were deserted now and I could expect to be stopped quite legitimately. I drove with great caution, trusting that my choice of a little old lady's car wouldn't attract suspicion. Even so, it seemed like hours before I pulled up near The Larches.

I huddled in the car for three hours, kept awake by the cold of an English summer's night. I waited until the first faint hint of blue was showing on the horizon then I crept out. It was a big house in mock-Tudor style with a carriage drive and a large bow-fronted entrance up three steps, quite a nice bijou 'gentleman's residence' but slightly outside the price bracket you'd expect a university professor to be able to afford. I crept all round the house, glad to note that, unlike Wilmington, the professor hadn't had burglar-proof double glazing fitted everywhere. This place retained its leaded lights.

There was no sign that Carver kept a dog or even had a burglar alarm. I remembered Greta Armstrong's comments about his life style. Hopefully, his security arrangements were in keeping with the sixteenth century, though I supposed rich Elizabethans had lots of wakeful servants to keep them snug. I could only hope that Carver didn't have a whole squad of flunkies kitted out in doublet and hose.

For the third time that night I broke into a building. A man wanted by the police in connection with several murders shouldn't be squeamish about a spot of breaking and entering, but I was. I smashed a back door window with a brick wrapped in my jacket. The key was in the lock.

I stood by the door for some minutes aware that I was about to commit a serious crime, but what was my alternative? I couldn't run for ever. I had to find the truth. There were creaks and cracks such as you normally get in any old house but no sound of detection.

Emboldened, I pressed on. I didn't allow myself to think about what I was doing. I was like a tightrope walker who knows he'll fall if he looks down for a single second. Once inside I took my shoes off and walked on tiptoe through the downstairs rooms. I paused at the foot of the staircase. Someone up above was snoring loudly. I'd no idea how many people Carver entertained on his premises. He might have had the whole coven with him for all I knew. I went upstairs, again looking neither right nor left, walking as if I had every right to be on the premises. One of the doors was open and it was from here that the stertorous sounds were echoing. I risked a peek inside and saw a large four-poster bed with the curtains drawn. All the other rooms were piled high with junk and clothing and bits of machinery made out of wood. It was as if Carver had hired out his rooms as storage for a theatre or museum.

I couldn't risk approaching the four-poster, so I didn't know if anyone was sharing Carver's noisy slumbers.

Anyone unconscious under that torrent of sound had to be a heavy sleeper.

I went back downstairs. One room held a massive hand loom, spinning wheels and other assorted bits of antiquated textile machinery. The main living room was on the right-hand side of the entrance. It was furnished with heavy oak reproduction furniture, a real time warp. The walls were panelled and adorned with tapestries and the ceiling covered in moulded plasterwork. Ashes of a wood fire smouldered in a wide stone fireplace. Pride of place in the room was given to a collection of Elizabethan folios and manuscripts housed in a glass-fronted bookshelf that covered one wall. The doors weren't locked. Ignorant though I may be, I was clued up enough to recognise a valuable library.

One large folio volume stood open on a lectern. A crude woodcut picture showed someone being burned at the stake. I guessed that fitted in with the professor's interests.

Seeing it gave me an idea.

There was no phone in the room but knowing there must be one in the house I went in search. I found an old-fashioned phone in an alcove by the front door and ripped it free from the wall. There was a slight noise as I jerked the connection free from the plaster but the booming and droning from above continued relentlessly.

I went back to the loom. There were some thick ribbons. I took them and tied up the handles on the front door as best I could. I did quite a thorough job. Carver wasn't going to get out of his front door in a hurry but then there were always the windows. I didn't intend to trap him in the house, just point him in the direction of the rear exit. I returned to the large drawing room and began carting the books and manuscripts out to the back garden. This consisted of a low stone wall facing the house backed by a spacious lawn with an

Elizabethan knot garden in the middle. There was even a viewing mound in the far corner of the garden. I could see at a glance that everything had been done in compliance with Carver's obsession with life in Elizabethan England.

Well, he was shortly going to come into collision with the nastier side of Elizabethan life.

I carefully stacked the books on the stone wall and then spotted what I'd been looking for. There was a garden incinerator on my left side close to a vegetable patch and a tall leylandii hedge, which sheltered the neighbouring garden from this one. Trying not to make much noise, I dragged the incinerator across the lawn close to the pile of books. All I needed now were combustibles.

Fortunately, Carver believed in open fires.

A brass ornamental chest in the weaving room contained kindling, firelighters and matches. I transferred them to the garden and with the help of some timber and branches lying in a corner I soon had a fierce blaze going in the incinerator.

I went into the house, stood at the foot of the stairs and shouted loudly up the stairs. By that stage I was as mad as Carver had ever been. I racked my brain for an appropriate Shakespearian quotation, but nothing much came.

'Come on now, you secret, black and midnight hag!' I yelled inaccurately, and then, suddenly becoming aware that I was in danger of foaming at the mouth, shut up.

There was a terrific crash from upstairs and I retraced my steps to the garden. I'd included modern texts along with Carver's prized rare book collection and trusted that the dim light of dawn would obscure which was which.

The man emerged at his back door with a loud crash. He didn't look very diabolical, more like ridiculous in a homespun nightshirt.

'What the hell do you think you're doing?' the

379

academic roared in a high-pitched voice, carefully closing the door between us but leaving a crack through which he could shout.

'Book burning!'

'Are you mad?'

'No, I'm having an old-fashioned book burning party,' I roared back. 'Very Elizabethan.' I tossed one of his books into the flames.

The effect on Carver was dramatic. He opened the door, took a couple of steps forward, hesitated, rubbed his eyes and then darted back inside. From my position I could see him frantically looking for his library.

'Greta!' he bawled.

Even at the distance I stood, I could hear the sound of heavy feet pounding downstairs. Greta Armstrong emerged at the French windows, which she flung open with a crash. Her mighty bosom, released from all restraints, was swinging about as if she'd pushed a large bolster up the front of her loose white nightie.

'Doug,' she ululated, 'it's that private detective I told you about. Keep back, he's crazy.'

'He's burning my precious books,' Carver screamed, as if in mortal pain.

'And I'm going to carry on burning them until I get some information,' I rejoined.

'You Nazi!' he yelled, starting towards me. Not very tall or robust-looking, he wore his dark hair in an elaborate style and sported an unusual parti-coloured beard. The white patch under his chin and the nightshirt made him resemble the nursery rhyme character, Wee Willie Winkie, and he was just about as menacing.

I picked up one of the heavy folios – '*Actes and Monuments of these Latter and Perilous Dayes*' – and held it close to the flames.

'Come a step nearer and this joins the rest,' I warned. 'All I want is some answers to questions.'

'That's an invaluable first edition of John Foxe's *Book of Martyrs*,' Carver screeched in horror.

'Then he won't mind it being burned,' I snapped, holding the book as close to the fire as I could. I'd already picked up that neither of them had threatened me with the police, the first action of a normal householder dealing with an unwanted visitor. 'Talk, or in it goes,' I concluded. 'Why did you have Meg Hands killed?'

He clapped his hand to his mouth as if he'd swallowed a wasp.

'I know nothing about that. It was nothing to do with me.'

'Say nothing,' Greta advised. 'He's cut the phone off. I told you to get a mobile.'

'Who were you phoning?' I demanded.

'We have friends,' she said defiantly.

'Friends like Percy Pullman?'

She looked stupefied at this, then gave a weird giggle.

'According to the police you're responsible for what happened to him,' Carver yelped defiantly.

'But you know different, don't you? Admit it, you're the head of this group of loonies going round killing people.' Even as I spoke my words seemed fantastical to me, but I had to press on. Whatever Carver was, he wasn't the Napoleon of Crime, nor even the Al Capone. I picked up two of the smaller modern books and threw them in the fire. They blazed up immediately. In the smoke and confusion Carver wasn't to know that I hadn't destroyed his first edition.

'You criminal lunatic,' he wept with rage. 'You foul Nazi barbarian! If only you knew the truth. I've nothing to do with those deaths. I've done everything I could to stop it.'

'Everything except the tiniest practical step,' I said, picking out another folio.

'That's a third folio of Shakespeare. You wouldn't . . .'

381

'I will. I want to know everything you know about what's been going down. Why are you on the board of Black Cat Services? What's your relationship to Neville Fraser? They'll do for a start.'

Carver seemed to crack. He slumped to his knees and curled up on the doorstep.

'I'll tell you,' he said. 'I never wanted to be involved in the first place, but just leave my books alone.'

I took a step towards him but Greta Armstrong hurtled through the French window like an avenging Valkyrie, far more life-like and menacing than anything Wagner thought of. She was whirling a long sword round her head and shrieking.

I dodged backwards, and fortunately Shakespeare took the wicked thrust of her rapier or I would have been kebabed through the heart. As she struggled to free her point I stooped and, picking up a log, smacked the hilt of the rapier out of her hand. That didn't stop her. She closed with me, her meaty arms whirling in search of a target.

I stepped back again, feeling carefully for my footing on the wet grass, and then gave her a perfect right hook to the side of the jaw.

She subsided slowly and majestically and went face down on the grass. Carver made no move to intervene.

I surveyed the scene. For once things seemed to be going my way. I picked up the rapier and pulled it free from the book.

'Pick her up!' I ordered, making a fine flourish with the sword.

'What about my precious books?' he quavered, indicating his priorities.

'Pick her up!' I repeated.

'I can't,' he whimpered. Nevertheless he made an ineffectual move to haul Armstrong by the shoulders.

I rammed the rapier into the soft turf of the lawn with all my strength.

'That's a fine Toledo blade, sixteenth-century Spanish,' he said with far more indignation than he'd mustered over his mistress.

Between us we lugged Armstrong's whale-like carcass off the lawn and into the living room. We dumped her, none too ceremoniously, on a rug in front of the stone fireplace. She moaned and stirred but was definitely out for the count, which suited me.

Carver looked at me with pleading eyes. 'At least let me pick up the books that are on the grass,' he begged.

'Talk, and you can bring them all back in,' I offered.

He rolled his eyes. 'This has all got out of hand. Please let me bring the books in before they get soaked in dew. I'm begging you. Some of them are irreplaceable.'

'So was Meg Hands but you didn't mind doing away with her.'

'That was an accident. It was never meant to happen that way.'

'Rape and murder, an accident?'

He buried his face in his hands. 'It wasn't me,' he wailed. 'I warned them not to go too far.'

'Who was it? Fraser?'

'Him and others.'

'How did it happen?'

'I can't say. I wasn't there.'

'You know, though, don't you?'

He nodded.

'Look, there's a fire in here,' I threatened, chucking some dry sticks into the embers. 'I'll burn your whole bloody library, book by book, unless you talk.'

Unfortunately genuine brutality's not my scene. I haven't got the face for it. Even with my shaven head I didn't look savage enough to be convincing. Nevertheless, Carver flinched as the flames took hold and the fire began crackling in the hearth. I went over to the shelves and selected an expensive-looking volume.

'Please no,' he whined. 'That's a rare *Daemonologie* of King James the First with marginal notes in Tudor secretary hand.'

'Tell me what happened to Meg.'

'A charming girl . . . wonderful old-fashioned manners . . . she came to several "at homes" here but unfortunately her brother was keen that she should be initiated.'

'Initiated?'

'It was a completely harmless idea at first. We have a little society devoted to study of some of the more obscure aspects of Elizabethan life.'

'Satanism.'

'No, no, anything but. We sought enlightenment through exploration of the senses.'

At this, I looked down at the senseless form of Greta Armstrong. She'd started snoring loudly. It was she, not Carver, who'd supplied the industrial sound effects in the four-poster.

'Was she in this society?'

'Yes.'

'So how did you go from dancing round the Maypole to sacrificing virgins in one easy move?'

'We didn't, or at least I didn't. Some people got the wrong idea. They went too far.'

'Who? Names please.'

'I've told you enough. I'll be ruined.'

'Percy Pullman?'

'Yes.'

'Jack Rix?'

'Heavens, no!'

'Who then?'

'Let me get the books. You don't understand. Some are worth many thousands of pounds. I believe the notes in my *Daemonologie* are in John Dee's own hand.'

I decided to let him get the books and bring them in. I thought that I'd get more out of him that way. I stood guard as he garnered in armfuls. He resembled a mother protecting her children.

'That's enough,' I said, tapping him with the Spanish sword which I'd retrieved.

Sweating freely in the early morning light, he trotted back into the living room and reverently replaced the books on his shelves, sighing with relief when he found that the *Book of Martyrs* hadn't been burned.

'Right,' I ordered, 'just who was in on this initiation of Meg? It wasn't only Fraser. He hasn't got the brains.'

Carver nodded agreement and then sat down heavily on the wooden settle. He began breathing hard, gulping in air. His face turned as grey as one of his old parchments.

'My heart!' he gasped. 'Pills by the bedside.'

'Who was it? You're not getting out of this so easily.'

'Pills,' he murmured feebly, and slipped off the seat. I looked at him. His eyes were closed but were fluttering behind his eyelids.

'Damn!' I swore.

Armstrong was coming round. She tried to sit up.

Brandishing the rapier I dashed upstairs. There were pill bottles galore in a cupboard by the bedside. One was labelled 'HEART' in red letters. I grabbed it and ran back. When I reached the living room Armstrong was cradling Carver in her arms.

'You murderer,' she snarled. 'He was told to avoid all excitement. Give me the pills.'

'He shouldn't have started killing innocent young women if he wanted to avoid excitement!' I shouted.

At that point Carver's eyes blinked open. 'My son,' he murmured. I leaned forward to catch what he was saying but Armstrong gave me a push.

'Get away from him,' she yelled. 'You're killing him. Give me the pills.'

I pushed her back and she snarled like a savage dog.

385

We faced each other. As long as Carver could talk I wanted answers. 'My son,' he croaked again, and then he said something like, 'I want my son,' or 'It was my son.' I couldn't distinguish. Anyway, I gave in and handed the pills to Armstrong who immediately stuck one under her lover's tongue. His face relaxed at once, losing the expression of intense strain. Greta hugged him and he seemed to be unconscious.

'You tell me then!' I ordered her, raising the sword.

'Or what? Burn all his bloody books, if you like. I don't care.' Her face was lit by a malevolent light as if an evil presence had entered her.

I didn't want to leave with so many things still unresolved. I wanted to squeeze every particle of information out of this vicious old stoat, who might well be cleverly shamming, but in the distance I heard multiple police sirens. The sounds electrified me. They seemed to be creeping nearer and nearer. Hairs prickled on the back of my neck.

Greta Armstrong peered up at me with a gloating look of triumph and I decided it was time to beat a hasty retreat. Without a word, I dashed out through the back door, hurling the rapier across the lawn like a javelin. I came round the side of the house and paused for a second, expecting to see police cars arriving in the drive but they didn't. Trying to compose myself and look normal I walked out onto the road and got in my car.

I sat still for a moment, feeling the blood pound in my ears. The noise of sirens was close but the police must have been called to an adjacent street because no flashing blue lights appeared. I was grateful that the sound had provided me with the excuse to leave that dreadful house. I now knew where to get answers. Arthur had been involved in Meg's death. I'd already known he was involved. Harry Sirpells' letter had said that the conspirators would know if he sent anything but blank paper to Ruth Hands. They could only have known about Ruth's mail through Arthur.

I drove slowly to the motorway and joined the traffic jams approaching Stockport. It was almost ten when I arrived back at the Mumbhai.

Mr Mistry raised his eyebrows speculatively but said nothing as I went in.

I took a bath and changed my clothes. The outfit I'd bought at the Arndale was nondescript – fawn slacks and grey jacket. I thought I might pass as an unemployed PE teacher, or something of the sort.

I had to meet Ruth Hands. She had to be told that Arthur had been involved in his sister's death. I dialled her number on my mobile.

'Ruth,' I said when she replied, 'I'll meet you where we arranged. I'll be in a green Micra. Give me a half-hour start.'

The arrangement was that she'd drive to the Trafford Centre, park in the corner of the rooftop car park, then make as if she was going into Selfridges, but in fact transfer to my car in the lower car park.

It had all sounded simple when I'd explained it to her but I was on tenterhooks as I took the M60 counter-clockwise to the Centre. When I saw her coming down the escalator she was carrying a yellow Selfridges bag. I got out of the car so she could spot me and seconds later we were driving away. There didn't seem to be any signs of pursuit.

'Are you sure all this cloak-and-dagger stuff is absolutely necessary?' she drawled.

'I wouldn't be doing it if it wasn't,' I said peevishly.

'So what did you find?'

'Later,' I muttered.

'My, we're tight-lipped today,' she scoffed.

'It's very awkward.'

'Bad news, huh? That figures.'

When we reached Aston-under-Lyne I parked the car on the street round the corner from the Mumbhai Hotel. I suppose we could have gone to a public park or open space somewhere, but I felt more secure with four walls between me and prying eyes.

'What is this, Mr Constable?' Mistry exclaimed when I walked in with Ruth. 'Nothing was said about you entertaining ladies on the premises.'

'Er, this is Mrs Constable,' I said slowly and deliberately, gripping Ruth's forearm. 'We've come to sort one or two things out. Neutral ground, you know?' I felt her stiffen and prepared myself for the instant denial she was certain to make but she kept quiet as we walked towards the stairs. Mistry's eyes were almost revolving in his head. However, he made no move to stop us. We were a mismatched pair, me in my PE teacher outfit and Ruth in an immaculate green Versace jacket and trouser suit with matching blouse that must have set her back the best part of a thousand.

'Excuse me,' she snapped, jerking herself free of my grip as I opened the room door. 'This had better be good, *Mr Constable*! If you've got me up here for –'

'Will you listen?' I said. 'It's not good. Arthur helped to kill Meg.'

She took the one comfortable chair in the little room and I perched on the bed.

'How do you know?' she asked crisply.

I related my discoveries, including about Rix.

'So it comes down to this!' she exclaimed when I'd finished. 'You took the word of this wretched college professor that Arthur was involved but then you let him off the hook just like you did with Wilmington. There's nothing signed, nothing that would stand up in a court of law. The only tangible things you have are some incriminating photos of a cop we already knew was bent.'

'What should I have done?' I asked, trying to rein in

my anger. I realised that she was prepared to put a lot of mileage into maintaining her misperception about her precious son.

'You could have burned half his blasted books and made him write down a full confession to preserve the rest.'

'So you've had training from the Mafia?' I said indignantly. My anger was sharpened by the realisation that she might be right.

'Oh, keep your anti-American cracks to yourself! They're so cheap. If we'd been back in the States I'd have had legal redress against your laid-back bunch of bent coppers and got to the bottom of this long before now.'

'I doubt that,' I said angrily, 'and it's only one copper that's bent, not the whole force.'

'According to you!'

We faced each other in an angry silence that lasted for a full minute.

'Is it possible to get a drink in this dump?' she asked.

'Alcoholic?' I asked.

'Idiot! Tea, coffee, water, anything. I'm thirsty.'

I phoned Mistry.

We waited in silence until he tapped on the door and then came in with a tea tray. He stepped over Ruth's legs to place the tray on the bedside table. As he did so he kicked over the Selfridges bag Ruth had laid on the floor near her chair. A box fell out. It was clearly labelled 'Smith and Wesson .38 automatic pistol' and included a picture of a chrome-plated gun.

Mistry said, 'Oh, my,' when he saw the gun, and slapped the tray down. Then he backed out of the room, still saying 'Oh, my'.

'Thanks a bunch!' I said, leaping to my feet and cramming my few clothes into the case. Immediate flight seemed in order.

'Stay where you are. I'll sort this,' Ruth said, and she was out of the door before I could stop her.

'What a sweet man!' she cooed when she returned five minutes later. 'I managed to persuade him that he saw nothing.'

'How?'

'Don't ask,' she smirked, rubbing her forefinger against her thumb, 'but I think he believes you're high up in the secret service.'

I subsided onto the bed. I'd been on the go for most of the previous twenty-four hours. The strain was beginning to tell. I may have sighed.

'Don't you want to look at the gun?' she asked, passing me the box. 'A friend at the embassy sent it me by special courier.'

'Nice,' I agreed, unpacking the box and testing the slide on the neat little automatic. It was loaded. It fitted snugly into my hand and I felt a certain comfort from it.

'I didn't want to think about you going up against this group without protection.'

'That's kind of you.'

'Oh, stop being so British! Here, drink your tea!' she ordered, pouring me a cup.

'Ruth, I'm afraid everything does point to Arthur being involved.'

'I know,' she said wearily, 'but not being a parent yourself, you don't realise how hard it is to believe anything bad about one of your own.'

'Ruth, I'm not totally insensitive,' I protested.

'I know. I get everything wrong, don't I?' she said softly.

To my surprise tears began running down her cheeks. To my further surprise I found myself holding on to her and not being pushed away this time.

'Oh, Dave, I've no one to turn to. I don't want to believe this about Arthur but I've had it in the back of my mind from the beginning. He was so unwilling to grieve or tell me what Meg had been like in those last few days of her life.'

390

'Oh,' I murmured.

She held on to me tightly.

I tentatively began to free myself from her arms.

'Don't let me go!' she said fiercely. 'Comfort me – that's what you do, isn't it, Dave? Comfort me.'

'Ruth, this isn't the time or the place.'

'Yes, it is. It might be the only time or place either of us ever has. I've got a feeling that things are going to get a whole lot worse for us before they get better, if they ever do.'

'Ruth, you mustn't do something you might regret later!' I said urgently as she pressed her hand against my back and started kissing me.

'I need this now,' she said, undressing swiftly. 'Lock the door!'

With visions of an armed police squad charging into the room when Mistry had second thoughts about my secret service status, I did as I was told. In addition I put a chair under the door handle, and then got into bed with her. This was not how I'd thought things were going to turn out but I felt too weak to alter the course of events.

Ruth made love passionately and I responded in the same way.

Afterwards we both fell asleep – tension, I suppose.

It was almost seven in the evening when I woke to the sight of Ruth putting her bra back on. She gave me a sort of half-smile, neither warm nor cold.

'I thought you were going to sleep the clock round again,' she observed. 'You'd better get up, we've lots to do. Now, listen,' she said in a matter-of-fact voice, 'what's happened has happened. I put it down to human weakness. I don't want you to get the wrong idea . . .'

'Oh yeah!' I observed. 'It's an everyday thing for me, being made love to by a wealthy American client just like it is being holed up in a grotty hotel with the entire

391

Greater Manchester Police on the lookout for me, not to speak of Carver's bunch of sickoes who must have been informed by now of my activities at The Larches. Everything's coming up roses! Never finer!'

I sprang out of bed and began to get dressed. I felt that I'd been manipulated more than a little. My intention in bringing Ruth to Ashton had been to prepare her for the next step, which would have involved seating dear little Arthur in a hard chair and getting him to sing for his supper. He was the lad with the answers. Instead, I'd ended up in bed with his mother, an unexpected but not entirely unpleasant outcome.

I decided to leave the issue of Arthur for a more opportune moment. Not for nothing does the code of the Cunanes involve obliging ladies in distress.

Mistry bowed respectfully as we left.

20

'Off the Case!

'Rumours deepened last night that the Home Secretary has given in to public demands that the Greater Manchester Police be forced to give up the lead role in the ongoing Mangler Case. Speculation is rife that a squad is being formed of detectives from Scotland Yard, Regional Crime Squads and even MI5 to take over the inquiry as public pressure on the Government mounts.'

Report on BBC Greater Manchester Radio breakfast programme

The first thing we did was to drive back to Rochdale and retrieve the photos from Harry's office. Ruth examined them carefully.

'Rix was being paid to drop the Aycliffe murder investigation,' Ruth explained decisively. 'Just like he probably got a kickback to drop the investigation into Meg's death. We get this all the time in the States. The police pick up some poor person, probably a black, as the fall guy for a killing and then they tap the real perp for a healthy handout.'

'Corruption common, is it?'

'Isn't it everywhere? I know it's rife in Africa. One of my many illusions about England was that this country was different with your unarmed "bobbies" and little old ladies gently solving crimes in beautiful country villages.'

'My old man was a copper,' I confessed. 'I don't think he ever took bribes.'

'Oh, I've really offended you now, haven't I? All those things I said about the police and you must have taken them personally, yet you never said a word. Me and my big mouth!'

393

'No offence taken,' I assured her. 'The coppers here are far from perfect but they're not all like Rix. Thick maybe, messed about with by the politicians until they don't know what they're supposed to be doing, but they're not routinely corrupt. Rix really is the "one bad apple" they talk about.'

'You hope!' she said, punching my arm. 'I want to see this Carver. I might be able to persuade him to say more than he blabbed to you. I can appeal to him as a woman.'

'You're an appealing woman,' I agreed. I remembered Greta's spiteful expression. 'His lady friend guards him like a savage dog. I doubt you'll get past her.'

'Let's try,' she insisted. She looked like General Patton commanding the armoured breakout in Normandy, or at least like George C. Scott's rendition of that event.

I'd nothing else to do and no reason to disagree with her opinion about what Rix was up to with Fraser so once again I set off for Hale Barns. It occurred to me that I might've found a cheap hotel in those parts but I told myself that police activity would be more intense so near the airport. As well as being an unlikely spot for a desperate fugitive, Ashton is closer to Rochdale, which I think is why I chose it. I turned off the M56 and followed the roundabout onto Hale Road, then threaded the Micra along the winding Chapel Road. When I rounded the bend that would bring The Larches into view, I slammed on the brakes, and pulled into the kerb under the dense shade of a tree.

There were four police cars drawn up on the pavement. I could see a scene-of-crimes van parked in The Larches' drive.

'Oh God!' I moaned.

'Don't blame Him!' Ruth said in her practical way. 'Let's do something.'

'Like, race away from here?' I suggested.

'No, I'm going to ask a few questions. You stay here. You look suspicious with that prison crop!'

'You did it to me,' I protested, 'and besides, they don't cut your hair in prison these days.'

Ruth got out of the car without further argument.

I watched apprehensively as she strolled up to the police tapes in her confident way. A constable guarded the gateway and there were several members of the public, neighbours probably, gathered on the opposite pavement. Ruth immediately engaged the copper in conversation. The chat seemed endless and then, even more chillingly, a uniformed inspector came out and also chin-wagged with her.

A moment later the police tape was withdrawn from across the entrance and an ambulance emerged. I cowered low in my seat as it passed. The thought that Ashley Gribbin might be present was making me nervous. Ruth walked back towards me and got in the car. The inspector stared up the road after Ruth, possibly admiring her rear end, and then gave her a friendly wave when she turned. I let out a long breath.

'Both dead!' she announced dramatically when she opened the car door. 'A suicide pact. They took two whole bottles of his sleeping pills and swilled them down with whisky.'

'Suicide?' I mumbled disbelievingly.

'No, not that kind of suicide. Not like Wilmington, apparently. They each left a note, even copies of their wills with the latest alterations.'

'Oh yes!' I said. 'They would.'

'Whatever it was, murder or suicide, that pair had it coming,' Ruth replied in a way that left no room for argument. 'They're both where God can take care of their punishment now. I'm only sorry I can't give that stupid college professor the benefit of a few words in his ear. If he hadn't encouraged Meg to join his circle she'd be alive today.'

'Right!' I said, just as firmly as she.

'Now we need to do something about this creep,' she said, tapping the envelope containing the photographs of Rix.

'Send him to hell with Carver and Armstrong?' I suggested.

'Find out what he knows,' she replied, taking me perfectly seriously. It was dangerous joking with Ruth. She might decide that Rix would benefit from ventilation of the thirty-eight calibre kind; after all, I was now armed.

'Yeah, I might have an idea or two about that,' I commented. 'If you're right and he deliberately suppressed the investigation into the Aycliffe killing and possibly the other killings, he must have all kinds of information about the merry folk who were in Carver's Elizabethan glee club. Remember Carver never denied that there was a group going round murdering. He just kept whining that he wasn't responsible.'

'Wasn't responsible,' Ruth repeated grimly, 'and him a college professor!' She seemed to consider that Carver's profession added a dimension of horror beyond her earlier fears of Satanism. If I'd hoped she'd dropped that idea, her next words corrected me. 'If only I'd been with you this morning. I'd have toasted the fiend's nasty cloven hoofs in that fire until he gave us every name connected with his band of devil worshippers.'

'Yes,' I remarked.

'I hope you weren't taken in by his cant. Don't forget what I told you before, Satan is the father of lies. Nothing Carver said can be taken at face value.'

'No,' I mumbled.

'Well,' she said aggressively, 'what's this big idea for fixing Rix?'

'Have you got a scanner?' I asked.

She frowned. 'You want to transmit the pictures? To expose him?'

'No, just to hold the threat over him until he spills the

beans. Remember those photos do nothing to get Rix off my case. If he's arrested on the spot for corruption I'll still be wanted for questioning about the death of Percy Flaming Wilmington Pullman.'

'OK, and where d'you want to shake down your rotten apple?'

'My flat?'

'Better at mine. They'll still be watching yours.'

'And yours.'

'But I've got the benefit of a certain status, which you don't have. Even Rix'll think twice before putting the cuffs on a rich Yankee like me.'

'I'm not so sure about that.'

'Whatever, it's got to be my place. There's something I've decided, Dave. You'd better know before things go any further. It's Arthur. If things point to his guilt in a way that might mean serious jail time I intend to help him to escape.'

I must have looked pensive at this move.

'I know what you think, and I know what I said, but he's all I've got and I keep telling myself that he was misled. This college professor, I mean . . . Well, I'm as much to blame myself. I should have been here for him and Meg. He was too young to be left to fend for himself. Some can do it, he can't.'

'So?'

'So, if we get to the end of all this with God's help, I intend to take him back to Africa with me and straighten him out.'

'What if he doesn't want to go?'

'He will,' she stated with ominous certainty.

I almost laughed out loud. I had the police force and a gang of heavy-duty criminals systematically tracking me down but I had Ruth Hands on my side. What had I to fear?

'This isn't funny,' Ruth complained.

'You've got to laugh, though,' I said. 'I've told you before, Ruth, I'm not the police force. If you want Arthur to skip that's all right with me as long as there isn't more to come about his activities. If I find out that he was part of this scheme to fit me up for killing poor Annie –'

'Don't even say that!' she warned. 'I'm sure he's not deeply into this evil. He's still redeemable. He must be.'

Getting into Ruth's flat without being seen presented certain problems. I was sure that Mr Heritage and his crew of licensed Peeping Toms in the CCTV control centre would be sitting on their chairs with their narrow little buttocks clenched staring at those screens for any tale or tidings of me. No doubt supplementary cameras had been deployed near Ruth's flat.

I drove into Manchester, noting with pleasure the number of other anonymous green Nissan Micras that we saw, and dropped Ruth off near Piccadilly station, from where she could take a black cab to her home. Her flat overlooked the River Medlock and I hoped to approach it from there. She'd leave a light in Meg's bedroom window if the coast was clear. I drove round aimlessly for a while, then left the car in a side street in Ancoats and risked a quick walk to the Rochdale Canal where it passes under Great Ancoats Street, and took the steps down to the towpath. It was a long walk through central Manchester along a gloomy but secret trail which I hoped was not being overlooked by any CCTV cameras. I met a few dossers and a few underage drinkers and ganja smokers but no one to cause me any alarm.

When I reached the Whitworth Street West stretch of the canal it felt weird to be following the same route Meg had taken before her death, or so the camera claimed, and the camera can't lie, can it?

I still ached to know just how those pictures of Meg had been produced.

I bitterly regretted not questioning Carver more closely

about the circumstances of Meg's death but I'm a private investigator, not a professional interrogator and besides, I'd had no backup. I'd done well with the means available, well enough for someone to decide it was time the professor took early and permanent retirement.

I followed the canal right to its end at the ninety-second lock and emerged in full view of La Venezia. My throat tightened as I caught a glimpse of Neville Fraser's head gleaming under distant sodium lamps. He wasn't looking at me. I hurriedly turned up my jacket collar and walked away, taking the steps down to the Bridgewater Canal and then under the viaduct to the point where the Medlock joined the canal. After that, I waded into the water until I came to the wall of the luxury apartment block where Ruth lived. The developers had anticipated that someone might try entry by this route and they'd built a high wall as a barrier, but Ruth had left a knotted rope hanging down and I was able to gain access to the basement car park. She was waiting anxiously.

'Arthur's come home,' she said.

I'd no intention of retracing my steps, particularly with Fraser on duty outside La Venezia.

'That's OK,' I muttered as she led me to the lift. 'Does he know I'm on my way?'

'No, I told him I had to come down here to check out some storage arrangements. He doesn't seem to take much interest in my movements anyway.'

She held the door of the flat open.

'You stink,' she confided.

Fortunately, she still had the clothes I'd changed out of on my last visit to her apartment and she led me into Meg's bedroom to dry out and change.

Noises of violent struggle were coming out of Arthur's room.

'He's playing one of those blood-thirsty computer

games,' Ruth explained, 'horribly spooky and violent. They're made just across the road.'

I nodded. Just as long as it kept the young master quiet until I set up my arrangements I didn't care if it came from China. She handed me the clean clothes out of the airing cupboard and made no move to leave so I stripped off the sopping garments and handed them to her.

'You still stink,' she whispered. 'You need a shower. He'll not come out of his room unless there's an earthquake or something.'

She seemed very anxious that I avoid meeting Arthur, and having come here to do something else I didn't feel like insisting that we get the rubber hoses out and start giving the lovely lad the third degree. I took a shower, towelled off, dressed and then padded back to Meg's room where Ruth had already scanned the photos of Rix on to Meg's laptop.

'What email address are you going to send these things to?' she asked.

'Janine White at the *Manchester Evening News*.'

'Oh, that woman!'

'She's my best contact with the press,' I explained as I keyed in Janine's address and placed the pictures on attachment. 'One touch of a button and she gets the pictures. A few seconds later everyone in the office will have them. Not long after that they'll be in every newspaper and media office in the country.'

'I see, but I don't see, Dave. Getting in touch with White's completely out of left field. I don't like it. The woman's unreliable. Suppose she doesn't want to receive a message from you?'

'Look, all we need is the threat. Rix won't know. Anyway, the pictures'll download to Janine's office whatever she wants. Now have you got that tape recorder?'

She flounced out and returned a second later with an

expensive tape recorder. We hid it in the desk drawer and checked that it recorded adequately. If I was ever going to get free and clear of the morass I was in I needed more evidence.

There was no point in me phoning Rix. Despite Ruth's confidence that her American passport gave her special status I knew that Rix would arrive mob-handed if he thought I was on the premises.

I listened nervously as Ruth phoned from Meg's room. 'Mr Rix, I need to see you right away. Something's come up. . . . No, it's not about Mr Cunane. . . . I need to see you urgently about . . . I don't like to say on the phone but I'll tell you if you come on your own. . . . It's something about Meg, there's new information from one of her friends. I'm thinking of leaving the country and dropping my campaign.'

'That'll grab his attention,' I said, as she put the phone down. 'Remember, don't let him in unless he's on his own. We'll never get him to talk if he has someone with him.'

'The little rat will talk or I'll –'

'You'll do what, Mother?' Arthur demanded, standing in the door. Ruth went to embrace him but he held her at arm's length. He saw me. 'Oh, it's him! I could smell that there was something unpleasant in the flat. Why have you brought this sewer-rat in here? I'm phoning the police.'

He moved to take the phone out of Ruth's hand but I blocked him.

'Mother, tell this ape to behave himself,' he entreated.

He then tried to get round me and out of the door. I grabbed him and pushed him towards a chair.

'Sit down, you toad,' I snarled. 'I've been talking to your dear friend Professor Carver. Before they carted him off to the mortuary, that is. He had a lot to say about you. '

401

All the colour drained out of Arthur's thin face and he collapsed into the chair.

'You killed him!'

'No, we think his friends may have taken care of that, but he did tell me that you volunteered your sister for initiation.'

'Dave!' Ruth said sharply. 'Remember what I said.'

Her face was screwed up in a mixture of anger and sorrow. I realised that despite hiring me to discover the true circumstances of Meg's death, that was now the last thing on her mind. At any rate, she didn't want Arthur making an admission that would put them at odds for the rest of their lives.

I shut up.

'Arthur,' she warned, 'Inspector Rix is coming here in a moment . . .'

Arthur looked as if he was about to wet himself.

'Not for you!' I growled.

'. . . and it's very important that you keep quiet,' Ruth continued. 'Do you understand?'

Arthur made no reply.

'Do you understand?' Ruth screamed.

Arthur almost jumped out of his chair in shock, but then nodded submissively.

The door chime rang and Ruth left to admit Rix.

'Don't make a move,' I warned Arthur, as he stirred.

I heard Rix come into the flat. There was a buzz of conversation for a moment and then Ruth ushered Jack into Meg's room.

'You!' he snapped. 'I should have known.'

Dapper as ever in a new Armani suit, anger flared in his face. His colour matched the red of his tie.

'You're under arrest,' he thundered.

'What for?' I asked.

'What for? You only had your fingerprints all over Pullman's car. That's what for. What is it? Are you getting

402

careless? Were you strapped for cash? Did you hire your-self out to hold him down while one of your drug-dealing friends injected him?'

'I think it was one of your friends who dealt with Pullman,' I said calmly.

'What are you on about, you bald-headed twit?'

'I may be bald now but mine's growing back, Jack. Yours never will.'

'Piss off, Cunane! I asked you a question. You may as well tell me here as at the station.'

'No, you're going to answer some of my questions.'

I turned the laptop towards him so that he could see the picture of himself counting Fraser's money.

'What the fuck . . .' he shouted, pushing his way for-ward. I shoved him back.

'Watch your mouth and stay back,' I yelled.

'Or what, big man? I can take you any time I like. I've been looking forward to this.'

I slipped the pistol out of my belt and pointed it at him. It wasn't loaded but he couldn't tell that. He backed away. To his credit, the smile that made most of his antag-onists yearn to smack his face switched on. He wasn't a man to be easily rattled.

'Well, isn't that the price of you, brave lad? I suppose you feel tough now you've got a gun?'

'Not particularly, but I want your full attention while I ask a few questions. You'll give me straight answers or I'll transmit these pictures to the press.'

'Mr Fraser bought a car off me,' he said quickly. 'The pictures mean nothing.'

'Oh good, so you'll have records, registration docu-ments and what not?'

He turned deep puce with rage.

'What we want to know is, who was Fraser working for?' Ruth queried.

'Ruth,' I cautioned, realising that questions from her

were meant to divert from the detail of Meg's murder and her son's involvement. I held my hand up and she subsided for the moment.

Rix missed none of this by-play.

'Jack,' I said in a more friendly tone, 'you're up the creek without a paddle. Whatever you say, you'll never be able to explain that photo. You'll "lose the confidence" of the Chief Constable. Isn't that what they say when they have a bent copper but can't quite prove it? For God's sake, the man you're taking cash from has got a string of convictions as long as your arm.'

'He may have,' Rix admitted, 'but what's in this jolly little reunion for me?'

'Ruth and I are interested in two things and when we get satisfactory answers the photos are history. We already know Fraser had a hand in Meg's death. We want to know who put him up to it.'

'And?'

'I'm fairly sure he did Pullman as well.'

'Another of your hunches?'

'A little bird told me. Check the marks on Pullman's arms against Fraser's hands. I think you'll find they match.'

'So you had nothing to do with it? How come your prints were all over that car?'

'Pullman gave me a ride a couple of days before he died. I can prove that. It'll be on CCTV.'

'You're saying these pictures won't be released if Fraser becomes number-one suspect instead of you?'

'He is the number-one suspect! I know I didn't do it,' I said indignantly.

'Your word doesn't go a long way with me, Cunane.'

'Likewise, Rix,' I snarled. 'Come on! Make your mind up. If I touch this button the pictures will be all over the national press tomorrow.'

'OK, OK,' he muttered. 'All right, Fraser makes a good

404

suspect. One or two things have emerged which point to him. Castlefields, for instance.'

'Could Fraser have been at Castlefields when Meg died?' I asked.

'He might have been,' Rix admitted sulkily. 'What I told you about Fraser being in custody at Bakewell in Derbyshire at the relevant time was correct as far we knew, however it's since come to light that he was released on his own recognisance that weekend. It wasn't recorded due to a system error.'

'Was that the kind of system error that you buy with folding money?' Ruth asked sarcastically.

'You can stow that!' Rix snapped. 'I notice you aren't asking what sonny boy here had to do with his sister's death. At the time it was as plain as a pikestaff that he knew more than he was saying, but to spare his mother's feelings I let him off easily.'

'How generous of you!' I commented as Arthur blushed crimson.

'It's true.'

'Arthur will answer later,' Ruth said grimly.

'But not to a court, is that it?' Rix rapped back, with a rising note of triumph in his voice.

'You're the one who should be in court, for taking bribes from a murderer and for trying to frame Dave,' Ruth said hotly.

'I didn't frame him. The evidence was all there,' Rix replied, ignoring the bribery charge.

'But you didn't pursue the investigation that might have cleared him. That was because Fraser bribed you,' she insisted.

'Think what you like, lady. As far as I'm concerned you're crazy.'

'We want to know who put Fraser up to his crimes,' I interjected. 'We know he wasn't the only one involved.'

'Now you're up a completely different gum tree,' Rix

405

said. 'Why don't you ask him yourself? He's only across the road.'

'Dave, send those pictures out now!' Ruth ordered in fury.

Rix looked slightly abashed at this. The perpetual irritating grin that had given him his nickname flickered off his face for a moment as I steered the cursor to the 'SEND' button.

'The deal is this, Jack,' I said slowly. 'You phone Fraser and get him here. You can let him think that he's home free, or whatever, but I must have those names.'

'But I can't clear you without incriminating him!' he protested.

'Double-cross him, Jack. You're ace at that!'

Rix looked at me and then at Ruth. Seeing no way out, he finally spoke. 'I'll have to go and get Fraser. He won't come for a phone call.'

'Don't let him out of here,' Ruth advised.

'What choice have we got?' I said. 'Rix, if the electricity goes off or there's any funny stuff, these pictures still get transmitted. These things run on batteries, you know.'

I'd no idea if that was true. It sounded good and I hoped Rix was as computer illiterate as I was. 'We'll give you ten minutes, then I'm pressing the off switch on your career whether you're here or not.'

He was back in just over ten minutes. The Smith and Wesson was in my pocket when I heard the entrance bell ring.

'What's this bastard here for?' Fraser snorted when he saw me. 'You said nothing about him. You said this bitch would pay me and there'd be no more trouble.'

'That's right, Neville,' Rix said in his most coaxing tones. 'Cunane's just here to protect the lady. However, if you're scared of him –'

'Scared of him! I'll rip his head off and piss down his neck.'

'Calm down. We're all in this for the money, including Cunane. Isn't that right, Mrs Hands?'

Ruth had enough self-possession to say yes.

'How much?' Fraser bellowed.

'Ten thousand a name,' I said, 'and more for the name of the top man.'

A look of keen calculation passed over Fraser's blurred features.

'Have you got cash up front?' he demanded.

'Tomorrow,' I said.

'Forget it then. Am I supposed to grass and then take an IOU?'

'Neville!' Rix cajoled. 'Don't look a gift horse in the mouth. I'll see they pay you.'

'You! No deal!'

'Think of the money,' Rix suggested. 'You'd be able to retire to Miami or set up your own security firm.'

I could almost hear the cash bells ringing in Fraser's cauliflower ears. Greed smouldered in that austere room like embers waiting to be fanned into flame.

'They could hand over the money at that barge where we met,' Rix continued.

'The *Virgin Queen*? Hah!' he leered. 'I don't know about ten grand a name. I'd want at least half a million for the lot. There's a whole long list of names – doctors, lawyers, even a judge. They liked watching me doing things they hadn't got the bottle for themselves. Listen, missus, if you come to the *Virgin Queen* with half a million in used notes I'll give you the name and description of everyone that was in our little band of brothers. I'll tell you exactly what we did and when we did it.'

'What about my daughter?' Ruth asked in a choking voice.

'I didn't kill her. I was in police cells that weekend.'

'No, you weren't. You were released in time to be in Manchester. Rix has told us,' she objected.

407

'Happen, I was,' he admitted, with a sly laugh. 'Happen, I wasn't.'

'What about Pullman? Was he in this bunch?' I asked. Ruth looked as if she was ready to explode at any moment.

He nodded.

'Did you help to kill him?'

'That was just in the line of business. They all knew that the penalty for grassing was death. You could say you killed him, Cunane, making the little shite talk like that.'

'Who was with you?' I demanded eagerly. 'You weren't on your own.'

'Here, who's paying for this? I've said enough to you, Cunane,' he muttered stubbornly.

'Was it the same person who put you up to killing Annie Aycliffe?'

'That was the stupid bitch's own fault. If she'd just said she wasn't your tart we'd have left it at that but she had to come at us. Who the fuck did she think she was? Some sort of SAS woman?'

'Did you rape my daughter?' Ruth whispered.

'I had nothing to do with that. Ask him, he knows,' he said, pointing at Arthur.

Arthur cringed. 'No, Mother!' he screamed. 'It wasn't like that. I did nothing.'

Ruth howled and ground her nails into her fists and then she leaped at Neville Fraser like a wild cat. She took him by surprise for a second and managed to scratch his face but he'd had too much experience in fighting and killing women. He grabbed her by the throat, lifted her off her feet and shook her.

Arthur dived forward to rescue his mother but Fraser casually threw a punch that sent him reeling against the wall. He crashed onto Meg's bed, which collapsed under him, and then he stayed where he was.

I pressed the muzzle of my gun against Fraser's fat neck. He looked at me through the side of his eye.

'Got a gun, have you? Well, I don't give a shit. I'll snap this bitch's neck like a dry twig. I don't give a shit if you shoot me or not.'

His massive hands closed round Ruth's neck. She made a sort of gurgling noise.

'Put the gun down and back off or she's dead,' he warned.

I believed him. Even if I managed to club him senseless with the pistol he'd still kill her. I threw the gun at his feet. He slowly released the pressure on Ruth's neck and let her go. I caught her as she fell.

The gun was in his hand in an instant.

'Cunane, get her out to that barge with the money by twelve tomorrow or you're both dead,' he snarled. 'Rix knows where it is.'

He turned to the door.

'Fraser, don't go!' Rix begged.

Fraser gave the detective a slap across the mouth that sent him to his knees.

'That's for you, pig!' he laughed.

'Don't go outside!' Rix screamed through bleeding lips.

By this time Fraser was down the stairs and at the outer door.

Rix pulled himself to his feet and went after him, still yelling 'Come back!'

I realised what was happening and charged after Rix.

'You bastard,' I shouted. 'It's a setup!' I elbowed Rix to one side but he grabbed my arm.

'Too late,' he muttered as Fraser reached the doorway and flung himself through it.

I heard an amplified yell of 'Armed Police' coming as if from the mother of all megaphones. It sounded like Gabriel's Horn summoning everyone to the Last Judgement and in the case of Neville Fraser it was certainly the final sound he ever heard. He turned towards the voice with the gun still in his hand, slightly raised. I

409

wasn't sure if he was even aware of the weapon. His mental reactions weren't the quickest. Two shots rang out. I saw them hit his chest.

Fraser looked stupidly down at the wounds. Too late, his fingers let the pistol slip. He went down onto his knees, then tried to struggle to his feet, failed and fell forward face into the gutter.

Arc lights flicked on, reflecting off the shiny bald head of the dead man. In an involuntary movement my fingers stroked my own hairless scalp.

'That was meant to be me, wasn't it?' I spluttered. 'You thought he'd chase me out of the flat then, bang. No more Cunane!'

'Steady, lad!' Rix cautioned. 'Don't let your imagination run away with you. Come back upstairs. You've had a shock.'

I noticed he wasn't showing any symptoms of shock. He mopped his bleeding lips with a handkerchief. If I'd had a shock, it was nothing to the voltage that was coming Rix's way. I ran back up to Meg's room. Doors were opening, heads emerging along the corridors.

Rix chased after me but he wasn't in very good condition.

'Dave!' he wheezed.

The laptop was still on, but the screen had gone blank. I fumbled with the mouse until the email page came on again.

'Dave, old son,' Rix gasped over my shoulder, 'in fuck's name, what good will that do?'

I turned.

'It'll let everyone know what a murdering scumbag you are.'

'You fool! I can clear you of the Pullman business and remove any lingering suspicion about you and Annie Aycliffe but if you press that button everything comes out, including dear little Arthur's part in his sister's death.

Do you think he'll last five minutes under questioning?'

I looked at Arthur. He was sprawled on the wreckage of his sister's bed, unconscious. Ruth, though, was struggling to her feet.

'Listen to him, Dave,' she croaked.

I looked at her, shook my head and then jerked the connecting lead out of the telephone socket and switched the laptop off.

'Nice one, laddie,' Rix said, with a sigh of relief. I could hear sounds of heavy feet pounding up the stairs towards us. 'Say nothing,' Rix suggested urgently. 'Fraser saw you. He followed you here and then tried to blackmail Mrs Hands into handing over money. Young Arthur here called me, and I arrived in time to save you all. Got that?'

I nodded.

As the police entered the flat Ruth turned to her son.

21

'Shot Man Guilty!

'In a dramatic incident on the streets of England's vaunted second city, Neville Fraser (32), whom the Manchester police have now named as the Mangler killer, was shot dead last night. Fraser, who may have had links to extreme right-wing racist groups, was named as the man behind the Mangler killings. He was shot dead by police while attempting extortion from the family of one of his previous victims.

Right-wingers deny links with Fraser: Barrie Hardbottle, (a.k.a. George Jones) (67) leader of one Britain's most well-known anti-immigrant groups denied that the Mangler killings were an attempt to stir up hatred against the asylum seeker community. "We know nothing of this Fraser," claimed Hardbottle.'

Report in the *Independent*

I trust Marvin Desailles.

He's acting as my solicitor in the case against Peter Snyder and his wife. Marvin's having some success in persuading a court that Peter acted wrongfully in winding up Pimpernel Investigations and transferring the assets and goodwill to his own firm without any compensation to me.

He's being helped by the fact that my name is now clear of all suspicion.

I trust Marvin even though he is Celeste's cousin.

You have to trust someone, though it'll be a long time before I completely trust a client again. The way Ruth moved the goalposts wasn't easy for me to swallow. For months she'd pressured me to find Meg's killer. When I was almost at the point of success she changed her mind. A verdict of accidental death was now acceptable.

I asked myself if that meant she'd decided that Arthur killed his sister. Sororicide it's called. I looked it up. I doubted that Arthur had the bottle for murder. The evidence pointed to him being part of a conspiracy and I thought his motive was jealousy because Meg was so superior to him in every way. The virtuous attract the envy of the vicious. She was training to fulfil their dead father's dreams in Africa and at the same time she was everything their mother hoped for. Her way of life must have been a daily reminder to Arthur of how far he fell short of their unattainable ideals. In the end that burden was too much for him.

According to Patricia Manningham, Arthur had been the dependent one in the sibling relationship. Perhaps Meg felt that Arthur's interest in 'scrying' and Tudor magic wasn't so innocent. As a would-be missionary would it have been out of character for her to decide that her own brother should be her first convert to the paths of righteousness? If Meg was as confident and aggressive as her mother, Arthur's reaction became understandable. From being supervised by the 'Old Queen' at a range of ten thousand miles he suddenly found himself living ten feet away from a domineering sister.

I couldn't be certain that was the true scenario but it felt right. If only Ruth hadn't changed from vengeful fury into protective mum I could have found out exactly what Arthur had done. As it was I had to make do with guesswork about his role.

Whether it started as a mean prank, or was a deliberate act of spite, Arthur entangled his sister in the web of circumstances that led to her drowning. He wanted to drag her down, to splatter her pristine façade of purity with filth.

So, if not directly responsible, Arthur was a major

player in the drowning of his sister. Meg's body was raised in silence from the murky waters. I'd managed to briefly penetrate that wall of silence. Now silence was to reign again as far as Ruth was concerned.

Ruth's a moral woman, a very moral woman. She'd slept with me for one reason only. It certainly wasn't love, or need, or simply the prevailing fashion of our times. Ruth stands apart from all that. She wanted to save her son. Dear, meddling Celeste had given her a very overblown account of my reputation and so Ruth calculated that sexual desire was the one card she could play to ensure that I wasn't hard on Arthur.

I tried to raise those issues with her but she wasn't having any. I was hired help again.

Arthur had told her everything, in detail – or so she said. I'm not his mother so I don't have to believe that. She told me that he'd had a conversion experience and as a born-again Christian was giving up his studies and was joining her in her work as a missionary combating Aids in Africa.

I asked her what those significant details were but she wouldn't tell me.

'Dave, it's best if you don't know. Arthur's making a fresh start and I don't want anything to spoil it.'

I learned later that the Hands Jam money was only a small part of Ruth's fortune. She'd inherited many millions from her abusive stepfather, so perhaps great expectations were helping to keep Arthur off the primrose path and firmly tied to her apron strings. He was welcome to them.

This was after the sensational revelation of Neville Fraser's starring role as the Manchester Mangler, deceased. More evidence piled up linking him to those killings. That was a nine days' wonder. I did quite a few television interviews and Jack Rix did even more. Something happened to him, though. The wheel came off his chariot.

He lost the confidence of his superiors. I don't know what the details were. Someone at GMP Force HQ had added things up and found that two and two didn't make four in Jack's case. Possibly someone twigged that he'd set up the shooting at Ruth's apartment.

I still nervously stroke my hair when I think of that. Fortunately, it's all grown back, dark and curly as ever. I often wonder what pretext Jack was going to use to get me to step through that fatal exit. His fertile brain had no doubt come up with something and but for the impulsiveness of Neville Fraser I'd be pushing up the daisies now. I was duly grateful that it was his bare scalp and not mine that the police marksmen saw first.

Rix was given six months' leave for stress-related problems. I heard that he was considering an important post in the private security industry.

Some time after most of the fuss had died down I went to see Arthur and Ruth off at the airport.

When he thought Ruth wasn't looking Arthur scowled at me like a convict awaiting transportation. In a way that was what he was. All he lacked was a T-shirt with broad arrows and a pair of leg irons. I knew Ruth wasn't deceived about him because when she kissed me goodbye, she said, 'I know what you're thinking, Dave, but believe me, I'll get to work on him. The Lord works in mysterious ways and he's his father's son. I've got to believe that there's the right stuff in him.'

It occurred to me that this was what she'd wanted all along – the means to ensure that errant Arthur stepped into Meg's shoes. Maybe this was what Arthur himself had subconsciously wanted when he lured Meg to the so-called 'initiation'. I supposed I shouldn't complain. Ruth's financial settlement with me was generous, but not overgenerous, considering that I'd temporarily lost my business and was almost sentenced to life imprisonment in her service.

415

I nodded and smiled and waved to them from the departure lounge. Arthur turned his back but Ruth waved. There were some of her support workers standing nearby. It's nice that people no longer move away when they recognise me.

I even go drinking in public bars like La Venezia, which is still pulling in the rich and the famous and the wannabes. Cosgrove's no longer in charge. Michael Coe gave him a clean bill of health but, in fact, he was stealing the stock and when the business went belly up he was found out and given three years in jail. Michael must have known that Cosgrove was 'at it' but he'd kept quiet. Of course, he wasn't being employed to protect the finances of La Venezia but he must have had a reason for not giving me the truth.

That was just one more of the loose ends that teased me when I drove home from the airport.

It was as if the veil of mystery surrounding Meg Hands' death and the Mangler killings had been partially lifted but then replaced. In the public mind, Neville Fraser had now firmly taken his place in the rogues' gallery alongside the other serial killers of the last twenty years, and if the police had any doubts they weren't saying. Neville wasn't here to answer questions. In a way, that freakish man fitted in perfectly with current obsessions. If he'd been a left-wing militant, a violent struggler against 'globalism' or whatever, there might have been more questions but his own nasty little joke, the letters N F tattooed on the back of his hands, put him irremovably in the frame as a racialist killer. His birth name was Barry Thwaite.

Instead of turning off at Chorlton and going to my flat to brood about the absence of Janine, Jenny and Lloyd in addition to all my other unsolved problems, I carried on down to Castlefields. It was mid-afternoon, there were only tourists on the cobbled streets and parking the car was easy.

The sun was warm and I drank a pint of lager at the La Venezia beer garden, where I'd sat while Jack Rix pestered me months ago. Looking out at the towpath and the still waters of the Canal Basin, an image that I couldn't blank out returned to plague me. It was a vision of Meg floating face up with her hair splayed out as in a Pre-Raphaelite painting.

I knew that it wasn't just Arthur and Carver and Pullman and Fraser who were responsible for that girl's death. Ruth Hands might claim to be satisfied but she was away in Africa and could put these scenes out of her mind. I couldn't. There were others involved in the killing and they were still out there.

Trust is a two-way street.

I finished my drink and walked back to my car.

It happens to me often now, this moment of abstraction during a busy day. Unfortunately, I've read enough medical and forensic texts to know about post-traumatic stress disorder, but that doesn't cure me of the symptoms. I feel genuine anguish. Often, I think of Meg hurrying down Whitworth Street West and looking over her shoulder. Then there's Pullman, who I'll always think of as Wilmington, who I see running towards that presbytery door to be met by a strange clerical figure, still unidentified. At other times I think of Annie Aycliffe boldly tackling Fraser.

I look at the faces of the people I meet and wonder which one of them is a member of Carver's little band. Fraser had claimed there were many, including lawyers and judges. It's true that he was trying to extort money from Ruth Hands and it was in his interest to exaggerate.

Still, my failure to reach a conclusion cast a pall over everything I was doing. Recreating Pimpernel Investigations, persuading the insurance companies that had gone over to Snyder that it was safe to transfer their business back, hiring

417

new staff, finding new accommodation – none of this gave me any great pleasure. The only entertainment I got was hearing on the grapevine about the long faces at Snyder Investigations as their business dwindled.

Because I was unable to concentrate for long stretches I decided to take a partner. Harry Sirpells was the obvious choice. He got in touch with me after the death of Fraser. I offered him a share in the business but he replied from Spain that he was enjoying life there too much. He refused to go into detail about the circumstances in which he'd come to be there. I got the impression that he was still nervous about returning to Manchester.

So was I. I found myself jumping whenever I spotted a CCTV camera.

I spent a weekend with my parents. They were both looking a lot older since my incarceration in Strangeways and my fifteen minutes of fame as a serial killer. My bike was up there and I hoped that uphill pedalling and upland breezes would help me snap back to normality.

It didn't, but things did come to a head.

'Kate Mackenzie's back home for good,' Eileen said conversationally during Sunday lunch. 'I was speaking to her mother in Sainsbury's.'

'Uh!' I grunted.

'Eeeh lad, what ails you?' Paddy asked. 'We've hardly had a civil word out of you all weekend and you've a face on you like someone who's just won a wet weekend in Wigan as first prize in a raffle. Your mother's only trying to be helpful.'

'Yes, David,' Eileen scolded. 'You're not getting any younger, you know. Don't think you're such a catch that you can pick and choose.'

'Mother!' I protested.

'Well, we'd like to see you settled. All this business has been a bad shock for us . . . seeing and hearing our son constantly denounced as a vicious killer.'

'That's all stopped now, hasn't it?'

'But you don't seem right in yourself, David. There's something troubling you. Is it because you don't see Jenny and Lloyd any more?'

I shrugged. That had been a blow but it wasn't the cause of my malaise.

'You're still not too old to start a family of your own,' Eileen continued, riding her hobby horse that domestic life is the cure for all psychic ills. She was probably right, but it wasn't a frustrated longing for the patter of tiny feet that was grieving me.

'Charlie Chaplin was having kids right on into his seventies,' Paddy commented.

'So?' I said. 'Is that intended to console me? I'm not intending to start a family at the moment or in forty years' time either. Why don't you start another family yourself if you think it's so great? You're nowhere near seventy yet. Maybe your new kids will give you more satisfaction than I do!'

'David!' Eileen said softly. 'There's no need for that.'

'No need, whatever,' Paddy intoned, though I thought he looked secretly pleased with himself.

We ate quietly for a few moments and moved on to the sweet course. Then they returned to the fray . . .

'David, you're not leaving this house until you tell us what the trouble is,' Eileen said firmly. She may not have a fortune running into hundreds of millions of dollars like Ruth Hands but she can crack the whip when she wants to.

'It's not something I can discuss. The case . . .' I mumbled.

'It's that American woman, isn't it?' Paddy asked. 'Well, nothing you can say to us will upset her. She's buggered off out of the country, hasn't she?'

'Yes,' I murmured.

'Is that the problem?' Eileen queried. 'You weren't

419

thinking of taking up with her, were you? She's a Protestant preacher.'

'As if that would stop me, but no, it's not her.'

I had to smile. My mother wasn't concerned about our differences in wealth or nationality, or even age, only with Ruth's religious persuasion.

'But it is her case. You're not happy with the outcome, are you?' the astute former senior detective, who happened to be my father, asked.

'Something like that.'

'Eileen, clear the table and get the whisky bottle out. I'm going to get to the bottom of this,' he ordered.

'Yes, Detective Chief Superintendent,' Eileen replied with mock meekness. 'Any other orders?'

'You'd best go out for a walk or something when you've finished. I fancy that what our David has to say isn't for a woman's ears.'

'Ooooh! Paddy Cunane! I'll swing for you,' she said before unexpectedly running round the table and grabbing him by the ears.

He quickly offered an unconditional surrender, getting to his feet, siding the pots and loading the dishwasher. When I moved to help him my mother took my arm. 'No, you sit down. David. You're a guest. This is good for him. He's got to remember he's not in the police force any longer, with people at his beck and call.'

Later the whisky bottle did come out and I related every incident of the case to Paddy. He was a good listener, only occasionally interrupting with a question. Eileen sat hunched over her knitting but she didn't miss a word.

'Legwork! That's what this case has lacked from start to finish, legwork and thoroughness,' he complained when I concluded.

'That's not fair. I was on my own most of the time.'

'Exactly. You should have sacked Snyder as soon as

420

he started whinging about you getting help. He'd do well in the force today, that lad. That's all they do now, sit counting their budgets and then sit counting the people who're counting the budgets. Bloody accountants, most of them, who couldn't investigate their way out of a wet cereal packet.'

'Dad, we aren't exploring the deficiencies of the police service.'

'Aren't we? I rather thought we were. Do you think there'd be all these killings if the force was anything like it was when I joined? We were actually in continuous contact with the public, not charging round in cars.'

'I did quite a bit of charging round myself,' I said, remembering the journeys back and forth to Rochdale and Hale Barns.

'That's just what I'm saying. Did you think to go back and have another chat with the O'Carrolls, or Jed Eagles, or even this Cosgrove now he's got nothing to lose by telling the truth?'

'I hadn't got the time.'

'That's what I'm saying! You're like a bull at a gate, no time for anything. Oh, I'm not blaming you. When I was younger we had more time because we weren't filling in PACE forms night, noon and morning, and we didn't have the press on our backs to anything like the degree they have now.'

I was getting weary and a little sozzled by this time but Paddy seemed to have fire enough in his belly for both of us.

'Listen, David,' he said, continuing his lecture, 'you've done well . . .'

'Thanks,' I murmured.

'. . . but this was a botched investigation . . .'

'But no thanks.'

'. . . because although your client was a millionaire many times over you and your daft employee . . .'

421

'Ex-employee!' I corrected.

'. . . insisted on doing everything on the cheap. I don't know if there is such a thing as a Satanic influence which makes people do murder –'

'There is!' Eileen interrupted fiercely from her corner.

'I know there's wickedness and evil people. I should know that,' Paddy replied, turning to her, 'but I mean a force that's outside people, that tells good people to do bad things.'

'There is!' Eileen insisted. 'I'm constantly tempted to throttle you!'

'If you ask me, some of those that do wrong – and I mean really wrong, murdering and torturing kiddies and what not – have always had it in them. All they needed was the opportunity.'

'The Hands case?' I suggested, trying to get him back on track.

'Yes, David. What this case needs is a spot of good old-fashioned coppering.'

'You volunteering?'

'I am. I've got a few friends who won't mind wearing out their shoe leather on the pavements of Manchester. We'll go over everything and pick up what you missed. There must be something because I don't know if Old Nick's out there doing things invisibly but I do know that whenever something happens there's always someone who saw or heard if you spend long enough looking for them.'

'Who's going to pay your pals?' I muttered.

'I don't mind spending your money. You've got plenty. What do you want, peace of mind or a fat bank balance? Anyway, they won't want much. Most of them are retired.'

So that was it. I stayed the night with them and, I must say, slept better than I'd done for weeks. It was convenient that the lease on the empty Dutton Street office Ruth had provided for me still had months to run so Paddy agreed to make that his headquarters. Remembering how Celeste had been paid to spy on me I thought it was best if Paddy got to work at some distance from me and my affairs.

Over the next few weeks, apart from signing a few cheques to settle pay demands that came in the post to my flat, I heard nothing more from Paddy's private police force.

It was on a weekend in the middle of July that Paddy turned up at my flat unannounced.

'Right, a few things,' he said, taking out a small black notebook. 'Everybody's been visited and everybody spoken to. Ariel Ngwena, heard of him?'

'I've met him.'

'Did you know that he's listed at Companies House in Cardiff as the main shareholder and managing director of Black Cat Services, the security outfit that employed the bouncers down at La Venezia?'

'Michael Coe went into that, but he didn't mention anything about Ngwena.'

'Yes, Michael Coe,' Paddy said grimly, turning a page in his notebook.

'Oh, come on, Dad, this isn't *This is Your Life*.'

'It was very nearly your life, son, so just listen for once. Michael and his good lady have recently bought a house in Didsbury for which the deposit was at least fifty thousand. They moved out of a council flat in Moss Side, so where do you think he raised the readies for that? Michael was hardly going to tell you something that would lead you in the direction of the people who were paying his wife so well.'

'I can't believe it. Michael's straight.'

'Believe it. Celeste paid large cash sums into her bank account. The bank manager wondered if he should report her for suspicious sources of income but the amounts were always just under the limit.'

'I don't want to hear this.'

'David, you were his friend but Celeste is his wife and the mother of his kids. Anyway, back to Mr Ngwena. We managed to trace that furniture removal man. He spoke to the Vauxhall driver – you know, the one who was so interested in your relationship to Annie Aycliffe.'

'Yes, that was Neville Fraser,' I said.

'Wrong! The man helped us draw a Photofit of the driver and this is him.'

He handed me a drawing showing an African with a bulbous nose.

'Recognise him?'

'It's Ngwena. I spoke to him that same night.'

'And you must have convinced him that you intended to go on searching for Meg's killer despite the CCTV pictures he so carefully showed you?'

'I don't know,' I said, holding my head in my hands. Had I sentenced Annie to death?

'It gets worse,' he said sympathetically. 'This part-time removal man, a very rum character by the name of Hamish Morgan, was questioned by the police, as were all the witnesses who saw the two confrontations between yourself and Aycliffe, who had a lengthy criminal record for assault, by the way. A hunt saboteur and local tearaway, was the late Miss Aycliffe.'

'That's no excuse for killing her.'

'Did I say it was? I'm suggesting that there was plenty of reason for the police to look for other evidence about Annie's killer besides that which pointed at you. They interviewed the onlookers and Morgan gave them a good description of the man who asked if Annie was your wife. They told him they'd follow that up. He was expecting to be asked to an identity parade, but he heard nothing from them. He phoned the contact number he was given and was told to forget it. He was a persistent bugger. When he heard you'd been arrested he couldn't believe it. You know what he said? He thought you were a patient bloke like himself and he couldn't see you killing Aycliffe, however much she was asking for it.'

'So?'

'So he phoned again and this time a senior officer came round to see him. This officer told him he was a publicity seeker trying to get his name in the papers and warned him that wasting police time is an offence.'

'Name?'

'You know the name.'

I went to the drinks cupboard and poured us both a large glass of malt.

'There're only two explanations of Rix's behaviour,' Paddy continued. 'He was either determined to fix you, no matter what the evidence, or –'

'He was already on the take.'

'It looks that way.'

'Is that it?' I asked, draining my glass and returning for another. Paddy declined a top-up.

'I'm afraid not. I'm not doing this to show you up, you know. You were inside when Rix should have been investigating Ngwena, and you were betrayed by those that should have been helping you.'

'Go on, say it!' I said angrily. 'I'm a fool to myself and I shouldn't be allowed out on the streets.'

'Don't get dramatic, David. I didn't bring you up to become one of these psychological cases,' he warned.

I had to laugh at that.

'OK, stiff upper lip from now on, I promise.'

He looked at me with a certain glint in his eye. Between the two of them, my parents had an answer for everything.

'So, what about Ngwena's mate, Hobby Dancer?'

'In a word – nothing.'

'What do you mean, "nothing"?' I demanded, secretly pleased that his 'official' detection methods had failed. He actually looked embarrassed.

'Just that. Strange though it may sound, Mr Hobby Dancer doesn't officially exist. His name appears on no electoral roll. He's said to travel a great deal but there's never been a passport application in his name. No local school has any record. It's as if he just popped out of nowhere twelve years ago when his firm started up.'

'That's it! You can surely track him through his firm.'

'Yes, the registered ownership is a corporation with an address at a lawyer's office in Vaduz, Liechtenstein. It's just a name on a wall.'

'So Hobby Dancer's an assumed name. He's probably called Smith.'

'No way of proving it. Whenever anyone calls at his offices down in Castlefields they get the brush-off. He and Ngwena were seen going into that place on the viaduct he calls his home but no one's seen them coming out. I've had men watching there for up to three days at a stretch and they haven't seen him come out.'

'He likes staying in a lot?'

'No, that's the whole point. He's been seen going in. Then he's been seen jogging in the streets but no one's ever seen him coming out.'

'Obviously the building has another exit,' I said irritably, 'unless you're claiming he's got supernatural powers.'

'If there is another exit it isn't shown on any building records. I've had a surveyor out there pretending to be checking the alignment of the viaduct and he couldn't detect another exit.'

'A man of mystery eh? Anything criminal listed?'

'I've told you there are no records of this guy, with the police or anyone else. Bill Platt even tried to check if he has a National Insurance number or Health Service number. There's nothing.'

I looked disappointed.

'Actually, there is one thing. Joe Norton's a bit of a

426

Shakespeare buff and he reckons that the name Hobby Dancer's out of Shakespeare. I can't see it myself but that's what he said.'

'Go on.'

'I don't like to say. It sounds daft.'

'Go on!'

'Hobbididance is one of the five fiends who possess Poor Tom in *King Lear*.'

'*Fiends*, you said?'

'Yes, there's five of them . . .' he consulted the notebook '. . . Obidicut, Hobbididance, Mahu, Modo, and Flibbertigibbet. I'd look well reading those names out in court, wouldn't I?'

'And that's it?'

'Joe says Hobbididance is the Prince of Dumbness, meaning demonic possession.'

'So the guy has adopted a made-up name, unless you believe he really is a demon.'

'Dave!'

'Dad, there must be something in the local press about him. He's got a big firm.'

'All we could find was that Hobby Dancer sold his first computer game called *Wild Ride* when he was seventeen. *Wild Ride* became a bestseller in Japan. It concerns a battle among demons to control hell.'

'Photos?'

'None anywhere. Nothing in the company brochures, nothing in the files at the *Evening News*.'

'Dad, if this Hobby Dancer is the one who's "at it", how are we going to prove it?'

'That's the problem, lad,' he said drily. 'It's up to you now.'

Though he didn't say it, Paddy obviously felt that he'd gone as far as he could go and still keep within the law.

It was five days later that I got my first crack at solving the problem and that wasn't of my devising. I'm very busy these days. Before, I had people I trusted. I delegated to them. Not any more. I do nearly everything involving a decision myself.

My new secretary, actually an office temp, Miss Holt – I don't know her first name and I don't intend to – knocked timidly on my door. These days I'm cultivating reserve and distance as far as my staff are concerned. At any rate, Miss Holt, a pale, bespectacled young woman in a Marks and Spencer's navy-blue office suit, tapped ever so gently on my door. I yelled at her to come in. She seems a little deaf – either that or she's terrified of me. It doesn't matter really; her approach is preferable to Celeste's – barging in and telling me what cases to take.

'Come in!' I screamed, but in the end I had to get to my feet and open the door.

Miss Holt passed me a card on which the words 'Hobby Dancer' were written.

'This man, he's not got an appointment, but he said you'd see him when you saw this,' she squeaked, hitching up her glasses nervously.

'Show him in,' I ordered.

It was only the second time I'd seen the elusive entrepreneur. Slightly built, not at all imposing, this time he was wearing a Nehru-style jacket and trousers in some expensive grey material. I offered him my hand but he didn't take it. Instead, he greeted me with a long piercing stare. I think I was meant to be intimidated but I was determined not to be.

'Sit down, Hob!' I said cheerfully.

'I'll thank you to use my correct name,' he said coldly.

'Sorry,' I murmured, 'Hob . . . you know? Short for Hobby, seems a bit soft calling someone Hobby, but if you want me to, Hobby, there you go.'

'My name is Hobby Dancer!'

'OK, but I saw you in a tracksuit and it said O.R.G.

Hobby Dancer across the back, so you do have a handle to your name.'

'If you must know, my first name is Orgoglio.'

'Italian, eh? Love Italy myself. So what do your folks call you? Orgy?'

'If you must persist in playing the buffoon, stick to Hobby Dancer.'

'No, Org, I insist. Names are important. Yours, for instance, it doesn't exist in any database throughout the United Kingdom. So you don't exist, yet I see you sitting in front of me. Anyway, how about Oggie? That has a vaguely Welsh ring, doesn't it?'

'Leave my name alone!' he hissed.

'Sorry, no offence. I just think it was cruel of your parents, knowing you were going to struggle through life as Hobby Dancer, to lumber you with Orgoglio as well. Some parents, eh?'

He looked ready to start spitting feathers. I felt pleased. If he was who I thought he was he'd caused me sleepless nights for months. He seemed to be making a conscious effort to control his rising temper. I didn't want him to succeed.

'My name owes nothing to any parents. It's original to me.'

'Really? Not one of the Somerset Dancers, then?'

'Cunane, I came to see you to –'

'Yes, why did you come, Oggie?' I interjected.

'To tell you that I'm well aware of your pathetic attempts to have me watched.'

'Oggie, you're going nuts. Don't you know that's the first sign of paranoia, thinking people are watching you? Why on earth would I have you watched?'

'That's what I ask myself,' he said vehemently. This time his face was red with anger and I was well pleased.

I laughed and that was just enough to tip him over the edge.

'The police are perfectly satisfied that the Mangler Murders were committed by Neville Fraser. There's no need for further inquiry.'

'What are you on about?' I asked in feigned surprise. 'The Mangler killings, that's all over and done with, Oggie. But as you've brought them up is it widely known that Neville worked for Black Cat Services, which is controlled by your close friend Ariel Ngwena?'

'Whatever you're implying is rubbish! Fraser had help from racist groups. The police are investigating them.'

'Hold on, though, Og. I'm the last one to be fair to racist groups but they're not exactly a collection of intellectual giants, are they? More like mental pygmies. I mean, think about it. Neville himself barely had two brain cells to rub together, poor chap. He could hardly speak, let alone plan complex murders. He was typical of them. No, my money's on the idea that he had help from some really, really clever person. What do you think?'

'I think your stereotyping of my friend is unforgivable.'

'Neville?'

'Ariel Ngwena's a pygmy, as you very well know.'

'Sorry, it was just a figure of speech.'

'I came here in friendship to offer you some advice. Now I see you need something stronger than advice,' he snarled, and then left.

That wasn't part of my plan.

I skipped round my desk like lightning but he was just as quick. He was out of the door and into a red Range Rover before I could stop him. As the door opened I saw that Ngwena was driving.

Hobby Dancer wound the window down and shouted inarticulate abuse in a foreign language as he drove away. I offered him a two-fingered salute. It was only later that I learned that he was trying to cast a spell on me.

If he was a demon, then I was an angel, only I know

that I'm not. I wondered if he did. I decided it was time I took a holiday.

I fancied cycling round the West of Ireland but my bike was at my parents' cottage. I packed and then drove to the moors beyond Bolton.

22

There was a car I didn't recognise parked in the muddy lane outside the cottage.

'David!' my mother said in confusion when she opened the door. She blushed to the roots of her hair.

'Whatever's the matter?' I asked.

'Kate's here with her mother.'

'Kate who?' I queried.

'Kate Mackenzie! This is so embarrassing! They called on their way to Preston.'

'And so you took the opportunity to do a little match-making?'

'No, no! Kate would be just as upset as you were if she thought anything like that was going on.'

'So you thought you'd just stoke the fires secretly and then let things develop?'

'No, we were just naturally talking about you and your recent troubles. People do.'

'Mother, I'll be no trouble to you. Just give me the key to the garage. I only want my bike. I'll fix it on the back of the car and then be away to Heysham to catch the ferry to Ireland.'

'Just come in a moment,' she coaxed.

'The key!' I said.

She scuttled back indoors and returned with the key.

'This is so rude of you, David,' she said when she returned, but she was on the back foot and she knew it. 'Just come in and say hello. They won't bite you.'

'No, Mother,' I said stubbornly, 'you've got to learn that I'm not in short pants any more.'

432

She threw her hands up, handed me the key and went back inside.

I opened the garage, wheeled out my bike and started fixing it on the carrier.

Paddy came out.

'What's your hurry?' he asked.

'I'm going to Ireland. I decided to take a holiday.'

'A bit of a sudden decision, isn't it?'

'If you must know, your investigation's stirred up Hobby Dancer. He was in my office today to give me a warning.'

'Then if it's my fault I need to know about it. Come here,' he ordered, indicating that we sit on the low wall alongside the living-room window. I didn't realise at the time, but the window was open and neither my father nor myself have particularly soft voices.

Reflecting that Paddy was harder to brush aside than Eileen, I sat next to him and related my conversation with Hobby Dancer almost word for word.

'And now you're clearing out, are you?' Paddy asked when I finished. There was an undertone of contempt.

I started up indignantly. 'I need a break,' I snarled.

'And very wise you are too,' Kate Mackenzie said. She stood framed in the window, a perfect picture.

It was on the tip of my tongue to tell her to mind her own business but she looked so strikingly attractive with her long dark hair that the words froze on my lips.

'Listen, David –'

'Dave!' I corrected. 'Only these fossils call me David.'

Paddy snorted.

'You were David in school,' she said with a pleasant laugh.

'That was a while ago.'

'Yes, it was. I'm sorry for eavesdropping but I'm a psychiatric nurse these days and what you've just described fits the symptoms of acute obsessional behaviour perfectly.

433

I know from your job that something criminal must be involved but by challenging this man's beliefs about himself you've put yourself in great danger. He's certain to want to lash out at anyone who challenges his assumed identity as provocatively as you did.'

'Really?'

'Yes, certainly. I had a friend at the hospital who was stabbed to death because she smiled at a man in the wrong way. He thought he was the Prophet Mohammed and that by smiling at him she was challenging his status. He broke into the kitchen, stole a carving knife, and then killed her.'

'God!'

'It's true. The only way to control people who have these intense fantasies is by medication and then, as my friend found, it doesn't always work. Is this man on medication?'

'I doubt it.'

'So do be careful,' she warned, and then disappeared inside.

'There! That's you told,' Paddy said.

In the end I decided to lie low in Bolton for a few days. I needed to do some research of my own. Bolton reference library contained as much detailed information about eighteenth-century canal building as the library in Manchester and there were the county archives in Preston. After I completed my research I decided to return to Manchester and hope that Hobby Dancer was visiting the South Seas or Nepal.

Even as I drove back to Manchester I knew I was making a foolish move but I couldn't see any alternative. I needed to make a living and there was always the chance that he might have cooled down.

I had no such luck.

Hobby Dancer and Ngwena picked me up the day after I returned. I was leaving the office after six when they casually walked up to me on the street. Ngwena took a small pistol out of his pocket and pointed it at me. I couldn't take in what I was seeing. There was a CCTV camera focused directly on us.

'Just walk quietly behind me, Cunane,' Hobby Dancer said. 'We need to have an extended conversation.'

'You can't expect to get away with this in broad daylight,' I snarled. 'What about the CCTV cameras? The police will be here in seconds.'

They laughed at this. Then Ngwena positioned himself behind me and prodded me in the back with the pistol.

'Come with us now or we'll shoot you where you stand,' Hobby Dancer said in a gentle voice. Thoughts of the man who killed Kate's friend flashed through my mind.

I started walking. All the way I was praying for the sound of a police siren. All I heard was the roar of traffic.

We ended up in the room at Hobby Dancer's house above the viaduct where Ruth and I had spoken to Ngwena about the CCTV tapes. I didn't feel terribly threatened. Ngwena was tiny and Hobby Dancer so slightly built that he didn't seem very menacing. That shows how mistaken one can be. The smallest snakes are the ones with the most dangerous venom.

'You're wondering why we've brought you here?' Hobby Dancer said.

'That's right, Oggie, there'd better be a good explanation.'

'Yes, there'll be a full explanation and then we're going to persuade you to dispose of yourself.'

'In a pig's ear you are! Your mate Pullman tried that and look what happened to him.'

'Ah, but poor Percy didn't have all our tricks up his sleeve. No, it's surprisingly easy, as you'll find. But first explanations.'

He clicked his fingers at Ngwena, who pressed a button and a large section of panelling on an internal wall began to slide upwards revealing the familiar shape of a massive CCTV monitor. The screen showed people at a pavement café in Albert Square. The familiar backdrop of Manchester Town Hall gave my situation a nightmarish quality.

'Observe!' Hobby Dancer ordered gleefully, holding the gun to my head. Ngwena fiddled about with a console and suddenly my own image filled the screen. I was walking along Deansgate towards the viaduct. It took me some seconds to realise that I was witnessing the stroll I'd just taken with a gun at my back because there was no sign of Hobby Dancer or of Ngwena. The only indication that it was the same walk was the odd way I kept twisting my neck and glancing over my shoulder. I'd done that to see if Ngwena was relaxing his guard. Now, according to the evidence before my eyes, he wasn't there. I was walking on my own.

Ngwena clapped his hands in childish pleasure at the confusion on my face.

'Show him the other stuff, Ariel.'

The screen changed. This time it was Meg Hands walking along Whitworth Street West looking nervously over her shoulder at an empty street. That scene was already etched into my memory.

'And again,' Hobby Dancer requested.

Meg was walking along the street just as before but this time Ngwena was behind her, prodding her along with his automatic. Near the end of the street Ngwena forced her into a Range Rover, which drove away.

'And the supplementary footage.'

Meg was back on the empty street again. There was no Ngwena. She walked right past the spot where the now non-existent Range Rover picked her up, reached the pedestrian crossing and staggered drunkenly against the traffic lights.

'I believe you guessed at something on these lines,' Hobby Dancer said condescendingly. 'The girl at the pedestrian crossing is an actress standing in for the unfortunate Miss Hands, although she'll never know what a star role she had. She thinks she was helping to compile footage for a public safety film. You put us to great expense by doubting the CCTV cameras. Even when we arranged for you to see additional footage of the double going down the steps to the fatal waters you clung to your irrational scepticism.'

My mouth felt very dry. There was no way Hobby Dancer was going to let me walk away after I'd seen this.

'How did you do it?' I croaked.

'Nothing you would understand, Cunane. Eigen numbers, subtraction of certain designated pixels. It involves tremendous computing power.'

'But how are you getting these pictures from the CCTV centre?'

'There you have it. The power of money.'

'You mean you bribed Heritage, the CCTV centre manager to let you –'

'No, not him, he proved resistant, for some reason, but there are many tunnels under Manchester and I was able to procure access to the Post Office tunnel along which the feeds for the CCTV centre run. From there it was easy enough to splice into the cables and run my own material into the centre.'

'You're a genius, Oggie.'

'Modesty forbids . . .'

'Who else did you try to bribe?'

'Well, I tried with you. A pity you weren't amenable because you wouldn't find yourself sharing your last evening on earth with Ariel and myself if you'd been sensible. There's an art to bribery. To have offered you more than I did would have provoked suspicion. Others are different. Mrs Williams-Coe was scornful when she

437

was offered ten thousand, interested at twenty and really on fire when it came to a down payment of forty thousand and extra payments for each piece of additional material.'

I jerked forward off my chair, intending to grab Ngwena and hold him as a shield. But the African twisted away from me and Hobby Dancer brought the butt of his revolver down sharply on the back of my head. I stumbled to the floor, dazed.

Between them they pulled me back into the chair. Ngwena produced a length of cord and tied my wrists behind my back and my ankles to the chair legs. I thought Hobby Dancer would finish me there and then but he didn't. His obsession with his own genius demanded that he prove how much cleverer than me he was.

'Yes, Cunane, you'd be surprised what people will do for a hundred thousand or even much less. I'm thinking of starting a TV show on those lines – bribing individuals to kill their nearest and dearest – not for public viewing, of course, but for private distribution among certain connoisseurs of the human condition. Rix was easy. At first he thought he was giving a group of property speculators helpful advice but once the first transaction had taken place it proved surprisingly easy to persuade him to turn his inquiries in certain directions. It helped that the ideas I was feeding him chimed with his own prejudices. Right till the end he found it hard to credit that there could be a serial killer just as clever as he thinks he is.'

'You mean he didn't know that it was the Mangler who was actually paying him?'

'Hah! We claimed to be a secret citizens' committee concerned about the public image of Manchester.'

'And he believed you?'

'Not me! I never spoke to him personally. Our arrangement was conducted through an intermediary.'

'Neville Fraser?'

'Of course not. Rix would never have accepted helpful advice from the likes of Fraser. Our man claimed to be merely giving Rix a helpful steer with his inquiries.'

Hobby Dancer laughed delightedly at this point. The African chortled along with him. They were thrilled by their cleverness.

'Well, who was it then?' I shouted angrily.

'You've met him! You almost sat in on one of their meetings.'

'Carver?'

'No, you fool! It was Percy Pullman, a genuinely wealthy businessman. A fat cat Rix believed was speaking on behalf of monied folk. You tried to barge in on one of their meetings down at La Venezia. That's why it became important to find out exactly how much you knew.'

'I can't believe Rix deliberately wrecked his own investigation for a bribe.'

'He must have had an inkling that he was being misled but I'm sure he rationalised any doubts away, especially when his cash flow improved so dramatically. Having decided there was no serial killer it was easy for him to mentally play down matters that pointed to the existence of my little band.'

'Such as?'

'That all of our victims, such as your client's daughter, had a loose connection with saving the environment and that many had edible body parts removed.'

'The bastard!'

'As I say, he was easy and all too typical. What were those women to him? They were just grey figures from the grey hinterland of a vast city. You were the stubborn one. You turned your nose up at twenty thousand but you thought you had a prosperous business then. I wonder what you'd say now if, in return for your silence,

439

I offered you your life, a hundred thousand in cash and the total ruin of your former friends Snyder and Coe. Tempted, eh?'

He put his head back and roared with laughter. The sound was truly Satanic.

'Well, that's not on offer,' he continued with a cackle. 'No more bribes! Here's a story for you . . . a few years ago when I was still young and green I met a pretty student. She was a nice girl but she got awfully upset about the number of children being born, our vanishing wildlife, the state of the rainforests, global warming and all that. She was a Friend of the Earth, she said. I took her on a picnic to a remote spot on the moors. I suggested that she might like to make a personal contribution. "How?" she asked. I offered to strangle her and bury her under the tree we were sitting by. She didn't like it when I said I had a pick and shovel in the car. "Of course you won't do it," she said. But I did. It still hurts me to think of lovely Lauren mouldering into a rich manure, but there it is. She was a Friend of the Earth.'

'You're quite mad, you know,' I said. 'Why don't you turn yourself in to the police. You must have nightmares when you think of all the people you've killed.'

'Not at all,' he scoffed. 'Are you upset if you accidentally squash a bug?'

'Yes,' I muttered. I was now desperate to keep him talking. One never knows what might turn up. The building might be struck by lightning.

'It was you that killed those priests beside Strangeways, wasn't it?' I asked.

'That took some orchestrating, I can tell you.'

'What about Douglas Carver and Greta Armstrong?'

'My father and his companion?'

'Your father!' I groaned. How had I failed to find that out?

'I thought you knew.'

440

'No.'

'Then how did you trace me?'

'Through Ngwena and Black Cat Services.'

'This is doubly unfortunate, Cunane. For you, because now you must die, and for my father because he's already died! I thought you'd persuaded him to divulge my identity.'

'He mumbled something about a son but it was hard to hear. He could have said anything. I didn't have time to check.'

'In a way it's appropriate that my father didn't tell you my name. I often wondered if he knew he had a son. He was so wrapped up in his Elizabethan fantasies.'

'As you are in yours?'

'There are similarities, I'll admit. But my main influence was my mother. She was a fanatical eugenicist. She believed the lower classes and lesser breeds were having too many babies. Strangely enough she didn't put her faith into action by having a large family herself. Oh no, that would have been too simple. Instead she campaigned about overpopulation. I think I came along more or less by accident but she never missed a chance to tell me how much of the world's diminishing resources I was consuming. I believe it was a relief to her when she drowned.'

'Did you kill her?'

'No, it was a boating accident.'

'But you were in the boat with her?'

'How did you guess?'

'I'm getting used to the way you operate. How did you kill your father?'

'There I must admit I wasn't directly responsible. My father and his coarse acquaintance followed the path you will be taking shortly.'

'What do you mean?'

'Suicide . . . well . . . assisted suicide, shall we say.'

'Both of them? You were taking a chance.'

'The police seem happy. Dear Greta was being paid to tell me what my father was doing. Nothing too much, of course, but I liked to keep an eye on the old fellow. Well, after your impetuous visit she phoned to say that the dear man had finally lost his marbles. I presumed, wrongly according to you, that he'd revealed all. We went round to Hale Barns. It was a kindness to help him take the final step. The old sweetie took his medicine like a good boy.'

'They were part of your group?'

'Oh, yes. Surely you know that all secret organisations have two parts? There's the open front visible to the world and then there's the secret group who use the fools as a cover. My father and his crazy, organic, back-to-the-Tudors, mystical, magical mob provided a very good screen for what I was organising. It was through them that I was able to learn the identities of many of my . . . er, victims.'

'You're pretty mystical and magical yourself. You took your name from a demon mentioned in Shakespeare's *King Lear*, didn't you?'

He suddenly smacked me hard across the face.

'Fool! My name is my own! Shakespeare learned of my identity by accident.'

'So you *are* this fiend, Hobbididance? A likely tale.'

He hit me hard for a second time. I strained against my bonds. Ngwena nervously fingered his gun.

'Clown that you are, Cunane! You'll shortly learn that there's another existence besides the merely corporeal. I've always existed.'

'Sorry I spoke, sir!' I mumbled through rapidly swelling lips.

He looked at Ngwena and I thought my time had come. I braced myself for a bullet in the back of the neck, only you can't brace yourself for that. I tried to think of some way to keep him talking. Perhaps someone had noticed them prodding me along at gunpoint, even now not an everyday sight in Manchester. Perhaps police were surrounding the building. Even a second might be precious.

The phone rang. I thought salvation had come.

Ngwena picked it up and listened.

'How long?' he said to Hobby Dancer.

'Make it twenty minutes or so.'

Ngwena relayed the message.

Hobby Dancer turned to me. My eyes must have been shining. 'Hope springs eternal, eh?' he said. 'That was only the taxi we've called to help us deliver you to your final destination.'

My mouth felt very dry but I forced myself to speak.

'But Greta? You're not telling me she went quietly.'

'How astute you are now that it's too late to do you the slightest scrap of good. Greta! Oh, my goodness, suicide wasn't part of *her* plan. She thought she'd be inheriting!' he chuckled grimly. 'You should have seen her face when I told her it was best if she joined my father in his eternal slumber. Positively demonic in her rage she was, though I say it as shouldn't! Ariel had to be at his most persuasive to convince her.'

'How?'

'I understand your natural curiosity. Ariel, will you oblige him?'

'I merely told her that I would slit her belly open and then roast her intestines on a charcoal fire while they were still attached . . . She was convinced when I showed her the knife,' the African chortled.

He gave his sleeve a flick and a knife appeared in his hand. He put the point to the tip of my nose. I squirmed in the chair and he laughed cruelly.

'Ariel's a cannibal, you know,' Hobby Dancer said conversationally. 'There's nothing he relishes more than a slice of human haunch basted slowly in its own juices. She knew that. Yes, Greta understood the reason why

443

most of the Mangler's customers were missing a little part of themselves. "Trophy taking" the police called it when they finally admitted there was a serial killer, but it was much more primal than that. Ariel knows what it is to hunt for a living.'

'Pig!' I yelped.

'No, human,' Hobby Dancer corrected me. 'That's how we met, at the dinner table, you might say, and that's why we decided to dispose of Meg Hands. The missionaries have a lot to answer for in Africa. Of course, we didn't have the pleasure of consuming Meg along traditional lines. She'd have made poor eating, I'd have thought, but Ariel and Neville devoured the poor girl in every other way. Then we half drowned her in the bath here. The canal's just outside the door, so we popped her in.'

'Bastards!'

'Not at all! She was the daughter of missionaries and must have considered the traditional fate of unwanted missionaries – death at the hands of reluctant converts.'

'You absolute monster!'

'No, I must insist not! Cannibalism's part of Ariel's culture. Why shouldn't he indulge in it? This is a multicultural society, don't forget!'

'But you –'

'I'll admit it's not to my taste. Once was enough. I tend to be a vegetarian.'

'Was her brother involved?'

'Ever the detective, eh? No, Arthur's too weak for anything like that. He was involved but he was careful to preserve a certain distance. My father had some pretensions as a mage, a sort of Tudor conjuror, and Arthur was deeply impressed by him. He believed my father could see into the future with a crystal ball. Scrying, they called it. Wicked boy, he later claimed he thought she was going on some kind of dirty weekend. He believed that my dear father would be looking after her.'

444

'Did Arthur know she was going to be raped?'

'He was certainly aware that others had met that fate.'

'How could he do it?'

'He may have believed that it was the price of initiation into the group.'

'For his initiation or hers?'

'His, of course.'

'So he knew she might be killed?'

'He was ready to let her take the risk.'

'Did he know about the Mangler?'

'It can't have escaped his notice that the names of some of the Mangler victims were mentioned at Hale Barns both before and after his sister's death.'

'The little swine.'

'Arthur was well aware of what might happen to him if he spoke out, but as you say, he is a little swine. Actually, what sealed the girl's fate was when Arthur revealed that she'd been secretly photographing my father's little gatherings. We couldn't have that. He must have known what the conclusion would be, but when he found the photos plastered over her room he could have saved her. With the resources available to his family he could have made it difficult for us to find him but he chose not to.'

'And Pullman?'

'Never mind about him,' he snapped. He was becoming bored by the parade of his superiority.

'He was in Carver's group, wasn't he?' I persisted.

'I know you're only trying to postpone the inevitable but as you insist I'll tell you. Percy was originally attracted to my father by an interest in insects, of all things. It seems that the Tudors were positively overrun with the things. A man of some ability, unlike the dreamy academics, would-be literary figures and poets my father surrounded himself with, he was one of the few who graduated to my inner circle. He had a taste for harming people.'

'Who was the phoney priest who met Pullman at St Jude's church?'

'Now you're asking too much. There are other colleagues whose identities I'm not prepared to reveal even though you're going to die shortly.'

'Did Pullman help you to kill Meg?'

I looked at Hobby Dancer, or Carver Junior, or whatever he was called. He was almost salivating. It was disgusting watching him gloat but I had to know the details.

'Yes, he did. The girl was in a frightful state of nerves when Ariel brought her to my father's house. Pullman was able to calm her down and persuade her that she was taking part in an elaborate hoax. I don't think we'd have ever got the alcohol into her without his skill in administering certain drugs. Once she succumbed, he didn't avail himself of the opportunity to enjoy her physical charms but he watched as Neville and Ariel did. He brought her back to Manchester in the boot of his car and helped Neville to carry her to the canal from here. We all watched while she drowned. I believe it was Neville who actually gave the final push which helped to keep her head under water.'

'Did you burn Pullman's house down?'

'Enough!'

'It's a simple yes-no question.'

'Ariel, to work!' he ordered with a click of his fingers, then he struck me again.

Ariel first checked my bonds and then brought out two bottles of Lagavulin malt whisky from a cupboard.

'Your favourite brand, I believe,' Hobby Dancer said. 'You see no expense is being spared.'

He and his acolyte then donned breathing apparatus complete with masks and air bottles and carefully tested each other's kit. I looked at them in dread. I strained to free myself but the chair was rock solid and the ropes were tight. They hadn't pulled the masks over their faces but as I watched Hobby Dancer's hands moved upwards. It was almost as if time was slowing down. Then his long fingers were on the mask.

'One last question!' I shouted. 'Condemned man's last request?'

'My, you are an inquisitive chap! Go on then, one question.'

'Why?'

'Why?' he repeated.

'Why have you caused so many deaths?'

'Why did Hillary climb Everest? It was something to do. It manifested my power and, besides, I had to supply Ariel's dietary needs. No, don't say another word, Cunane. It may be an unsatisfactory answer but the truth is I don't entirely know why I did it. Computer games lose their power to enthral after a time and it may be that solving these real-time problems gave me back my competitive edge. You saved your best question till last, Cunane, but as they say, that is definitely it!'

He snapped the mask over his face.

Ngwena went to another room and returned with an incense burner. He inserted several cakes of self-igniting charcoal and lit them. They sizzled and glowed when he blew on them. I thought of the choice Greta had been offered. Then Ngwena took some green powder from a packet and sprinkled it on the charcoal. The room filled with intoxicating fumes. It was some kind of very powerful cannabis or related substance. I could feel my head spinning and my consciousness evaporating. I stopped struggling. After a moment the fumes began to disperse.

'Open your mouth,' Hobby Dancer ordered, his voice booming hollowly through his mask. 'Drink!'

I shook my head but I didn't resist when Ngwena pushed the neck of the bottle against my lips. I drank deeply.

My recollections after that are clouded. I have an

impression of being driven back to my flat and staggering up the stairs with my new friends on either side. No one seemed to be about. Later, I was conscious of being immersed in warm water.

When I came to I was lying on the floor of my bathroom with my father bending over me and vigorously slapping my face while Kate Mackenzie looked on anxiously. My head seemed to go from side to side. I felt no pain. In one hand I was still gripping an empty whisky bottle. I giggled.

I tried to speak. Nothing came out but an awkward gurgle. Through the shaving mirror I could see that the bath water was bright red. It seemed all wrong.

'He's coming round!' Kate exclaimed.

'Thank God!' my father gasped. 'What next?

'Hospital, what do you think!' she snapped. 'He seems to have consumed two bottles of whisky and slashed his wrists. He needs a stomach pump and a blood transfusion.'

'No!' Paddy grunted.

'Yes,' Kate replied. 'It's the first time I've had a man slashing his wrists to avoid taking me out but that's what this is. I don't know why I let you persuade me not to phone for the ambulance right away.'

'For the very good reason that this is a murder attempt, not a suicide. No Cunane worth his salt would ever deliberately avoid meeting a lovely creature like yourself. Hobby Dancer's tried to kill him and he would've succeeded if you hadn't been here.'

'He still needs the hospital,' she insisted.

'No ambulances though. I want Hobby Dancer and his mate to think that they've succeeded or they'll try again.'

I passed out. When I woke up next time I was in a bed in a private hospital in Bolton. My wrists were bandaged and I was attached to a drip. My head was splitting.

It took several blood transfusions and two weeks before I felt normal. Kate and my parents visited every day. My survival was entirely down to chance, as such things usually are.

Before my foolish foray back into Manchester I'd agreed to take Kate to Tiger Tiger, a bar-restaurant at the Print Works, catering for an older, more select age group than students and teenagers. I asked her out because it seemed the right thing to do. I didn't particularly fancy her at that stage but calculated that an invitation would get my mother off my back, and I realised that my behaviour at the cottage had been less than charming. Dad was going to a police function in Salford and as Kate didn't know her way round Manchester he agreed to drop her off at my flat before going on. When they found I wasn't answering, Dad let himself in to find why I was skulking in my flat and breaking the code of the Cunanes.

That's why I'm still here.

All that remained was to sort out Hobby Dancer and Ngwena. As I lay on my back in that hospital bed, I thought of a thousand ways to destroy them until the perfect answer finally came.

Paddy had told me that he'd insisted on transporting me to Bolton in a private ambulance such as are used to convey corpses to undertakers, so if Hobby Dancer had kept my flat under observation he now probably believed that his plan had succeeded. My absence from work and Paddy's single-handed efforts to keep the firm going would have provided confirmation of that if he needed it.

I'd already made my preparations. Paddy wanted no part in them when I told him that they didn't involve the police. How could I go to the police? I had no evidence. An allegation that misfired would leave me to face Hobby Dancer and his circle of 'colleagues' on my own. To my mind, what I was about to do came under the heading of legitimate self-defence.

During my previous researches in the musty bowels of Bolton Reference Library I'd been able to study copies of the eighteenth-century plans of the building of the Bridgewater Canal Basin. Hobby Dancer was right when he said there were tunnels under Manchester. One was the old Salford Navigation, connecting to the Basin, which was drained a hundred years ago. The tunnel remains to this day and was used as an air-raid shelter in the Second World War. Another was the one Hobby Dancer had discovered. When the old engineers used the waters of the Medlock to help feed the Bridgewater Canal they had to leave a small tunnel alongside it for overflow waters. It was this tunnel running under the Bridgewater Viaduct and Hobby Dancer's home that he'd converted into a personal bolt hole.

I guessed that the curious lift that was the only entrance to his bunker-style dwelling went down to a deeper level giving access to the tunnel. That was the only explanation for his trick of entering the bunker and then emerging elsewhere. To his twisted mind it would suggest the demonic power of being in two places at once.

With the plans in my hand it hadn't taken me long to discover where the tunnel exit was. It was on a lane called Jordan Street behind Deansgate train station, a stone's throw from the Medlock. The area's a survival of nineteenth-century Manchester with lots of small factories, warehouses and workshops. I was able to identify the location thanks to the red Range Rover. It was garaged in a disused workshop with a sliding door behind a chain-link fence. The giveaway was the new padlock on the outer gate. By climbing up on the fence I was able to spot the Range Rover through a cracked window in the workshop door. Alongside the car there was a steel plate set into the concrete floor. To the casual eye it looked like an old inspection pit but on the wall behind, a notice read, "Caution! Do not enter, Unsafe Tunnel". There was an eyebolt for a padlock to keep the entrance shut but the padlock that should have been fitted was missing.

It was three a.m., on a moonless night exactly three weeks after the murder attempt when I returned to Manchester. I was equipped with jumbo-sized bolt cutters this time, and a full set of burgling tools. My first trick was to cut into the old workshop on Jordan Street and, after confirming that it was the entrance to the tunnel, I fastened the steel door with a padlock. Then I returned to the viaduct and climbed onto the roof of Hobby Dancer's bunker.

I thought I was alone so my heart almost stopped when a gruff voice said, 'Hey, what you doing up there?'

Scarcely daring to breathe, I looked over the edge of the roof.

It was Jed Eagles, complete with his rucksack and shopping baskets.

'I'm doing a spot of maintenance, Jed,' I croaked, in what was intended as a whisper.

'If you ask me, maintenance is long overdue in that quarter,' he said quietly. 'Friends of yours, aren't they? I saw you with them a couple of weeks ago. Still, it's none of Jed Eagles' business if you've got a surprise for them. They're a right pair of bastards.'

He then shuffled away towards the Canal Basin with a good turn of speed.

I lay down on the roof for a full five minutes after that. Nothing happened.

I wasn't intending to break into the apartment. My target was the concrete structure on the flat roof, housing the works for that vital elevator shaft. A padlock secured the steel door and it was the work of a moment to snip it off.

Inside I found the normal winding gear, motor and a large fuse box protected by a hatch. I unscrewed the hatch, discovering an array of fuses and a large lever for

451

turning the electricity off for maintenance purposes. A notice warned that the switch should not be thrown while passengers were in the lift. I took out my mobile and phoned Hobby Dancer's number, which I'd retained from the time he phoned me to offer a bribe.

'What! Who is it?' he barked. Hobby Dancer's voice was unmistakable.

'It's me, Oggie, Dave Cunane,' I said. 'I'm outside. I want to see you and settle what's between us man to man.'

The phone went dead. Almost immediately the lift motor began to hum and the wheel to turn. The passenger compartment was descending. My heart missed a beat as I wondered if he was going to accept my invitation and appear at his entrance alongside the Wharf Café. But he didn't. The compartment went on down to a lower level. I waited until the sound of the door opening and closing echoed up the shaft and then threw the switch. Whoever was in the tunnel at the bottom of the shaft now had no mechanical means of returning to the upper level.

To cover my tracks, I damaged the equipment, and then closed the door.

I took my time getting off the roof. Although it was quiet, and Jed Eagles was long gone, I didn't want to appear on any screen. Fortunately, the boundary of CCTV coverage had still not been extended past Deansgate. I crossed the road and went along the familiar street where Meg Hands had shared an apartment with her brother and where one of her killers had ended in the gutter. When I reached the Jordan Street workshop Hobby Dancer and Ngwena had already arrived below the steel plate. When I put my ear to the plate I could hear them banging and cursing.

I smiled in satisfaction. That plate was half an inch thick, set in a steel frame surrounded by concrete. They weren't going anywhere. I shut the garage door and secured the outer fence gate with a new lock. Out in the street no sound carried from the two desperate men below. It could only be a short time before they discovered that their route back to the flat was blocked.

I'm not a cruel man but the thought of Hobby Dancer's clever face when he discovered that he was trapped in a tunnel with a knife-carrying cannibal pleased me considerably.

It was six weeks before Ariadne Witherspoon, Hobby Dancer's not-too-alert gatekeeper at Wild Ride, reported him missing. It took the lift company little time to restore the elevator to operation. The withered body of Ariel Ngwena was found at the bottom of the shaft where he'd been licking a damp patch on the wall for moisture. It was estimated that he'd survived for some time.

Of Orgoglio Hobby Dancer there was no trace at all, not even a scrap of bone or gristle. I wondered if it was too much to hope that Ngwena had consumed all of him, right down to his boot laces, or if I would be hearing from him again.

I crossed my fingers.

THE END